FLORES AT BAY

Malag peered more closely. His brows furrowed as he noted the un-washed clothing, the lack of noble headgear, the common sandals, the dagger belted in the style of a poor man, and the unkempt beard of one of the pedestrian class. The intruder wore neither the skirt nor the leatherwork of a slaver. Malag felt anger rise within–the slaughtered bore the bandoleers and baldrics of his comrades. The slave-driver spoke, making no effort to disguise his contempt, but apprehensive lest more intruders lie hidden in the darkness.

"Aside!" Malag said. "You have no business here."

As if chiseled in stone, the intruder made no move.

Malag grimaced. "Speak, man. What do you here? You are not of Tumset, and you do not work for me. By what right do you interfere in my affairs?"

The man said nothing, but fingered the butt of his sword.

"I warn you. Only once more shall I ask. Who are you, and from where do you hail?"

A moment passed.

"A stranger."

The slaver's lips twisted with sarcasm. "Nothing more? You have no name?"

The intruder lowered his eyes until they rested on a ring upon one finger. The ring bore the sign of the Turlicum. He glanced up again.

"You need not know it."

Malag's eyes narrowed. Again he took in the common raiment and style of the intruder. Stepping back, he turned to his men. "Cut this dog to pieces. Then scatter them throughout the valley."

Without hesitation, the two axe-wielders leapt forward. . .

MAALSTROM

–REVIEWS–

"Glenn Lazar Roberts is one of the finest writers of un-conventional prose in contemporary fiction. His wonder-fully inventive plots and mastery of the language place him in the company of Calvino, Burges, Gass... The story is a hair-raising adventure... Highly recommended."
—CT

"A beautifully written fantasy saga. The excitement devel-ops in such a way as to make the reader keep turning pages."   —Writer's Digest

"Glenn Lazar Roberts has created an imaginary world filled with exotic creatures and strange customs [that is] drastically different from anything the reader has experi-enced. The suspense and the action never let up, always a new twist and a mystery... This book will keep you up all night reading it."   —M. Kilgore

"In the tradition of Burroughs and Howard, Roberts gives us an exciting story...inventive, absorbs the reader and takes him or her to places never dreamed of."
—R. Paulding

"The action is unceasing, the sex torrid, the violence grue-some, and the religion detailed and bizarre...Guaranteed to surprise down to the last page, the last paragraph, the last sentence."   —Sirius Reviews

"Using an incredible writing style, Roberts has created a fantasy that is bloody, vengeful and engaging."
—Anthony Downen, author of
The Forgotten Scribes

And more fevered dreams from the mind of
Glenn Lazar Roberts...

ADVENTURES
OF THE
RADIATED LESBIAN NUN

BOOK 1:
'JUDGE CRATER
TAKES A POWDER'

The most mysterious disappearance of the 20th century is solved as Judge Crater goes undercover for the FBI in this hilarious satire set in mid-century America, with an eccentric cast of characters including Amelia Earhart, J. Edgar Hoover, Orson Welles, German spies, Japanese submarines, space-folding transvestites, Masonic mafia, and recipe-obsessed nuns, exposing a galactic conspiracy of aliens intent on flooding the Earth through global warming.

"Nuts!" —Sirius Reviews

MAALSTROM

by
Glenn Lazar Roberts

Dark Lotus Books
Home of the
JUST PLAIN WEIRD

If you enjoy MAALSTROM
please post your
REVIEW
on the following websites:
www.amazon.com
www.goodreads.com
www.siriusreviews.com

DEDICATION

To my mentors:
Edgar Rice Burroughs, visionary,
and story-teller extraordinaire
&
Robert E. Howard,
master of brevity and
craftsman of the bloody encounter

ISBN 978-0-9675809-0-6

www.darklotusbooks.com
Home of the Just Plain Weird

Cover Design and story art by Glenn Lazar Roberts

CONTENTS

CHAPTER   PAGE

PROLOGUE   1

1   THE CITY OF GLASS   2

2   THE ASSEMBLY   15

3   THE MOONLIT TOWER   25

4   CALLING FOR SONS   37

5   THE VOK-TAIL CLAN   49

6   "TRUST ONE, TRUST NO ONE"   59

7   IN THE WILDS   73

8   UNEASY ALLIANCE   86

9   EMPEROR OF THE VENSORS   94

10   UNDER SIEGE   105

11   IMPRISONED   112

12   AMINA   121

13   THE TEMPLE   127

14   CATACOMBS   144

15   ESCAPE   156

16   WILDERNESS   164

17   THE REVEN CLAN   179

18   MACIUS   186

19   BONES AND IRON   200

20   TUMSET   217

21   THE ENIGMA   228

22   ILLUSIONS   248

23   HALL OF MIRRORS   254

24   "THE TURLICUM IS DEAD!"   268

25   THE HALL OF VIM   281

26   VENSA   290

MAPS & PICTURES   302

NOTE BY THE AUTHOR   307

I flee to the Lord of Dawn,
from the Evil He created,
from the night when it falls,
from gilas who twist what should be straight,
from the One that Envies all.

I flee to the Lord of Man,
the King of Man, his God,
from the One who sneaks through portals,
who whispers evil in the hearts of men,
and the ways of selks and mortals.

—The Holy Quran
Surahs 'Falaq' and 'al-Nas'

The dark man paused. A sparkle of glass caught his gaze, and his sweaty palm closed and slid within a pocket. With a last shallow breath he stepped forward and slipped the length of the shadowed hall till an open threshold loomed, his amphibian features sterile of emotion in its soft trapezoid of light. An empty courtyard, overgrown with weeds and worts and lit by a trio of gibbous moons, led to a massive gate. Silently he crossed. At the portals he halted, his gaze impaled by the mad leer of Atasan thrusting gargoyle-like from the carved rorewood, in its hatred of Vensor mocking all with egalitarian indifference. He gripped the jagged tongue and drew back the jaw to reveal an aperture set within the gate. He breathed deep...one more step. A smile might have played on his face, had the shadows beneath the pediment been less dark, or had his face been capable of smiling.

He placed one leg within the aperture–and froze.

CHAPTER 1

THE CITY OF GLASS

"How could they do it? Not in a hundred years has such an outrage been permitted. Have Assemblymen become slaves and servants, crawling to perform every whim of my enemies?"

Flores stalked the narrow avenue, his lean legs again outpacing his companions. About him rose chalky clouds of dust and a raucous clatter of beasts and children, grunting and shouting with abandon. A knee-length vest of intricate blue and silver, drawn about his tunic, proclaimed his role in the Municipal Assembly, the supreme ruling body of the city of Ven. His appearance, from tanned boots to close-cropped beard, portrayed wealth, dignity, and privilege, his almond-colored face, an alert intensity tempered by patience and pain.

At his side jogged Mosum. Friend, and loyal to Flores in the Assembly, Mosum informed his colleague of its happenings between wheezes, his arms aloft to prevent dragging his tunic's voluminous sleeves in the street. Behind strode Lasmer and Isav. Of common origin, they were employed by Flores as captains of militia, and grown rich for their talent. Only Flores and Mosum sported the apparel of Simet-sa, the aristocracy of Ven. Only the nobles had not been raised in the Orphanage after their spawning in the Temple of the double sun.

Lasmer jostled merchants and commoners, who halted to stare, curious to see nobles on foot. "Calm, Flores. I think we should be cautious."

"Yes, caution," broke in Mosum. "They are angry and have closed the debate."

"Caution? Vacillation, you mean," said Flores. "No, that would end us."

A clump of struggling children overtook them and squatted in their path, tossing dirt and dust in the air. They stretched out empty hands.

Flores scowled and the boys dashed away.

"Petition to address the Assembly," suggested Mosum.

"Petition?" Flores' eyes popped in disbelief. "Like an embassy from conquered vassals? Crawl before insult? Pffft! Not a day will pass but the city will hear of this. I'll batter their ears with my speeches. In the marketplace or in the Assembly, I'll speak, petition or not. All of Ven will know–and especially the Assembly. The name of Sruk will be as of the god of fire–"

Mosum and Isav caught their breath and halted.

"–odious and shunned."

They resumed their march. The little band turned off the avenue onto a thoroughfare lined with spires that led toward the plaza and the marketplace. The traffic grew with throngs of grimy peasants, indolent watchmen, nobles in sun-shaded litters, and mobs of tradesmen and poor. More urchins sighted their expensive trappings and followed in their wake calling for money.

Lasmer addressed Mosum. "Who introduced the motion?"

"It was the Venerarch's."

"I had guessed."

"The man is mad for gain," said Flores.

"He questioned the purpose of your speech on Soorkrul," wheezed Mosum.

"Who assuredly assassinated our colleagues, Jaz and Clesp."

Mosum nodded. "Then you accused the Triumvirate of undermining the authority of the Assembly."

"When they accused me of undermining the morality of Ven."

"And you left in protest."

"A mistake–and Sruk was prepared. But what of our faction: Sorel, Hem, and Latkin? How did Sruk sway their votes?"

"He did not, Flores!" exclaimed Mosum, slowing. "They are loyal still. But after your dramatic exit, Sruk turned the debate to... 'domestic issues.' Most unkind things were said of the personal lives of all. It was then that Sorel and Hem decided to, um...defer to your 'tactical example.'" Mosum toyed with his fingers as Flores rolled his eyes.

The fat aristocrat nodded. "Yes," Mosum continued, "they too boycotted the Assembly. It was commendable, but rash. I stayed, but the Triumvirate shouted me down. I protested till I was hoarse, then Sruk seized the floor and in his speech tried and hanged you. He blamed the House of Turlicum for all the city's woes. Disrespect for the Eunuch Guild and the Holy Law of Ven became the worst of evils, and finally all condemned it. He even criticized your toll on the city gate."

"Was it voided?" inquired Lasmer.

"Abolished."

"And what of our fees for dock space on the Suma?" asked Flores.

"Untouched," wheezed Mosum, falling behind again. "Sir, they are all aware of their importance to your house. Your enemies have influence, but the day has not come when Assemblymen would deprive each other of their sacred rights as noblemen."

"Perhaps. But the day *has* come when they will abolish my seat in the Assembly," clipped Flores.

The walls and shops that lined the thoroughfare retreated to either side as the street emptied into the city's central plaza. The traffic flowed without pause into the square where it merged with a tide of masculine faces.

Flores and his companions turned leftward, proceeding along a wall of baked brick and mortar that separated the plaza from the Assembly grounds. Eight feet the wall rose, shielding the brain of Ven from the city proper. Behind were gardens where trees swayed, occasional branches drooping over and down to shade passers-by. Beyond the trees rested the Assembly Hall. Like a hill of gems, the edifice sloped, bright, domed and glinting. The oval dome was composed of *irsrem*, 'tear-glass,' called such because once its essence was annealed with the mineral corta, the glass formed a cross-worked pattern of lucent drops, each tear forming an iridescent prism stronger than iron. Irsrem had made Ven great. Luxurious and cheap, the city's inhabitants erected irsrem plates over walls, irsrem domes over roofs, and fused the material into high pinnacles, so that the city seemed to shine with starlight at mid-day. Even the priests of the Temple, the citadel in the midst of Ven, as dark and silent as the city was light and alive, would nod with appreciation when offered the glass-smith's treasure.

A trio of guardsmen behind the Assembly grounds-gate grew nervous at the little band's approach.

"Ultem," said Flores. "Why so slow? Open, if you please."

"Sir Flores," the man averted his gaze. "I have been directed to forbid you from–"

At a signal from Flores, Lasmer snatched the keys from Ultem's belt and unlocked the gate. Flores swept into the garden, strode up the broad steps of the Assembly Hall, swung wide the portals, and paused at the end of the corridor. For a moment he listened. Then he pushed past the protesting doormen into Ven's debating chamber.

The chamber was a large oval room with several tiers of benches abutting the walls between the several entrances. Upwards of a hundred Assemblymen, with their retainers, scribes, and consorts, sat in attendance to the city's affairs. Most were attired like Flores: jewel-encrusted vests over delicate tunics, rich embroideries of blue and silver covering their garments. Pelts, cushions, and voting boards lay scattered upon the floor and tiers.

Before the casual attention of the nobles clustered a delegation from the subject city of Nasvetin, waiting to be noticed. An elderly Assemblyman of lush and impeccable appearance spoke in a dry monotone.

"In total, the capital counted, in tribute and in toll, 158,500 mir this past year. For each of the last several years we have discharged about 135,000 mir, and therefore we have accumulated–"

"Sirs, I shall not waste your time." Flores turned to show he addressed the entire Assembly. "I come to bear you a warning."

The Assembly lapsed into silence, awaiting the words that would prove insanity or treason and complete the ruin of the noble House of Turlicum.

Flores threw his hands high in a flourish. "Yes, you may loll in dignity, though I stand violated before you. But don't weep on my behalf. Weep on yours! Sirs, what is a man without his tribe? He is alone and pitiable, but remains a man. But what is a man without his divine father, Vensor? He is less than pitiable–he is nothing. He is without soul, honor, sustenance. When a loose brick falls from a wall and hits a man, he knocks the wall down or repairs it so others may not be hurt. If a ros seizes a child and rends it, men know to kill the beast before it hunts again.

"Simet-sa, as I have warned you many times before, I shall warn you again. There is a conspiracy in Ven that seeks all our liberties–a conspiracy of vain and ambitious Simet-sa who scorn the holy laws of Vensor, a conspiracy aimed at nothing less than the imposition of a tyranny in the style of Nesos of Neset!"

As a rising squall, a chorus swelled to drown him out, offended and disbelieving Simet-sa laughing and mocking Flores. However, many were quiet and some nodded agreement. The men to whom Flores referred were well known. Termed by their enemies the Triumvirate, Numsenmur, Sruk, and Sendas sat close together, their advocates and allies about them. Calling themselves the Loyalists, they now led, after their recent parliamentary victory, the strongest faction in the Assembly.

Sendas rose. He was of average height, but heavy, and frequently said more than he meant, which best explained the continued attention of his audiences and the distraction of his co-conspirators. His wealthy and powerful Molersal clan best explained his comrades' continued allegiance. Gripping his sides, he thrust out a shaven chin.

"Those words are lofty indeed for one who but a few hours ago placed a few gold nuggets above the most sacred traditions of his city!"

The noble Simlet rose to join him. "Sirs, I repeat the charge our good colleague Numsenmur made earlier. The man you see before you, this self-proclaimed 'exemplar of righteousness,' refuses to deny the charge that he harbors a gila. By his own words, this man is in violation of the law!"

A second noble, Ust, rose from his seat near Numsenmur, his sleeve flapping. "Begone, beggar!" Ust glanced at Flores' hand, then sneered, "You have no right here."

"Sirs," continued Flores, ignoring the interruptions, "I now need no omen to foresee the future. A new evil shall emerge, one born out of the cabals and intrigues of the traitors in our midst, one growing like a rose of death from the ruins of Vensor's laws and justice. Slander me if you will, but none here shall forget my words." Flores whirled and strode out of the chamber.

The Assembly buzzed. Disgruntled opponents of the Triumvirate clamored as shouts and jeers sounded after the retreating party.

Flores and his retainers returned to the bustling plaza where they were swallowed by the multitude. Ven, the gaudy capital of the Three Valleys, teemed with wealth and sprawled far beyond its ancient stony parapets. Caravans of hulking beasts, laden slaves from subject towns, swarthy dealers, irsrem armorers, and others hurrying on a thousand errands mobbed the square, crossing to the market or to the many narrow alleys that opened on every side. The wealth of the wide valleys of the Tlaam, Hedronmas, and Suma, occupied by Ven's potent garrisons, drew them to the capital. And the city's population multiplied as Vensor rewarded their success with infants in burgeoning numbers, the Temple cranking high its gate and sounding the call for sons more often than any could recall. Irsrem glittered from a thousand structures. Of the cities of the three valleys, Ven surpassed them all in its taste for public gaudiness.

As the party walked back to Flores' estate, armed men in Flores' employ joined them, their martial purpose unconcealed. The Way of Murfenmas ran parallel to the Hedronmas. Estate walls angled outward, crowding the street, marking the sprawling villas and private court-yards of the Simet-sa of Ven, here, as in the rest of the city, encom-passing too much, their lots too large. The stony walls of Ven being too narrow to contain them, the wealthier nobles bought villas in sub-ject lands. But those who chose to reside on those far estates paid the political price for absence from their legislative Assembly, so most did not, but remained within the confines of the capital.

As Flores and his retainers passed under the sculptured lintel of the Turlicum estate, several clansmen overtook them, manhandling a pair of somber and defiant youths. Lasmer spoke with the newcomers, then approached Flores.

"Another recruit was found," Lasmer said. "Stabbed." He nodded toward the captives. "These two were near the body. They are Ser-claslers."

Flores gazed at the double suns, which were once again beginning to merge. Their rays outlined his slender features, accenting his full, protruding lips. His eyes narrowed.

"Make the proper introductions. Then return the bodies to our col-leagues." He stepped away, and paused. "Since the Assembly cannot keep the streets safe from ruffians, it falls on us to do it."

Flores' estate was similar to those of most Simet-sa, but larger. The dwelling itself, rambling and cloistered behind glittering walls and grilles, possessed four floors above ground and several below. The bright ancestral hall occupied much of the estate, gardens and exercise yards the rest. At its apex, a gang of laborers installed more plates of irsrem and put up rafters for the installation of a huge glass dome in imitation of the Assembly Hall so that all Ven could see the high rank of its owner. Waving aside a party seeking audience, Flores, body-guards in tow, climbed ramps past armed sentinels.

Sandol, head of the Turlicum estate, stood near the entrance to Flo-res' chambers. "Storl is waiting."

Flores nodded and entered the adjoining room.

"Flores? Ah, my Flores!" Storl took his arm.

Flores returned the clasp coolly. "Is there something more that you wish, Storl?"

"No! You've done enough! The crisis has passed and I'm grateful. I shan't keep you. You're busy. I have brought gifts." He jerked his thumb toward the next room. "Something special." He grinned. "If you don't like them, send them away. You're busy. I'll go."

Storl exited and Sandol re-entered the room. The chief opened another door, and Flores, having guessed the nature of the gift, gazed upon a pair of castrated youths, gaudily painted.

Flores turned to Sandol. "Send them back to the Eunuch Guild." Once they had gone, Flores shook his head. "Will Soorkrul never cease his attempts to infiltrate this House?"

Flores entered his private chambers and pushed the heavy door shut. The rooms of the head of the House of Turlicum, lineage unbroken since the awakening of Vensor, lay in a T-shape. The first several were conference room, antechamber, and bedroom. These were sparsely furnished. Crossing the T was a single chamber of simple construction and unassuming decoration. Flores' study was built with tear-glass windows opening on three sides of his property in one wide sweep so that he could view gardens, barracks, and exercise yard with but a few steps. On the left flowed the River Hedronmas. On the right, crags climbed to the Falls of Sish. Between lay the city, with the vast dome of the Assembly Hall glinting among a forest of domes and spires. Beyond, at the highest point of the city proper, loomed the Temple of Vensor.

Objects lay about the study haphazardly. An enormous slateboard bearing smeared impressions of characters was half-filled with a cylindrical scheme, interspersed with notes and entries. A jewel-studded helm with preserved reven talons embedded on the crest hung from a rack, framed by iron and irsrem weapons. Several iron were blunted or chipped from use. A portable lattice-frame supported hundreds of parchment scrolls. Within a recess that protruded into the room from the nether side of the irsrem window was a small, translucent sphere made entirely of tear-glass, housing a species of hornet called leroosa. A glass panel separated the room's interior from the nest's denizens. The hornets arrived and departed as usual, taking no notice of Flores' entrance.

Flores sat and rubbed his right hand and forearm where a network of scars reminded him of the once-ripped flesh. With an effort, he straightened the fingers. He grimaced, and permitted them to re-curl. He kicked off his boots. As manservants hurried to proffer more comfortable garments, he discarded the entangling vest. The austerity of the room was relieved by a vast soft couch and the recent addition of a golden, thick-piled carpet. When the expected knock came upon the door, he was ready. He joined his captains: Lasmer, Sandol, and Isav. The Turlicum Heir, Mesret, sat reluctantly. Too young to share in the decision-making, he glowered from some solitary concern.

"Lord Mosum has delivered interesting news," began Flores.

"And how can we deal with it?" replied Isav.

"I refer to other news," said Flores. "Hama of the Venholis has refused to adopt at the next Temple spawning."

Eyebrows raised.

"Some in the Assembly did not expect this, but it does not surprise me. He is old, a minor noble. Now much encouraged, his eunuch hopes to gain control. But a man named Sorotir–a commoner–runs his estate. This Sorotir is our way into the Venholis clan. If Hama's consort and his cronies in the Eunuch Guild succeed in their plans, then Sorotir will soon be unemployed. His consort is a young man and will run things himself. If Hama's consort gains control of the Venholis, the Triumvirate, whom all eunuchs and consorts support, will be strengthened. We can prevent this by recruiting Sorotir. We may offer him rank in the Simet-sa. Or perhaps even the Assembly. If he fears Hama's consort, so much the better."

"Yes," said Lasmer, "but of course the houses will never accept a commoner among their ranks."

"That is so. Still, some probing may find he has some famous ancestor whose son was inadequately treated." Flores' expression was unchanged, though his tone was unctuous. "Besides, commoners often show themselves more favored of Vensor than Simet-sa. More than one house has become indebted to their inferiors and their leaders forced to seek employment with other nobles. This Sorotir is doubtlessly mulling over his uncertain future. He may be interested in an administrative position, the water complex for example. In any case we could put his influence to good use."

"What is the Venholis tax base?" asked Isav. "If Hama adopts no one before he dies, the house will dissolve. We could move to replace our lost revenue."

"If the Assembly allows us," said Sandol. "It is difficult now merely to guard the interests of Turlicum."

"You know their base, Sandol," rejoined Flores. "They supply and regulate the public weights in the marketplace–a most lucrative business. Their income is growing rapidly, even with the nobles' exemptions. Anyhow, he may retire soon. He almost ignores public affairs as it is. The Loyalists themselves may move to appropriate. If that occurs he will resist, and his clan become our natural ally."

"Either way–adoption or no adoption–there will be a scramble for the spoil," added Lasmer.

"Let us not overestimate the rewards, though," Flores said, "Until I regain our house seat in the Assembly, we can neither help nor hinder in any debate, which is more important. This must happen. I have made the Simet-sa to understand what they have done by ejecting me, so let us hope my seat in the Assembly will soon be restored. The power of the Triumvirate increases without such acts."

"I heard the Loyalists plan to give food to the commoners," said Mesret.

"Perhaps so," interrupted Flores. He chuckled. "No worry. We can buy them for less."

Mesret closed his mouth and looked away.

"However, something must be done soon. Though we have accomplished much, the Triumvirate intend to wreck Turlicum. If we lose, life will become dangerous for our clan. And if our faction in the Assembly lose to the Triumvirate, it will be worse–nothing will then stand between Sruk and the absolute subjugation of Ven. A massacre would ensue such as would strike the tyrant Nesos with envy. Ven and all the valleys would become too small for those on Sruk's list."

His gaze drifted to the ceiling. "It is not the spoil of the Venholis that we need most, but rather my seat in the Assembly. So let us use the impending crisis in the Venholis clan to create a diversion. We shall deliver a message to, let us say... Numsenmur. For the benefit of Numsenmur and Sruk, we shall claim that this Sorotir of the Venholis possesses information on the defection of one of the Triumvirate to our cause. Which one does not matter. We shall apprise Sruk and Numsenmur of this in some subtle fashion. Then see what may follow. In the meantime, I have other irritations arranged to keep the city away of its true enemies."

The others nodded.

"Now," Flores leaned forward and pointed a finger at Isav. "I want a new levy from the Orphanage. Two dozen–ten year olds–healthy only. Lively, but no troublemakers." The finger moved to Sandol. "Go to the docks. Post men on our quays, get what's owed us, make it clear to all the boats that the docks are still ours." The finger continued to Lasmer. "Visit the glass-smiths. They think they are the nobles and we the commoners. Tell them we'll see the tax on irsrem doubled if we lose our privileges. We've got to move fast now and show the Triumvirate that Turlicum's interests were unaffected by my ejection from the Assembly. Sandol, when you return, we'll discuss the garrison payments–it's time we rewarded our vassals."

The meeting ended and all exited. Except Flores. He entered his workroom. Crossing to the hive of the leroo-sa, Flores sat upon a small stool and awaited a moment when the surface of the nest was clear of hornets. He slid the glass panel to one side. Ignoring the angry buzz of the hive's inhabitants, he placed his palms on either side of the nest. The hornets ceased moving. Flores shut his eyes and allowed his mind to wend through the tortuous path in search of the center. Hexagonal chambers enveloped him, beckoning, blocking, opening, closing about him as he sought the innermost chamber through dark and glittering tunnels. He felt an obscure tug and turned down a previously unexplored path, only to encounter a cul-de-sac. Suddenly he could not move. As if enmeshed in clay, he stared upon a vast clouded hexagon, unable to turn, while a buzzing grew, churning his mind, then a wind leapt up and a shadow loomed upon him from behind.

He opened his eyes. In the bright daylight of the afternoon suns, he looked upon an orange hive cooling rapidly to green, then blue, then violet. When it had again assumed its former iridescent state, he released his grip. The hornets stirred and resumed their activities, again oblivious of Flores.

Once again he had failed to find the invisible, elusive core.

Grunting, he procured an irsrem dagger, and departed by way of a back stairway. Descending slowly in thought to the ground floor, he entered the rear gardens. Here flagstones trailed to disappear among trimmed bushes, trees, and blossoms. A pond rippled, fed and drained by a meandering rivulet. From the right, hidden by a belt of verdure, a dull clacking drifted, accompanied by occasional shouts and thumps. The house militia trained constantly in the exercise yard; their mounts, the amphibious reven-na, required unstinting attention. A high wall encompassed Flores' land. The stream, channeled from the Hedron-mas, flowed through an iron grating set in the wall.

A warbling of birds drifted on the breeze, and Flores paused to savor the moment. He sighed. Though he had seen only fifty-six of the short Maalstrom years and wielded extraordinary influence for such limited experience, it seemed the years were slipping by at an accelerating pace. The callow youth, who had stared wide-eyed as his father lay dying on the steps of the Assembly Hall, cut down by rival Simet-sa, was gone. His father's assassins too had passed, assassinated in turn. In Ven, rising stars had a way of being suddenly extinguished. The warring factions had swelled and collapsed, then reformed under new ambition. Of his father's enemies, only Sruk remained, one of the two power brokers of the Triumvirate, self-advertised as the 'Venerarch' for his donations to the poor–with funds collected through the grain tax, Flores noted cynically. Sruk's arguments frequently swayed the Assembly of the Simet-sa to the Triumvirate's purposes. Then there was Numsenmur. When Flores thought of the chief of the Serclaslers, he saw in his mind's eye a mausoleum–unadorned, rock-cut, silent, at its gate an invisible presence, topping it a life-sized figure of Numsenmur standing motionless, soldier's pike by his side.

The image faded and Flores paused beneath a leafy tree to rest in its shadow, which lay across a low stone bench beside the estate wall. His eyes drew shut, and he slept.

When he awoke, another brief day of sixteen hours had passed. The suns were gone. Dusk's heavy pallor was deepening rapidly, and a gathering of moons etched the tinseled sky. Flores rubbed his eyes before realizing that something had struck him. A pebble had caused him to wake. Above the garden, spires of the palace glittered. To the right, the estate wall vanished in rows of thick greenery. To the left, the wall turned the corner at the riverbank and doubled back. A soft bubbling wafted as the rivulet cascaded over artificial falls. Belatedly, Flores realized his peril. Lulled by the garden and the quiet vastness of the Maalstrom night, he had committed the gravest error possible for a Vensor politician–he was alone.

A second pebble bounced. Eyes darting, Flores leaped to his feet. Then he saw it–a figure beside round bushes, edging closer. It waved its arms. A scroll unrolled and flapped. The man seemed unarmed and again gestured. The intruder was startling. Almost naked, his limbs and torso were strongly muscled, his hair trimmed short, and he had evidently just come through water, as attested by the water dripping from his limbs.

Flores thought he looked like an assassin and grew calmer. If assassins looked like themselves, they would kill no one. A lost petitioner, he thought, or a new reticent underling. He could summon the estate guards with a shout. Some would doubtless be near, though invisible in the twilight. Noting that the man was unarmed, Flores approached. Stepping forward, the stranger pointed behind Flores and upwards, as if to direct his glance. Flores was reluctant to turn. The man continued to say nothing but worked his mouth, waved the scroll, and pointed. Finally, curiosity prevailed, and Flores turned to look.

The man sprang. A hand clamped Flores' mouth. Another gripped an arm, and Flores was dragged into the bushes where the stranger crooked one arm about his throat as if to throttle him. Inexplicably he paused. He looked at Flores, arched his brows and nodded toward the bench the noble had just quit.

In the gathering darkness, a dim silhouette could be seen upon the bench, a stubby iron sword weaving evilly. Flores noted: iron for evening; an irsrem blade would spark with starlight. The figure hopped to the ground and peered while a second shadow descended from the tree. For half a minute, the pair searched. Finally they exchanged glances, re-climbed the tree, and were lost to sight. Moments later, they reappeared at the coping and slid over the estate wall.

Flores let his breath go. The Triumvirate had never come closer to ending the House of Turlicum. Only now did he realize the habit he had formed of resting on this bench at twilight. It was inevitable that his enemies would learn of it. As the twin suns' last pale light died, his savior turned and discovered Flores' upended dagger resting just behind his neck while they lay. The stranger went limp and released him. But for the arching of his brows, the stranger–and likely Flores as well–would have died.

Flores stood. "What is your name, servant?" His distrust had only subsided, not vanished. Surely the intruder knew the penalty for assaulting a noble. "Well, speak. You have done your duty well. I am not like some other nobles. I reward those who assist me, even if they violate the law by laying hands upon me."

The intruder did not answer, but pointed to his mouth and worked his lips. Then he placed his hands about his throat.

Flores' eyes widened. "You're mute!" He scratched his head. "Still, you are a good man. How lodng have you worked for me? You do not? Then how did you get into these gardens? They are off limits to all but my retinue."

The man pointed to the back wall of the estate, the parapet by the river, then pointed up and made pantomimic gestures to indicate climbing. Flores glanced at the parapet. The vertical surface was blank with no adjacent trees or handholds.

"I don't understand."

He handed Flores the scroll.

Flores read the caption scrawled in spidery Vensor script. "FST. That must be Flores-Sumvensor-Turlicum."

The stranger nodded, and Flores resumed reading:

> I need to speak with you. I have information that may be worth your life. Only in person. You can trust my slave, Tilsis. If you permit, he will bring you to me tomorrow evening in secret and in safety. Only alone. Please trust. You have nothing to fear. —CNS

Flores' brows crawled up his forehead as the intruder again motioned toward the back wall.

"You climbed the wall, ten feet high, to deliver this?"

The servant spread his hands and bowed.

Flores sheathed his dagger. "Can you tell me who this CNS is?"

He shrugged his shoulders.

"Can you return tomorrow after dark, the same way? In secret?"

He spread his hands.

"Then do so." Flores gazed at the shimmering stars that spanned the horizon. "Some say that nought occurs by chance. But others that there is nothing *but* chance. I wish to know. I will come with you to meet this CNS."

As Flores watched, the damp body turned and loped through the garden. With little effort, the intruder hurdled a low hedge, and, attaining the rear wall, scrambled nimbly up the sheer face. Within seconds, he sank over the top. Flores was glad it had not been he sent to murder him.

CHAPTER 2

THE ASSEMBLY

The following day, the Assembly noticed the delegation from Nasvetin. The surrounding terraced dais was packed with nobles of Ven, nimble-fingered scribes squatting at their feet, lackeys and servants nodding agreement with their respective employers, or fetching refreshments. Overhead, the light of day shone resplendent through the tinted arched dome that rimmed the chamber.

"So, kind sirs," one ambassador said, bobbing his head in the suffuse rays, "we appear before you as commoners, for our city has not the wealth for dignified dress. Large numbers of our men suffer from a lack of sufficient food. Our harvests have failed miserably. I cannot see from where the money will come to pay our tribute."

A low murmur carried through the room, accented by periodic calls for service, and an occasional peal of laughter as listeners harkened to the animated vignettes of a colleague.

"Last month the rum-na herds trampled our fields again. We labored many days to drive them away, and some penetrated almost to the city's outskirts. Such multitudes of beasts I have not seen in years."

Several Simet-sa paused from their private conversation. "Must he whine so?" complained one, casting a disdainful glance upon the supplicants.

"Gill sickness has spread among our reven-na," added another ambassador. "Our country is high and less humid than Ven, our reven-na more sickly." He was an aged man of august carriage and graying hair.

The aristocrat Numsenmur rose and directed his attention toward this emissary. Numsenmur-Nidrenmor-Serclasler was a hulk of a man, immensely strong and sure. A fair-haired beard awned his massive chin and cheeks to frame humorless and calculating eyes, poised, like the iron jaws of a hunter's trap, to snap upon the unwary limb. His penetrating glance and trim appearance illustrated the preference he held for forced solutions, this martial trait being further revealed by the brace of unadorned irsrem daggers thrust in his belt. Bodyguards, whose watchful eyes all important statesmen in Ven found necessary, stood behind in silence. Numsenmur had trained his personally. They were three out of hundreds–kin by custom rather than blood, as all Vensor clans–and were called Serclaslers, the most numerous of the aristocratic tribes of the city. The number covertly employed, or allied, would be known only to Numsenmur himself, or his single true relation, his Heir. Unlike others, the mass of Numsenmur's wealth went to augment that which he understood best–the number of his blades.

"Matan of the Malamut."

The murmur in the chamber quieted as the emissary briefly bowed.

"Time passes quickly."

The ambassadors bobbed their heads.

"Which perhaps is good, because injuries heal slowly." Numsenmur placed his fists on his hips. "Living citizens still remember the crimes of your fathers. They still bear the scars which your fathers inflicted upon them. Sometimes I think your memories are unaccountably short when I hear you speak to us thus of your problems. The struggle our fathers had rooting out the subversion which your people spread near impoverished our fair town."

Matan bowed his head. "Kind sir, we are too well aware of the depredation of our ancestors. It is humiliating to have to appear before you, bringing a history of transgressions. Our bandit ancestors did wrong. We know this. They thought selfishly to think they should keep the Mountain's quarry for themselves."

"They were foolish and evil," said the Serclasler Lord, "and they have condemned you to pay for their weaknesses. The mines belong to all now. Like the rest of the Three Valleys, we hold the pits of Maanus in trust for all. The corta is ours by right of conquest, and, believe me, that is best for all Vensor-sa."

The noble Sendas of the Molersal rose, handing a cool drink to an underling. "Sir Delegates," he paused to adjust a sleeve of his blue official gown. "What you say may be true. But look at yourselves. Do you think you are the only Vensor-sa on Maalstrom with troubles? Why, we have to run the affairs of a dozen cities the size of yours, and each one of them has grain fields as dry, and suffering, as vulnerable as yours. Each and every one has sickly reven-na–the steeds of Lunsen are very sickly. I have seen them myself." Sendas breathed deeply as he warmed to his speech.

"The city of Ven also is subject to these calamities. They could strike at any time. Indeed, our city has assumed the heavy task of running both our own affairs and yours. It isn't easy. Now, whatever difficulties Nasvetin might have, in all likelihood, will weigh on the rest of our lands too. Your city rests by the same River Suma as Ven. And if your city experiences poverty, I fail to see why you bring your woeful tale to us–whom your fathers injured so wantonly. Whatever poverty you have, in my opinion, is deserved."

The delegates craned forward, spines arching.

"Lords of Ven," Matan's voice quavered, "we have fulfilled our obligations as efficiently as we can. We have supplied riders to drive off the Empire's enemies when needed. We have saved many citizens of Ven from bandits and other ruthless nomads."

"The fulfillment of obligations is to be expected. Sickness is in the normal course of events. Rum-na herds must be anticipated. And debts must be paid."

"Ohh!" Matan collapsed to the floor. The rest moaned and covered their eyes. "Have mercy! We are poor!"

"Ambassadors," called Numsenmur, "I would like to call your attention to a rumor I have recently heard. The rumor is that there has been political subversion in Nasvetin, and that a public demonstration occurred where our garrison was subjected to cowardly threats and taunts."

The men shook their heads vigorously.

"Don't your people realize that there are benefits to being ruled by Ven? In your days of independence, you had only your own men to rely upon. Now, in times of trouble, the warriors of not only Ven, but every city of the Hedronmas and Tlaam will hasten to your aid!"

Flores' supporter, Mosum, had now returned to the chamber and begun to whisper vehemently with his colleagues, Sorel, Hem, and Latkin.

The Nasvetin emissary continued, "Oh, sir! There has been no demonstration. Our people are well aware of the benefits of our mutual alliance. There have only been a few anti-social hooligans whose minds are closed to logic and civilized persuasion. These have been caught and reprimanded."

Matan started back as Mosum leaped to his feet. "Simet-sa!" he bellowed, "I am going to tell you what these delegates cannot for diplomatic reasons. Cannot and dare not, though they wish they could.

There is a movement throughout the valleys. It has already spread to every city we control. It even affects our citizens themselves. We have now witnessed the first twitchings of its awakening, the first trial of its strength, the first intimation of what well could overwhelm our State.

"The city of Nasvetin is ripe for revolt! After an attempt to use captive gila-sa to seduce and subvert our garrison, we had to forcibly suppress a full-blown rebellion, an assault on their very quarters, which the authorities of the city made no attempt to control."

The ambassadors turned beet-red as the Assembly voiced cries of consternation.

"Sirs, the entire state, from Sipan to Nasvetin has been squeezed dry," Mosum declared. "Their patience hangs from a thread and our safety balances precariously." He grasped his vest in dignity. "Why do they feel thus? Why are they dissatisfied? Because the tribute system imposed upon them is starving them to death!" He slammed the dais at his side. "The tribute system designed and perpetuated by our own notorious Triumvirate." His eyes leveled at the culprits. "Our own secret conspiracy that will yet wreck our fortunes."

Sorel and Hem jumped up and shook their fists at their enemies, shouting, "Death to the Triumvirate!" Half the Assembly leaped up, yelling support or opposition. The rest snorted in condescension. Sruk spoke with Sendas and Ust as Numsenmur stood and pointed at Mosum and his faction.

"We should have taken your seats too, beggars!" yelled the Serclasler chief. "You disgrace the rank of Simet-sa!"

This was precisely the wrong thing to say before an enraged Assembly, its members already fearful of losing their offices. The remainder stood and shouted. The Triumvirate's supporters were swamped by the clamor of the opposition, whose faction swelled with turncoats, the nobility regretting the precedent they had set by ejecting Flores.

In vain Sendas sought to be heard. Someone screamed a proposal that all tribute be halved, and the Assembly turned and fumbled for their wooden blocks, black for approval, as Numsenmur's objections of illegal procedure were shouted down (a favorite tactic of the Triumvirate). The act of fumbling, however, distracted the chamber's attention momentarily so that the Simet-sa began to perceive the soothing voice of Sruk, droning, aged but steady.

"–and I will repeat once more. We have armed garrisons in every city of our State, to deal with the threat of revolt. We have our own army. We have important persons hostage in every city we control. We used to have them here, and we can bring them here again if necessary. We have governors in every city for the express purpose of dealing with armed resistance before it spreads. We have preserved the purity of our land from the corruption of Atasan, bright beneath the pristine gaze of God's angels. But my colleague Mosum is right when he speaks of violence in Nasvetin. Our garrison has been assaulted. But friends, this is no rumor. Our messengers brought the news this very morning for this body to consider. They have been in Ven all day for any to consult–I see few have done so."

Mosum leaned to a colleague and whispered, "He must have hidden them better this time."

"My dear sirs," continued Sruk, "have we forgotten that with the gold we take in tribute, we buy grain for the Temple and thus keep God's acolytes fed? Their demands grow without pause, and we, God's chosen people, have the duty to fulfill them as best we can. It is for this that Vensor grants us our children. Such are the pronouncements of God.

"So, my esteemed colleagues, we again encounter the manifold problem which I have sought for so long to solve." Sruk's voice grew sorrowful as he shook his aged white head. "What has become of the high principle of duty to one's city? What has become of the loyalty of Vens to their divine father Vensor? Has no one truly noticed how the integrity of our chamber has been corrupted by hate and greed and jealousy?"

He leaned on the dais for support.

"I am old, but I remember well a time of unity and pride when Vensor-sa would rather praise their divine Father than slander an esteemed colleague, would rather strive to please God's priests than give ear to the sniveling of vassals, and would never take foreigners' gold to line the plush interior of their clansmen's tribal coffers."

"The gold your colleagues have taken, Sruk, would fill this hall," called a voice. The murmuring began again.

Sruk's back straightened and he set his jaw. "I will not surrender to the despair of these times–"

Another stood. "Sirs, the exactions of this Triumvirate will engulf our city in revolution if we don't act to stop it." A chorus of voices echoed agreement.

"However, I agree that something must be done," hastily concluded Sruk. "My proposition is this: that the annual tribute from Nasvetin be reduced from 2000 to 1800 mir, that the garrison there be doubled, and that Flores-Sumvensor-Turlicum be reinstated with full honor and privileges, and be asked to head the investigative Public Commission without further delay."

A hearty burst of approval followed as the chamber hungrily devoured the raw meat of appeasement. Mosum breathed deeply and cast the first black block onto the marbled floor. The rest of the chamber followed suit. The vote was near unanimous and the Nasvetinian delegates, disappointed but relieved, departed the Assembly Hall for home. Token achievements were better than none.

Flores heard of his reinstatement while in the Avenue of Murfenmas. Aloft in palanquins, he and his heir, Mesret, lumbered toward the plaza on the shoulders of slaves, beneath linen bonnets spread to break the suns' glare, shielded by hired blades.

The Assembly had dispersed. Statesmen and other Simet-sa mingled with the mob, in plush sedans or on foot, which to them was unseemly if unavoidable. The plaza and the adjoining marketplace were strewn with skirted Vensor-sa citizens visiting the state House of Prostitution, or children fleeing the discipline of the state Orphanage for the state public baths. The municipal police dismantled makeshift dwellings of the poor or homeless on the square's outskirts. It was the policy of the government to keep the plaza free of barriers; no debris or construction, however transient, was allowed to break the level space. In contrast the marketplace was a labyrinth of platforms and stalls, formally temporary and removable, but which had become permanent through official neglect. Here, itinerant traders and merchants, mostly foreigners swarthy from their travels and not permitted to leave the market after dark, blazoned commodities and a galaxy of skills, under the neglectful eye of indolent guardsmen. Occasionally one glimpsed weary refugees from the far valley of the Tlaam–there was a new king in Neset.

The toiling bondsmen brought their regal cargo to rest before a platform in the bazaar. A network of canvas tents framed the platform and the goods it displayed–chattel, stripped bare and manacled with iron, were led and exercised for the perusal of potential buyers, for the most part Ven nobles. Vensor convicts and Vensor captives taken in war from other cities, including a few Vaw-sa from the southern ocean, were presented for the rich to renew their stock of domestic labor. Many golden ingots changed hands. At one side, Flores noted the nobles from Nasvetin buying workers for the Mines of Maanus; for those unfortunates he felt pity. The proceeds, however, would help keep the poor of Ven alive, and, without the corta the Mines produced, the glass-smiths could make no irsrem.

"Barbarians!" said Mesret. "They are but wild animals." The youth looked upon the trade with an expression of unutterable boredom.

Flores nodded. "Yes. It would not be wise to stray within their reach. Still, their fate could be worse. At least their souls will live in Heaven...except for those." He indicated the ones being purchased by the nobles from Nasvetin. "They will be sent to the Mines. There is no succor for them–how can the malkops take them to Heaven if their bodies lie beneath the ground?"

Mesret made no sign that he had heard.

Just then the viewers were joined by more sedans, and Flores' retainers, as well as those of the newcomers, bristled with wariness–Sruk and Numsenmur had arrived. Flores' men gathered about their two litters and readied for a brawl, while Isav began to clear a path for retreat through the mob. Flores waved him back.

He leaned to Mesret. "What luck. I think we'll have a most entertaining afternoon." He straightened, smiling wanly as his arch-rivals closed.

"Flores, good sir!" Sruk said. "Where is your Assemblyman's vest? Has no one told you? You've been reinstated."

"Ah, Simet-sa, indeed I have been told. And I have you to thank for voicing that gracious suggestion." Flores bowed his head slightly.

"I accept your thanks." Sruk bowed lower. "My heart reaches out to those who lose their social standing."

"And besides, none other seemed willing to do the deed!" Numsenmur winked at Sruk and they both laughed.

"You are louts," Isav fumed.

Flores motioned him silent. "I don't know if you've had the privilege. This is Mesret–my Heir. The next generation of Turlicum glory. In fame, perhaps, destined to rival the original Murfenmas."

Numsenmur and Sruk perked respectfully. The exploits of the ancient hero were widely celebrated. Numsenmur summoned a litter from behind, in which a young man reclined, his guards reforming tensely about them. The young man took casual notice of Flores.

"And this is my Heir, Lirsus, who rivals him now," Numsenmur regained his pugnacity, "and who is sensible enough to live only in the present."

"Well, gentlemen. I can only express my gratitude again for your concern," Flores said. "It is a courageous man who risks the loyalty of friends to voice his opinion. May Vensor give him strength to weather it and hold to his convictions."

Sruk glanced at Numsenmur, puzzlement on his face.

"And I accept your praise and your concern," said Sruk. "May Vensor grant you strength."

"–in your trials to come," grunted Numsenmur.

At that moment, a strident voice commanded their attention. A pedestrian had mounted the slaves' auction block and interrupted the transactions. Brusquely, he shoved the two slave dealers off the platform.

"Vensor-sa, listen to me!"

The audience groaned. Though violating the law, public speech-makers were common, and in the turbulent state of Ven politics, increasingly vocal. Few of the crowd were interested, but they were less inclined to leave their shaded seats–the police would grab the speaker momentarily anyhow.

"Nesos, the child-killer, the butcher of Neset and Lim, Nesos, the bloody-handed terror of the Tlaam. He is but a few days' journey to the east. He is restless and hungry, his men clamor for the ritual of Atasan, and he searches for new foes this moment."

Several yelled, "Who cares?" and "Let him come!" Many began to depart as new pedestrians stopped to take in the harangue.

The demagogue flapped a white scroll in the air. "I have proof that certain Vensor-sa have met with the Neset child butchers and sold them sword and wine, armor and reven-na. At this moment, the Triumvirate count their ingots as Nesos counts his spears."

Sruk turned to Flores. "Oh, Flores, how vulgar. He is a good speaker, though. Wherever did you get him?"

Flores smiled. "He does impress one, doesn't he?"

"Quite. The form. The style. The timber of the voice."

A murmur rose from the listeners and a crowd began to gather.

"Ven totters!" the speaker yelled. "The Triumvirate wait like carrion, playing with gold as they plot the destruction of our city." The crowd began to ply him with questions and buzz among themselves. A laborer stumbled against one of Numsenmur's guards, who fell against his bearers, causing his litter to sway. Numsenmur puffed.

The speech-maker sighted Numsenmur swearing at his guards and bearers. "There!" He pointed. "There sits one in his litter, his hands dripping blood!"

The mob buzzed angrily and looked about, unsure whom the demagogue had meant. Loiterers and rabble shouted threats at the well-to-do and several shopkeepers shook their fists at all the Simet-sa in their palanquins. Several offended patriots cast stones at a swarthy merchant and drove him off, and others, not believing the speaker could have meant the Venerarch, slipped between Numsenmur's guards and kicked his bearers, trying for Flores' before being thrust back. Numsenmur's slaves lurched to avoid them and jostled him again. He reddened and began to curse.

"Lieutenant!" Numsenmur called.

"Sire!"

"I want that man." Numsenmur aimed a finger at the platform and his attendant collared several henchmen to obey. But the market police were ahead of them. They elbowed through the crowd, swords drawn and bucklers ready, and clambered onto the stage from both directions to arrest the rabble-rouser, who lost no time in bolting. A sweating slave-owner briefly tried to hold him, but was pushed aside, and the speaker leaped into the tangle of tents behind the platform. The encumbered police, joined by Numsenmur's men, clumsily pursued but soon emerged prey-less. A gaunt police captain gestured to his men to disperse the mob. Scuffles broke out and the police began to club them as another squad trotted up.

Sruk remained calm but alert as he eyed the author of the incident.

Flores coyly smiled upon the hubbub.

"Captain!" Numsenmur commandeered the militiaman, who approached and bowed. "Well? Where is he?"

The officer drew back in surprise. "The man, sir? He has hidden in the crowd. I don't know where he is."

A callused paw struck him across his face.

"Find him, man, or you'll take his place!" Numsenmur roared as the officer reeled back. He clutched his jaw, then bowed again, more stiffly. At that moment, a larger scuffle erupted to one side of the platform and it was evident that the offender or at least a facsimile had been apprehended.

Numsenmur gloated. Sruk seemed anxious and peered at his colleague as if to read something unspoken. Several police, one for each limb, hauled the man free of the mob which, though cowed, continued to murmur. The guards halted before the Serclasler clansmen and argued until the captain intervened. They handed over the suspect. The henchmen dragged the struggling and disheveled man forward. Numsenmur glanced at Flores, who straightened, unable to mask his dismay.

"A fair exchange?" Numsenmur shifted his muscled bulk, causing his litter bearers to stagger. "You rough up mine, and I rough up yours?" His expression grew crafty. "The news will be interesting tonight with such a talkative new acquaintance."

For a moment Flores seemed disoriented. His eyes flitted from the broken man to the crowd. Then they narrowed. "Captain..."

The gaunt officer approached.

"What is the law on public incitement to riot?"

"Imprisonment... until public execution."

As if announcing the taking of a pawn, Flores called, "Then you will do your duty... as the Assembly has ordered."

The captain took in the situation. He turned a malicious glare upon Numsenmur, then turned and barked orders to his squads. Quickly they reclaimed their captive and packed him off.

"The Assembly's will is law," pronounced Flores. "None may disobey."

He breathed contentedly.

For a moment Numsenmur seemed about to intervene, but stopped when his gaze fell upon Sruk. The aged man appeared distracted. Senile? thought Numsenmur. Even he?

As they moved away, Mesret, who had found the interchange of passing interest, spoke. "What will happen to that man, Flores? Will they kill him?"

The Turlicum Lord remained silent for a time, his litter swaying as they rejoined the flow of traffic.

"Kill him?" he said at last. "No...you forget. I am now Public Commissioner. I will pardon him in the morning."

CHAPTER 3

THE MOONLIT TOWER

"Reflex! Reflex! Pivot...to the right! Reflex–don't cabré!"

The reven descended and the staff held by Mesret's opponent clacked against the youth's glass-plated midriff.

"Have you got it?" Flores approached. While Mesret watched, he spun his hand in demonstration. "When in doubt, reflex. Never pivot right, always left. If you turn right, then reflex." Flores backed away. "Isav–again. This time, cant him if he errs."

Isav pulled his reins and the grey beast rippled its massive tail. The reven stepped backwards. Mesret perched on his mount uncertainly, his legs barely able to cling to its barrel-like flanks. His bare skin was drenched with sweat and he held a blunt staff in his right fist, a heavy rod ill-suited for sparring.

A tender splashed water on the youth's reven, then poured it directly on its gills. The animal spluttered through the muzzle.

Flores pointed. Isav spurred his mount and the reven leaped, seeking to ram its opponent with its chest.

"Reflex!" barked Flores.

Mesret's reven sprang backwards in response.

"Propel!"

Isav sprang forward.

"Reflex!"

Mesret leapt back.

Flores raised his hand while Isav propelled again.

"Pivot!"

He flung his hand down. Mesret snapped his mount to the left.

"Good! Now cabré!"

The youth lifted the staff. He lost his hold on the reven and dropped the staff to regain his seat. Isav pivoted and raised his weapon–too slowly. Flores saw the opportunity and opened his mouth to shout encouragement to Mesret. The youth cabréd and Flores grinned. Weaponless, a rider could still rear his mount to crush his enemy–if the enemy were slow he would miss his chance to cant.

The smile faded.

Mesret had slipped off and fallen to the ground, where he lay groaning and clutching his leg.

Isav dismounted.

Flores examined his son–nothing broken, but he had fallen heavily. As Mesret limped off the yard with the aid of his teacher, Isav shook his head.

Flores followed the youth with his eyes. "He'll make the ritual, Isav. You'll see. He is still young."

"There is time, Flores, yes."

"He has his grandfather's blood! When I have given my own for Turlicum, he will lead the tribe. Responsibility follows necessity!"

With a strigil, Flores scraped the dust off his torso in great sweeps from neck to loin-skirt and flung the sweat soaked grime aside. He unsheathed his irsrem rapier and deftly split the air. He inhaled deeply, closed his eyes, and concentrated. In an instant, the artificial bonds of rote instruction fell away, to be replaced by the emotionless conditioning of the Simet cult of violence. The prisms in his blade flashed in the light of the suns: blues, orange, ultramarine. Flores felt his hand tingle as the glass responded to his mounting lust for battle. Pausing to mount reven-na, he and Isav crossed swords in a series of swift hammerings, a single spark flashing briefly at each contact. Minutes passed and a warm breeze rose to ripple dust across the yard at intervals. Pausing, they mounte reven-na.

The two sparred in a trance-like state, repeating the traditional movements in all their permutations, maneuvers rooted in the natural abilities and inclinations of the amphibious beasts they rode: propelment to rush, reflex to spring back, pivot to counter a move by swiveling on a flank, the cabré to drive home the blade while one's mount crushed the mount of the enemy, or the cant–the attempt to lever one's opponent from the saddle. Finally, they halted. The breeze vanished, the dust ceased rippling, and the two warriors allowed their beasts to return to their water-filled stalls. Flores and his captain bathed in the militia barracks and Isav accompanied his chieftain to the Turlicum's apartments.

Flores took in the view of the city, then paused before the glass cage.

Antennae shifted with his approach.

"Do you have compunction?" Flores kept a covert, expressionless eye upon his captain.

"None, Flores."

"You understand that as of this moment I only suspect–I must be certain. If I am right and we ignore it, we could find our hides nailed to the city wall. Watch, but do nothing. Only after I obtain final confirmation, when I know for sure, will I act."

"I understand, my lord."

"As a Turlicum, I am not in the habit of asking such from my clansmen."

"Turlicum is my life and my clan as well as yours. For the sake of us all, we must know."

Flores nodded. "Let me know tomorrow what you find." He straightened several scrolls. "I myself will be gone by midnight."

৯ ৪০ ৫৪ ৶

After the suns had vanished, Isav emerged from the shadow of a tenement and crossed a broad avenue to a ponderous porte cochere that threatened to engulf the avenue. Pornographic iconalia marked the entrance of the House of Prostitution, gilded phalluses and genitals of chalcedony and rorewood protruding from the structure. Isav passed several eunuchs loitering beneath its veranda and, with head lowered, entered the domain of the Eunuch Lord.

The interior was bathed in steam and shadow. The Turlicum warrior traversed a series of rooms without event and without accomplishing his purpose. He paused. His lips projected and rippled as he observed the occasional customers who were always to be found in the State House. The sacred profession did not evoke from him the same degree of emotion that it did from others. Isav was of that rare middle ground to which the oldest loyalties, the most inviolate institutions, and the newest innovations evoked the same response. Formal support or opposition was sufficient. That he insisted upon, and would have been sincerely outraged had anyone suggested he might be disloyal to his fatherland, or his city. But in private he held with equal conviction that his feelings were his own, and reserved private praise or condemnation for anyone or any custom that he felt deserved such judgment. The State House itself deserved indifference. Its lord, on the other hand, merited else. Soorkrul the Eunuch Lord counted his enemies and adherents in the thousands and did not conceal his support for Ven's Triumvirate. That support was enough to incur the wariness of Flores. But Isav also recalled the tales of assassination which the Eunuch Lord's wards had allegedly committed at his command. That was what cemented Isav's opposition to Soorkrul, and angered the Turlicum officer.

Isav shook his head, still brooding. Had he lost his quarry?

Several forms materialized. Three thin youths painted like bright demons coalesced to block his path. Their hair was dyed green and twined with feathers, their skin was blue or crimson, and bland, smug expressions were upon their shining alien faces. One approached and laid a red-palmed hand on Isav, then held out his empty palm for the customary payment.

Without effort Isav disengaged the youth's flaccid grasp and pushed past, pretending to be in pursuit of some particular object of passion. He passed numerous rooms and cubicles into which the common-folk of the city passed or departed. He turned a corner of hewed stone and caught sight of a broad back with a cape. The caped man stood by a painted youth, and for a time their lips moved in silent conversation. The man removed his cape, and together they entered an apartment, a cubicle too small for a third to enter unobserved.

Isav approached the entrance. He again paused and listened. No sound emanated from the room. Finally, his face covered by an arm, he glanced about the corner in a seemingly casual manner. The room lay empty. Isav stared. How could they have left? The only solution was an alternate entrance. Isav entered. He examined the far wall and soon found what he had suspected—a green feather projecting from a crack in the masonry near the floor. The youth had recently passed through an opening that was now hidden.

Pressing his ear to the wall, he listened. He heard nothing. He felt the wall around the feather, pressing, peering, then stumbled. A portion of the floor where he had been standing, almost contained by the corner of two walls, had dropped beneath the weight of his foot. A wave of steam descended from the ceiling, temporarily blinding him. Isav grasped the wall for support and lurched as his grip closed upon emptiness. The wall had gone. A section the size of a small door had opened before him. Isav passed through the opening.

He found himself in a damp tunnel, dark except for the flickering torchlight that penetrated from a bend at its far end. Advancing, he peered round the corner into a wide and broad room, sparsely furnished and dimly lit. But the light was sufficient to make out four individuals who stood and spoke at the far end. One was his quarry, the man with the cape. Another the prostitute whom he had seen moments before–Isav caught his breath in speculation of the identity of the third. It all fell into place. Who else could it be? A man in dark cassock that covered all flesh except his hands, and the cowl which hid his face, gave close attention to the man with the cape, nodding from time to time in the direction of the fourth figure, a eunuch servant-assistant apparently committing the conversation to memory. After a time he ceased speaking, the robed one nodded, and Isav supposed that beneath the cowl he could see Soorkrul the Eunuch Lord smile.

The caped man and consort turned and made for the spot where Isav stood.

Quickly the Turlicum warrior retraced his path to the steam-room. A simple push opened the door from his side, relieving his anxiety on that score, and Isav plunged into the steam. Soon the man with the cape exited the porte cochere and, with a short pause to ascertain whether he had been seen or followed, was again enveloped by the tenement's shadow. Isav waited till the cape vanished. He had seen all he needed.

꙰ ಖ ಚ ꙰

At the same moment that Isav departed the domain of the Eunuch Lord, the heavens cast a flush radiance over a pair of silent figures across the city. One of the figures released an iron grating and quietly pulled it ajar. Beyond the grating was a rocky bluff that descended sharply to a wide and deep river where night-torches of the city glimmered, snaking with the banks into blackness. The pair silently descended. Cached in a muddy alcove lay a shallow pirogue, and the two conspirators slipped into the flowing stream, their paddles dipping noiselessly until they floated with the current. Sometime later the foremost figure turned and motioned to his partner. The two steered the pirogue toward a low bluff and breached it. Approaching the shallow grade, the first of the two pulled aside a profusion of dry brush and plants to reveal a circular hole in the earth. The two slipped inside the crumbling pipe to vanish.

Tilsis and Flores emerged in an abandoned privy with dust and grime piled in the corners. A perforated bench ran along the walls. The pipe through which they had come ran underneath the bench where a gap opened through the masonry. They wriggled through, avoiding a gaping black pit in the floor, brushed themselves, cautiously crossed an adjacent chamber which was equally disused, and crept to an open doorway on a wide, dimly lit corridor with swept slabs of stone and solid walls of brick. The servant strolled casually down the corridor and opened a wooden panel. He gestured for Flores to approach. The mute followed Flores through the aperture and shut it as muffled footfalls drifted from behind.

They stood between the walls of a cylindrical tower. A narrow stone staircase curved above and to the right, almost obscured in the darkness. After several revolutions, Tilsis paused and pressed a hidden release. The entrance swung open and Tilsis led Flores through a darkened room into a larger chamber, the green emanations of Tumsenet setting the interior aglow through a broad bay window. Lights of the city twinkled beneath them.

For a minute Flores thought the servant awaited someone else's arrival as Tilsis stood with folded arms and stared out the window, seemingly ignoring him. Flores turned to inspect the room and was startled to discover a figure in dark clothing observing him from behind a partition. Flores stepped forward. His observer swiftly pulled a section of the partition to block his approach, then the servant stepped between and indicated that Flores was to sit upon an adjacent divan. He sat.

An engraved section of the partition, perforated by several convoluted gaps, was between him and his mysterious observer. After a moment the other drew near. Through the gaps in the woodwork the green rays of Tumsenet fell upon a face. The visage was youthful and delicately proportioned. Healthy, thought Flores, if pale. He noted the high neckline and compassing folds of cloth–the traditional garments of the eunuch house. Amber eyes penetrated through the green-tinged gloom, curled eyelashes contrasting with straight locks clipped short. For a moment it seemed to Flores that the youth's gaze reflected hopeful optimism as the delicate eyes searched his own, but the impression faded, or was forcibly suppressed, to be replaced by a more habitual hardness. Flores frowned and turned to his guide.

"Is this who wrote the note? It is but a child."

Tilsis spread his hands in assent. He turned and bowed humbly toward the figure behind the partition.

"My name is Crestal-Nidrenmor-Serclasler."

Flores reeled as if struck. "CNS. Crestal-Nidrenmor-Serclasler!" He glared about him. "And this–the palace of Numsenmur!"

"Yes."

"Vensor curse you!" Flores leaped to his feet and made for the door to the inner chamber.

"No, wait!" called Crestal. "We haven't harmed you. I wish to help."

In his haste, Crestal disturbed the partition and it shuddered and fell. In the doorway Flores paused. No guards had appeared, and the youth spoke rapidly through a fold of cloth hastily drawn over his face as Tilsis replaced the partition.

"Numsenmur doesn't know you're here. He isn't on the estate tonight. You're perfectly safe. No one knows of your presence here but us." Tilsis remained attentive to the youth, while Flores peered at the darkened corners of the room.

"Why did you ask me here?"

The cloth was lowered and the youth's illumined face returned to the protection of the partition.

"To save your life."

The Turlicum's puzzlement increased. "How?"

The youth breathed more easily. "Won't you sit? Please? Tilsis will escort you back whenever you like. Hand him your dagger, Tilsis. We must make him feel safe."

Flores acquiesced and cautiously returned to the divan. Tilsis approached and proffered his weapon handle-first as Flores eyed the servant with fresh distrust. He accepted the weapon and placed it beneath his belt.

The youth peered at him from between the ribs of wood and his voice assumed an indulgent tone. "Flores, I don't wish to address you like a slave. Have some wine, some fruit. You must be hungry after your trip." The Turlicum stared in surprise. The incongruity of eye and ear struck him as absurd. That a child hiding behind a curtain should speak to him thus! Tilsis indicated a low table by the divan. With a smile, Flores sat, ignoring the food.

"Tilsis, I need my chambers now. No one must see us here." The servant withdrew to the far side of the chamber out of earshot, but close enough to respond if needed.

As Flores' eyes adjusted to the darkened interior, his gaze wandered about the room. It was large, luxurious. Rugs and cushions littered the place. The huge windows alone were worth a fortune; they were real glass, clear and fragile, not irsrem. Flores could see spires glinting with starlight in the surrounding estates. Spurs and complexes of Numsenmur's palace stretched before the window. Not as wealthy as

Sendas, the Serclasler was still one of Ven's richest men, and outdid Flores in the opulence of his estate.

"So a consort of the famous Numsenmur invites his master's enemy into his harem at night. Why? To dally? A diverting evening of unlawful relations? I think it absurd that a man who cannot govern his own harem would govern a city."

The luminous face paled. "What is said here will not pass beyond these walls. Even so, I would not violate the guild laws of consort fidelity. As for diversions," his voice crinkled, though he remained unsmiling, "I have no need. But if I did–the chief consort of Numsenmur is refused nothing."

Still suspicious, Flores glanced about the chamber. "How long have you been with Serclasler?" he finally asked.

"Six years."

"And how old are you?"

"Forty."

Flores' skeptical expression resurfaced. "Are you sure it's not thirty-five, boy? Or thirty?"

"I'm forty... that is, I will be on the next day of spawning. I look younger, I know–but I am not a boy." His voice became thin and sharp.

"Forty is an appropriate age for a consort."

"Not of the famous Numsenmur."

"Oh?"

"Numsenmur's favorites are young."

"You are younger than thirty?" Flores' tone suggested moral indignation.

"I'm forty. And still his favorite. That is all I meant." The eyes lowered. "Don't you want to know why I asked you here?"

"I have asked once."

The youth reached forward, grasped the end of the partition and folded the last leaf back, then rested small delicate hands upon a cloth-enshrouded lap. After a moment, he grew more cautious and pulled the partition forward so that only sandaled feet were visible next to Flores' boots. He looked back to Flores, again through the restrictive carving. "I learned something the last time I was with Numsenmur. He confided something in me. It has to do with you."

"Oh? How?"

"He told me...that he intends to kill you."

"And–"

"And what?" The green eyes turned yellow. "Isn't that enough?

That's all." The youth's voice returned to a high pitch.

"There is more. Tell, me, really, why did you ask me here?"

"I have told you. Numsenmur is going to try to take your life!" The youth's voice trembled. "Don't you care?"

Flores began to chuckle. He stood and laughed. The youth peered as at a lunatic, the recovered with an icy haughtiness as understanding dawned.

"So that is it," laughed Flores. "This is why you dragged me on hands and knees through sewers and down rivers in the middle of the night, stealing like a common thief, and risking my life. To tell me something that not only I already know, but that the entire city and half the world knows? Of course Numsenmur is trying to kill me! He has been for months. And I am trying to kill him. And Sruk, and Sendas, and a dozen others!"

Crestal's gaze lowered again, nursing bruised pride. "You should be grateful. I didn't have to do you this favor."

"I wonder just how unselfish your 'favor' was."

The youth stood, his chest heaving. "You speak to me thus. In seconds I could have Numsenmur's guards within this room. Maybe then you would show some manners!"

A vile curse exploded from Flores' lips. He backed away, and turned.

"Wait! I'm sorry." Crestal stepped from behind the partition and caught his arm. Flores pulled away roughly, making him cry out. As Tilsis turned near the window, the partition again collapsed. Seeing his master stumble and Flores disappear through the door to the inner chamber, the servant charged, his mouth working mutely in rage.

"Let him go!" Crestal rubbed his arm. "He didn't hurt me." For several moments the youth shivered. Then, as an inner structure sacred and delicate, crumbled to ruin, he withdrew once more into darkness, drew the comforting folds of cloth about his face, and coughed bitter tears.

❧ ಖ ಛ ❦

In another part of Ven, a young man fumbled nervously at the door of a crumbling house, and slipped within. His eyes focused on a lambent glow that seeped through torn curtains and a misaligned door, and a rickety table appeared along with several unreliable chairs, some uncertain furniture, and split walls. A pair of doorways loomed opposite and the man planted himself within one, fingering the butt of a dagger.

The seeping light abruptly dimmed as shrouded figures converged on the outer door. The panel opened and a shadow entered. The young man sank deeper in the gloom. At a clandestine signal, the remainder of the group streamed in, compassing the table and the entrance and directed their attention to the windows and the narrow alleyway beyond. A flame sprouted from a portable lamp–the bearded face of Numsenmur-Nidrenmor-Serclasler flickered redly, bellicose and stern. His cohorts drew their blades about him. The hidden man silently unsheathed his, hissing to himself.

"We'll wait in the positions as I said," Numsenmur said. "In the dark so that nothing will appear suspicious–"

Hands grabbed the young man from behind and thrust him headlong into the room as they wrenched away his weapon.

"So, we won't have to wait after all," Numsenmur crowed as more ruffians entered through the third door. The captive was subdued and bound. "We can start the night's business right now."

Numsenmur confronted his prisoner. "Why did you come here? Whom did you expect to meet?"

Silence.

"Who sent you?"

The young man hesitated. He set his jaw.

"Son, if you want to grow up, you'll cooperate." Numsenmur poised jauntily, then sank a first into the prisoner's belly. The youth gasped and doubled over. The warlord punched him again, then motioned for his men to take over as he returned to the table.

"Take him into the next room." Numsenmur rested and pulled out a slip of vellum to read it one more time. Soon the men returned and he resumed his questioning with patient confidence.

"Why did Flores send you?"

"To...to meet someone." The captive mumbled painfully through swollen lips.

"Who?"

"Just someone...alone, and without arms."

"Why?" The guards shook him.

He winced with pain. "I don't know."

"You're lying. Into the other room."

The henchmen dragged him off and Numsenmur turned up the lamp. Soon another group of shrouded figures arrived and the tired and cranky voice of Sruk sounded at the entrance.

"Numsenmur! Why all the skulking about at such an hour?" The orator approached and removed his hood as Sendas joined them.

"This." Numsenmur handed them the vellum. "Note this well. This was tossed, tied about a stone, onto my property two days ago. It says that a man sent by Flores will meet at this spot a man who is to arrange the defection of one of the Triumvirate, in secret, but that the meeting is merely a ruse to sow distrust among us. And signed: 'a friend.'"

Sruk looked up. "This is preposterous!"

"And here is what I have found." He gestured to his men who brought in the captive. "He doesn't like to talk, but I think he has about changed his mind."

He turned to the captive, who was propped erect, bleeding. "Once more. Who sent you?"

"Turlicum."

"Why did he send you?"

"To meet an agent of the Triumvirate."

"For what reason?"

"One of them..." He struggled to catch his breath. "...is defecting to the Turlicum."

Numsenmur waved him off again.

Sendas chuckled. "Why, this is completely silly! To think of such a thing. The very idea."

"Yes," echoed Sruk. "I don't believe it. But let's hear from our spy. Has he had anything to say?"

"Yes. But first–I want to say a few things." Numsenmur offered them wooden chairs, sat on one backwards, then leaned forward. "When my men brought me this note, my first thought was to reject the idea that either of you had defected. You know that Flores is a greater threat to each of us than we are to each other. After coming this far, it wouldn't make sense for us to split when our victory is so close and Flores' defeat so near. I thought there could be but one explanation for this sneaking around: Flores was laying a trap. I had already decided to alert you and accept this invitation, despite the risk, but I wanted to receive word from out traitor. This is what he said: There is a man named Sorotir who works for the Venholis. It is he who is the 'agent of the Triumvirate' whom this dupe is supposed to meet. But it all means nothing because the man is a mere commoner who was chosen at random for use as a 'front.' The truth is that Turlicum planted the note and fully intended us to capture this messenger. His only purpose behind all this conspiring is to try to split us by sowing distrust, by pretending that our split has already occurred. That is all!" Numsenmur grinned as Sruk and Sendas listened open-mouthed.

"That young man in there really believes that one of us is defecting, and doesn't know which. Sirs, Flores has shown himself willing to sacrifice his own followers in desperate, childlike attempts to end our cooperation before we crush him utterly."

Sendas exploded in triumph. "My tongue tingles with the sweet smell of success!"

Numsenmur slapped the table with an open palm, still grinning. "This is a desperate attempt by Flores to salvage something from his situation. The man hurts more than we had hoped."

"I do admire his tenacity, though," said Sruk. "I had expected him to go into voluntary exile before this."

"And perhaps he will. But now," Numsenmur gripped his friends' shoulders. "See this man? He is young, impetuous. He is eager and gullible in his foolishness. He would as soon have run a dagger into our vitals as pursue errands for his master. Flores is not impotent. Again, I implore you, let's stop wasting time–surely now we are agreed."

Sendas spoke. "And how silly for him to accuse us of recruiting the Eunuch Guild for assassination. He knows the Assembly would never stand for it. And why should we? We all know the Turlicum has no harem. How could a eunuch get near him? These are all mere inventions of Flores."

"Yes," replied Numsenmur. "Soorkrul insists that he has no assassins, but who knows what game he plays with the Turlicum, or with us? We may one day find killers planted in our own harems. We must protect ourselves from all, therefore it is time for the real game to begin. We should move before Flores does something out of desperation that we shall all regret. Agreed, Sruk?"

The old parliamentarian rubbed his chin. "This is too quick. I need more time to think."

"We haven't time," said Numsenmur. "The longer we wait, the more support we lose in the Assembly. We must strike while we still have enough votes."

"Yes, that is right. All right, agreed."

"Sendas?"

"With utmost enthusiasm."

◈ ❦ ◈

CHAPTER 4

CALLING FOR SONS

The following day at mid-morning, beneath circling malkops, a gong sounded from a spire within the Temple and rolled like muffled thunder across the sky. As the last waves died, Ven gathered to another calling for its sons. The day was the fifteenth of Nevneset, a special holiday for the clan of Turlicum. It was on this day a century earlier that Flores' grandfather had crushed the men of Ror with reven-na bought from a coastal town, introducing the beasts to the middle Hedronmas. Grimly they burnt the temple of their foe and slew all within. Its ruins now lay deserted. On the same day in the hazy memory of folklore, a Turlicum resisted the entry into Ven of a mob of refugees mad with plague, by barring the gate with arrows until the portals could be secured. His rusted clan helmet still rested above the pylon.

Now, answering the summons, Flores passed through a new Ven of jutting irsrem spikes and scutate domes, riotous with the clashing of ritual timbrels and the whistling of many flutes. Vensor was pleased. His wakefulness danced on glass as He drenched the files of worshipers with His breath. Flores had donned his state apparel–the public had a right to see its leaders in their best, though he looked haggard in his litter, having returned to his estate only in the early hours before dawn. At his side walked bodyguards and an elderly slave waving a half-moon fan of brown rum-na feathers. Mesret occupied a second litter, his expression morose–typical for the Heir. He glanced toward his father reproachfully, till Lasmer looked his way. The boy keened on Lasmer and would stare at him when he thought the officer's attention was elsewhere, but could not endure the man's direct gaze. As befit a retainer, Lasmer walked with a blank expression beside Flores' palanquin; the Heir's affection had placed him in an uncertain capacity. At the last moment, Isav joined, watching the streets and alleyways for attempts on the life of his feudal master, Flores.

The shrill voices of criers relayed the approaching celebration to the throng of Vensor-sa converging before the Temple gate. Eunuchs with shaved heads, accompanied by the head of their Guild, appeared on a raised walkway that led from their complex to the plaza. In the center of the platform rose a tower of brick and mortar; they quickly found their places and raised their arms to stare into the burning orbs without respite, long blind from their devotions, and consequently unable to view the interior of the sacred cloisters. Clangs and gongs sounded as latecomers shoved, swaying nobles hastened, and the magistrate rushed to assume his post. The wailing became shrill and thin, then piercing as the suns neared zenith.

Above the gate spanned a carven entablature surmounted by an onion dome. Here were balconies, and a swarm of dark priests moved behind crenelated ramparts, over rutted arabesques of limestone and granite. The priests were wrapped head to foot in black swaths of circling cloth that revealed only a faint glimmering of eyes and vague outlines. Whether they were humans or animals none could say. They were stewards of the rites, guardians of the sacred spring, and deliverers to the children of Vensor of His endless bounty, their sons–His sons.

The gong within the Temple rang a second time, and the gate cranked skyward, inch by inch, huge gears squealing to heave it aloft. Within was a courtyard, bare and paved with flagstones, upon each a wide flat altar, and solid ramparts as hard and imposing as the walls without rose on either side. Huddled figures passed upon them. A loud squalling and crying emanated from the courtyard. On the altars, hundreds of male infants too young to crawl were placed, each without clothing, in the center of a single flagstone cupped and eroded from long eons of use.

The magistrate of Ven drooped the rattan cane and a crier called forth the first name: "Toosel-Nibpantis-Tooselwat!" A man of some youth passed under the portcullis and walked to his ancestral site. The man located an altar with a specific inscription and gently lifted the wailing infant from the alter. As he exited the gate, a second title rang forth: "Fursel-Flortumset-Leredol!" Fursel was older and a son stood by his side. He made no move and the caller proceeded to the next.

The Serclasler Heir stood beside his father. When the Serclasler's name was called, neither moved. As the crier came to Sruk, Flores barely noticed. For long years he had expected the older man to adopt—since no son had ever appeared on Sruk's ancestral stone. But Sruk had not. Now the elderly statesman declined even to appear. Though Sendas was present, he too already had a son. As Flores had expected, Hama of the Venholis also had not appeared. When the crier had finished reciting the titles of every warrior clan of Ven and all the Houses had had an opportunity to renew their blood, the magistrate motioned and those of the common people who wished a son entered and chose from among the remaining infants, which were still a great number, to raise as their own. When this was done, more than half the original number remained—these were collected by state functionaries and transported to the city's Orphanage to be raised as slaves or eunuchs, or eventually to be released en masse at the appropriate age to till the City's fields and collect the harvest.

After the removal of the infants, the nobility proceeded to the far side of the Temple court, which was bounded by a gallery of narrow lanced arches overshadowing a dark interior. From each arch a thread of steam wisped. The men filed beneath the arcade and entered a spacious brooding chamber, the ceiling of which swam with steam. Glowing braziers put forth a red effulgence which illuminated the images of the Urlis, the Tribe of Heaven. Here the faithful pled for mercy, called forth thanks, or renewed their grace, dropping prostrate upon a floor of stone so worn and ancient that it sloped and undulated like a frozen sea. Pitted visages of Maalstrom-bone gazed silently: white Nantifus of the mountains, frowning with contempt; winged Talen of the wilds, baring claws and reptilian tail; Tumsenet of the forests, smiling, with roots for feet; enigmatic Nvediteg, resting on clouds with rain and lightning in his hands; and oceanic Gethos, his scales a deep-sea blue.

Towering over all was the yellow idol of Vensor. Its ponderous bulk squatted, its hands—minuscule in comparison to its massive body—resting on the flexed knees of equally small legs. The head was absurdly small. Constructed of gold, the massive statue joined with the wall, seeming to continue beyond the stone into the Temple proper. The steam emanated from a grill positioned between the feet at eye level. A wide staircase of mortared stone arrowed from the floor to end in a platform just below the chin of the idol whose eyes glowed redly in the steam-laden shadows. From the head, a fan of gold rays projected in imitation of the suns' exudence.

The magistrate pointed the rattan cane and a long queue of brawny laborers and slaves dragged in the Assembly's offerings. Soon the laborers had filled the chamber with the spoils of the three valleys, a dazzling array of tribute collected from a score of subject cities. Some left wicker baskets of grain of ses and rore-rush, others tubs of dunmelons, pickled hen, and flesh of reven and lyart. The more wealthy clans did not miss the occasion for public advertisement of their status. Turlicum clansmen deposited barrels of ses, lyart flesh, and rich cloths of lyart-hair and karakul of Vok from Nene. Flores, perhaps to counter the charge of lack of patriotism stemming from his opposition to the Triumvirate's exactions and the Eunuchs' Guild, had again surpassed himself in his personal contributions.

The Serclasler chief, not to be outdone, had bushels of grain, an iron sword inlaid damascene, and demijohns of waistwood oil for lamps. The magistrate and several nobles were scandalized, for arms of any kind were not supposed to pass the portcullis. A dispute on this most sacred of ground might bring disaster on the entire city by causing Vensor to disown his children and turn his attention elsewhere. Several nobles fidgeted and made moves as if to speak to Numsenmur, only to be confounded when Flores revealed his offering–a matched rapier and corselet of irsrem tinted beryl. The other nobles forgot their speeches and interposed themselves between the two, who ignored them and each other, quite content with the outcome.

The Assembly then placed finely worked ornaments and ware of gold and silver for the priests' use–nothing that the inhabitants of the Temple might fancy or desire was omitted.

The magistrate summoned Flores and Numsenmur, and the trio mounted the steps to the face of the idol of Vensor, the rivals keeping the official between them as they climbed. At the top of the stairway was suspended a small railed platform upon which rested a gong. The magistrate took the hammer and rang it. When the sound had dissipated, the official unrolled a scroll and read, "Our Lord Vensor, Father of the Universe, Just and Merciful Giver of Life, Protector of the Sacred Spring, Bringer of Victory, Imposer of Order, God of Justice, Master of the Malkops..." Flores inspected his nails as the droning continued. Numsenmur stood piously with eyes closed and hands folded. "We beseech thee today to give your attention to your unworthy children, in the following: There has been revolt in Nasvetin. What course should we take?"

They waited silently for a considerable time. Finally, emanating from the mouth of the idol came a thin but commanding voice.

"The creator commands: Food."

The three looked at each other and waited. Nothing more was heard. They stroked their beards in thought, then descended. After departing the Temple, the portcullis staked shut behind them.

❧ ଔ ଓ ❧

Afterwards came the traditional feast of thanksgiving, which all the Houses of Ven attended, in the hall of Vim. The elite entered the building by clusters, each personage accompanied by glass-sporting guards, burdened servants, nervous food-tasters, dark-clothed consorts, and bedecked concubines. The hall was an elongated affair with a carved ceiling, and a row of irsrem windows on either side. Down the center of the hall, hewn from the stony outcropping upon which Old Ven was built, gaped an open, shallow trench, cut in the shape of a sunken galley, whose only access was two short flights of steps, one at either end. Running the length of the trench at floor level was a walkway of two meters' width. No commoner was allowed to set foot within the trenches, and servants hurried along the walkway between them depositing trays of melons, lyart and vok for the assembling nobles.

Lord Flores lowered himself into the trench and sat cross-legged in the location reserved for the Turlicum near one end of the hall. Directly behind him, his taster positioned himself, squatting upon the floor between Lasmer and Isav. Gradually the other nobles found their places and the banquet began.

Numsenmur made some requests of a servant before taking his place on the same side of the trench as Flores, but out of earshot, and Sruk and Sendas took their customary places opposite Flores, one and two positions to the right.

"Gam!"

Flores watched as a servant responded to Sendas' request. The latter wrestled free a hen-leg and passed it overhead momentarily, which his taster sampled. Then he held aloft a tankard for the servant to fill. After exchanging brief pleasantries with his companions on either side, Sruk addressed Flores, as if he had only just noticed the Turlicum Lord.

"Ah, Sir Flores!"

Flores did not bother to answer.

"I simply must say, Flores, if I may..." Sruk glanced at his colleagues, "that you are one of the–should I speak frankly?–strangest fellows I have had the privilege to know."

Flores finished chewing a bit of vok-meat. He cocked an ear to hear over the noisy requests for service bellowed by Sendas.

"I really don't understand you, Flores," continued Sruk. "I'm not sure anyone can."

"Life is full of mysteries, is it not, Sir Sruk?" Flores sampled his wine, swilling it in his mouth before swallowing it.

"But that's just it, Flores." Sruk leaned forward. "Life on Maalstrom is Life from Vensor–the boon of God, from Him, of Him, and when we die, back to Him. Yet you bend His laws in the heat of politics. (Some would be more blunt, but we are all friends here). For political advantage, mere heat of the moment, in the excitement of our earnest contest you become–should I speak frankly?–mean-spirited, on occasion at least. In the Assembly, you speak as if it were the city breaking the laws of Vensor, and which you, on the contrary, are seeking to restore."

"Is that not so?"

"Indeed not, Sir Flores," laughed Sruk. "The city of God must always represent the Will of God. It cannot be otherwise."

"Then are you asserting, if I understand you correctly, that Vensor's will can be determined on the basis of popular votes, or on the size of one's fortune? Or perhaps the number of trained mercenaries in a clan's barracks?"

Several other celebrants suspended their conversation to listen.

"There! That is just what I mean," Sruk laughed again, less with mirth than disbelief. "You live in Ven, observe the ancient customs, call yourself a son of Vensor, denounce your most popular and esteemed colleagues and public servants in the name of rightness and truth, then question and denigrate His will–the wisdom of centuries, when you find it inconvenient, or unpleasant, or beyond your understanding, or too distasteful, or... Or, I don't know why!" Sruk sighed in exasperation.

Flores looked up from his plate, which steadily grew with portions distributed by the gangway-bound servers.

Sruk resumed his colloquy. "For example, you criticize the Eunuch Lord, Soorkrul, and accuse him of murdering our colleagues, Jaz and Clesp. Now, my dear sir, I am a Simet noble. Don't you suppose that if there were a modicum of truth to that foul rumor, that I would be the first to embrace it? Indeed, I would vote to toss that whore, Soorkrul, into the street in moments, and nothing would please me more than to turn over his State House to you for administrative purging. But I will not. Because, my friend, you have no case! Our colleague Clesp died at the hands of his own consort, when out of jealousy he poisoned him in secret. The fact that the eunuch had recently been delivered by Soorkrul is of no significance–the Eunuch Guild trains and delivers all the consorts in the city. Really, Flores, this type of rumor is easy to spread, and easy to believe, but most difficult to stop. But stop it must. You claim that Soorkrul picks your faction off by ones, and thus draws the city into Loyalist hands. But what if the incident was only a passion of the harem and nothing more? You would then be risking civil war over a mere lovers' quarrel. Vensor knows such are common enough. Where is your evidence, Flores? Would you turn the city upside down on mere rumor?"

Flores nibbled at the vok-flesh.

Sruk turned to his friends. "See Numsenmur there. And Sendas." Numsenmur, occupied in conversation, thumped the gangway with his first, startling his neighbors. Sendas paused and looked up.

"Are these good people the dire threat you fear so greatly, that you would attack the very institution of the House of Prostitution, beloved by God?" Sruk asked. "Oppress and eject those who have already endured so much contumely from the intolerant, the narrow-minded?"

Flores passed a glance over the trio of glass-plated guards behind Sruk. Other guards stood behind Sendas and Numsenmur.

Sruk glanced quickly to either side and lowered his voice. His companions leaned forward. "My friend, we all know that some have broken the ancient laws, the rumors are rife. Gilas in private harems, the forbidden sex once more here, in Ven. I can feel them. They are here even as we speak." Sruk stared at Flores. "But you would not know of that, would you?" Turlicum returned an enigmatic, bemused expression.

Sruk broke his stare, then laughed. "You bait me, Flores!" He shook his head. "No, you would not know. You are too single minded. And it is that very single mindedness that frightens me. If only you relaxed and enjoyed life, like the other nobles."

The two seats at Sruk's right, previously unfilled, were claimed and occupied by the nobles Endel and Misenta.

Sruk continued his chat with Flores.

"Your calculated opposition to everything I and my colleagues undertake is making you extremely unpopular in certain quarters," continued Sruk. "And your reinstatement seems to have encouraged you unduly. Might I suggest something?"

"Please," replied Flores.

Sruk puckered his brows in thought, then smiled and nodded. "Numsenmur, you know, claims that it is a mistake for one to be too helpful when one has a friend in need." Sruk arched his brows receptively as if awaiting a response. When none came, he continued, "In brief, he believes–and I agree with him–that every person is already doing at all times exactly what he most desires."

"Indeed?" Flores passed a melon above his own head to be tasted.

"Indeed!" The Venerarch peered at him. "Therefore, if you were to assist a friend in need, what you are really doing is harming him–even if he doesn't realize it–since he already is doing what he in fact most desires."

"What is this?" Hem spoke from beside Flores. "In all circumstances?"

"Yes!"

"But sir," interrupted Flores, "what if the gentleman in question is being imposed upon by someone else? Surely you are not suggesting that justice requires the allowance of interference by a third party, or the indulgence of criminal passion?"

"No, of course not. However, one can imagine a reply which an advocate of this position might give–that sometimes it is not so simple to distinguish victims from criminals, and that in some cases he who at first glance appears to be the innocent party, may in an abstract sense be, how shall I say, 'holding the reins'?"

Flores smiled. "Well, then. We must do as we see fit, and let posterity decide where the right lies."

Sruk looked crestfallen. "I see that my words will not dissuade you from your purpose."

"Indeed not, Sir Sruk, as you should know by now."

The Turlicum Lord turned to Sendas, who had been busy downing melons and drumsticks since the conversation began. "What do you think, Sir Sendas?" called Flores. "Does this theory of Numsenmur's hold water?"

"Theory?" Sendas rinsed his fingers in a shallow bowl. "Oh, yes I would agree with that. You would be robbing him of his rights as an adult to be independent, because then he would have no opportunity to develop himself and learn how to accept responsibility, something every son of Vensor must do."

"Well, who could disagree with that?" said Flores amiably as Sruk sighed and looked away.

Endel and Misenta, both aristocrats opposed to the Triumvirate but who had persistently refused to coordinate their activities with Flores' faction, now joined the discussion.

"You mean to say," queried Endel, "that if you have a friend, and he appears to be unhappy, one should not believe him in the least, because he brought himself to such an end?"

"Yes, you have it," said Sruk. "So can you imagine a greater fool than the one," Sruk looked back to Flores, "who would meddle and seek to turn one friend against another?"

"Not I," said Flores.

"Perfectly put," said Sendas. "And the world's greatest fool is the professional philanthropist who dribbles golden mir left and right just to help those less fortunate than himself. What a waste!"

"Oh look," Isav called, pointing down the aisle. "The Venholis did come."

"Oh yes," said Sruk. "There is Sir Hama now. And Kal, and Melat, and Sorotir as well."

Flores made no sound, but turned slowly to gaze at Sruk.

"Sendas," Sruk said, "I'm afraid I must disagree with you. The 'dribbling' of gold, as you put it, is not philanthropy. In fact, it would be the purest of self-interest–the purchase of power."

"What? Are you certain?"

"Quite certain. I believe Sir Flores would agree with me on this point."

Flores had returned to his meal.

Finishing some sweetwood, Endel brushed his hands together. "It is my turn to disagree, sirs. Philanthropy is just that–philanthropy and no more. You see, one cannot purchase power if power is not there."

"Don't be so quick to dismiss the rabble, Sir Endel," said Flores. "They are far from powerless."

"But, dear sir, the Assembly itself has no power–no real power, I mean to say."

Sruk looked at Endel askance. "The Assembly has no power?"

"A colleague of mine has done some interesting analytical studies. And after careful research he has made a momentous discovery. The fact is that the entire population of Ven are not only a disadvantaged class, but a downtrodden minority."

"Everyone you say?" Flores stared at Endel through the passing legs of a servant. "But we are a sovereign state–the most sovereign in the valleys of the Hedronmas, Tlaam, and Suma. You mustn't mean the Assembly, but only the commoners..."

"Yes, I mean the Assembly."

"Of course," anticipated Sendas, "I know what he means–that we are all servants of Vensor, and that only He has true power."

"That is true, but that is not what I mean. There is a majority which literally represses us and violates our rights as free men every day of the year." Endel leaned back and gloated over the puzzlement of his companions.

"But who, then, is oppressing us?" asked Sruk.

Endel grabbed his older colleague by the arm. "Why our ancestors, my man! We are the downtrodden victims of a monstrously huge and exploiting class–our dead forefathers from the beginning of time. Think of it. All those voting blocks cast on the marble floor of our Assembly, all those legal precedents set, all those cyclopean walls erected to impede our every action. Why, the sheer weight of our cultural heritage, being the accumulated generations of all our dead ancestors, outvotes us on every issue!"

"So those blocks we cast are not our own?"

"No. They are the votes of our ancestors, whose ghostly tyranny prevents us from exercising our full rights as Vensor-sa."

Flores and Sruk exchanged glances.

"A great crime has been uncovered," exclaimed Endel.

"You mean to say," queried Sruk, "that when we go to the Assembly and cast our votes in what we believe to be the interest of the city, or the valleys, or ourselves, or in the interests of all, we in fact are not representing the interests of any living being at all, but on the contrary are voting exclusively by and for the dead?"

"Indeed!"

"But what of those who insist they vote by and for the city, or themselves, or their tribe?"

"Duped."

"Unless, of course, it is your vote, I presume," exclaimed Flores.

"Our ancestors were wrong."

"Our ancestors are dead!"

"Same thing." Endel folded his arms. "They still must be tried for their crimes."

Sendas grasped his tankard and hit the table. "Sirs! Endel has hit upon something. Pardon me, Sruk. Gam!" Sruk sighed and returned to his meal as Sendas-Moredin-Molersal, bold epicure of a hundred banquet bloodlettings, raper of numberless lox, leapt into the fray.

"Sir Endel! What remarkable intuition! What unsurpassed insight! I agree wholeheartedly–why this very morning I was speaking with our good colleague, Sir Numsenmur, of the tyranny under which our fair city labors, feeling the pain our native land suffers, penetrating to its very sacred spring which Vensor willed should never know discomfort or violation. Feeling intuitively, yet vaguely, without a proper name to label this feeling that–" Sendas craned to circumvent a passing servant, "–some vile conspiracy, some incontinent cabal, some evil association had reared its impertinent head and caught our land in its unholy grip, attempting to inflict a crime of hideous barbarity." He cupped his hands to call through more hurrying legs. "What joy! What progress! That we can now put a name to the unspeakable danger threatening our fair city, peaceful and innocent under the bright leadership of the Venerarch and his Loyalists. Dear colleague," Sendas waved to Endel. "How would you sum up this notion of yours?"

"The excessive influence of our forefathers?" suggested Endel.

"Anti-patrimonialism!" Sendas yelled. "That is to be our battle-cry."

"Anti-what?" pleaded Sruk.

Flores placed his hands behind his neck and grinned.

"The Loyalists' enemies," continued Sendas, "have finally been exposed for what they are. Anti-change; anti-progress; anti-justice. Patrimonialists! Vile creatures that would turn the world back to barbarism and savagery in cruel violation of every right known to the children of Vensor–"

"Sruk, why did you not tell me you had entered Sir Sendas' name for election to the Commission?" asked Flores.

"My apologies. I had meant to."

"As a Public Commissioner, I must see that form is observed."

"I shall inform your scribe tomorrow."

"–well, after all, they are dead, Sir Hem," Endel was saying.

"Yes, but Numsenmur is not, and we need assistance. I have been conducting an expensive public campaign to get across the idea that the Loyalists thrive on publicity and that we should ignore them in order to lessen their influence."

"–let us not lose all to these wretched criminals!" Sendas plowed on.

"Sendas!" Sruk grabbed his friend's sleeve.

"If not this...what? If not now...when? Pardon me, Sruk. Yes?"

"Sir Scroy is giving the testimonial."

"...have enabled us to achieve the most stable and incorruptible of societies on Maalstrom..." Scroy's voice wafted across the chamber as the celebrants grew quiet.

Flores turned his gaze from Sendas to Sruk while a slave filled the old noble's glass. Sruk was old and decrepit. But how sharp those aged teeth! His own servant offered a plate of lyart flesh and Flores carefully pushed aside the more tender morsels to choose what he judged to be the leanest and toughest piece. Lasmer whispered something and his clansmen doubled with laughter. Flores strained to hear, failed, forced a smile, then returned his attention to the hall. His glance paused on Numsenmur. At his side sat his son, Lirsus. Flores nodded with respect. How like him is his son, and how unlike me is my own. While Mesret still could barely sit a mount–in fact, feigned greater incompetence than he had by falling and risking injury–Numsenmur's Heir already wore a sword. A paradox, he thought, rubbing his forearm. One man has progeny too many, another has none. One is rewarded and becomes a loyal clansman, while another, after similar reward, slips his blade into your back.

In Ven, while the suns shine, Vensor reigns supreme and all the world is right. But when the twin orbs sink beneath the Falls of Sish, Atasan stirs with corruption, plots, and lust, and then each soul must fend for itself as rum-na become prey of the ros. Flores breathed out quickly through his nose. A distorted hive took shape in his mind. His play required concentration. Nevertheless, he found it diverting. What if he did eventually succeed in finding the one correct path to the center? Since irsrem was indestructible, no one had ever seen what lurked there–it was probably empty. He didn't wonder that his father had finally abandoned the game as dangerous and useless.

When the speeches ended, midnight had passed and the Simet-sa dispersed gossiping in small wary convoys, Flores and the Loyalists among them. Within the city, not far from the Temple of the Suns, a growth of broad green leaves grew heavy with moisture as dark cloudbanks rolled in from the distant sea to release their burden. The stalks leaned pendulously, shredding streams of water as several grey, rootless specters briefly paused and then departed, leaving one of their number prostrate in the rain.

❧ ❧ ❧ ❧

CHAPTER 5

THE VOK-TAIL CLAN

Dos-Senelwat-Hutsutsem felt greatly refreshed after a long night's sleep. The puffiness in his face had receded, his thighs were less raw, his back had stopped hurting, and his large, round eyes no longer squinted from the glare. Even his potbelly seemed to have shrunk during his protracted journey. If only these drylanders had a little cold water to splash one's face with. But where were they? Except for the small party of mounted escorts, he had seen no one. The rows of sun-dried brick apartments lining the avenue through which he guided his reven seemed empty, several being burnt-out shells with charred beams overhanging pink and yellow painted facades. His escorts seemed unconcerned, though well-equipped with irsrem armor and rapiers. Dos did not ask and they offered no explanation of why all had not returned to normal despite the passage of months since the accession of Nesos to the leadership of the Vok-tail clans. With passing interest, he speculated that, perhaps for Neset-sa, all that he saw, including the burnt-out dwellings, *was* normal.

They arrived at the city's central plaza, a design common to all the cities of the children of Vensor. It appeared to be littered with timber and debris; small vague movements suggested some kind of infestation to Dos. The party entered the plaza and began to thread a path through upright poles when suddenly, with a great flapping, birds took to the air in a wave that rippled across the square and revealed a forest of flesh whose jagged figures were suspended like torn puppets in frozen torment upon stark stained poles, their withered mouths open in mock surprise with the startled birds. Some puppets were new, many were old, a few were collapsed in heaps of bones upon the pavement, torsos still transfixed. Dos assumed the most bland visage he could muster and glanced unobtrusively at his escorts. Theirs were blander. He noted that true indifference required practice and resolved to dedicate himself. On the far side of the plaza, beside the brooding stone Temple of Neset, stood a wide edifice of several stories of the same dried-brick construction. The front of the building was alternately pillared and blank like a frieze of triglyphs and metopes with occasional windows punched, and a gateless entrance lay squarely in the middle with broad-stepped porch of packed cobblestones before it. The men dismounted, taking the reins of Dos' reven, and the traveler followed his escorts as they crossed the porch. His bland expression did not waver as he perceived the cobbles beneath his feet to be skulls encased in mortar.

The interior was a large square chamber ringed with balconies. In front and to the right, a second entrance led into a smaller, though still large and somewhat spartan chamber. Dos' hosts disarmed themselves and handed their weapons and Dos' robe to heavily armed soldiers who approached with bared blades and searched each with informal efficiency. Within this room stood an entourage of half a dozen servants who held plates piled with Dos' gifts: gold and silver mir from Lunsen and Vaw, scarce oils for lamps, rare cloth from far ports, delicate images of irsrem and glass, the reins and muzzle of a fine, war-trained reven, tethered outside, and a pair of young eunuchs for the king's harem, carrying baskets of feathers from albino rum-na. No gilas were included. Even had Dos been capable of securing such, it would have been a pointless gesture–the pious Nesos did not merely turn gila-sa back at the Neset border, but executed them without ceremony. The king was a loyal servant of his God.

Behind this entourage sat a figure on a heavy iron throne half in shadow. The seat was roughly cast and dull; brown corrosion spotted its base, and it rested on a platform of rough granite. The man was above average in height and more than usually heavy, though not impressively so. He sported a full, pitch-black beard and his expression was that of vast amusement. He sat at an angle, finger flanking face, in mute inspection of his guest. To the right of the figure stood a shorter, thinner man, a wrinkled countenance enfolding an experienced, unassuming gaze.

The hosts descended to their knees and announced their guest.

"Emperor of the Vensors, Brother of the Moons, First Born of He Most High, Leader of the Vok-tail Clans, Protector of the Sacred Spring. For your pleasure, I bring Dos of the Hutsutsem, Emissary of Ven."

The hosts rose and backed out the door, their gaze still averted, leaving several statue-like guardsmen near the throne.

"Good King Nesos, I bid you health and good fortune." Dos bowed and his retainers filed forward to place their burdens deferentially at his feet. The man on the throne did not shift his gaze, but watched Dos while the retainers withdrew.

The thin man spoke. "Nesos bids you welcome." He nodded slightly. "He bids you and your house good fortune likewise." The thin man narrowed his wrinkles in absorbed curiosity. Then, like a mobile mask, they assumed an air of detached indifference. "Noble Dos," the thin man said, "a long age has passed since we have seen emissaries from Ven. It is a pleasant change that now our people meet in the context of peace and not armed dispute. Such pleasant meetings should occur more often."

"Indeed," replied Dos, "sometimes the past can cling far beyond its time, like withered vines still strong though long uprooted. Yet vines and even iron must crumble eventually and old prejudice give way to new knowledge."

"Sir, any journey to a country is a bold undertaking, fraught with danger in the best of circumstance. There is no law in the wilderness and civilized people themselves are apt to entertain suspicions. One marvels at the hardiness and courage of the Ambassador. And one also finds intriguing the reasons that force one to take little-used and hazardous routes when safer ones are available."

Dos briefly pursed his lips. "O Nobles, my journey has been strange and difficult both for the beasts and bandits which assailed us and because we did not know the nature of the country through which we passed. But noble sirs, we did not tire. For the reputation of King Nesos is such that we knew the power of his arm, and the justice of his word, and had no doubt but that if we gained the safety of his lands, his presence would ensure our welfare, and our arrival in his brilliant capital would prelude a just hearing of our appeal."

Nesos glanced at the gifts and said nothing.

"It is pleasing to know that one's efforts have achieved such renown and have been so well rewarded, that even your famous and magnificent city holds us in esteem." The thin man's forehead stretched flat.

"The renown of Lord Nesos is spread far and wide," declared Dos. "Mok-sa clans we have seized in the far north know his name, and rank it with the Urlis, an equal in the Tribe of Heaven. Our rulers praise his name and thank the good fortune that has privileged them with such a beneficent neighbor. It would be a great calamity if our two noble peoples–"

Dos fell respectfully silent as Nesos grasped his advisor's arm and whispered.

"Um...the First Born would like your opinion as to who now rules in Ven?"

Nesos glanced back expectantly.

"The Simet-sa rule in Ven. They meet at the Assembly Hall where every important house–"

Nesos interrupted, speaking for the first time, in a gravelly voice. "Who is it who rules? What is his name?" An air of curiosity settled on the King's face.

"Lord Nesos, all the important Houses of Ven sit in the Assembly, whose duty it is to run and maintain the city's affairs."

"And how many is that?"

"Ninety and five, my King."

Nesos looked surprised, then skeptical. "And when they give their orders, do they all speak at once?"

Dos' remarkable impassivity weakened a little. "Lord, not everyone rules every day. Sometimes a few worthy men rule jointly, or even a single person if he can persuade the others–"

"Then he is King?"

"We would not call him that. Such is not our custom."

"Homd, can you imagine a worse way to run a country?" Nesos snorted to his advisor, who reshuffled his wrinkles.

"King Nesos, perhaps I can clear this confusion. Our state changes on occasion. Our city grows, our people need new land, we settle misunderstandings with neighbors. Vensor permits some to rule in Ven when they cause the city to prosper. When they no longer serve Vensor properly by failing his children, the Divine Will removes them, and places his new choice upon the 'throne.' At the present, his choice is three men whom we call the Loyalists for their dedication to Ven and Vensor. And his choices are in the process of eliminating evildoers, those who oppose them, and through opposing them, oppose the Divine Will."

"Yet, these evildoers have not received justice," said Homd. "They are at large in your country and could threaten the safer routes."

"Yes, noble sir. But such punishment is inevitable and necessary. The Loyalists are the instrument of Vensor's will in Ven."

"Even as I am the instrument of His will in Neset." Nesos smiled.

"Yes, First Born."

Homd spoke again. "Though our cities are distant, some matters fly like Vensor's breath touching all with ears to hear. Who could say but there may be an infinity of divine instruments? So good sir, as the representative of one aspect of Vensor's will, to the representative of another aspect, how do we reconcile our split, and unite to single purpose? What action must be taken, or perhaps refrained from, to ensure the triumph of rightness?"

"My masters in Ven, holy instruments and protectors of our Sacred Spring," Dos said, "would like the following event to occur: that a scroll of skin be inscribed with the seal of the First Born, Emperor of the Vensors–King Nesos. And that this scroll shall say that the King agrees to appoint one Flores-Sumvensor-Turlicum as Viceroy of Ven, to rule in the King's name, on condition that the said Flores seize Ven's Assembly, capture its gold and grain stores, and open the gates of the city to Nesos' armies. And additionally, that on the twelfth day hence, the King, or one of his captains, will gather armed men, march through the Tlaam valley, and encamp in the rough country overlooking Ven until a messenger should arrive from myself or my masters, which would require no more than three days at most."

Nesos and Homd exchanged glances, incredulity growing by degrees. Homd's face hung its dangling folds in amazement and Nesos rubbed the throne-arms, glaring craftily. "Your masters want me to invade their territory with armed men? My reven-na to trample your fields this close to the harvest?"

"The valley you are to traverse, the ancient Tlaam, Vensor wills your people to keep. Old Sipan will know new masters."

Nesos gulped as if swallowing bait. "The Vok-tail tribes will train the young ones! The reven-na will hiss with joy when we face again our old enemies in Sipan!"

Homd appeared worried as Dos risked a suggestion of a smile and bowed slightly. The secretary leaned and whispered hurriedly in Nesos' ear. He turned to address the Ambassador.

"Honorable sir, what you say pleases the King. Vensor is certainly guiding your masters. However, it occurs to us that whatever the outcome of this desired campaign, the valley of the Tlaam will be less prosperous than it now is, even if only for a season. Do your masters see the Divine Will as allowing for more dependable rewards for those whose lives we would risk?"

"Indeed, my masters would not be averse to a gift of ten thousand gold and silver mir."

Nesos' eyes widened as Homd interrupted.

"A remuneration."

"A remuneration," echoed Dos.

"Noble Dos. Every day our slaves multiply even as our own people grow in number," said Homd. "Our holy priests announce our sons more frequently and Vensor requires food and offerings in return. Calving time approaches and if our men are gone we could lose much. If Vensor permits us the joy of fulfilling His desires, then surely He would not do us injury while we perform His will."

Homd paused and glazed blankly at Dos. "Can your masters deliver to us the sum of forty thousand mir?"

Nesos gasped and for the first time Dos' mask dissolved. But he quickly recovered. He had been engaged not only for his unerring judgment and diplomatic skills, but for his intimate knowledge of his employers' affairs. Dos too was a noble, though of a House too small and poor to allow independence.

"Sirs–"

"King Nesos," corrected Homd.

"King Nesos. Vensor is indeed mighty and can work whatever miracles He wishes. If my masters can secure the amount you request, they would doubtless enjoy the very thoughts of the Divine Twin. But my masters do not seek to rival Him in His lordship over Maalstrom. Will the First Born accept payment of twenty-five thousand gold and silver mir?"

Homd paused. "Thirty-eight thousand."

Dos cleared his throat. "Twenty-eight thousand."

"Thirty six."

"Thirty thousand."

"Thirty-six thousand."

Dos breathed deeply. "Thirty-two thousand..." He was careful to give each syllable just the right intonation to avoid giving an impression of either weakness or hubris.

"Thirty...six...thousand..."

Dos swallowed. "Agreed. Thirty-six thousand."

Every wrinkle on Homd's ancient face curled upwards in a smile. Nesos stared open-mouthed and viewed his secretary with a look of new appreciation.

"Good King Nesos, my masters have not authorized me to deliver such a sum without their approval. However, I believe this can be obtained quickly. In the meantime, I can pledge half. Would a representative of the King be willing to undertake a journey to a place that lies some distance outside the city of Ven in the hills to receive it, and then begin your part of our... reconciliation? Time weighs most heavily upon my masters."

For a moment Dos paused to reflect upon the gravity of the transaction. If it succeeded, his masters would be considerably less wealthy than now. But the army of Ven would be intact and under their control. And as for the second installment of eighteen thousand mir–debts must be enforced to be collected. "And if King Nesos feels that we now serve Vensor adequately, it would be fit–"

Homd raised and lowered a hand. "Nesos bids you well. Good day."

Dos closed his mouth, then bowed low. With hands raised and head bent, he backed away from the throne until he was out of sight.

After Dos had departed, Nesos turned to his secretary. "Homd, your achievements astound me more each day. I will send you yourself to meet these Loyalists, and when you return with the gold, you will get a fifth of it!"

The secretary's eyes gleamed yellow as he bowed.

"Now bring me a scroll," Nesos added. "You will write upon it now and take it with you when you leave."

As evening fell, Dos found himself in a small suite of the palace, allowed his privacy but with a guard at the entrance. When the window was bathed in darkness, voices distracted his attention, and a few moments later the portiere drew aside.

"Noble sir."

Dos lifted himself with some difficulty from a soft cushion that had been placed upon the floor.

"You will excuse the interruption."

Homd stood, observing his guest. "Good Ambassador, the King has reflected further upon the affair and has instructed me to inform you of a second condition of our meeting in the wilds. It seems to the King that this rendezvous you mention is a secret, dangerous affair. Foreign diplomacy is unstable enough without far journeys and hidden meetings. For such sums as were discussed to travel through unpoliced wilds in the service of subordinates seems an unnecessary risk. We think that your masters should themselves appear–not to raise a question of your personal loyalty, of course. This vellum shall be deliverable upon this condition and upon receipt of the first half of the gold."

Dos had been snubbed and he knew it. Silently he cursed Homd, but bowed deeply, his owl-eyes fastened upon the ground.

"If His Eminence believes it necessary, then I'm certain it can be arranged."

"Good sir, your understanding knows no limits."

Homd backed through the opening and vanished.

Dos sat. A feeling of disquiet rose within. Had he served too well?

❧ ℡ ❦

The dark man turned. One leg through the aperture, he glanced back to stare across an open courtyard at a chateau bathed in moonlight. An animal howl broke the night. Answered by deep coughs from elsewhere, a string of figures appeared. They glimpsed the open jaws of Atasan and bayed and with a rush the figures converged on the gate, loping, despite their human-like appearance, like beasts.

The dark man crawled through and let the trap slam shut behind. He peered. Before his roving eyes, the empty plain rolled interminably, with no place to hide in the glare of the moons but shallow dips among grassy swells. He glanced behind, up. The exterior of the gate was carved in bas-relief. Sighting an open window three levels above, he climbed. Moments later, he drew himself within.

He caught his breath. In one corner stood a man–or what he thought was a man–till strong wings beat the air in agitation. A chain rattled and the creature stepped into the streaming moonlight. The legs were lithe and strong, the arms thin and well-formed. Two fleshy globes lay heavy upon its chest, outswelling, pendant, soft. From behind, its hands had been bound, upon its hips hung a threadbare dirty-brown cloth. His eyes sought their natural contact but failed and he nodded in sudden realization–the malkop's head was obscured by a sack.

The rest of the room took shape. One end of an iron chain confined the malkop's ankle; the other end was clamped to a bar set in the floor. Behind were a pole, a broad-bladed axe, several nets, and contrivances of bags, tubes, and cups. In the center of the chamber stood three empty cages and a gouged wooden table strewn with knives and remnants of flesh. Upon the table lay a framework of bones. The dark man shuddered. May it find rest in the Eye of Vensor, he thought–this malkop will take no more souls to Heaven.

Across the room a stairwell spiraled down to the courtyard. To his left, a second window opened at right angles to the first, revealing the castle's yard and the inner face of the small aperture through which he had crawled. The dark man glanced into the moonlit yard. The beast-men were clambering through Atasan's open jaws, their grunts reverberating as they penetrated the fields beyond the walls of the stronghold, sniffing for their missing prey.

Steps sounded.

The dark man jerked. His eyes settled on the chain. Pulling from a pocket an iron clamp that joined a clutch of glass rings, he pried the clamp open, and, before the malkop could react, snapped it tight about its ankle.

He twirled.

At the head of the stairwell emerged a man in voluminous red cassock, the hood thrown back. The man was of moderate height and build, his head crowned with dense white wisps, and his face stained like an ancient hill. The dark man noted that the hill had yet time to wear, being still supple with the moisture of youth—or something like youth.

The dark man nodded. In the months just passed, he had perceived the blend but slowly, and silently reproached himself for his slowness in understanding, and reaffirmed that all things are subject to the eternal will of Vensor. Again he looked into the veron-shaded eyes and noted how the yellow of the one balanced the blue of the other.

"So," the aged figure intoned, "beasts on occasion become men. Could it be that on doing so they no longer wish the company of their master? Tell me, my *'pet'*—or should I say 'guest,' since you no longer walk on four legs, but two—what moves you to depart without first paying the grace due the host?"

The dark man's face remained frozen as a mask.

"Tell me," the older man said, his voice a mellifluous sweetness, "why you tire of your host's hospitality and choose darkness for the time of your departure?" The eyes narrowed. "Something is missing from my rooms, my 'pet.' Vanished. Gone. *Stolen.* Tell me I err to think that one who has lived beneath my roof for all these months planned only to steal from me an item. Tell me now—"

The malkop beat its wings.

"—or hold your tongue—"

Two thin hands rose, each gripping a silver sphere.

"—inside your skull—"

The spheres glowed.

"—forever!"

A spark popped–with a snap the malkop's wings unfolded and it flapped toward the moonlit window, whipping its chain taut just within the sill. The dark man seized the axe and with a single smooth motion brought it down upon the chain.

The iron parted.

The old man gasped. He rushed to the sill–too late, the force of the creature's effort had propelled it through the window, and for one long moment he watched as it dwindled in the night, the rings that the dark man had clamped about its ankle sparkling in the moonlight.

"No..." the old man croaked. He turned. Rage twisting his face, his hands again rose and the globes glowed with renewed menace.

With a leap, the dark man pushed him out the window. Pausing only to close and latch the shutters, he flew to the staircase and tumbled to the floor of the court, where he ran to the visage of Atasan. The heavy trap rose. Throwing his weight upon it, he crushed the hand of an unlucky beast-man and locked the tongue of the fire god securely in its place.

The night rang with animal howls. From outside the gate, fists beat upon the carvings. Claws scraped at the iron hinges. As if they would shatter the rorewood with noise and temper alone, the portals thundered and shook from the beast-men's efforts to re-enter the stronghold.

At last silence reigned.

The dark man gazed hesitantly at the walls of the castle–walls that seemed suddenly like those of a prison. He sat. Placing his chin in his hand, his gaze was again impaled by the snarling leer of the god Atasan carved in imperishable rorewood on the inner face of the portal.

CHAPTER 6

"TRUST ONE, TRUST NO ONE"

Sruk Lurenmurg climbed the benches to his seat in the Assembly and listened as Numsenmur whispered in his ear. The older man passed his gaze over the nobility of Ven. With distaste he watched as Flores took his customary seat. Then his gaze passed on. Sruk cleared his throat. The old noble smiled with unexpected pleasure–for once the chamber had quieted.

"Simet-sa. Nobles," he began. "Blessed be the design of God, whose foresight, whose farsightedness, has preserved us thus far, and if it be His Will, shall preserve us all our days, the city and each member."

The multitude mumbled assent.

The grey-haired man looked up to enfold the broad expanse of sky shining through the irsrem dome overhead.

"Sirs, it is my duty to open our discussion this morning with an un-pleasant topic."

Flores glanced at Mosum. His colleague shrugged.

"Last night, several clansmen of the Serclaslers broke up a distur-bance in the marketplace where the foreign traders are quartered. Dur-ing this disturbance two slave dealers of unknown origin were found to be in possession of contraband–a most serious contraband. The pair had brought their cargo into Ven for the purpose of unlawful, immoral, and flagrantly irreligious behavior. This cargo, far from being brought to our fair country openly and in accordance with established law and custom– which as you know would not have been allowed entry under any circumstance–was smuggled in for the express purpose of circum-venting our laws, and with the intent of spreading its well-known and justly feared corruption among the good citizens of Ven. At the sug-gestion of our colleague Numsenmur–praise be to him, whose eye is ever vigilant in the suppression of immorality and whose sword-arm is ever quick in the cause of justice–the merchants were executed on the spot, and, I might add, before the gaze of much of the merchant class quartered in the plaza. An act that shall put the torch to those foul rumors which persist in characterizing our city as a place of laxity and corruption."

"Hear! Hear!" The Assembly bellowed its approval of the swift action of Numsenmur, and of Sruk's endorsement, and his eulogy of the fame of Ven.

Sruk waved the applause aside. He smiled to think that his plan might be accomplished with such ease. He risked a glance at Numsenmur and Sendas. The former gripped a knee with one hand and did not smile. The latter basked in the Assembly's applause as if it emanated for his benefit alone.

"But, my colleagues, there is more," Sruk continued. "I have not told you the nature of the contraband. The contraband was a *gila*."

Sruk paused.

The assemblage of nobles had again quieted. The Simet-sa, some of whom had already guessed the nature of the 'contraband,' turned to each other in amazement, fascination, and outrage. The assembled faces betrayed a wide mix of expressions. Some were transformed with disgust, some were fearful, but a few nodded with obscure smiles.

"My colleagues, it is true that we killed the carriers of the illness in accordance with law and custom, those merchants whose design or laxity would corrupt the city. But I have ill news to report concerning the gila. When the gendarmes attempted to enforce the holy law, a scuffle ensued, the animal near escaped, and the gendarmes, in defiance of our law, killed the animal as well."

The Assembly buzzed. Many exhibited a succession of emotions, from disgust for the ultimate weapon of Atasan against Man, relief that the creature did not escape to wreak destruction in the city, and fear while contemplating the abilities and temptations of the foremost representative of the animal world. Some were confused, some avaricious, and for those with eyes to see, some exuded purest lust, their prurient instincts aroused.

Sruk nodded. "Yes. Before the ancient law could be invoked–the gila was killed."

Flores rose to speak. "Sirs, with these three men and their intrigues the city will never rest. Have we not heard enough of skirting or breaking of the law on the part of the Triumvirate? Have we not heard enough of such excuses?"

"Yes, we have heard enough!" Numsenmur shouted at Flores. "Enough of the slanders of Turlicum, of the plots of the reven clan, of the schemes that keep our city in turmoil."

"Simet-sa," Flores declared, "this respected Assembly knows the impetuosity of Numsenmur's sword-arm. So let us omit formalities and open debate immediately on the gist of his argument–"

"–I had no choice," interrupted Numsenmur. "It was a threat to the city. Besides, it was the gendarmes who killed it, not I. So you now criticize the State. The Assembly should instruct its member Flores to cease opposing its will in all things."

"We all know how the beast survives," added Sruk. "It deceitfully twists others to its will."

"We should pass a new law at once," said Numsenmur. "Any gila encountered in the future shall be executed. We must ward off this threat, not coddle it as in the past."

Mosum rose. "That is sacrilege! Our colleague Numsenmur knows well what the law says. We may kill no gila at any time, but must escort them to the Temple where their fearful energies cannot harm us. Think well, gentlemen. Few Vensor cities would look with favor upon their execution, or tolerate such within their walls. Assassination, even of the children of Atasan, violates the holy law. Should we provoke our vassals in holy matters when the Empire is on the verge of rebellion?"

Flores stood. "Sirs, I have two questions. First, I would like to know what measures were taken against the perpetrators of the deed?"

Sruk answered, "The gendarmes who lost self-control were killed immediately afterward–I'm told that Numsenmur himself wielded the sword, a noble effort that demonstrates his lack of complicity in the crime."

Numsenmur smiled, accepting the expressions of approval from his supporters.

Flores twisted his lips in a cynical smile. "Of course, there would be no witnesses. My second question is Where is the body?"

"The body?" Sruk and Numsenmur exchanged incredulous glances. Numsenmur laughed with a tone of haughty but worried surprise, as if presented with the absurd and impertinent demand from a newly hired and expensive subordinate. "You won't find it, Turlicum. I suggest you find your entertainment in more socially approved ways." He sniggered and elbowed Sruk. The older man winced.

"I am not surprised at your answer, Numsenmur," said Flores.

"Then you should not be surprised at mine," said Sruk. "The body of the gila was delivered to the Temple in accordance with the holy law."

Flores looked at Sruk, then turned to address the entire Assembly. "Sirs, we all know the frailty and venality of men. For the good of their souls, I submit that the Assembly request its members Sruk, Sendas, and Numsenmur at once to open their harems to an investigating committee to be appointed by this Assembly. Alternatively, if the gila is dead, let them produce the body."

The Loyalist faction, being at least half the members present, snorted at this intrusion into what was considered the most private of matters. Numsenmur mustered his most truculent expression.

Sruk smiled. "A commission headed by Flores Sumvensor. How very convenient."

"As for myself," continued Flores, "I shall pledge as much as I expect from the opposition. I shall open my own private quarters to any commission which this Assembly may appoint–provided, of course, that the commission does not include Sruk, Sendas, or Numsenmur within its ranks, or a Loyalist at its head."

Sendas rolled his eyes knowingly, and he and Numsenmur laughed.

"Only someone capable of being bribed. So that is your plan!"

Simlet stood and shouted, "Kill all gila-sa!"

Mosum called, "Respect the law!"

Ust shouted, "Praise the State House!"

Latkin cried, "Clean out the assassins!"

"What nonsense is this?" chortled Sruk. "Flores would now have us repeat the debate in this Assembly on these so-called 'assassinations'! We have already established that the deaths of our former comrades were mere accidents. Flores seeks to use this as a weapon in his towering ambition to rise to the top of all Ven and install himself as Emperor Flores the First of the Empire of Ven. What charm the title has."

"Sirs," rejoined Flores, "we know that Soorkrul is in the service of the Triumvirate, and that he has assassinated Simet-sa. What sane person can doubt this? Who will now accept a consort from the House of Ven? Almost none. But witness the flood of consorts imported from foreign cities. Why? Because none wishes to succumb to poison!"

The Loyalist faction laughed and threw up their hands.

"Open their harems!" insisted Flores.

"Promote the Eunuch Lord!" shouted Numsenmur.

"Destroy the Guild!" shouted Sendas.

"Increase their allowance!" Numsenmur shouted, glaring in surprise at Sendas.

The latter stammered. "I mean *promote* the Eunuch Guild! At once!"

Sruk flung a sleeve in exasperation and sat.

Numsenmur leaned to Sruk. "If only Flores would do Soorkrul the honor of visiting the State House of Prostitution. Just once!"

Sruk whispered to Numsenmer, "If only Soorkrul had remained with his whores and spared us this mess..."

Sruk rose again. "Sirs! I believe we have been missing the core of what we should be concerned with here today. This is not some mere opposition of wills, a divergence of opinion, a traditional and meaningless debate, as our colleagues Flores and Mosum seem to believe, but something much more fundamental. This is a debate that goes to the core of our lives, of our society, of what kind of people we are, or should be. It is well-known that no sane man or person of moral fibre with an interest in the well-being of this city would deny that our God Vensor placed us here on Maalstrom, after choosing us to be His people, from all the life forms of the Universe. No person of respect and backbone would doubt that He gives us of Himself, that He gives us His own children, begat in His own mysterious way, that this manner of renewal is spiritual, not corporeal, and that it is age-old, existing since the Age of Silver, and that Vensor reserves this perfect joyous replenishment for us alone–His children. It is peculiar to us, a method immaculate, undefiled by the touch of corrupting flesh, a method holy, divine, incorruptible, a method of reproduction above all–*masculine.*

"Its opposite, femininity, where it is known, is the sign of Atasan, the sign of fallenness, the forbidden symbol of dark, of night, of emotion, of flame and fire, of unrestrained violence, of animal copulation–abominable acts common on Maalstrom, but utterly alien to ourselves, from which, thanks to the indulgence of God, we, the eternally undeserving and insufficiently grateful, are forever spared. We, as all Vensor-sa, are the sons of the Twin God. For us is daylight, bright suns, civilization, reason, cities, honesty, peace, and irsrem. For us handsome strength rather than brute force, dialogue rather than coercion and deceit.

"It is well-known, and God's priests teach us, that femininity is animality, and attraction to it–corruption of the soul. Femaleness, since it occurs only among animals, is contrary to the divine spiritual nature of Vensor-sa. And submission to it, feminality, a crime that we must forever be on guard against, a weakness which our ancestors knew will never completely vanish, a primal flaw which, though exorcised, forever creeps back to undermine society despite our vigilance. Still, the lust for feminine flesh remains deviation, perversion, a fall from God's grace into blasphemous degeneracy. Man with man is God's eternal sacred order–man with animal, his curse. His perfect image is the eunuch; his perfect clan, the Eunuch Guild.

"The forbidden word, the forbidden sex, the forbidden language must be eradicated where encountered, lest it prevail as it has so often in the past. We must expunge this disease–this creeping of the flesh– from His world, this unnatural craving which some fallen and disgusting Vensor-sa have allowed to fester and grow within them. The source of this temptation, this fiendish tool of Vensor's eternally ungrateful Child, must be dealt with in as strenuous, militant, and drastic a manner as necessary to preserve our way of life, indeed our lives themselves. Our colleague Numsenmur is right. We must pass a new law to preserve mankind from evil. True, the holy law should not be flouted or ignored–but its intent, on the other hand, is clear. The city and our way of life must be preserved. Not only should those who harbor gila-sa be killed, but the most effective manner of dealing with evil contraband must be instituted. When gila-sa appear in the future, as we know they shall, I submit that they be killed on sight and their bodies delivered to the Temple in accordance with ancient custom."

Flores applauded with mock seriousness.

"A fine speech, indeed, Sruk. And patriotic to the core. But there remain difficulties. First, how may we be certain that this is not merely another attempt to stampede this body of men to do the bidding of the Triumvirate, to distract us from the rooting out of more mundane, but more common corruption among its own members? Aside from the gila that you mentioned, none have been reported within the confines of this city, indeed this Empire, for a decade. And not one gila has been brought before this Assembly within living memory. I wonder how many Assemblymen present today have even laid eyes upon a gila? I have not. At this moment we have no reason to suppose that any reside within the city–if we choose to believe your testimony, Sruk. How are we to know that this renewed militance toward an ancient threat, this call to arms against such a rare opponent, is not designed simply to divert our attention away from the investigation at hand, the rooting out of the corruption in the State House of Prostitution, and the discovery of who delivered the poison that killed our colleagues Jaz and Clesp? In short, how much are we to make of this 'threat,' gentlemen? What motives do our leaders have in exciting our fears at this time?"

The faces of the Assemblymen remained thoughtful, their emotions mixed. None answered Flores. Each seemed preoccupied with private thoughts.

Flores continued. "Of course, the ban of the holy priests on gila-sa is necessary, since the vulnerability of men to the temptations of Atasan is well-known. However, this should not be allowed to divert our attention from the fact that the Triumvirate are attempting to use the issue of gila-sa to distract the Assembly from their own felonies. The ancient threat should not be ignored, but the equally ancient, wise, and merciful way which Vensor long ago commanded for us to deal with gila-sa should be adhered to. Vensor commanded firmness when dealing with the children of Atasan, but also kindness. We should protect ourselves, but the ancient law is clear–they are to be escorted to the Temple and delivered to Vensor's priests unharmed. This is both merciful and effective."

"You say there is no threat," answered Sruk, "but what of the gila?"

"What gila? We have seen no gila. Would you turn the city upside down without evidence? There are no witnesses except the hirelings of Numsenmur. Let our colleague Sruk produce the body. Then we shall address the problem in earnest."

A broad smile lit the face of Sruk as he silently acknowledged defeat. Shrugging his shoulders, he sat as Numsenmur rose to continue what Sruk now knew would be a vain pursuit. The next gila discovered would be delivered to the Temple in accordance with ancient custom– alive. And perhaps that was best, thought Sruk. For some reason he felt uneasy when Ven's politics impinged upon the Temple, as if the laws and principles that operated in Ven, which Sruk had mastered so well, gave way to rules of a different sort within the citadel's gate.

৩০

That evening three figures, closely hooded and casting stealthy glances, approached the entrance to the State Orphanage and, although the doors had long been shut and barred securely for the night, paused before its thick portals. For some moments they peered into the darkness. Satisfied that the few pedestrians on the avenue of Murfenmas had no interest in their doings, the trio moved up a side alley that separated the two principal state endeavors of Ven–the House of Prostitution, and the Orphanage. The south side of the alley betrayed a slice of deeper blackness. Nodding as if their expectation had been met, the three approached, pressed upon a portal, and entered a shadowy chamber adjacent to the alley. The last to enter shut the portal behind them and fastened the lock.

The visitors produced a lamp and lit it. The flame revealed a wide, low room, containing a spartan selection of furniture and woven rugs of lyart-hair. At one end a wide, thick plate of fragile glass threw their reflections back upon them. Numsenmur viewed himself flanked by two of his mute warriors, each attired in dark and unobtrusive clothing. To calm his nervousness, which persisted despite the familiarity of the surroundings, Numsenmur toyed with an irsrem dagger. Plans could change swiftly...

When their own flame had disclosed their identities, a door beside the glass pane opened and two men appeared, brandishing lamps in their hands. Each wore the uniform of the Eunuch Guild–ill-fitting dark cloth that covered all skin but that of head and hands, skirt hems dragging the floor to hide their feet. The head of each was shaved with pious thoroughness, and Numsenmur noted that even in the torchlight their fleshiness could not be hidden. He could not help but compare them to his bodyguards–efficient, muscled warriors whose gaze and arm were equally unwavering. But for his father's selection of them in the State Orphanage years before, these same bodyguards might have greeted him tonight in the rumpled clothing of a eunuch. The Serclasler fought down a growing revulsion for the Guild and all its works. However, he could not banish the feeling entirely. It reappeared with each visit to the home of the holy order. Tonight, at least, his hosts were not yet grossly obese.

One of the eunuchs signaled for the visitors to follow and disappeared through a doorway. Several corridors and rooms passed, all dark, all dirty, Numsenmur tramping behind while his mutes brought up the rear. Numsenmur noted with contemptuous disapproval the shabbiness of his colleague's estate. He, Numsenmur, son of Nidrenmor of the renowned and illustrious Serclaslers, should be intimidated, should pay money at the whim of this half a man? Once again he steeled himself. Tonight he would press his interests firmly. He would not be bullied or bargain away his interests for vague assurances of allegiance and safety.

Another door opened.

His guards remained in an antechamber with several eunuchs who were apparently unarmed, though Numsenmur knew they remained within reach of hidden weapons should the need arise. They mattered little. Numsenmur felt no doubt as to his ability to finish a roomful of them single-handed–it would be a mere butchering of swine. He waited, contemplating the room's sculpture. Golden phalluses and genitalia of rare minerals and metals decorated every room in the complex, standing free or springing from flat walls or woven in tangled labyrinths about paired golden suns. The salacious imagery of Vensor was as profuse among the eunuchs as it was rare within the city itself.

His host reappeared and signaled. The next chamber was ill-lit by a guttering torch and Numsenmur was escorted into the presence of Soorkrul, the Lord of the Eunuchs. The lord sat upon a three-legged stool with his back toward the door. Numsenmur entered and stood and waited. He glanced about with slowly growing apprehension, then with an effort of will again calmed himself. The Eunuch Lord rose and turned, his face hidden by a drooping cowl. Manicured fingers waved away his assistants–this conversation would not be trusted even to secretaries.

To Numsenmur, the lord was an enigma. The Serclasler gazed upon a man attired in identical fashion to that of the other eunuchs he had seen. The lord wore the same dark cloth, but in the case of the Eunuch Lord it seemed to fit poorly, relieved only by an almost invisible red hem. On the lord's limbs, the cassock appeared unnatural, confining, obstructing. The man stood at the center of a room meticulously decorated with irsrem and feathers, gaudy should one compare its ornamentation to the barren tunnels through which Numsenmur had just come.

Numsenmur felt a curious blend of respect and alarm, although, to be sure, mixed with the same unctuous slipperiness that pervaded the air when his underlings were present. Somehow, despite his confluence with the Guild, the lord had contrived to remain slender. Numsenmur could not guess the Eunuch Lord's age–he was rumored to be young. He had succeeded his predecessor only recently after the latter's 'premature' death, but his modest build and steady voice yielded no hint to Numsenmur of the lord's true age or experience. Numsenmur feared, now, as upon their first meeting, that the man might prove unexpectedly formidable if angered. But what cautioned Numsenmur most was the lord's consuming aura of purpose. When the lord moved, it was with a smoothness that suggested calm and hard precision–despite his blindness.

Through the tumbling shadows Numsenmur's eyes observed a well-proportioned neck, slim compared to his own. He speculated that he could crush that neck bare-handed, and at times longed to try. Soorkrul's unruffled and imperturbable confidence was what held him back, the confidence of one used to possessing information, intimate and private information, such as might be worth betrayal or murder—if the subject of that information believed those dark lips might one day divulge it. Numsenmur wanted to believe they would not. So, for now at least, the Eunuch Lord's neck remained intact.

Soorkrul smiled, his sightless eyes invisible beneath the woven convoluted hem.

"My Lord Serclasler." The familiar soothing voice greeted him.

Numsenmur approached and bowed stiffly. He realized that he was betraying his thoughts with his manner and bowed again, more smoothly. In time, even Numsenmur could learn.

"You heard?" Numsenmur asked.

The cowl shifted.

Of course he has heard, Numsenmur corrected himself. He hears all.

"The gila was discovered." Soorkrul said nothing and Numsenmur continued. "It was the fault of the merchants—*your* merchants. They fell to arguing over the gila. Each desired it."

"Yesss."

"You knew?"

"Yesss."

"The gendarmes came just as my guards managed to quiet them. I had to think quickly, so I...killed them all."

The cowl stared at him blankly

Numsenmur swallowed. "It was not my intent to interfere with your plans, but it had to be done. The gendarmes could have talked." He relaxed. He had spoken his mind.

"And the gila?" whispered Soorkrul.

"It is dead. I had it killed as well."

The thin lips frowned.

Numsenmur tensed again. We made a deal, by Vensor, he swore silently to himself, a contract between equals. I don't work for anyone, certainly not for this pathetic, emasculated clown. Let him do his worst—I know my consorts are loyal. I'll wager he has no one in my harem and never has had. "The gendarmes heard the commotion and searched the merchants' stalls and found it. Other merchants had already heard rumors and talked."

The hood inspected the floor.

"There was no other way. I ordered the gila killed–then I ordered the gendarmes killed. Then I killed the men who had killed the gila, and those who had killed the gendarmes. There is now no one who can speak of our part in the matter."

The cowl took a breath. "The gila was rare. I imported it from the far city of Tumset. The Eunuch Lord there prepared it well."

"What else was I to do? Would you rather have had it taken before the Assembly for interrogation? It knew it was to join another of its kind here in Ven." Numsenmur permitted the most defiant expression he dared use with the Eunuch Lord.

"No. However, it is a small matter." Soorkrul waved it aside. "I will have another soon. We can discuss my terms then." Soorkrul sat. "And the Turlicum?"

Numsenmur laughed. "Flores? He has nothing more than a suspicious mind. He will always suspect, reason or not. The Assembly mocks him."

"Yes, a suspicious mind...but patient." He smiled. "I await the outcome of your struggle with interest." Numsenmur paled and felt his anger rise, believing for a moment that the Eunuch Lord was declaring his withdrawal from their secret alliance to a position of neutrality. Soorkrul continued. "And I shall not pause in assisting Ven's Loyalists in their struggle to assert the triumph of righteousness in Ven."

Numsenmur breathed more easily. Of course, he thought. Flores alone pays no honor to Soorkrul and seeks to purge him from the House of Prostitution. Therefore Soorkrul will never make peace with Flores, no matter who wins the struggle in the Assembly. "And, Soorkrul, how successful are your efforts to infiltrate spies into the harem of our colleagues?"

"Sruk and Sendas?"

Numsenmur nodded. "This should not be neglected. It will provide us both with protection."

Soorkrul nodded and smiled. "Yes. All should have consorts." Numsenmur's skin paled again. He could not forget that most apropos aphorism of Ven politics: Trust one, trust no one. Meaning that the first person one trusts will be the last. He seeks to place his spies in my harem, just as I seek to have them placed in the harems of Sruk and Sendas and of as many nobles as possible. No matter. The plan of the Triumvirate still holds. However, I am aware of them while my colleagues are not. But Flores–he has taken the safest path of all. He has no harem. Yes, clever...if calculated. Otherwise it would simply reflect a corrupt and antisocial nature. Numsenmur nodded in his reverie. Could the germ of feminality lurk in the Eunuch Lord's breast as well?

The lord returned his vacant gaze to the Serclasler.

"Flores is proving more difficult," Soorkrul said. "He ever scorns my services, and my spies discover little–except for my one success." The hood returned to Numsenmur. "But have patience. We shall be rewarded. Now, it is time for another payment."

Numsenmur frowned. "Payment? Now? All my funds are committed to the plot against Flores. How can I pay?"

"No time is convenient to pay debts. But pay you must."

"Impossible! Now, of all times."

"I have my own needs. You have three days. Try. I'm certain you will succeed."

"But I require all my funds for our plot–we approach the climax." He clasped a fist before the Eunuch Lord. "We finally have the Turlicum where we can crush him. He cannot escape this time–but only if we have the money."

" 'The fulfillment of obligations is to be expected. And debts must be paid.' "

Numsenmur looked at the Eunuch Lord with widening eyes, feeling his face redden. Is there anything the Eunuch Lord does not know? He tried a different tack. "Get the information I need, Soorkrul. You shall have your money, but I expect something for it."

"Do not bluster here, Serclaser, there is no one to hear you but I, and I am not impressed." Numsenmur narrowed his gaze. He would remember that remark. Soorkrul continued, "You shall have results for your money–when you pay. Be patient. Do not lose hope. We shall have our way with Flores if only we are as patient as he."

Numsenmur breathed more easily. The Serclasler turned to leave, and paused as his eyes again glimpsed the vulnerable neck of Soorkrul. For a moment he experienced a wash of pleasure at the prospect of crushing it, stronger than before. Then he dropped his glance and directed his thoughts to other topics. Best not to take chances by letting one's thoughts run wild–should Soorkrul have the capacity to read minds as well. Numsenmur nodded, turned and exited the room. With his bodyguards in tow, he left the domain of the eunuchs.

႟ ୫ ୬ ౭

To the north of Ven, on the plateau above the Falls of Sish, the Eye of Vensor rose on a grassy meadow bordered by a chalky path that the steady crush of feet and wheels kept free of vegetation. As the suns' rays warmed the grass, transmuting dew to steam, a man of average height and build verged a rise to the west and viewed the path with a calm and penetrating glance. His hair was white and brittle with age. His skin cool and wet. One eye shone as yellow as the straw beneath his feet, the other as blue as the highest stratum of the brushed, cold sky. He wore a brown jacket and trousers of woven vok-hair, which fit so poorly that they could only have been cut for another. Over one shoulder hung a red scribal robe, in the company of scribes a badge of knowledge and ready means of employment. Several wagons already churned the dust, moving south toward the capital, and none of the Vensor drivers took notice of the wanderer when he stepped between them and turned his face southward as well. His grey lungs pumped and his thin legs swung putting the miles of dirt and rock behind him.

The Divine Twin had climbed far into the sky when the ponderous gates of the city came into view. The scribe pressed forward without pause and entered the customs queue. Upon a stool behind a low wooden table sat a bearded official, flanked by a half dozen police, sporting glass rapiers.

"Name?" Without raising his eyes, the clerk made a mark upon vellum and awaited the reply.

"Yezd."

"What clan?"

"No clan."

"You must have a clan. What is yours?"

The newcomer thought. "Sardonicum."

The officer looked up.

"I've never heard of them. What city is that?"

"Metropolis."

The clerk squinted, and shook his head. "Never heard of that either. What is your business here?"

Yezd lowered his head in a formal bow and spoke, his voice creaking. "I am here to seek employment with the scribal guild. I must stay for a time to prepare my further journey." Yezd held up his red robe to certify his status as a scribe.

The clerk looked him over, noting the absence of any pack for provisions.

"We have scribes in plenty here. You have no merchandise to sell?"

"No."

"Your labor alone is worth little, old man. Have you any money?"

Yezd bowed again and produced a golden chip, which the clerk promptly seized and pocketed.

"What is your further destination?"

Yezd smiled. "The Island of the Dead."

The clerk's face grew red with anger at what he at first believed was a sarcastic reply, but his eyes opened wider and he laughed. "Cheer up, scribe Yezd. By Vensor's will, you will not depart this blessed world for some time yet. I am certain you will be able to apprentice yourself to a master so that you may learn wisdom from the sages of Ven before Vensor finally calls you to the Holy Island. Enter, and enjoy your time in our city."

With a brief bow and crinkled smile, Yezd passed the wooden table and entered the city of glass.

CHAPTER 7

IN THE WILDS

The allotted days passed quickly. As the evening of the tenth day approached, a band of mounted men entered the hill country to the south of Ven, where the level fields soon were split by sharp ridges, and woody copses stretched their limbs into the sky, their shadows flying like birds before the hurtling suns. The reven-na padded softly, stretching sinuous necks, snaking massive tails. The group was composed of eighteen or twenty riders with a half dozen more reven-na burdened by heavy sacks. Brush surrounded the band on either side. Beyond, a grassy meadow melded into woods. The trail led up a short rise and, as the men watched, the suns sank beneath the hills and a host of white stars peeked.

Sendas was tired but confident, and took a drink from a flopping sack. "I tell you, Sruk, he has reason to lay low. Any man with brains would. The city is in an uproar since the treasury was pilfered. It isn't safe for him to do anything unusual. The Assembly wants to hang someone, and anyone would do."

Sruk remained sullen, his face puckered with recurrent worry. The others were silent, their weapons clacking softly against irsrem armor.

Sendas continued, "What surprised me most is that Flores and his party were so roundly blamed. Hardly a one believed my speech about starving bandits. I thought it was good. After all, it's not every day that I give a good speech in the Assembly Hall–and I hadn't a single cup of wine when I gave it. It appealed to all my noble guests' sense of achievement: the city under the present Assembly, especially with the leadership of the Loyalists, has been governed so efficiently that the robbers have been forced to abandon the forests and invade the city, where they–"

"Enough!" cried Sruk. "I heard your speech, but you should have shut your mouth and listened. Not a one believed it. They know a patent lie when they hear one and perceived it as direct evidence of the arrogance and condescension of our clique. You only attracted attention to us when we should have shunned it."

"But Sruk–"

"I thought we should have waited before, and now I'm certain we should have."

"Still–"

"It was not the time to move. Answer me this! Why was Numsenmur the one to receive the note?"

"I don't know."

"And why was Numsenmur the one to be contacted by the traitor in the first place? And why would the traitor deal with no one but him?"

"I can't imagine."

"And why did Numsenmur insist on sacking the city's treasury when we could have borrowed, or extorted from our allies, or even deceived Nesos? And what about the deaths of Jaz and Clesp–Flores is right. I too smell the hand of Soorkrul."

"And I don't care!" Sendas said. "Sruk. I know what you're saying and there is but one thing I see for sure. You're slipping in your old age! Don't you recall what our spy said? Flores is trying to split us up by planting suspicion, and you're falling for it! Numsenmur is right. Flores' opposition to our cause, with his money and his stubbornness, is far more deadly to us than we are to each other. He is still in the game and Numsenmur would not break with us until he is out. And Soorkrul would not move without us. His eunuchs cannot withstand any one of our clans."

Sruk shook his head. "You may be right. But something doesn't figure. We need to know now more than ever what Flores is doing, and now Numsenmur tells us that our traitor will not answer. And what about that man of his that Numsenmur seized? It is not like Flores to give up his own."

The party continued in silence.

An hour passed.

"Halt!" called Sruk.

The band paused.

"Did you see that, Sendas?"

"See what?"

"I'm not certain. Lights perhaps. Like the first flashes of a storm–or irsrem swords."

Sendas searched the horizon. The effulgent sky of the Maalstrom night shone bright and clear.

"You sound like an old eunuch. Forward! We haven't far to go." Sendas goaded his mount.

Soon the men neared their destination. The point of rendezvous was the Palmate Stone, a natural formation in the midst of a copse of trees with three craggy limbs like fingers thrust up along its back, and a fourth one flat on the ground like a thumb.

They met the dark stone and stopped. The trees rose about them like guardians, their straight trunks surrounding a moon-lit glade, dense thickets rustling in the breeze. Sruk pulled his ear and toyed with the reins, eyes peering. Sendas unstopped his sack and noisily offered some to the other men. One accepted. The others stared into the trees, their hands wandering to their weapons.

"All this for the skin of a new-born vok stained with the juice of weedwort. Too fantastic, eh, Sruk?"

The older man said nothing.

"How are we to recognize this Homd? What did Dos say again?"

"No need for that." Sruk counted the laden beasts again. "I only hope our Neset comrades have found their way without trouble. I want no delays–not out here. I would feel safer if Numsenmur had joined us."

"And I would feel safer if I were at home snoring. But Numsenmur was right. He had to stay in the city to keep trying to contact our traitor."

"Yes, that is what he said. But how convenient for Numsenmer if on our return we are waylaid and relieved of our document and our lives, out here in the wilds where our own tribes would never find us. Numsenmur gets the vok-skin with the seal of Nesos condemning Flores, he pays nothing to the Neset-sa, or takes the money back before they leave. When we fail to show in Ven, Flores gets the blame for our murder and Numsenmur creates a special office with emergency powers to deal with Nesos–it is all too easy. Four birds with one stone, and Numsenmur becomes King of Ven." Sruk counted their swords.

"I don't believe it," replied Sendas. "I don't believe Numsenmur plans anything against us, and I won't until his very sword is on my neck."

"What is that?" One of the men pointed.

As the party of mounted men peered into the gloom, a shadow separated from the blackness beneath the trees and proceeded haltingly into the open starlight. It seemed to be dragging something.

"Hello!" yelled Sendas. "Speak your name, sir, or we'll stick you."

The man jumped in surprise, then disappeared into the gloom.

"Ho there! Halt!" The men lashed their mounts. The reven-na hissed and sprang forward.

The first man reached the object and yelled, "Someone's been murdered! And another! And there!"

Sruk, who held back, hissed, "Shut up! Listen!"

The men froze and all heard a myriad soft thumping, like the pads of reven-na on dirt.

"Treachery!"

A score of armed men burst into the glade from the way they had come. They waved dull swords, barely visible in the starlight, and shouted in hoarse triumph on spying the group. Without pause, Sruk whipped his reven and dove into the wood as the others yanked at reins and swung out with five-foot irsrem rapiers. Sendas dropped his sack, clutched at his sword, dropped it too. The glade filled with twisting and pivoting figures, the darkness lit by bright flashes where hot glass touched iron. Two men had their mounts rammed. Pikes finished them. Sendas' reven spun beyond control, the noble lurching and staring open-mouthed as whistling blades sought his skin.

Sruk aimed his mount between two trunks. In a moment he was enveloped in blackness, his reven barreling through massive undergrowth, branches snagging his cloak. He could hear other reven-na snapping branches behind him. He whipped his beast again. It leaped across a fallen log, then halted before an impenetrable wall of growth. Motionless, Sruk clung to his mount with his eyes shut, hoping he might somehow be overlooked, remaining invisible in the night. Then he was rammed with what felt like the weight of a falling house and arms grappled him as he fell.

Sendas' reven finally calmed and he regained his balance. With a shock he discovered a pike protruding from his thigh, the far end wielded by a hooded assailant. His attacker yanked his weapon free while another took the reins from Sendas' hands.

The fight was over. Several had escaped into the thicket, followed by a dozen pursuers, the sound of a clacking sword receding, but presently all returned, with each of the victims' party accounted for. Two assailants appeared with Sruk. Sruk sighted Sendas and hissed in a venomous voice, "So was I right? Would Numsenmur miss his chance to finish us all at once?"

Two more reven-na padded into the clearing. A voice spoke,

"Sendas, I'm ashamed for you. You should have more sense than this. We heard your yelling from the other side of the hill. You should have held him in rein, Sruk. He was ever impetuous. Was it he who engineered the gold theft? A poor move, sirs. Hurt more than helped. But then I could not expect you to move with the same intelligence as before when you had Lasmer, your steambath spy, to help you."

"You!" said Sruk. "And not Numsenmur!"

"Numsenmur?" replied Flores. "Don't tell me you fell for my little trick, Sruk. I had hoped maybe Sendas or conceivably Numsenmur would, but you should have guessed that the object was to catch your traitor–Lasmer. You see, there is no Sorotir of the Venholis. But you knew the name anyway and voiced it at the banquet. You could only have learned that name from a spy in my Council."

"But," said Sruk sorrowfully, "Numsenmur...only he could talk with our spy. He would not let us write to or receive from him directly."

"Is that true? You mean you were not aware that my officer Lasmer was meeting with Soorkrul in the State House of Prostitution? Or that Soorkrul then passed his information on to Numsenmur?"

Blank expressions met Flores' gaze. "Not until now did we know how they communicated, or even what the name of his spy was."

"So you were sincere when you insisted that you had not recruited the Eunuch Lord! Indeed you had not–Numsenmur had. It seems you were not as united as I feared and that all along my struggle has been more with Numsenmur than with you. Oh, gentlemen, have you met Homd? He was to meet you, I believe. It was a fortunate day when his representative contacted mine."

From a reven by his side, Homd stared silently at Flores.

"And," continued Flores, "it was a clever move to send a party of warriors hours early. Unfortunately for them I have been here since yesterday."

Sruk looked puzzled, his expression still blank. "What party? We sent no warriors."

Flores looked perplexed. He glanced back toward the clearing, rubbed his chin, then shrugged. "Anyway, your secret meeting has now been accomplished and terminated in good faith. Sendas, you may return to Ven–if you can survive for a week in the wilds without food or glass. I hope to see you in the city." Flores chuckled. "Your continued allegiance to the Triumvirate is invaluable to my cause."

Flores turned to the Lurenmurg. "But you, Sruk, are too dangerous–to me and to Ven. I'm sorry. Goodbye." He waved his hand and muscled arms half dragged, half lifted Sruk away, without protest. Sendas, meanwhile, was escorted limping to the edge of the clearing. He was placed on a reven and directed toward Ven.

Two Vens rode up to Flores leading reven-na loaded with ingots as another party rode across the glade. They halted beside Homd and Flores.

"And now I must leave," said Homd. He handed Flores a scroll that bore the seal of Nesos.

"And now you must have your money, you mean. Very well," Flores motioned to a man leading another reven. "Eighteen thousand golden mir–plus ten thousand more, for you."

Homd took the reins of the wealth-laden beasts as his men gathered. The folds on his face reassembled. "Remember your pledge, Assemblyman. The Brother of the Moons has little time remaining in which to draw breath. When he departs, there will be many candidates to replace him–I will meet with you then and show you what you can do to assist me in my struggle to restore sanity to Neset." Homd's party turned and rode out of the clearing.

Flores wasted no time in returning to Ven to execute the remainder of his plan. Fortune had finally come, in the form of an unexpected visit from Homd, the Neset conspirator.

By next morning Flores was in the plaza, details of his plan meshing like clockwork, his criers announcing the drilled rote phrases. "*Vasa, vasa! Mavnes Nesos!* Treachery! Traitors! Spies of Nesos!" A dozen men spread the news through the marketplace.

Flores rode his best reven, his Assemblyman's vest obscuring its barreled flanks. In his wake trundled a wagon bearing two chained conspirators and drawn by another reven. A crew of mounted men surrounded the wagon, bare-chested, skirted and carapaced in irsrem armor. The hired callers told all: Sruk, Sendas, and Numsenmur had been caught bribing Nesos himself, paying him to invade the city, offering to open the gates. The proof was here! The seal of Nesos in his own hand! Their own clansmen, outraged by the act, had mutinied and seized them and Flores was going to the Assembly to demand justice and retribution.

The news rippled through the market with deceptive calm, like drops of rain catching men harmlessly in the open, giving little warning of the downpour to come. Observers at first ignored the bizarre cavalcade as yet another of the public follies of the city, but a crowd soon gathered to view the curious spectacle.

"Traitors of Nesos! The Triumvirate caught!"

A burly glass-smith tossed a stone shouting, "Damned of Vensor!" and the amused smiles faded. Abruptly, like a contagion, an ill mood spread through the crowd. People suddenly clotted the procession, pressing forward by the hundred, then fell back in panic as the shy beasts hissed through muzzles and extended sharp talons.

Flores urged his men to hurry. His triumph threatened to miscarry in the face of the crowd's worsening mood. The plaza rang with cries for vengeance.

The Turlicum Lord approached the Assembly where a cluster of nervous guardsmen peered between the irsrem bars of the grating. More men with swords and bucklers hastily traversed the garden. He kicked the gate. The guards jumped.

"Open, keepers. I am due at the Assembly." They stared dumbstruck until Ultem appeared and released the catch.

"Bring the wagon in, Isav! Hold back this mob!"

The guards yelled in dismay but the wagon rolled in. The guards grunted and hit the mob as it surged forward. Outside, the reven-na clumped together and refused to move. Finally, Flores' men coaxed them within the gate and truants who sought to evade the keepers were seized and ejected.

"Thirty-five thousand five hundred mir has now disappeared from our coffers–"

Flores and Isav entered the Assembly Hall with their captives and the Assemblymen threw up their hands and shouted.

"Flores! Your vanity will ruin the city!"

"This isn't a slave auction, Turlicum."

Flores led his captives to the center of the chamber. His companions stood one on each side of them, arms folded as guarding dangerous criminals. Numsenmur remained seated but was visibly shaken.

"Simet-sa. Assemblymen of Ven. I thought my informants had deceived me, but I now see that they were right. You do not know. You have not heard."

"Cease speaking in riddles," Ust, the die-hard Loyalist, replied. "You are now wasting our time."

"It is a riddle only to you, Ust. If you want answers, put your questions to your friend and colleague–Serclasler!"

Numsenmur paled and rose. One of the captives was his employee.

"Turlicum, your provocations have no end. What do you here?"

"I come to prove your treason."

Numsenmur reddened and began to puff, unable to speak.

"Simet-sa, you must know I do not speak idly. The men you see chained before you surrendered themselves to me this very morning. They have only just concluded an agreement with the representative of Nesos of Neset, Tyrant of the East."

The chamber began to murmur.

"Proof! You speak lies and slander! I demand proof!" Numsenmur exploded, scattering drinks and voting boards.

Casually Flores unveiled the scroll. His voice boomed, "In exchange for forty thousand gold and silver mir, I confide to Dos-Senelwat-Hut-sutsem that I shall occupy all the Tlaam valley, even to the city of Asan which land I shall keep, and that I shall despoil his capital, the city of Ven, take its grain and treasures, and break its gate."

The Assembly burst in a storm of consternation. "Forty thousand mir!" one cried. "Few could raise such a sum. Sruk is Dos' employer—surely he was the thief of the City's coffers!"

Flores smiled, glad they had made the connection themselves. He held up the scroll. "This treacherous document bears the royal seal of Nesos himself."

Ust spoke again. "Sir, you claim these men delivered themselves into your hands? They gave you the scroll? And why do you believe them? They look as farmers to me. I see not a conspiracy to crush Ven, but a pair of vagabonds soiling the good name of Sruk, and holding out greedy hands for their reward."

"But who robbed the treasury? Could it have been any but the Triumvirate? These men have received no reward. And the scroll bears the seal of Nesos."

Simlet, a sallow man and intimate of Ust, now rose. "Simet-sa, we see here a man of untrammeled vainglory. He knows who robbed the treasury. It was he, probably with these men, his paid accomplices. Doubtless the scroll is his own, written by his own scribes who forged the seal of the Neset Tyrant."

Assemblymen leaped to their feet and hurled accusations like missiles.

Flores rubbed the scars on his arm. "If you won't believe me, then listen to the testimony of others!" He pointed to a captive. The man spoke feebly. Flores breathed faster, then motioned. Isav slapped the captive on the back.

"It's true! I was there! Numsenmur did it. I am his man. I was with

Sruk and Sendas when they paid the gold to Homd. Homd gave them the scroll. They robbed it from the storehouse. I heard them speak of it."

Again the floor erupted. Someone yelled at Numsenmur, "Confess! You have been convicted!"

Numsenmur glared at the captive. With an effort he calmed himself. "Yes...yes, he is my man. And he has been missing for days. He was kidnapped by this rogue, who obviously put him to the torture and taught him what to say! I shall not submit like some old man to such blatant slanders. You, Turlicum: Where are our fellows Sruk and Sendas? They are missing. Did you also torture them? I believe you did, and when those nobles refused to join you in your subversive plots, you murdered them and left their good bodies in the hills!" Several men patted his back and gestured menacingly towards the opposition.

Ust rose again. "Assemblymen, I suggest we ignore this foul vagabond and let him put away his little seal and scroll. Scraggles on a paper prove nothing. This man is a lowly servant of Numsenmur's and undependable. The other captive—although Sruk's man—is again low and untrustworthy. Finally, for Sir Flores to privilege himself and offend this supreme body with his sweating slaves and his doggerel of open invitations to marauding conquerors is demeaning and pointless. Sirs, the city is at peace and I defy this man to produce his invader."

Flores frowned but motioned his men to remove the captives. He took his seat beside Mosum, Latkin, and his other allies, who had sat quietly during the exchange. Ust continued to speak, condemning any and all who would drag slaves and servants before the Assembly and commented that the prisoners were the only invaders he had seen. Mosum grew disturbed and seemed anxious, his gaze oscillating between the opposition and the Assembly Hall exit.

The noble Temes, who had developed a vague antipathy for Flores, resumed his speech. "Sirs, my suggestion is this: First, of course, we must increase the guard on our storehouse. Second, we must raise the taxes on foreign vassals and visiting merchants. Third, we must—" Temes groaned as a subtle murmur from outside the chamber grew. A vast angry clamor assailed the Assembly within the building's walls.

Attendants appeared, trembling and disheveled. "There are mobs!" said one. "The people are rioting!" He gulped, then added, "And King Nesos has invaded!"

The Assembly exploded. Servants dropped their fans, men pulled their beards, and several Simet-sa summoned their retainers and departed. Guards were sent to verify what each feared but knew was true. The guards returned with a band of panting and grimy soldiers who had ridden break-neck from Sipan. The soldiers relayed with frantic haste: a vast body of Neset-sa had ridden into the Tlaam valley, cut off the city of Asan, and now were crossing the hill country to the south. They were headed straight for Ven.

Mosum heaved his bulk up and addressed the Assembly. "This austere Assembly of nobles owes apologies and conciliation to its member, Flores-Sumvensor of the Turlicum. He has done no more than his duty and for his pains has been vilified and cursed. Much now is clear. The scroll is indeed authentic. The captives are indeed guilty of what they themselves confessed. Their masters, whose guilt is assured by their absence, have dragged this country into a bloodletting which shall require its utmost resources to survive. I submit that the persons Sruk-Nevneset-Lurenmurg and Sendas-Moredin-Molersal be placed under arrest and charged with treason if they ever again show themselves in this city, and that their estates be placed under Assembly jurisdiction until this body recovers its missing funds. Our colleague Numsenmur, whose complicity is assured, should be ejected from this body and his robe stripped."

A score of men groaned. Dozens more applauded.

"Furthermore, Flores, whose fathers have proved of military ability, I propose be appointed to lead the city's standing garrison against Nesos while the city mobilizes."

Seventy black voting blocks clattered to the floor in assent. Less than a dozen white blocks followed.

As Numsenmur stood, a host of fists waved in his direction. With armed Assembly attendants collecting before the dais to enforce the Assembly's will, he slowly removed his blue and silver vest and held it aloft in a ham-like hand. Pain on his face, he let it fall. What remained of his following softly groaned and Numsenmur stood in silence, his skin the color of ash. The Triumvirate was finally, completely crushed. Without a word, he walked out.

❧ ❦ ❧ ❧

Sendas gazed upon his reven with pity. He had not gone far and already the animal limped more than before. He shook his head. What could he do? His own leg throbbed and still bled. He dared not attempt to walk the many miles to Ven. The creature would simply have to suffer.

Poor Sruk! He had tried to tell him. If only Sruk, the orator and benefactor of Ven, the brain behind the Loyalists, the mind upon which the prosperity of Ven depended, had listened. In fact, Sendas wished he had been wrong. He had been wrong before, he reflected–Vensor knew he would be wrong again. But this time, for once, he had been right. And Sruk was dead. The plot with Nesos had failed; Homd had betrayed them to their enemy for a higher price, with the result that the struggle with the Turlicum was set back dramatically, perhaps even ended. Yes, Flores' power had grown far beyond what he or his companions had suspected, even unto the court of Nesos.

What more could they have done? At great risk they had robbed the city's storehouse to raise the sum owed to Nesos, though Sendas had never understood the reason for that, since Numsenmur had contributed little of his own enormous wealth to the bribe. But Sruk had acquiesced and Sendas rarely opposed the Venerarch. What would he tell Numsenmur? Sendas sighed, contemplating the rage that would seize him on learning of the disaster, despite the fact that Sendas had lost more gold than he.

How long might it take him to return to Ven, he wondered? He frowned. The situation was even worse than he had realized. When he should enter Ven, assuming he survived the wilds, Numsenmur would already have heard of the debacle from Flores. Who knew what plot Flores had cooked up in answer to the machinations of Sruk and Numsenmur? Feeling the cut in his leg bite, he was forced to admit a new appreciation for the capacity of the Turlicum to intrigue. He thought of what Flores had said, the reason why he, Sendas, had been allowed to live, and Sendas felt sad. He had tried to serve his city. He knew that his efforts at times frustrated or exasperated his colleagues, but he had always done what he thought best for Ven. And never had he personally profited from his alliance with the Loyalists. Bad judgment and incompetence were perhaps accurate charges, but not treachery, malice, or greed. Sendas held his head high. For his city had he struggled. For his city would he continue to fight–against any and all.

The Maalstrom night was passing; one by one the stars paled and vanished, and the day soon opened on a clear blue sky. Sendas sat taller, as well as he could, given the steady rocking of the beast, punctuated as it was by its limp. He raised his head and breathed deep the clean wilderness air. He smiled. Through pain and worry he found his journey revealing a side of life he had heretofore neglected: the pleasant aspect of the rustic countryside. A green meadow opened before him and Sendas picked his way along a path that seemed to lead in the direction of Ven.

He paused. Before him, prostrate in the meadow and blocking his path, lay a tangle of skin and limbs. He edged his reven closer and halted. To his surprise he gazed upon the body of an angel of Heaven—a malkop. It must have died but recently, as the bodies of malkops as well as Vensor-sa were promptly removed to Heaven by Vensor's watchers, two of whom circled even now, vulture-like, interrupted in their grisly task by Sendas' approach.

Something more arrested Sendas' gaze. The creature had apparently been used by some tormentor, for the torn remnants of a sack encircled its neck, and one leg had been caught in some mechanical device. Determined to reassert its freedom, the creature had gnawed off its foot. The severed limb lay beside it in a pool of dark blood. The device itself was still within its grasp, a rusted iron clamp the latch of which had apparently proved beyond its comprehension.

Peering closer, Sendas blinked. Upon the iron clamp was hooked a clutch of glass rings the size of bracelets, shining like burnished silver. With a nervous glance upward toward the distant dots, he composed himself and stooped. One ring remained solidly in the creature's grip. Easily undoing the latch, he slid the remainder off. He raised them to the sun, and smiled with boyish innocence. Dropping the rings and the iron clasp into his saddle pouch, he placed one foot within the stirrup, made the sign of God, and mounted. He spurred the beast forward, again sighing for the poor beast. For the beast, nothing. For him, Ven drew nearer by the hour.

Sendas had advanced far beyond the spot where he had dismounted, and the workers of the sky had reclaimed their own and vanished, when a disheveled figure emerged from a dense thicket. It pulled itself free of snagging branches and moss and stepped onto the grassy path. The figure glanced back, then turned its gaze forward across the open field where its eyes detected the minuscule and shrinking form of Sendas.

For a moment the stranger stood immobile, torn between a desire to summon him for assistance, as the stranger had no mount, and the desire to remain hidden, as he feared the diminishing figure might be the last member of a band of hostile warriors. Unable to decide he stood rooted and made no sound until the rider vanished over the ridge. For a minute longer he stood, still silently debating. In his exhaustion, there was little likelihood of surviving unarmed and unescorted in the wilds. On the one hand threatened hot glass and a human enemy; on the other white fangs and red death. And between, what could lie but starvation?

What indeed?

Something glinted by his feet. Looking down he noticed resting upon an imprint left by the stranger's reven what appeared at first glance to be a single glass bracelet, having apparently fallen from the other's pack without the rider's knowledge. He bent and took the bracelet up between forefinger and thumb. To his surprise it was light, almost weightless. It was not cold, but warm, and approximately the size of his palm. From the tingle in his fingers it might have been made of irsrem, but, instead of the usual iridescent sparkle of the iron-hard tear-glass, this was transparent as real glass. A slippery feel suggested wetness, but upon inspecting his fingertips he found they remained dry. The surface was unmarked and flawless; no mark of dust from the road clung to it. He held his new jewel high and watched with pleasure as it glinted and shone in the sunlight. The newcomer placed his hand within, and, despite the small aperture, it slipped somehow easily across his knuckles to stop securely on his wrist. Fearful, he hastily pulled it off, and then, reassured, replaced it. He flashed a broad smile, and, admiring his new ornament, he whistled, and began to walk in the direction of Ven—when suddenly the brush beside him crackled and the hissing of reven-na filled his ears.

CHAPTER 8

UNEASY ALLIANCE

That same afternoon, the battalions of Ven assembled. They gathered in the plaza, two thousand men on reven-na, feather-light plates of glass armor coating chests and limbs. They grouped in several regiments, each distinguished by the tint of its irsrem. A regiment of green milled about adjacent to one of blue and a third of red with totems displayed representing various aristocratic houses joining in for an early share of glory. Rum-na feathers, ros skulls, and isia stings adorned the warriors' helmets and headbands.

The men checked muzzles, tightened straps. Warriors on reven-na hopped to confer with colleagues before the gaze of spectators on the plaza's perimeter. Some went through the motions of the traditional dueling tactics: reflex, volt, pivot, cabré. Whistling sounded as riders cut the air with rapiers, though in battle these weapons were designed to pierce, not slash. These were the garrison of Ven, mostly well-to-do retainers of Simet-sa who owned their own reven-na and could be mobilized quickly. Banners proclaiming ancient dynasties were erected to gather recruits as they arrived. Many were veterans of campaigns in the eastern wilds or had helped quash the revolts of Toor and Lunsen. Some had fought against Nesos in the succession dispute with his brother, and a few had been mercenaries in the service of the tyrant when he sacked the city of Lim.

A week would pass before the full force of Ven would gather–if that became necessary. Contingents from subject cities would be assembled one at a time, and Ven would raise its own citizen army, the strongest of the valleys, the strongest known. A hundred thousand could be fielded, far more than the tyrant Nesos of Neset could produce.

Flores was solemn while plump and over-aged nobles gathered to officiate the war ceremony, but he was confident. After all, what was the original agreement but a ruse? None had reason to trust Nesos, but the king was not foolish. Impulsive and bloodthirsty perhaps, but not a fool. The full force of Ven would crush him, however long it took. And if his host turned back upon the arrival of Flores and his show of strength, the city would deify Turlicum, the Simet-sa follow at Flores' heels, obey him in everything, and his lineage, his clan, his city would have the final victory. Only the problem of Numsenmur and his Serclaslers would then remain. Flores looked down where his mangled hand gripped the reins of his reven. Painfully he extended the fingers. In another age, that hand had held the rapier. But there had been a statue. How fitting that matters have turned out thus, he thought. His struggle, he realized, had always been chiefly with Numsenmur.

Isav's mount padded up and the noble bobbed his head. Mosum and Latkin accompanied him. Ust and Simlet were in armor, and Lirsus, the Serclasler Heir, though not yet of age for war, was nevertheless present in full panoply. Of course, thought Flores. Numsenmur would not permit his rival to have free reign.

More nobles approached–Toosel and Nilsit summarily informed Flores of the limits of his responsibilities. Flores was to be a nominal head only, leader of the expedition, but not its commander. All decisions would be reached by consensus of full-fledged Assemblymen only, in consultation with their military officers. Besides those present there would be Laruca, another former Loyalist supporter, six in all, in sympathy evenly divided between Turlicum and Triumvirate. Flores noted wryly that he himself had demonstrated to Numsenmur the influence a stripped noble might still wield.

Without waiting for the gloating visages of his opponents, Flores motioned Sandol and Revd to confer. "How is Mesret?"

"Not well. He has not eaten for two days," said Sandol. "He is taking it hard."

"Yes," Flores said, "but at least he has stopped his puling. The traitor Lasmer would have had my son's life as well as ours. Mesret was too young for romance. I thought so even before I knew."

"You told me as much," added Revd.

"Listen." Flores pursed his lips as the ceremony neared its terminus. "We change our plans. I fear what may happen in Ven while I am gone. Take the youth of the clan and go to the villa. If there is trouble, ride north to Sish and Nasvetin. But take care. If you must flee, you may have to go in secret and under pursuit." He paused to view the malkops, which were already gathering in the sky, sensing a harvest.

"You know, we could lose this war."

"Impossible!" exclaimed Sandol. "As long as Vensor and Vensed rule in heaven, Ven will vanquish its enemies."

Added Revd, "The Creator made Neset-sa as he made all his clan. His Will cannot be thwarted by the Lesser Deity, the god of fire."

"Then let us pray to Vensor that the Envious One does not interfere but remains in the Abyss as Vensor commanded." Flores withdrew his irsrem rapier from its scabbard and concluded hastily, "Mesret may join the general muster if he wishes, but only with our contingent. I want him separate and guarded. He is not to join in any fighting. I daresay the event will not arise, however. If there is trouble, take him to Sish as well."

His men assented.

The square fell quiet as the ceremonies ended. Flores padded before the collected magistrates of the city and at a signal pointed his sword toward the twin suns, which were slowly merging as the season progressed. Two thousand swords flashed.

"Vensor! Hear your children! They go to war for your glory. Blind the eyes of our enemies. Burn their heads. Light the path to their destruction and ready your angels to carry our dead to Heaven."

The host prodded their mounts and Flores watched as the reven-na, necks arched and tails undulating, pranced toward the Way of Murfenmas. So they think I'll take the blame for defeat and give me no power to prevent it, he thought. So be it. If there is no war, there can be no vanquished—but there may still be a victor.

The settled fields south of Ven paralleled a wide irrigated lowland, the latest collective project attempted by the Assembly after the public baths and the Orphanage. The road followed the dike through a muddy plain beside a stagnant, elevated sluice-ditch. Frightened laborers were already climbing the banks and plodding towards the city. In the distance, Flores could see a glimmering whiteness—fields patched with salt where overseers neglected to drain the water in time.

The land rose and turned to sloping hills where woods appeared. With approaching dusk the detachment plunged into the wild ridge country, leaving behind the previous scattered hutments, and entered a vast land of half-light, the ground obscured by soaring trees. In the V of a deep rivulet and a sharp ridge, they halted for the night.

A tent was thrown up and furnished with chairs, a table, and a lamp for the army's generals. Flores, Mosum, and Latkin were soon confronted by their opposition, augmented by Lirsus and officers of both factions.

Ust opened the debate. "How soon we throw away our victory, Simlet. What a choice for camp! Lisrus, you are wise for your age, much like your noble father. Surely you can see the danger in this location!"

Flores sat and popped open a jug as Mosum defended his decision. Latkin interrupted, "Sirs, would you shackle this expedition so soon which serves the interest of your property and loved ones as well as ours?"

"I had wished," said Flores, "to leave the follies of the Assembly behind me, my friends, but I knew that would not be so." Isav and several carapaced captains collected on his side of the table.

Ust turned his harangue upon Flores. "If you mean you thought to lord it over this army as you do the Assembly, then indeed that would not be the case."

Laruca, a laconic man with a perpetual pout, added, "Here you must consult us. Commands must be issued jointly."

"Gentlemen," said Flores, "orders will be issued jointly. However, as appointed head of this body of men, routine concerns such as where to park our carcasses–and when to dispatch mounted reconnaissance– will be determined by me."

The three opposition members shouted in protest. Simlet sat and snorted to his colleague, "Did not I tell you, Laruca: Leave the city and see him work his bribes. Flores, this will be the subject of a report to the Assembly." He smiled spitefully at the Turlicum Lord. "I have already assumed the privilege of readying couriers in anticipation of such an event. We will see you recalled for this."

"And me too, sir?" rejoined Mosum. "My men, you see, have developed a strong affection for our Lord Flores."

Latkin stood and glared. "A most strong affection, sirs. I fear half the detachment would miss either Sir Flores or our Lord Mosum; enough to travel to Ven to nurse their loneliness. I wonder how your men would fare against Nesos without them?"

Men of both sides groaned aloud.

"Well, you cannot move without our consent," said Ust.

"And we will support none but Turlicum."

"Then we sit," replied Flores, "and await our riders' return. And I apologize for not consulting you." The Turlicum peered up from his chair behind the table. "And when we find the enemy, you will deign to advance against them, I trust? I would not wish to explain to the

Assembly why the army sat out the war amid camouflage while Nesos burned our capital to the ground."

"Well, I dare say you are capable of it," replied Ust.

Simlet added, "We are for moving on. Now–to any place but here." Ust grew silent, then drew aside his companions. A few minutes passed as they talked quietly and several officers left and had to be summoned again when the trio suddenly reopened the discussion.

"Commander, please accept our apologies," Ust said. "We have just discussed the merits of the campsite with our attendants and we now fully agree: It is indeed an exceptional one, perfectly defensible. In fact," Ust's eyes gleamed, "it is so good, that we have come to the unalterable decision that the army should await Nesos here, even if he is not sighted for a week. Unless, of course, our enemy should appear between us and the city, in which case we trust to your renowned generalship to conduct us upon the enemy's rear."

Flores drew his palm across his face in exasperation as the other nobles cried out and leaped to their feet.

"Treason!"

"Desertion!"

Mosum shook his head, and Latkin's slim arms shook. "You would wreck this campaign and risk the city's mobilization for your petty politics?"

However, soon it was seen they would not reverse themselves, though even a few of their own officers muttered complaints. The opposition withdrew from the torrent of abuse, leaving the tent to Flores and his men.

In two days the riders returned, panting and excited. The Tyrant of Neset had been found some miles to the southeast, across the roughest of the ridge country, a total of two days' ride, at the western end of a broad plateau that afforded access only from the south and east. The nobles learned with surprise the small number of troops accompanying Nesos, but the king was there. His blue and white pavilion was propped and decked in all its finery. Moreover, he had been there for some time as evidenced the growing refuse dump beside it.

The men were perplexed. The Tyrant, without warning, had violated the borders of Ven, trampled the Tlaam valley, assaulted their allies in Sipan, entered the hills leading toward Ven itself, and then inexplicably, halted to bask with pleasure in his royal tents. If Nesos had hurried, he might have met them in their irrigated fields instead of here in the roughlands.

Flores breathed a sigh of relief. There had been a scroll... True, if he advanced half the men would remain behind. They would think long before disobeying their feudal masters. But that still left a thousand under Flores' command–which, as it turned out, was as many as Nesos had brought. He did not possess another fortune in golden mir with which to appease Nesos, but a show of force to demonstrate his resolve should make some impression on the Tyrant. Nesos would have to be content with what he had seized thus far, or face a long and bloody war.

In the morning they mustered and prepared to depart. Flores was confident as he stood his mount in a patch of open sunshine. Mosum eyed the splinter group with envy; none too good on a reven, he now abandoned his mount for a ramshackle wagon, regretting his grab for glory, which he now perceived as more akin to foolhardiness. Latkin was discouraged, but patriotic. Flores had shared with neither the knowledge he had gained from Homd. Ust, Simlet, and Laruca were sullen and without arms; their men watched, shamefaced, while the departing warriors criticized them bitterly. As the column pressed up the rocky path across the ridge, a group of fifty broke rank and joined Flores' men amid shouts of praise, fame out-drawing fortune.

Once over the ridge, Flores relaxed. So much the better. Now he was commander in fact as well as name. Isav would direct the men, he would direct the diplomacy, and soon he would show the city and his clan a diplomatic 'miracle' such as would establish his house for generations.

A galloping reven disturbed his reverie and Flores halted and placed his hand upon his sword's pommel. He stared in surprise as Lirsus, youthful heir to the Serclaslers, reined his animal in beside the Turlicum. The youth gazed ahead without emotion and followed when Flores, wondering if he would yet be foiled by his enemies, again motioned his troops forward.

The march proceeded without event. Vast boles of trees obscured the path, dwarfing the riders as they threaded ravines and crevasses in perpetual twilight. An occasional beast withdrew into blackness, its slitted eyes winking from tangled thicket or gurgling cave. A small campsite was discovered and riders brought word: scouts of Nesos had found them as well.

They marched less quickly than they could have. Flores let them keep their strength, or so he said. On the third day in early afternoon, they paused below a broad slope that narrowed at the summit between two jutting peaks. Outriders waited patiently at the top to cover their approach and Isav motioned the men to climb. The slope was strewn with loose gravel, making the ascent difficult. However, within the hour, the entire force was drawn up before the peaks on the edge of a grassy sunlit plateau.

A thousand yards off, the Neset-sa had gathered. They seemed relaxed, though drawn in battle order. Behind stood their tents and camp pickets. Most were mounted on reven-na and armed, but some walked about without concern. The men of Ven advanced slowly, the Simet-sa before them. Unbidden, Lirsus had joined the nobles, though he kept some distance apart. Presently the Neset-sa took form. Simet nobles led them, diamond tattoos visible on their brows. Most of the Neset-sa wore thick beards, a rarity in Ven, where shaved chins or close-cropped beards were the norm. They displayed bare heads, without crests and their skirts were bordered similarly, and many wore bands of diadems about their brows to shield the suns. Vitreous armature similarly shielded chests, arms, and thighs. Their reven-na seemed smaller than those of Ven, a few almost stunted, their homeland being higher and less endowed with the water essential to the amphibious beasts. In the midst of the Neset encampment stood a large tent of fine cloth, ringed with sharpened poles, and swaying hirsute vok-tails.

The foremost Neset-sa seemed to grow nervous and Flores motioned his men to cease the advance. As if on cue, a band separated from the foreign line and approached with care. A man who lacked the diamond, thus signifying his common status, led the band. Flores summoned Isav and Latkin and rode to meet them.

"Hail! Who is your leader?" the man called.

"I lead these men! What do you say?" Flores noted that to send a commoner to meet a noble was disrespectful.

The ambassador reflected a moment, then dismounted, and Flores did the same. They met within earshot of their respective associates. The man was young and seemed to be pleasantly disposed, not haughty as one might expect the representative of a conquering army to be.

"I am the emissary of King Nesos, Brother of the Worlds, First Born of the children of Vensor, and Warlord of Maalstrom. It would please His Lordship to have words with you. He desires no bloodshed."

"I agree, emissary. I would know his mind." Flores turned to look upon his line readied for battle. "Will he meet us in the field, then?"

"He will raise his tent between our two forces, there, with a guard, and parley if you would have it. He is mightily concerned and does not wish to appear as events seem to betray him."

"Events betray him poorly, emissary. Our city regards itself at war with the King. But tell him we shall parley. Our concern is profoundly only that of peace. Have him set up his tent. You can do soon, I trust? Good."

"And pardon me, sirs. Have you some word," the emissary peered at Flores askance, "on events of importance among 'Assemblymen'?"

"If you mean the authority of the Assembly, yes. It is still there. The plot to install a tyrant has failed. Now be off. Summon us when your king is ready to parley." Flores turned and mounted as the emissary withdrew.

To direct the men to dismount and encamp seemed far too trusting to the officers. Flores and Isav agreed. The troops were instructed to stand or sit by their reven-na. The Neset soldiers were either more trusting or more confident, perhaps due to a partly fortified camp at their backs. Before long the vigil began to tell on some of the Ven warriors, having marched all morning. Food was produced from sacks, and here and there a man napped. The more experienced among them noted the suns crossing to the enemy's favor. By dusk, the light would hamper the Vens, but help the Neset-sa. They cast apprehensive glances overhead, where malkops had kept pace with the army, circling lazily, their numbers multiplying.

The tent of Nesos was a congeries of blockish cuts of cloth, each cut a deep blue or white. Once completed, the tent looked large enough to accommodate a hundred guests. It required half an hour to erect. An hour and a half later, when the suns had crossed decisively in favor of the Neset-sa, the emissary appeared before the now impatient Vens. Flores, Mosum, Latkin, and Isav were escorted to the entrance, where a single pair of guards accepted the reins of their beasts. As they relinquished their mounts, Flores suddenly noticed Lirsus at his side. Flores scowled and opened his mouth to speak, but saw that the emissary had seen. Gruffly, he snapped his head in acquiescence and walked inside.

"Ah, sirs," said Nesos. "I'm elated you are here. Sit."

ᔥ ᴤᴤ ᴄᴣ ᔤ

CHAPTER 9

EMPEROR OF THE VENSORS

A big man, black-bearded and smiling, spoke. The King of Neset sat ensconced in a great pale-blue pillow atop a low wooden dais, a long table before him set with wines and delights of the palate. The sides of the tent were hidden by thick tapestries, intricately woven in exotic designs, and piles of soft carpets overlapped about the floor without apparent order, their designs executed in hues that reflected the supernal source of Nesos' power. The First Born himself wore a flowing robe of azure and white, gibbous moons sailing in perpetuity across its surface. On his finger lapis lazuli glittered about his royal seal, a single sun symbolizing the king's unity with Heaven.

He motioned them to his left to low chairs with cushions where a second table formed an L with his dais.

"My entertainment troupe is about to begin." The king raised a flat piece of wood and slapped a bare spot on the table. The curtains parted.

"King Nesos, we have no time to spare–"

"Sit, please. You are my guests and the host must entertain. You will show proper respect." He waved them to the chairs again.

Latkin whispered, "The men are tired, Flores, and exposed."

"I am also tired, but Nesos is right." They turned as Mosum sat and emitted a loud sigh of relief.

"Permit me to introduce my other guests." Nesos indicated a young man immediately to his right. "Sedsednon, my son." The youth glanced up, then returned to his activity–he seemed engrossed with removing one of his shoes and replacing it as if it did not fit right.

With a pleading expression, Latkin glanced at Flores. The Turlicum stroked his chin.

"Sirs, all will be discussed in good time. Why, you have not even introduced yourselves. Come now, speak," said Nesos.

The diplomats chose seats. Flores said, "King Nesos, I am Flores-Sumvensor of the Turlicum, Assemblyman of Ven and commander of the troops camped before you in the plain. This is my friend of long standing: Mosum, Assemblyman, noted for his wise advice."

Nesos nodded.

"And Assemblyman Latkin, a warrior and renowned in Ven."

Flores paused. "Lirsus, noble. Doubtless soon to join us as peer."

The youth stood and bowed.

"Well-bred," said Nesos. "He knows how to please cultured people." The king grasped a goblet and drank, the liquor trickling in his beard.

"And my captain, Isav-Zeyd."

Sedsednon looked up, riveted.

"Isav is a descendant of one of the original Zeyds, the warriors who vanquished the giants before the beginning of time and made Maalstrom safe for the tribe of Vensor." Isav bowed his head deeply as Nesos beamed approval.

"And what, could you tell me, is an 'Assemblyman'?"

Nonplussed, Flores leaned against Latkin for support.

"King Nesos, an Assemblyman is part of the supreme body, the kings, if you will, of Ven."

"Ah, good. Then you have the power to treat with me. And we shall treat soon enough. Yes, very soon. But now you must meet the others."

The king looked to his countrymen. "Sterleric and Atlat, table companions and nobles in my court. And Tursan and Yendel. Yendel's great grandfather invented the spear. Then there is Meham, Rom, and Towt–all nobles of my court." The nobles sat attentively upon similar cushions to Nesos' right. Nesos slapped the stick again, and two entertainers who had been waiting with heads bowed, jumped forward into the light of the torches. Latkin shrugged his shoulders while Flores poured himself a cup of mead.

The two were acrobats, strong and clad in loincloths, one in green, the other blue, with flaps descending to their knees in front and back. The first produced a golden mir and the square ingot burst forth with a deep red flame. The flame swished and crackled. Turning towards each other, the pair began to circle. In a few moments the second man produced a flame. Simultaneously the acrobats tossed the flames in the air, which crossed, and each caught the other's flame, but the audience now saw that the ingots had vanished–only the flames remained burning steadily in their hands. The flames' color changed: one burned yellow, the other blue, then green, then yellow again. The magicians (for such Nesos called them) continued for many minutes, producing as much fire as needed. Once Nesos insisted on receiving a ball of flame himself. The king laughed and rubbed his hands. "It was cold," he said with childlike wonder, "actually cold."

Next came musicians with instruments, drums, and pipes, and dancers with small brass cymbals and rattles on their limbs. They sang and danced as Nesos and his nobles ate. After a time, Nesos tore open a bag of ingots, tossing half the contents to the entertainers. At this, Sedsednon leaped up. Roughly he tore the coins from their grasp. Nesos threw his head back and laughed. Summoning his son, he folded the youth's hand about a second bag of gold, as the entertainers gathered theirs from the floor.

As Sedsednon secreted his treasure, more slaves entered. They spread a heavy dun cloth over the rugs, and two scribes entered bearing a device of intricate manufacture with strange projections and knobs and a long, dull cylinder thrusting from one end.

"Emperor. Lord. Eminence. This device was found amid the ruins of Lim along with ancient scrolls. The scribal guild of Neset, and myself, whose sole pleasure is your entertainment, present it for your amusement."

The slaves produced one of their number who stood at the center of the dun cloth, his hands bound. Twisting the knobs, one of the scribes placed the device against his stomach. He looked up, noted the direction the cylinder was pointed and directed it away from Nesos and toward the bound captive. His finger sought a lever and pulled. Nothing happened. Glancing about, he muttered and peered into the tangle of instruments. He yanked the lever again. An explosion rent the air. The scribe dropped the device–the slave collapsed. A large red hole had appeared in his chest.

At the report the audience leaped in alarm, some falling backwards spilling drinks, others gasping; except Nesos who roared with hilarity and pointed at his abashed nobles.

"An excellent device! My scribes are miracle workers! May you avoid the grasp of Atasan for an age. May Vensor shine on your descendants." He flung another bag of gold, taking care not to expose the contents to Sedsednon. The others talked of the deed in amazement while the corpse was removed. Even Isav, son of a Zeyd, was impressed.

Nesos calmed and slapped his stick again. He leaned toward Flores. "This is the last event. My newest acquisition. Most marvelous!"

A wizened man withered with age hobbled before their gaze, dragging a length of iron chain. His face was dry and creased with sorrow. His joints cracked as he stood before them. The ancient one mumbled and his splotched forehead wavered, shaking beyond his faculty. From somewhere, Flores thought he could hear, barely audible, someone sobbing, sobbing with such great unhappiness that the moans must surely emanate from the gut of a broken soul, a tragic figure without a future and only a terrible regret behind.

Flores peered through the corner of his eye. Tears coursed the cheeks of his companions. The noble returned his attention to the center of the tent and blinked with surprise–the old man had gone. Flores felt suddenly that he must have been in error. What stood before the conclave now was a gawky young man with lanky limbs and a disingenuous smile. The young man's back curved, his belly protruded, and his wide, lower jaw jutted wapper-like. He lurched a few steps and guffawed, all elbows and knees. Laughter rose from the party.

Flores peered closely and noted that the chain had vanished. The youth's leg was free. The lad bent low and walked swiftly to the center of the tent. Suddenly a well-proportioned young man flushed with the vitality of youth and life drew their gaze. Beardless and muscled, his bare chest flexed as he went through the motions of the martial ritual of Vensor. The audience stared transfixed, admiring the strength and sureness of his sinews. The youth spun, jerked in mid-air, and collapsed upon the carpets to the sound of clanking iron as the original chains abruptly reappeared.

Rising to his feet, the old man hobbled again before their vision, his ankle shackled as before. Flores again felt the rending sadness and pity. Then, with the illusionist's exit, the feeling lifted like a passing cloud.

Nesos, who had been laughing quietly, opened his mouth and heaved. "An excellent talent. My new entertainer is also a miracle worker. I will enjoy his gifts for many years–provided I keep him chained. I only just found him in the wilds and he has already twice attempted escape." He summoned a slave and placed in his hand a bag of gold, taking care not to expose its contents to Sedsednon. The others murmured and slapped their thighs in amazement as the slave took the gold to the illusionist.

Nesos slapped his stick again. "Now it is time for business." He settled into his cushion and motioned the remaining entertainers away.

Flores and Latkin sighed with relief as the king turned toward them. At that moment a guard entered the area from behind the Neset nobles. He whispered in Nesos' ear a moment. Nesos replied quietly, then returned his attention to Flores.

"Now Flores. I will listen. What do you say?"

The noble sat up and clasped his hands. "King Nesos, I regret bringing matters which may seem unpleasant. But certain facts must be acknowledged and treated with due interest."

"I agree," replied the King.

Flores peered about the tent. The company had become very quiet.

"First, I must remind Your Eminence that you have marched into the territory of the Empire of Ven with armed troops, without warning or petition. Second, I must add that I have been appointed to detain your force until a greater host than mine will have been assembled, the gathering of which is certainly nearing completion even now."

Nesos leaned back, his finger on his cheek.

"In view of these serious events, I feel I must suggest that your warriors depart with all haste to their homes, in order to prevent a tragic climax to these proceedings. Either that, or I must request that your Eminence present to me a plausible explanation as to why these events have occurred and why the army and government of Ven should not apply a military solution to this problem."

Nesos nodded in his head and tapped his knee again. "Flores, my Assemblyman," he smiled. "You relate the facts accurately. And you are wise in perceiving that unusual conditions have caused them. I have something to tell you that is very strange." He leaned forward, very serious. "I was hired to invade Ven by some Vens!"

The nobles stared at each other, their mouths agape.

"I have already been paid–in gold–through my representative at a meeting not many miles from here, a meeting where he himself met these Vens. A very large sum, I might add. And as of now I have fulfilled my sacred oath to Vensor. I have marched across the border, occupied the valley of the Tlaam, and encamped in the hills above Ven even as I said I would. I have done nothing more. I have not killed your people–that is, except for those criminals in Sipan, whom the whole world despises. I have not burned your farms. I have not stolen your property. In truth, I have been the best of neighbors."

"With whom was your agreement?" demanded Latkin, rising in outrage.

Flores glared and gestured for him to sit.

"My friend," Nesos continued, "I have enjoyed our meeting and I am happy that we had an opportunity to talk, but certain problems have come to my attention which change things, to my great disappointment. Even though I occasionally perform for money like the lowest of my pets, I still despise treachery, and I reward loyalty. My employers were traitors and I hope they die for it. Your being here indicates that their plans have failed and I believe they have received justice. In fact, I think you may know more on that subject than I." He looked at Flores with a sly expression. "But now, I have heard of another meeting, one that again involves treachery, this time in my own court. And again I think you know as much as I. Even so, the meeting will take place."

Frowning, he slapped the stick and a guard ran up and placed a box on the table before Flores. The man opened the coffer and kowtowed. Framed within on cotton was the severed head of Homd with sand in his mouth and blank stones where his eyes should be.

Flores rose slowly from his chair. The other nobles and Lirsus, mystified by the proceeding, were stunned and angry at this unprecedented breach of protocol.

Nesos laughed in a deep, gravelly tone. He rubbed his knees. "And so our talk is through. Long ago, I consulted Divine Vensor about the machinations of Ven, and I was warned to be watchful and prepared. Vensor was right–treachery in my court, treachery in my guests, even treachery in diplomats who come talking peace but sneak in hundreds of extra warriors while we sit negotiating. Before today, my desire for peace was sincere. Now I want only war!"

To a man the nobles of Ven protested, incredulous and ashamed, even as they apprehended what must have transpired outside. The king silenced them with a shout.

"Your city is corrupt, Vens! You no longer worship Vensor but have turned to Atasan. You thought you could lull me while the rest of your men advanced but the Vok-tail clans have been summoned, and we still outnumber you. Now all has been said. There will be no truce. Leave this place, Flores Assemblyman, and go tell your city to prepare. Nesos is coming! He will cleanse it with blood and Sedsednon will rule it in his name!"

"Zeyd!" shouted Sedsednon and clambered onto the tabletop. He stood, swinging his bag of gold like a trophy, kicking drinks and dishes. Nesos drained a goblet and shattered it on the slab, then leaned back and roared with laughter.

The Vens stood. Warily, they backed toward the entrance. Seeing no attempt to intervene, Flores waved them to their mounts, Neset guards still tending them, and rode swiftly back, the sinking suns casting lurid shadows before them.

As they neared their lines, Ust, Laruca, and Simlet galloped to meet them. The former grabbed Flores' reins as he attempted to pass.

"What traitorous plan have you concocted? We heard of your plot! You meant to leave us so you could give Nesos the city's gold. This war is nothing but a sham."

"You fool!" Flores yelled. "They are about to attack! Get back with your men!"

Stunned, the newcomers halted. The others approached breakneck and reined in their mounts to a canter.

"Isav!" called Flores.

"We must get off the plateau!" shouted Latkin. "There is no place to retreat!"

Isav caught Flores' arm. "We can put the new men in the center. Ours can hold the flanks."

Flores glanced at the twin jutting peaks, growing dull as the suns sank over the western horizon. Dust already broke the ground in eddies as the tension began to excite glass rapiers and armor. "No. We've marched into a trap–and the trap has sprung. New men on the flanks. We will take the center." He sighted Mosum heaving upon his reven. "Sir, will you command the reserve forming at the rear?" The noble nodded, his face like a sweating strawberry, and hopped away on his reven. Flores and his companions followed, leaving the three interlopers alone in the growing darkness.

The warriors were already gathered for battle. A group of captains abandoned a frantic argument and rushed to their commander. "What happened? We thought you had been seized. The deserters rejoined us and the Neset-sa broke camp. They have been assembling for an hour; a thousand more have arrived. Our traitors are already beginning to desert again."

Even as they spoke a dull murmur rose across the field and grew louder.

Flores yelled, "It is war! Get our men to the rear! We must get off the plateau!" He dashed off again.

The first men were off the plateau when the Nesets hit them. Like a tidal wave they came, broad and massive, the last rays of the suns behind their backs. The shock squeezed the Vens against the far ridge; within minutes they were jammed thigh to thigh. The soldiers shouted, waving swords, desperately seeking the foe in the dying light. Cries of "Vensor! Do not desert us!" pealed from the stricken army as myriad flashes silhouetted animals and men. The carnage was worst just behind the line of contact. The beasts hissed and snapped in the crush, burying fangs in human legs and other reven-na. Their massive tails whipped, breaking men and staggering their mounts. Clouds gathered to deepen the darkness and a hot wind rose, whipping brush and debris among the dirt-bound warriors.

At the rear, men poured through the narrow pass and down the slope, Flores among them. Isav found the Turlicum totem of flayed reven paws nailed to a pole and called to clansmen to rally as Flores galloped about the slope in an effort to halt the rout. As the dusk turned to night, a continuous stream slid down, escaping the slaughter on the plateau in the deepening gloom. The stream fluxed; now more came, now fewer.

After a time, seeing no more survivors, Flores turned his mount to leave, then heard a cry. The dim shapes of two reven-na appeared. Glittering rapiers met and clattered, flashing with each contact of the blades. The pair slid parallel among the stones; the Neset warrior found a foothold and propelled his reven into the barreled side of the Ven's mount. The Ven collapsed and rolled barely escaping being crushed by his animal. The blades met again and spat sparks–the upturned face of Ust stared in horror at a glowing Neset pike raised for the kill.

Flores spurred his mount. The Neset released Ust and faced Flores. Grinning with sly malice, the warrior detected the flaw in Flores' attack and maneuvered his reven to Flores' unprotected side. In anticipation the foe reared his mount in the trained cabré to crush his opponent with its weight while his pike struck home. Seemingly oblivious to the deadly move, Flores rushed in. The Neset's grin froze in the midst of his descent as he saw–too late–Flores uncross his hands so that the pike that had appeared to be in his right hand now lay upthrust on his left. The grin did not fade even as the weight of the Neset's mount colliding with Flores' reven drove the Neset's body upon the Ven's blade.

Ust breathed heavily and said nothing. He stood. Retrieving his sword, still humming with transferred energy, he snatched the reins of his trembling mount and climbed into the saddle. More figures slid upon them.

Flores engaged two and shouted, "Sir Ust! Take the other!" The glass rapiers scraped and the Ven noble found the combined weight of his opponents pushing him down the slope, gravel rolling beneath padded paws. At the bottom his tribesmen waited. There could be no more left on the plateau above, he thought–surely none still living.

"Ust!" He turned his head.

Ust was gone.

With a scrambling motion, Flores' mount slipped and fell, scattering rocks. His foes yelled in triumph. One drew near. The bearded figure leaned to thrust at Flores with a sword when a pike transfixed the Neset from behind lifting him from his saddle. The weapon was withdrawn and its owner fell upon the other Neset with several companions while someone with bloodstained armor handed Flores the reins of his mount. Flores descended the slope, unable to make out the crests of his saviors, who quickly vanished in the gloom. Behind them the pass filled with Neset-sa. A dark mass, barely visible against the sky, lit sporadically where glass touched iron, flowed after the retreating Vens.

For two ferocious days and panicked nights the Vens fled, pausing only when too exhausted to climb the next ridge, resisting desperately when Neset-sa assaulted their rear, scattering before sudden midnight onslaughts, numbers dwindling, leaders lost, detachments abandoned, banners left in obscure ravines amid the dead. On the second night of the rout, a storm broke and plunged the hill country into a cold, dank labyrinth of shadowed woods and crevasses, as if the gods themselves had judged against them. The clashes gradually lessened as the Vens found secluded places to rest and rising mists hampered their pursuers.

A single thought obsessed Flores–he must get back to Ven before his enemies. The Assembly must hear his version of the battle, not that of Ust or Simlet. Luck had joined his rivals; they could not have planned his defeat better. With Isav's help he managed to keep a nucleus of Turlicum together. Most of his clansmen had survived the battle, though many had been killed during the rout, and more burned by charged glass. More had simply strayed or dropped away to seize some rest in tree limbs or beneath rocky ledges. Now, as they splashed through an irrigated field under a cold grey sky, perhaps twenty mounted men struggled alongside the Turlicum. They hunched over saddles or clung to necks of reven-na, many weaponless; even as Flores stared, another reven and rider slowed and stumbled into the morass, the animal's gills working convulsively in the muddied water.

Twice Flores had accepted mounts when his own collapsed in a shudder. He himself was dazed and barely conscious. Isav and Latkin tied him to his present mount after he had lost his hold and fallen among rocks, opening a gash in his scalp.

Far behind, a string of black dots followed as hunters do wounded prey, keeping them in sight, the Neset-sa hoarding their remaining energy for the kill.

A dike rose before them. Grunting, men and beasts clawed the bank. They had to dismount, for the reven-na would not go. Several turned and slid into an irrigation ditch.

Isav spoke to Flores. "You've turned a claw. Yours cannot go further. Take mine."

He took his head. "Don't try. We cannot make it."

"You must, or we are all dead!" Isav called another to help and together they cut the knots and pulled Flores onto another mount, tying him again to the saddle. "Only a few of us can continue. The rest will stop and fight the Neset-sa here."

Flores stumbled away on the exhausted animal, noting only that Isav had no sword. Unsheathing his remaining dagger, he let it drop, unable to tell if Isav had seen.

The Turlicum Lord had vanished in the direction of Ven and Isav and his men were resting upon the dike awaiting the arrival of their pursuers when a body of fresh cavalry cantered from the opposite direction. They were Vens, and the men cheered as the distant dots halted and receded.

As he neared, the leader shouted, "Man, have you seen Flores of the Turlicum?"

Isav eyed him with distrust. "What is your concern?"

"We must warn him. Numsenmur holds the city. Hem and Sorel are assassinated. We are Nevsonhet. Our leader, Nilsit, holds the main gate and its armory, but we cannot defy Numsenmur for long without Flores' help. The Serclasler controls all else and has arrested the Assembly."

Isav whipped a reven to its feet and mounted as he spoke. "He is on this road. Hurry! We may already be too late." The company hopped towards Ven.

Time passed in a cloudy haze for Flores till the scattered outlying dwellings of the city stood a few hundred yards away. He motioned fitfully to his men. "Rest...we must rest. We cannot enter Ven like this." His men seemed to handle him roughly as they loosed his bonds and dragged him off the reven. Dimly, he perceived warriors sprawled in the road in what should have been very uncomfortable poses.

A harsh voice rang from a row of surprised faces. "Flores-Sumvensor of the Turlicum. In the name of the Assembly and the People of Ven, we arrest you for treason!"

ↀ ଊ ଓ ↁ

CHAPTER 10

UNDER SIEGE

Shouts mixed with hard crunches and repeated flat whacks like wood on earthenware drifted from beyond the wall. A man in downward gripping reven claw headgear steadied his hold on a pale marine sword and readjusted the overturned tabletop that he had propped for use as a shield. The room was a shambles. Torches revealed desultory furniture and racks throughout, scattered and upended, a hard-breathing warrior refuged behind each. Some were Turlicum, but most wore different headgear, with mineral encrusted caps surmounted by circlets of iron. Many of the warriors were bloodied despite the flaring plates of glass armor flickering with torchlight.

Revd wondered silently why the Nevsonhet should now fight with such vigor when they had previously refused to oppose the Serclasers in the Assembly. He shrugged. Self-preservation knows no timing but its own, he mused. A warrior with finely leaved concoidal obsidian discs set in his cap–delicate work for fighting–glanced at Revd as if to reassure himself of their venture's outcome. The man, Nilsit, chief of the Nevsonhet, nudged a collector's repertoire of weaponry that littered the floor to rework his footing. Well, thought Revd, we may not have the numbers but we at least have the weapons. He sniffed. The acrid air, heavy and still, smelled of ozone.

A creak of splintering wood penetrated the walls and was followed by more shouts. Without taking his eyes off the twin doors before him, the Turlicum captain scooped up a dagger and placed it within his belt. Several Nevsonhet trod heavily at his rear where another door opened on an antechamber–more shouts drifted from beyond, drowning the noises at the threshold.

One of the warriors spoke. "They have begun. And another troop of Turlicum have joined."

The Simet Lord smiled. "Numsenmur will rue the day he struck us both at once. Or rather whip the man who reminds him, since that is more his mind."

He looked back at the cluster of men who stood poised, watching the vibrating doors. "Good. Once we gain the street, we shall get upon the ramparts above the gate. From there they will never move us."

The paneled door split with a shattering report and the butt of a makeshift ram protruded through the crevice. The men about the rear exit scrambled for cover as the ram levered and rotated, then withdrew. The shouts on the far side rose again and a clacking of swords resounded. Through the gap the men could see flashes and dark shapes struggling, but they soon subsided. The room had settled and grown quiet when the portals burst at the hinges and fell in a cloud of dust. Whirring shafts sprayed the room. A Nevsonhet who stepped forward at the wrong instant collapsed transfixed. Others staggered under the toneless impact of arrows on irsrem armor.

Like a sundered dike, the gap disgorged a current of primal-passioned warriors, wielding rapiers and pikes under the Serclasler insignia of rum-na feathers. The defenders rushed to stem the intruders. Revd emerged from the darkness of his table, slipped between two of the enemy, hamstrung one, deflected the thrust of the other, then drove him back, pike in neck, the greater charge of his opponent's glass causing his hair to rise. The captain smiled grimly–after running for half a day with his kin dying about him, he finally was able to level the score. Between thrusts and parries he saw the struggle fragment into a score of private duels, bodies surging, sparks hissing, deaths mounting as on a spiral staircase each step crumbling as one climbed, to permit no return.

In the torchlight the oscillating limbs threw dragons and chimeras across the walls. Revd's blade grew hot as it burned with his own blood lust–this was the ritual of Atasan. Like a desert twister, the fire god had awakened. He could see it in the knotted arms and drawn pupils, feel it in the guiding hand that helped each successful thrust. The smell of ozone grew stronger. The chamber grew livid with the hungry presence of the unmentionable god, He who, though banished by Vensor, remained dormant in each man's breast, waiting only a lapse of reason to rush forth again in all His rage and chaos.

A third victim collapsed before the Turlicum captains to reveal a ponderous image in the shattered doorway. A large man with archaic iron helmet and massive iron axe, oblivious of the charged glass around him, stood patiently, as in the center of a storm, blade balanced on tip, face obscured by rigid cheek and nose guards. Crude wings like those of a falcon slumped from the Temples to bulging shoulders. A Serclasler chief, thought Revd, and highly placed. More Serclaslers pressed into the chamber and forced Revd back with jabbing rapiers. The defenders began to back toward the exit, whether under the pressure of the Serclaslers or in response to some unperceived signal, Revd could not tell. He looked again at the silent figure. Here is my greeting–sorry I haven't time for better introductions. Whipping the dagger from his belt, he flung it. The chieftain saw the motion and turned his head a fraction–with a resounding clang the missile glanced off his helmet. Then, his eyes exuding confidence and contempt, he resumed his stone-like pose. At least I woke you, thought Revd, as he parried another thrust.

The Serclaslers were winning the armory. The pushed forward, climbing over the fallen, and Revd withdrew under the cover of friendly blades at the invitation of Nilsit, who himself retreated to the adjoining room.

The rear chamber led to a wide corridor that angled to reveal a single large ground-level window at its far end with casement open. Tightly massed within this hall a crowd of Turlicum and Nevsonhet warriors clambered over dispatched Serclaslers and poured out of the aperture. Revd and Nilsit joined them and swung over the sill into the avenue of Murfenmas where the cold autumn air was tempered by the breath of Atasan.

Revd halted. His eyes were smitten by an image of outsized nightcrawlers wriggling half in shadow inside a monstrous box. A huge handle or arch rising from one side of the box took the form of the city gate of Ven. It piled high and gaped beneath the overcast sky, gargantuan and hoary, its maw made for the triumphs of giants and not the charades of mere men. Its portals were wide as a section of street; they stood poised on two axles that seemed capable of spinning worlds. The portals were constructed of solid irsrem, four feet thick and flawlessly cast. The armature was compassed by two high towers; a primordial lintel spanned the lot, lined with crenelated ramparts. Blockish tenements formed the other sides of the box, dominating the avenue and throwing their umbra over the struggling mob.

While Revd edged away from the armory, the sill poured forth men. Revd remembered the event which–hours before–had drawn him within its walls. All morning, since the dawn raid of the Serclaslers on the Turlicum estate, he had followed Mesret. Dragging the youth from the palace in the midst of flame, he had broken through the Serclaslers as they sought to block the clan's escape through the garden, then he had lost the Turlicum Heir in a panicked rout of the Turlicum along the Hedronmas. He found him trailing with a limp; the whack of a sword had summoned his health at a run. As the clan passed the city gate and some Turlicum warriors had joined the fighting at the gate, Mesret had rushed in, weaponless. Swearing, Revd had pursued. The youth saw him and climbed within this window, and Revd followed. A lengthy search proved fruitless. Then the Serclaslers rushed the armory and cut its defenders off from the street. Now Revd, having lost the youth, retraced his steps.

As the captain watched, more Turlicum, exhausted and just returning from their rout before Nesos, rode under the gate and added their small difference to the hundreds of men slashing and dying in the city. Even as Revd perceived Isav on a reven next to a Nevsonhet chief, he heard screams and feet thumping in the corridor behind him. He chilled. Beyond the milling mass in the avenue, a fresh swarm of Serclaslers approached, scuttling like crabs on a beach. A wave of hot charged air washed over him.

Revd ran and clutched one of Isav's boots. "Where is Flores? We heard of the disaster in the south."

"Where is *Mesret?*" the other shot back.

Revd was surprised by the insistent tone of the returning leader, overshadowing his fatigue.

"Mesret!" Revd swore. "I wouldn't know. The whore has been playing cat and mouse all morning. Each time he sees me, he flees."

Isav leaned and gripped the other's arm.

"We've got to find him. The Heir..." He stared hard, communicating more than he had said.

Revd wondered, then understood.

"Flores?"

Isav nodded. He glanced toward the interior of the city.

A rising chorus of clattering earthenware interrupted as the enemy closed about them. The defending warriors were spent, their reinforcements exhausted before they joined, increasing numbers fell with burns, their glass unable to match the energy of fresh troops. The Serclaslers' number was bolstered suddenly by a flood of Molersal who emerged from side streets and loosed a cloud of arrows. A shaft jounced off the pavement at Revd's feet and the surviving Turlicum backed toward the gate.

From the direction of the plaza a party of cavalry appeared, not executing massed propelment for the confused nature of the combat, the duels rather playing out in volts and thrusts without regard for lines or sides. Each warrior of the new party was taller and heavier than those who clashed in the street; each wore the rum-na feathers of Serclasler; each voiced no sound. They paused while a huge Serclasler chief with iron-winged helm emerged from the burning armory and mounted a sinewy reven. He moved to the forefront of the mounted ranks, an enormous axe upon his shoulder. Though he walked his mount and had not yet lifted his weapon, the line gave before him like putty. Three carapaced warriors blocked his path. For several moments he swung the two-pronged blade in a revolving arc, then savagely spurred his beast forward. While Revd watched in horror, beast and man smote the nearest victim with such force that the irsrem plates ripped from the victim's body and skidded across the pavement and his reven stumbled on broken limbs and collapsed. Another propelment overthrew the second defender; and a single blow from the axe broke the third man, shattering his torso behind the still intact vitreous armor.

The chieftain's henchmen fell upon the stunned enemy with increased fury, cheering as yet more Serclaslers and Molersals appeared. The best efforts of the defenders to hold dissolved and the tired line collapsed. The Nevsonhet Lord Nilsit lit a mount and snatched a pennon from a follower. Spinning a stained sword, he waved the flag and yelled, "Out the gate!"

His men fell back rapidly, sweeping the Turlicum along, seeming more to sally forth than retreat rearward. Isav and Revd joined the flow. The armory was lost, and, having abandoned it, the Nevsonhet and Turlicum lost their last foothold in the city. Beyond were the suburbs of Ven–more commonly referred to as slums–temporary dwellings thrown up by the poor, and, as all acutely realized, soon likely to be thrown down by the King of Neset.

Outside the gate, Isav and Revd paused as the disaster took on the aspect of a drama's denouement before the dropping of the final curtain. Isav glanced at Revd.

"How did it happen?"

Revd thrust his sword upright in the hard scurf where it sparked and grew dull.

"They surprised us in the morning–killed the sentinels and flooded the garden before we knew anything was wrong. We fought them. Gained a little time–just enough to get the young ones out through the back grating."

Isav nodded.

"We got out just in time–the rain was cold and the stream rising–the Serclaslers almost rode us down. But we got out and jammed a blade in the lock. Several fell, pierced by Serclasler spears thrust through the grating. We followed the north road, before the front gate. But, as we passed, Mesret ran back into the city. I lost sight of him." Revd looked up at Isav. "I cannot understand. Unless...he prefers the enemy to his own clan." He motioned toward the city.

"Flores has been taken by the Serclasler, at the south gate. Both Lord and Heir lie there–"

"Then they will both soon lie in graves," he sighed. "The Turlicum clan must prepare to disband."

Revd sank to the ground, oblivious of the soldiers retreating around him. He did not notice when the direction of the retreat changed, the warriors no longer fleeing out the gate, but rather north, away from the city, and not just recently bloodied Nevsonhet, but compact bodies of tattered and haggard garrison cavalry, who glanced often behind them down the southern road.

Revd froze. He re-sighted a familiar figure.

Mesret, Heir to the illustrious clan of Turlicum, strolled casually away from the city toward a decrepit hovel, still unarmed, ignoring the stampeding groups of reven-na emerging from the south.

Revd swore. Isav spurred his mount. Overtaking the youth, he slipped off his reven and landed squarely upon the boy. Revd ran to him, gripped his collar, and unleashed a series of cuffs about the boy's head. He lifted him to Isav who placed him behind him on his reven.

"Get him away! I'll find a mount and follow."

Isav made a motion as if to leave but paused again. A large party of fifty riders or so, many of whom were weaponless, dashed towards the gate as the last defenders attempted to turn and flee, for the most part overwhelmed and cut down by the Serclaslers. With cries of shock and outrage, the arriving troops halted–before their eyes the vast world-turning portals of Ven moved slowly, noiselessly before the pressure of many hundred hands, narrowing the aperture. Even as they watched, the gap lessened to a strip, the strip to a slit, then the slit to nothing as the only path to safety shut definitively, uncompromisingly, with a muddy, anechoic thud.

The exhausted riders sat motionless before the solid wall of glass, They stared dully without comprehension. Suddenly a knot of dusty brown warriors with fillets and thick beards exploded upon them and the Vens broke in all directions, some scrambling madly up the north road, some diving into huts, others bolting to the south along the road they had just traversed. An arrow appeared in the arm of one and his reven responded to the unfamiliar jerk on its reins by tumbling. The animal rolled twice, crushed its rider, then rose. Revd grabbed its saddle and clung as it tried to shake him, then hopped madly away while Isav, with Mesret behind, kept pace. Revd mastered the beast, and looked back–the Neset-sa were closing. Shafts whirred and the Turlicum beat their mounts, rushing north, the road sloping unevenly upward to the first crusty ridge of the Falls of Sish.

The pursuing warriors cried out. On the crest of a ridge, Isav and Revd glanced back to see Mesret of the Turlicum raise himself from the dusty roadway and await the enemy with unruffled calm. Two of the pursuing Neset-sa halted. They surrounded the youth. The remainder shouted and lashed their beasts toward Isav and Revd, who, with a single last glance, descended the far slope and were lost to sight.

Down the roadway, had the Vens remained another moment they would have seen rise above the camber the main army of Nesos, a grey crawling mass like a centipede sarcophagus for towns, or an insect city on the move, with scattered glinting and sparkling of the suns' rays on glass amid myriad hopping of amphibious reven-na.

The square before the gate of Ven had emptied when a small party of reven-na materialized on the southern road and flew before the cool wind to the portals' brink. Their riders, like the others before, were tattered and weary, but they rode straight and clung firmly to their saddles. They still possessed their blades and pikes, and were still panoplied, some green, some blue, and many wore the dark proof of bravery in stains about their bodies and limbs, while most still displayed their kinsmen's crests. Their leader separated himself. Advancing to the towering pylon, Lirsus-Nidrenmor of the Serclaslers smote the glass with the butt of his sword.

Silence answered.

CHAPTER 11

IMPRISONED

Flores awoke to the rattling of keys and the turning of an iron lock. Sullen guards pulled him, hands tied, from the littered floor and stood him on his feet. One muttered "Neset-friend" and pushed him so he nearly fell. He was cuffed and roughly hauled out under the grey sky of a cool autumn day.

Several moments passed before he could walk. Not much time could have elapsed since his 'trial'; he was still deathly tired and sore, and blood caked his head where he had landed upon the rocks. His captors pushed him across a well-manicured park ringed with men to where the neglected portals of the Assembly gaped, more warriors efficiently blocking the entrance. Through the lattice of the grounds-gate, Flores glimpsed a column of reven-na across the plaza hurrying in the direction of the city gate. They bore a familiar crest–rum-na feathered head-gear–the clan totem of the Serclaslers. The Turlicum noble recognized several of his escort as they dragged him through the portals. He stared. They were not Serclaslers, but Molersal, employees of Sendas.

His jailers shunted him into an Assembly that awaited his arrival in silence. Seated in a high, massive throne upon an upraised dais where the tiered benches had been roughly hewn and hastily reconstructed was Numsenmur. His fair beard thrust from an archaic iron helmet that obscured his face with rigid cheek and nose guards, crude falcon's wings slumping from temples to bulging shoulders. A massive iron axe overlay his knees and a full dozen of his captains stood about his person beside a score of mute slave-soldiers, each carapaced in irsrem armor. Flores noticed the chief of the Molersals, Sendas, at Numsenmur's side, head nodding in fatigue. He was scratched and haggard. Flores surprised himself by smiling. He was glad Sendas had not succumbed to the wilds. He had not wished it. But, although to return sooner would have been inconvenient, the return of Sendas as it happened could not have been more poorly timed. An elbow nudged the epicurean's side and Sendas raised his chin weakly from his chest.

The Assembly had been decimated. Sorel, Hem, Selim, Misenta, Nilsit, Endel, each a leader of an important faction, anti-Loyalist or otherwise, were missing. And, ironically, a few chiefs known to be loyal to Numsenmur. Mosum and Latkin had also not returned. At least Flores hoped they had not–for their sake. But Temes was present, deigning not to recognize Flores. There would be no more interruptions in this Assembly, Flores reflected. And here was Ust, bleary-eyed and sneering. From his appearance, having barely escaped the Neset-sa; his tunic was torn and soiled though he himself was uninjured. Ust rose to make certain he had been seen. With a glimmer of satisfaction, Flores saw that Simlet and Laruca were also missing.

"Flores-Sumvensor, you have forgotten your robe." Ust delicately adjusted a tattered sleeve. "But that only saves us the trouble of stripping it off your back! Man, you are accused of the murder of the respected Simet and Assemblyman, Sruk-Nevneset-Lurenmurg; of the attempted murder of our good colleague Sendas; and the theft of 50,000 gold mir from the coffers of the city, which act involved murder and trespassing–"

Flores noted wryly that the amount had grown since his departure.

"–of creating numerous public disturbances resulting in much loss of property; of slandering the good name and reputation of His Lordship, the Public Benefactor, Numsenmur-Nidrenmor-Serclasler; and –"

He paused. Numsenmur pointed a finger at an Assemblyman across the chamber who had grumbled under his breath. A trio of thugs converged upon the wretch and beat him about the head with clubs. He was unceremoniously dragged from the tiers and through the exit. "–and initiating a war with Nesos of Neset with the intention of delivering the city of Ven into his power, over which you were to rule as the creature of the Tyrant." Ust finished.

The tired prisoner omitted asking why he had returned so quickly, weaponless and bound and injured, if that had indeed been his purpose.

"Do you have a reply?" Ust almost screamed.

Visions of his bonds snapping and of him striding heroically up the benches sword in hand surged briefly in his imagination–to fade and die.

"Then," chuckled Ust, "that is the first time."

Flores saw only a mausoleum with a frozen, menacing statue.

Sendas rose painfully to his feet, favoring the leg that had received the pike. His chin bore several days' growth. Chin and finger alike pointed across the chamber. "It was Flores who almost killed me! Me—a Simet noble of Holy Ven." He extended his hands to the accused, palms upward. "Flores, my friend, my colleague... Why?"

Sendas sought to rest his hands on the lapels of his vest, but wore a casual street tunic which had none and his jeweled rings became entangled. With an effort, he pulled his hands free and placed them on his hips. "I cannot understand how a Simet noble—and a friend and colleague at that—could commit such an act. This fellow with his ruffians burst into my palanquin and kidnapped me—and Sruk—kidnapped us at sword point, then hauled us into the night far into the wilderness without regard for our health or safety in the awful wilds with beasts and birds."

Numsenmur turned and Sendas paused. He breathed deeply to calm himself, though whether his distraction was due to his facing his enemy again or due to fear of bludgeoning from Numsenmur's minions Flores could not tell.

"Indeed, I saw the entire evil deed. This boastful fellow, whose head swells bigger than this room, gloated, mocked, and insulted us and the city of Ven, and then murdered my good colleague, Sruk. Dear Sruk..." Fat tears came to Sendas' eyes. He sniffed and wiped them away.

"This fiend, this criminal, this robber who would steal the nose off your face, robbed us of the vok-skin and all our gold—"

Numsenmur slammed the throne arm and Sendas stammered, "I mean robbed us of the vok-skin and Nesos' gold."

The Serclasler buried his forehead in his palm.

Sendas looked to the ceiling and poked the air. "Robbed us of the gold in our purses, took the vok-skin from Nesos—or his assistant—and gave him the gold which he, Flores, had taken from the coffers of the city. Last week." He beamed at Numsenmur for approval.

The Serclasler glared and Sendas fell silent.

Ust cleared his throat. "Flores of the Turlicum: the Assembly wills that you be confined in the new state cells beneath the palace of our Benefactor, Numsenmur, whom you have so mercilessly and wantonly persecuted, to be interrogated at length concerning your role in provoking the present war and your history as an enemy of the state, until such time as our foes of Neset are defeated, when you shall be burned before the public, your bones crushed to powder, and the powder tossed into the Hedronmas." Flores stared quietly ahead. "And that your tribe be disbanded and its members sold into slavery, and that you be stripped of your estate and all your property, which will become the property of the state, pending a decision on distribution by His Eminence, the Public Benefactor. And, finally, that your heir–"

Numsenmur leaned forward.

"–who is now imprisoned in the state cells, will suffer a fate even worse. I leave it to you to speculate upon it." Ust's expression turned cruel. "So the reptile has lost its fangs. Crawl, beast, back to your moldy lair."

The hall was silent. Numsenmur stared at his rival with a face like stone and the great majority of the nobles present looked away, anywhere but at Flores and the carnivore that now ruled them. The guards took Flores' arms and hauled him out of the chamber.

Once he had left, the Simet-sa in the Assembly redirected their unwilling senses to Numsenmur. The imperious warlord raised a muscled arm and pointed. Rushing to obey, his thugs laid their hands upon the person of Sendas-Moredin of the Molersal. Ignoring his squeals of protest, they dragged him bodily down the tiers to the floor of the chamber. A ruffian brandished a club and looked to his lord questioningly, but Numsenmur waved him back. Sendas shuddered and collapsed. His captors shook him and made him stand respectfully before his former colleague, now his master. Throughout the assault, four Molersal chiefs had stood quietly. They now walked calmly to Numsenmur's side.

"Molersal!" the king bellowed. "You have burdened this Assembly too long with your weakness and your timidity. You are not what this august body of leaders and men needs. No longer can your incompetence be tolerated. This city requires strength and loyalty. The first I will supply. The second, the Simet-sa of Ven. From this moment, those who will not give all to the cause of Ven will rest in the Eye of Vensor. As for you, Molersal, you are banished from the Assembly. Your life is spared only in view of your previous contributions. Do not appear in this Assembly again or you will forfeit that as well."

Sendas gazed at the floor. He struggled to regain his composure. With a single melancholy glance at his former colleagues arrayed before him, he shuffled slowly out the door.

ೞ ೱ ೲ ೬

The villa of Numsenmur was located some distance from the Assembly Hall on the western edge of Ven. In transit to his new cell, Flores and his escort were pushed to one side of the Way of Murfenmas to make room for more groups of warriors, hurrying now in the direction of the Hedronmas. Shouts carried dimly from the river and he supposed that Nesos had already arrived and penetrated the southern suburbs. Arriving at the Public Baths, Flores recoiled in horror. Corpses, many of old men or boys too young to pose any threat to Numsenmur, lay in windrows upon the esplanade. A squad of executioners in Serclasler rum-na gear casually piked shrieking victims as they were brought. A chill began to creep through Flores in anticipation of what must lie in store for him.

The Serclasler's estate was larger than that of Flores, but not greatly so. It was certainly smaller than the acreage surrounding the Assembly. Several stories piled toward the clouds, pinnacles still glowing with fading sunlight as the short Maalstrom day drew to a close. Behind the complex would be the barracks, exercise square and shelter for the reven-na. His guards pushed him past the now familiar coterie of armed attendants and into the villa, where he was ushered below ground level and into another familiar milieu–a mortared cell.

Here the most desolate of thoughts assailed Flores. From the pinnacle of success, but one remaining step from leadership of his city and his peers, he had fallen to the level of condemned criminal, mistakenly renowned for losing a battle that he did not initiate, with an army that would not obey his commands. Now the gods had placed him in the hands of the one man on Maalstrom whose ambitions required his removal and whose hatred knew no bounds. His son, who thought him mad with ambition, lay in chains within the city, perhaps within this very building at the mercy of his same enemy. His closest companions and allies were exiled. Or dead. Foreign emotions welled up and Flores fell to his knees, buried his head, and beat upon the floor of the chamber with his bound fists, scattering dust and refuse in the still air. Coughing convulsively, he wept bitter tears.

Flore woke when cold gruel slopped over him.

"Bon appetit!" cackled a voice.

This pair, Flores observed, were assuredly picked for the pleasure they showed in their work. One was short and nimble, with a projected visage that reminded him of a small annoying animal, The other was a great hulking brute, a scraggly beard hiding his expression; tufts of hair showed through his tunic's orifices in surprising places. The fur split into a wide grin.

"I am Molo," he introduced himself. "Would you like to meet my friend?" They laughed, exchanging glances. The grating was opened and the two pulled Flores to his feet. A rope was twined about his bonds to lead him and they dragged him into the waiting corridor where Molo yanked the rope to signal that he was to walk. His bonds bit into his wrists and Flores cried out.

Molo said, "Superb, good Snivet! That will hurry his feet."

Flores slipped and Snivet cursed. Up they dragged him, the rope biting deeper while the smaller man kicked his calves. From somewhere came a movement of scorched air.

"Listen! Snivet looked at Flores as they paused. A faint sound of hammer on anvil carried on the draft. "They ready your bed, my man, your kindly servants and valets, just as instructed. The wagers on how you like it are already being taken."

A dank mustiness filled the air. The hall through which they passed was long and narrow and dimly lit by oil lamps set in alcoves. Rooms opening upon the corridor were equally gloomy and almost devoid of people. Heads thrust briefly out a doorway. They were quickly withdrawn and the door slammed shut. The two guards and their ward reached the end of the hall and turned to view another corridor with more rooms stretching ahead. For several minutes the trio walked. Flores stared, uncomprehending. Gradually he realized he had been here before. On the right was a section of wooden paneling with wainscoting, old and creaking, and, at the end of the hall, a door. Behind would be the tower with its narrow staircase leading up to the rooms of the consort Crestal and his slave Tilsis. And on the left–this was more intriguing–was the room with the crumbling mortar that had lain unused for a generation.

Snivet leaned forward and clutched his arm. "You know the clan of the Urlis claim their own, man? As Vensor is their master, they each claim their own. Tumsenet stoops and pulls up the plants with his hands, and Talen spreads his beasts over Maalstrom. But Atasan! Atasan is supreme! Only his work is forever. Only his will is perfect. What does he claim? He claims carrion. The decaying plants and the rotting flesh."

Flores shook him off and Molo sneered, pausing to grin in his face.

Snivet continued, "The Workers of the Sky take the dead from their biers, take them to live with Vensor in Heaven. But those that rot the malkops will not touch–for they belong by right to Atasan. And those that die in prison cells must pray the Workers get their bodies before their flesh grows soft–if not, they live forever with the eternal god of fire."

The guards looked at each other.

"He doesn't like us, does he, Molo? I think he detests us." They laughed and started off again, dragging Flores along.

Soon Snivet wormed around and sidled up again. "Look here!" He thrust his neck into Flores' face. Three great weals ran to his back. Flores eyed him with disgust. "That's a scar that runs all the way to my legs," he said proudly. "Know how I got it? I was lashed."

Molo turned again. "Tell him why you were lashed, Snivet."

"By the love of Divine Atasan, it was something I did to a chi–"

Snivet gasped and hit the wall. As he collapsed, Flores swung hard and also struck Molo in the neck, who coughed and stumbled back, clutching his throat. Then Flores was gone. He dove into a dimly lit door, bounded across the room and through another open door, for which he gave thanks to whatever gods may be.

Behind him the guards screamed in rage and pulled their sword free of their scabbards, clacking them against the sooty walls. Flores ran in a cold sweat, too witless to consider the tangle of unoccupied rooms and halls opening before him.

He hit a dead end.

Quickly he retraced his steps and thought them through again. Down the hall–to the left–through the door–through another... again nothing.

A blank wall.

He stepped closer, barely able to see in the flickering light of a single torch in the hallway. Then it dawned on him. This was indeed the room where Crestal's slave, Tilsis, had led him to the youth's tower months earlier. In the corner lay the crumbling pipe that opened on the river Suma. However, now, for the first time in a generation, at the very moment when his life depended on it, the room had been repaired! The pipe was blocked. A chill rose from the bottom of his spine; several rooms away, he heard the sound of hurrying feet and heavy breathing. He turned. Better to confront them in the dark where he would have the best advantage and could surprise them with a sudden ambush. He stepped forward. If only he had a sword...

With a crash the floor gave way. He fell, even as a fleeting memory surfaced of a dark pit that Tilsis had carefully instructed him to avoid.

For an eternity he dropped. Twisting, turning, head up, head down, drops of clammy sweat drifting before his eyes. An ocean of ink and mustiness took his breath away. He did not land, but began to slide. A vast slope of gravel slanted and curved and rushed about him, crushing his ribs and rolling him down an endless mountain. Gradually the blackness took on a grayish tinge, as if a cloud from stellar gulfs had sought refuge within this subterranean pit. After an age had elapsed the rumbling and trickling ceased and the last echoes retreated into the distance as if loath to remain.

It was long before Flores attempted to move. For what seemed hours he lay, exhausted. Finally his eyes opened. Nothing presented itself and he breathed and coughed a cloud of dust. Then he moved and when the stones ceased shifting, rolled and sat upright. His eyes adjusting, he found he could see. Light must be seeping in from somewhere, he thought. He looked up and saw a small grey patch, no more than a pinhole, flickering as from dulled starlight. The lamps of searchers. A great greyness sloped upward toward the pinhole.

Drunkenly he reeled to his feet. As the darkness receded, walls appeared, towering slabs of dark on black, marching interminably into darkness. Walls with no roofs, no doors, no windows, without purpose or direction, reeling and tottering in ancient decay, as shattered as he.

He began to walk, limping through soil that was desiccated and lifeless. Gradually he made out a roof of live stone. In places the roof sank quite low, though without connecting the ambling walls, and in some places was too high to see, having vanished in shadow. Quiet echoes drifted from his feet, each sounding briefly before taking leave, dissonant chords in an ancient amphitheater. Flores walked further and, still surrounded by the mindless architecture, came to what appeared to be the side of the cavern. He turned and stumbled on.

He drifted aimlessly, sinking into despondency. So this was his sentence—if not of Numsenmur, then of the gods. To live out his life in this dusty hole, with no chance of rescue because none knew of his whereabouts, to shrivel without water, perhaps even to remain un-rotted, his countenance retaining its last hopeless expression, forever beyond the reach of Vensor and his angels. At the moment, his tormentors chased each other somewhere overhead down sagging halls and through unlit rooms, waving lamps and glittering swords as they bellowed in rage. Perhaps they too would continue, eons after he had long since dried and stiffened.

All about was silence and desolation. Nothing was visible except a heavy encroaching greyness that leaned and fell in great broken carpets. Flores knew his fate. This was the night of eternity, the night with no stars, the night of Atasan. He had fallen into the Abyss, he was indeed in the grasp of the Envious One, He who would be Equal, the inciter of war, of murder, of lust, the deity whose crime had thrown it from the heavens and whose brooding regret drove it to malice for everything alive. Flores, crushed and broken, sat and waited for His touch to descend.

A rasp sounded before him. He looked up slowly, agonizingly, to view the image of the god of fire. As from a great height through a shuddering haze, or through shimmering water refracted to a distant miniature, he perceived a delicate hand reach through the gathering veils, palm up, and grasp his arm. Breathing hard, he stumbled back against a wall. The bricks crumbled. In a moment of lucidity, he realized that fatigue and shock were causing his knees to fold, and he collapsed upon the rocky floor of the cavern.

CHAPTER 12

AMINA

Flores was explaining to divine Tumsenet why he could not depart his sun-drenched forest, adding insistently that he must remain awake for when the other god returned. The green face, massive and spanning Flores' vision, broke in two, and uttered something incomprehensible, but the rumbling betrayed a detachment and unconcern. A flume of smoke veiled the image, and Flores realized he was not talking to Tumsenet, but to Atasan, and its round mouth spewed lava. He watched his arm shrivel in flame and felt he must have taken the wrong path in the Amanus Mountains. Unable to bear the pain any longer, he shouted, crying for help, then fled through an endless jungle, his clothes ripping, until enormous arms snared him and he was lifted and thrown with sure strength into the sky, higher than he had ever been. He was caught again and his father grinned and took him up to the highest pinnacle of the palace, where Flores gasped at the expanse of all that he the One the only heir would someday possess, even the impenetrable jungle of gardens with its denizens and its grandeur.

All went black. Then, two yellow ros eyes gleamed. The ros grew a beard and the Serclasler stretched his insolent face into an animal snarl. Then the beard expanded and the eyes grew subtle. Nesos threw back his head and roared with laughter, and yelled, "Sedsednon will rule! Sedsednon my son!" The maniac offspring of God's First Born sat upon the throne and ordered his headsman that all should lose their feet. Then some distant province began to burn, whole forests igniting, their flaming limbs writhing against the crowded Maalstrom night, the lust of Atasan rivaling the calm stars of Vensor. The flames spread, consuming all that would burn and melting what would not, until the earth itself seemed to melt and run. The world scorched and flamed without respite, and Flores gave up hope that it could ever be the same, feeling nothing but his own incorporeal spirit, a pan-world-soul hovering like a malkop, but burning with the world itself. Then the world grew even hotter. The sweat beaded and Flores felt the flames burrow and search out every unspoiled region that the fires had missed, searing him until nothing remained of the vast empire that had previously existed. Then the flames receded and vanished into blackness. He screamed. The night of Atasan! For the sake of your soul, crawl free, find a way to the suns, your soul must rest with God, it must return to rest in the Eye of Vensor! He shuddered and struggled, but arms restrained his own, and a cool voice soothed his ears, and as if in answer to his cry a small light appeared, a flame not searing and raging as before, but dull and calm, reassuring.

Gradually Flores woke and became aware of the outline of a rough chamber shifting in the light of a single candle. He was alone. Then the light grew suddenly remote and soon was overshadowed by nightmares and phantoms that returned again and again to wrestle him, though they could no longer subdue him. Slowly the images faded, and the candle returned, and Flores learned to watch and wait for food and water, and to listen for the familiar voice that invariably accompanied them and comforted him. And when his savior would come and bright eyes appear in the darkness, he knew that his head would be lifted and cool water gently poured into his mouth, or the blood cleaned from his brow, and his savior call to him and encourage him.

Then the planks beneath his feet again gave way and he was dropping from an endless height, and great drops of sweat swelled to encompass the world. They finally coalesced into limpid eyes of night, and flawless skin the color of leaden seas and storm-laden cloud banks. In a nameless cove, two dark eyes shined like pools and he grew enraptured with the desire to possess them and was filled with gratitude for what he had received. In a strange, silken voice, the phantom whispered, "My lord, you've given me life," as deep within him something long dormant and unsuspected betrayed itself. Strange thing for a god to say, thought Flores. The deity smothered his face and neck with kisses and he slept.

The light steadied and he knew it was a candle, and the candle revealed a ceiling of rock and chiseled walls. A spray of minerals glittered pink through the darkness. Beyond the mouth, a low craggy ceiling extended ridge upon ridge above aimless brickwork whose tallest rows were just visible from the elevated floor of the candle-lit hollow. For a moment he thought he heard the flames hissing again, then realized that what he heard was water, the soft sound of water flowing over unpolished rock. A blanket had been laid upon the rocky floor and Flores lay upon it, the edge half drawn over him. He awoke to the sound of a voice softly singing.

"My lord, Mamnia, Son of the Goddess, Father of his tribe, King of his wife." The voice continued as his eyes fluttered. His brows perked at the strange words.

Then Flores felt the hair on the nape of his neck rise. A few feet distant a mysterious figure sat, nude body rocking gently on heels with eyes closed and hands folded, a dark cloth discarded at its feet. Vokcheese and shredded lyart lay before him on a blanket. He gorged on the food. Presently his mind cleared. His bruises ached.

"Who, or *what* are you?" he asked.

The figure rose to one knee, its eyes averte. Then stood. It crossed to the entrance of the cave and gazed upon the desolation of the open cavern and listened, then returned and sat again, legs folding. It opened a small pouch and dipped in its hand, then drew it out and applied broad streaks of blue over its dusky cheeks.

"Mamnia, Son of the Goddess, King of his tribe," it sang in a soft, melodic voice, its gaze alternating between the eroded stone beneath their feet and Flores' half-closed eyes.

"Did you not hear me?" Flores repeated, willing himself to full alertness. "I spoke to you." It continued dabbing and Flores lost patience. "Can you speak at all? Or are you just an animal, like a bird, singing all the time?"

The pain showed. Rejected, it looked down.

"So you do understand." Flores sat upright, then groaned, clutching his head. Once the pain had eased, he examined his companion more closely, gazing through unfocused eyes and wondering whether his companion would prove to be but another fever-induced illusion. He nodded, more in wonder than disbelief. The beauty of the creature was undeniable. He followed the minutiae of its form in the flickering light–the supple legs, well formed and strong narrow waist, swelled pendant globes of flesh, cascading locks black as the swirling shadows, the creamy blue paint accenting leaden skin.

"Such a delicate face," he whispered. "Yes, you do possess beauty–the beauty of the malkops."

It smiled again and resumed chanting.

"Wait!" he cried.

It paused and looked at him.

"What are you doing in these caverns? And what manner of creature are you? Malkops have no speech, but you understand what I say." The obscure smile returned. "If you are not an angel of Vensor, then what are you?" He stared deep into the blue-streaked pupils shining back at him.

Slowly it took his hand and stroked it.

For a moment Flores watched. He pulled away and his expression became clouded. "I do not understand. You have returned my life to me. *Why* have you helped me?" He swung his arm to encompass the cave. Its brows remained perplexed. He attempted to raise himself, but grew dizzy and lay again upon the blanket where he gazed through a haze of pain. Once more he strained and succeeded in lifting himself to a sitting position.

He smiled and nodded. "Yes. Now I know. I have guessed your secret. You are a recluse, a deformed Ven who has hidden himself in these caverns to hide your body from the world. You have my sympathy, and shall have more–that is, more tangible evidence of my gratitude–once I have returned to the city."

Its eyes clouded with tears and Flores ceased speaking.

"Why do you weep?"

The eyes remained downcast and wet.

"Do not weep. I shall not leave yet. Here, I grow hungry again."

Casually he raised a piece of meat to his mouth without dropping his gaze from his companion. He bit. A jet of blue burst from his beard and coated his arm. Flores stared in horror. He shot to his feet, then cried out and bent over, clutching his head again. He fell back to the blanket.

His companion watched, open-mouthed, then pointed and laughed. Flores gazed at the blue cosmetic on his arm and chuckled. They both laughed as his companion wiped the paint with a cloth, saying, "Amina will help you, My lord. She is your wife, and you are the father of her tribe."

"Wha–?"

Amina dropped the cloth. Smiling, she placed her hands upon his shoulders, and pressed him slowly upon his back. Flores turned suddenly white and pushed her off. He crawled to one side of the cave.

Amina sat, still puzzled.

"I don't know where I am or how long I've been here, and I don't believe that...I mean I don't know how customs are where you come from, but here in Ven we have other customs." She moved as if to touch him and Flores again recoiled with an instinctive glance upward for a glimpse of Vensor. He glanced out the cave's entrance and across the cavern.

"Crippled recluse or wingless malkop or Maalstrom spirit or whatever you are, you may go about your business. You have saved my life and I shall not forget it, but now–you may return to wherever you came from, for I am well and there is no need for–" Moisture gathered in Anima's eyes again.

"Of course, I am not ungrateful for your assistance–" He took a step toward the entrance of the cave. The tears rolled down, beading over the blue grease. He stopped and peered into the gloom. He returned to the blanket, sat, then leaned against the wall of the cave.

"However, I do need rest. Do you think you can bring me more food? There is none left."

With a sniff, she cleared her tears and smeared the paint with a cloth. Despite his continuing hunger, Flores closed his eyes and within a few minutes slept soundly.

Removing the paint from her face with a cloth, Amina glanced quickly about, took up a thick garment of coarse black cloth, and pulled the tunic over her head. Carefully adjusting the spiraled garment, she let the cowl fall over her face, then stepped through the mouth of the cave.

When Amina next appeared at the entrance, Flores was awake and sitting. Amina, who had brought no food, opened her mouth in a surprised smile.

"My lord? Oh, I am so pleased you will live!"

Flores stared, his brows narrowing.

"You...Amina."

"Oh. I forgot. I must not speak to you." She glanced down and her cowl hid her face.

"What is this you're wearing?" Flores reached up and touched a hem of Amina's black garment. "Amina–if that's your name–do you know what this is you are wearing?"

She waved and shook her head silently.

"You wear the robe of a priest of Vensor, an inhabitant of the Temple!" He glanced aside then looked back. "Do you not understand its import? It is forbidden for Vensor-sa to wear such. They are woven for the Temple priests only–you cannot know what the priests of Vensor would do to you if they found this on your person. In truth, I don't even know what a priest of the Temple looks like...." His voice trailed off.

Suddenly he realized.

The sound of crunching pebbles reverberated through the cave, and Flores heard a bright, short laugh like tinkling bells.

"Was I right, my Sisters? Did I not say that she had no proper business in the cellars? Now we have found where Amina has been sneaking off to...and why!"

∾ ₨ ₧ ₭

CHAPTER 13

THE TEMPLE

Amina wilted like a dry blossom. Dark figures in voluminous black cassocks crowded the entrance, thrusting spitting torches from their midst, cowls flung back to reveal a row of smooth, delicate faces, dark and expressive, like that of Anima. Clutching a wooden crosier, a thin figure whose ancient visage was like sere leather, drilled Anima with her stare.

"Profanity! Ingratitude! Self-hatred!"

Flores still sat.

The old woman turned here glare upon him. "You were right, Nara. She has tainted her soul with a defiled one." She raised one arm. "Bring them both. Put cloth about the eyes of the male–but be careful of his violence, Sisters."

She turned and disappeared and the tinkling laugh rang again. Flores looked at its source. A young woman with a face of striking beauty smiled down upon him. He soon felt uneasy beneath the contemptuous gaze emanating from those sculpted features.

The priestesses entered the cave and pulled Anima to her feet. The beautiful one snatched something off the floor. It was the blue paint.

"Sister Anima!" she said in mock alarm. "How far you have fallen. Vensa will never forgive this. But since you are my Sister, I myself will ask her to."

"That is for Wijah to do," Amina said through tears.

"That is not for you to say, my Sister–not now!"

The priestesses ushered Amina out of the cave. She did not resist.

Flores staggered to his feet. He had not yet recovered his strength, and felt dizzy. The priestesses hesitated. Wooden poles emerged from behind the intruders and were leveled at him, the nearer end of each resembling a cartwheel of projecting blades surrounding a pivotal point. Fashioned by Ven metal-smiths, Flores noted, and intended for use in ceremony, but effective against a defenseless man. He heard a length of cloth being torn from a garment.

"We are prepared for your violence."

"I mean no harm, priests, but if you try the blindfold, I'll break you."

They exchanged nervous glances, then ringed him with their weapons and motioned that he walk.

Obscured by a haze of dust raised by the priestesses' robes, the cavern yawned luridly in their torchlight, the crumbling remains of a deserted city shifting in the feeble flames, their ears lulled by waters hissing in a narrow crevice that bordered the broken architecture.

Following the commands of his captors, Flores climbed a series of stone ledges paralleling the rushing stream. Soon they left the cavern, traversed a series of twisting tunnels and hewn steps, and entered a corridor through a broken door of wood. At the corridor's end a second door, in better repair, led the party into a storage chamber stacked with sacks and barrels and adjoined by a second room. A broad, open hallway opened before them. It gleamed with treasured minerals lit by alcoved torches: networks of hammered gold ran from floor to ceiling, encasing slabs of chalcedony, onyx and marble. The priestesses paid no heed, their hand-held brands dropping glowing embers upon the polished rorewood beneath them.

Several priestesses halted in surprise when Flores' party approached. Upon sighting the intruder from the city of men, they drew cowls over their faces and withdrew.

The hall led to a large, hexagonal rotunda with an open skylight. Five other halls radiated outward. Here Wijah waited with a dozen dark-robed companions, her head held high, her expression disapproving. "Sister Aleka," she shrilled. "How is it the murderer is not blindfolded?"

A priestess with a large, round face lowered her eyes and motioned to those still holding the ceremonial pinwheels.

"He threatened us, Sister Wijah. We could think of no way to follow your instruction."

Wijah exhaled impatiently and snapped her fingers.

Flores bowed. "Sister Wijah, please forgive my interruption, but–"

"Quiet!" Wijah shouted. The old woman stared at him as if she had been struck. She clapped her hands to her mouth. "I spoke to it!" She howled and waved her arms.

"I must pray! This criminal must know that if he tricks Holy Ones in this fashion again he may find himself condemned. It is not for the unclean to taint the air with their speech, nor for a barbarian from outside to soil the Temple of Vensa. But," she reluctantly waved them on, "the Goddess herself has commanded us."

Crossing the rotunda, the priestesses entered another corridor of equal opulence to the first, identical to it except for a clerestory of irsrem plates high on one side through which a wash of sunlight flowed. They came to an open threshold leading to a flight of deeply worn stone steps. The priestesses motioned Flores to climb. Several flights later, they paused before an open door. Flores turned to speak to Amina; she was gone. He blinked, then stepped forward and his escort closed the portal behind him. A heavy bar rasped into place. Not taking any chances with violent criminals, he mused.

He glanced about him, startled. He stood within a large and luxuriously furnished chamber, glittering with such a profusion of wealth that his eyes dazzled, imagining Ven could pay all its debts with such reserves. Finely made objects of gold and silver and glass lay about in casual disorder, leading him to wonder if his captors had enclosed him in their treasure room by error. If not, could this be other than a poor example of what the Temple must contain? The finest crafts of Ven's treasure-smiths paled in comparison to the exquisite workmanship of what lay outspread before him, yet the style was familiar–indeed, as his eye followed details of craftsmanship and theme, he realized the style was the same as in the city proper, only subtly altered. As they were finer than what Ven's smiths currently produced, he realized that all he saw was the product of centuries of worship, philanthropy, and profligacy from uncounted generations of 'defiled ones' to the priests of the Temple of Vensor.

Crossing to a soft golden-gilt bed, he collapsed and slipped into a deep, perplexed sleep.

Flores awoke to the sound of a gong. Its tone was familiar but carried to him louder than he could remember. Somehow he took this as an indication of urgency and he hurried out of bed and rushed to the window to see if he was late to another calling for the sons of Vensor. In the cool breeze of an autumn morning, he swung open the casement and nearly fell over the sill.

An alien city lay below.

Three stories down was a small plaza. Bordered by crenelated ramparts, wings and annexes of the Temple extended leftward and climbed the acropolis of Ven, where, from the highest peak of the city, the Temple spire soared, rivaling the Falls of Sish in the distance. With peals from the tower echoing in his ears, and malkops circling the spire in broad, lazy circles, Flores turned his gaze back to the plaza, and recognized the courtyard of the calling for sons. Dozens of black priests moved across the square with infants in their arms, their wailing coming to him clearly. More figures scuttled above the portcullis and ramparts that overlooked the city beyond. Even now, he thought, the populace must be gathering before the gates, the magistrate preparing to signal the beginning of the celebration.

Following the movements of the priests, Flores fought to control his pounding heart. No mortal had ever glimpsed the interior of the Temple and lived. Involuntarily, he looked about to see if any observed him. If so, the fact that he watched was of no interest to those below. Peering cautiously, he made out the altars of various aristocratic houses: Selemnev, Furselim, Nevsonhet and...Turlicum.

He caught his breath.

There, on the Turlicum altar, clearly visible in the afternoon light, was a son. He calculated the approach again, counting the altars from the front gate–yes, he had a son. Ordinarily, he would ignore the child, for he had Mesret. By tradition, houses had only one heir; more than one caused succession struggles such as had occurred between King Nesos and his brother. If one's heir died, it was simple to adopt a second, since infants appeared on most clan altars with predictable frequency. But Flores' son was dead. Or if not yet, soon.

A dark-robed figure with a baton entered the courtyard and sat upon one of the altars. Others had placed food and drink about the seat of the priestess with the baton, and she, apparently supervising the others, began to sample a cut of vok-meat. A short distance away, another priestess lifted Flores' son, his gift from Vensor, from the altar of Turlicum and placed it on an adjacent altar. The priest swept the Turlicum altar clean. Then a second priest placed a different child upon Flores' family altar. Both moved on.

Flores stared in bewilderment. Proceeding down the row of alters, the two priestesses shifted and moved infants and swept under them without regard for order or location–not once did they return a child to its original altar. Frantic, Flores felt that someone else must have seen the culprits–surely they would inform the overseer of their error! Someone must be told! One of the priests, haphazardly it seemed, did return an infant to its original altar, and Flores breathed more easily.

Then more priestesses approached with more infants. They sat and talked, several chatting with the overseer and laying their charges upon the altars beside them as they did so. After a time they stood, retrieved the infants, and proceeded to the far side of the courtyard.

Flores slid down. He squeezed his eyes shut.

In full view of the overseer, some of the priestesses had retrieved those infants which the altars had previously held–not those which they had temporarily placed beside them. The overseer had seen their actions and had said nothing.

Flores peered over the sill to watch the overseer. Carefully, he counted the rows and columns. When he realized where the supervisor sat, he grew dizzy and sat again. The overseer's altar, apparently the current director's favorite location for supervising the distribution of infants, was the ancestral seat of Sruk of the Lurenmurg. Sruk had never had a son!

He had made a momentous discovery, but with whom could he share it? Certainly none in Ven would believe him. Again he peered over the casing. The priestesses were stirring and beginning to drift toward the chamber of the idols. Even now the citizens of Ven prepared to enter the sacred courtyard. If he could somehow disguise himself and descend to the courtyard while the gate was raised he could perhaps exit the Temple with the worshipers, though he realized he would only have traded captors. Still, mortal enemies were something that he could fight–priests and goddesses he could not. He leaned out the window and inspected the wall. The wall was smooth, lacking windows or gaps of any kind, offering no opportunity for him to negotiate its surface. However, as Flores watched, a hidden door at ground level opened to admit a laggard priestess and then shut, leaving no trace to betray its existence to the outside. As the second gong washed across the city and the Temple gate cranked upward, Flores rose and walked to the opposite end of his room, across from the portal that was guarded and barred by the priestesses. He pulled the handle. It slid quietly open and, to his surprise, Flores stepped into an empty corridor.

Walking the halls of the Temple, Flores felt his blood pulse. For the first time in weeks he was well and rested. As his spirits rose he examined the extravagances of the Temple. Halls with floors of polished rorewood and murals of intricate marquetry led from room to room. Some chambers were comparatively barren, others had been executed in tasteful simplicity. Still others he found breathtaking in their squandering of rare minerals and wealth. A stairway of polished diorite drew Flores downward to unlit levels, and for a time he carefully had to feel his way. Then the passage brightened and he entered a large chamber where massive spandrels flew skyward to prop capstones. They bounded a large lunette of gold-ground hexagonal tesserae and bossed silver plate on a background of chalcedony and sard. A narrative theme was evident, perpetually lit by a high aperture of clever design; Flores recognized the figures in the theme from other ornamentation that he had glimpsed inside the Temple.

Central to the mosaic was the unclothed figure of a priestess of the Temple of Vensa in idealized form. Her skin shone with reflected gold leaf, her hair glittered like the Maalstrom night, with star-specks of silver intermixed. She reclined in a garden of green trees and rippling brooks. One arm underlay her head, while the other stretched forth seeming to beckon. In the representations that he had viewed thus far the woman had lain similarly, always reclining, always beckoning, her gaze fixed skyward, tresses fanned out upon the ground, one knee flexed, inviting. Elsewhere she had reclined alone, no other figure being present in the delicate design. Here the narration was complete. Exquisitely executed in silver plate, the hammered figure of a man– or something like a man–prepared to meet his lover. His face was smooth and noble, his chest trim and muscled, his physique flawless and as human as any son of Vensor, except for the immense stiff wings emanating from his spine holding him effortlessly aloft.

Flores stared, transfixed. Silently, he praised the artists whose labor had created the masterpiece, the mind whose invention had supplied its essence. A twinge of regret passed through him at the wide split that wandered across the face of the work, fracturing the torso of the goddess and seeming to render impassable the short distance that sep-arated lover from beloved. The quake that produced the crack must have occurred long ago; the tiles at his feet were almost obscured by dust and grit, and the neglected silver plate of the winged man had deepened to a deep rusty black.

Flores shuddered. Although not explicitly sexual, there was no mis-taking the fact that the unifying theme of the mosaic was the abom-inable and supposedly extinct heresy of feminality. What mystery had placed women–*gila-sa*–in God's Temple, he wondered? What lapse in universal order had permitted a monument to intercourse in the cult-center of celibacy? Flores shook his head and proceeded.

Ascending a second flight of steps he re-entered unlit areas and found himself blocked by an archaic wing of the Temple. The granite rose in distinct layers of rusticated stratigraphy, to form a tall massive wall running parallel to the Temple proper. For some distance a banquette or catwalk ran along the face of this wall, which was accessible from another flight of stairs. A handrail with sockets for torches paralleled the catwalk. In one socket a hand torch still burned.

Flores took a step, then paused. A muffled droning emanated from nearby. He shrugged and climbed the stairs. They led to a small poorly lit room set in the archaic granite, in the midst of which crackled aromatic wood and resin deposited in a large iron pit. The far side of the room was bounded by a wall of mortared brick with a large breach in the center. Though the ceiling slanted back and expelled most of the smoke along a groove incised in the ceiling over the entrance, some of the smoke escaped in a steady stream outward through the breach. The breach did not open freely into space, Flores discovered, but was itself obstructed by some exterior projection, hollowed and exhibiting two further apertures that were oval and symmetric. The droning came from beyond the obstruction.

Flores bent and gazed through the apertures.

A minute passed and a shrill voice from behind indicated that he had again been discovered by the priestesses of the Temple. He turned to find Wijah, petulant at his disappearance, entering the room along with Aleka and several other priestesses. At their subdued but insistent gestures, reinforced by menacing movements of more sharp pinwheels, he left, retracing his route back to his room overlooking the plaza.

As evening fell, Flores watched the suns, now almost merged into one ball of light, verge the western horizon, weaving loops of grey through the Temple galleries and cloisters. The sky was swept clean of clouds and the temperature had again begun to drop. Soon winter would come. The time raced by, sixteen hours to a day.

Flores shuddered at the blatant use of the forbidden language that he had heard in the Temple of Vensor. He did not know why, and was not certain what the words signified, but he knew, as all Vensor-sa did, that certain words, for example 'her,' 'herself' and 'she' were of the tongue of Atasan and that Vens were forbidden to use them. The language was spoken by gila-sa, apparently even here in the Temple.

He forced his mind to face the question that increasingly troubled him. Were the priests of Vensor gila-sa? The answer seemed as obvious as it was unfathomable. No priest he had seen thus far was of the size and shape to be expected of men, but were smaller, slimmer, and their voices higher, much like Vensor youths. While not defenseless, the priests were physically weaker than most men and, like eunuchs, more easily intimidated; Flores felt that with a small band of soldiers he could take the Temple in half an hour. Yet many possessed the special powers of gila-sa, the powers that had gained such repute across Maalstrom, making them both feared and coveted. He knew what that power consisted of, and felt he could give it a name: It was the power of the ideal, the fatal grip of irresistible beauty. He had felt the power with Amina. Fortunately, his strength had held. Still, he could no longer avoid the obvious conclusion: these were not priests. They were priestesses—women—gila-sa.

This presented an insoluble mystery. How could the Holy Temple of Vensor, to whom the very existence of gila-sa was an offense, contain the children of Atasan, the fallen and despised heir of God? Of course for millennia, wherever gila-sa were found across the face of Maalstrom, the sons of Vensor had brought them to their Temples, each Vensor city obeying the command with respect to its own sacred spring. That was the law, set down by Vensor Himself at the beginning of time, a law which as far as Flores knew was followed everywhere on Maalstrom without exception. But to find gila-sa dressed as priests, and to learn that every priest was a gila, and that none were present who were not gila-sa—this Flores could not accept. Still, he himself had seen gila-sa deliver the next generation of the sons of God to the Temple courtyard, and do so badly.

Could this be part of Vensor's plan?

He pondered. In the ancient, renowned, muscular city of Ven stood the Temple. Its wings and annexes and garden sprawled before him in the twilight, its darkness and shadow emphasized by the brightness of the glass city that surrounded it. The people of Ven, governed by the Simet-sa, received the boon of Vensor from Ven's Temple—His sons—to renew themselves. And in return the people of Ven fulfilled the ancient covenant and laid gifts before the images of Vensor and his tribe, the Urlis, in the holy room of the idols. In each ritual, which occurred every month or so, the magistrate of Ven and the current heads of the strongest clans mounted the steps of the idol of Vensor and addressed Him concerning some measure of current interest. And, with few exceptions, He always answered with the single word: "food."

And they brought food, without asking who consumed it. Food in limitless quantities, food without end, until the populace suffered and the poor went hungry, and the republic was driven to secure the food of other cities by tax or tribute, cities that also had Temples, and idols to which were also addressed urgent requests and which also doubtless replied in similar fashion, desiring that one simple, unadorned, most basic, but most political of commodities. And if they ever slackened or delayed, the bounty of God was withheld, the portcullis did not rise, and Vensor ceased delivering His sons, and the abandoned city would plunge into despair and beg for the return of Vensor's favor with all the fabulous gifts it could muster. Food for whom? Gila-sa? Flores snorted. Such things were not possible. But then who spoke through the idol? Apparently a priest. That meant a gila. Whom had he seen? Only gila-sa, all similar in appearance to Amina–and she was not a man, that he knew. Could the few priestesses he had seen, only a tiny fraction of the ill-housed, hungry masses of Ven, consume such vast amounts? It seemed impossible, but who else?

There was only one possible conclusion. A thought began to coalesce, or rather the feeling began to rise, despite resistance, that the entire Temple was a massive deception, that at some distant time, too many gila-sa had been brought to Ven's Temple, and that the gila-sa had indeed usurped the Sacred Spring of God, killing or expelling God's true priests or imprisoning them, though Flores was at a loss as to when or how this could have been accomplished. For ages since, Flores supposed, the gila-sa had deceived and manipulated the men of the city to their own advantage, in secret defiance of the laws of God and Man, while they corrupted His plan in the courtyard below, disrupting and confusing the priests' ancient function of delivering sons. Even now, they elaborated on their deception with childish schemes to frighten and intimidate. Who knew how long they had given their advice through the mouth of the golden idol?

Flores' mind reeled with the implications of his discovery, his shattering conclusions. Who would believe him? Since he had discovered the priests' secret, could they ever let him go? And what of Amina? When Flores thought of the woman who had saved him in the cavern, who had sat by his side with patient strength while fever devoured his body, he felt none of the distrust and hostility he felt toward the others. Whatever she might be, her actions were not those of the Fomenter of Evil, but were worthy of Vensor Himself. She had indeed denied that she was gila. This was doubtless an admirable, though unbelievable attempt to dissociate herself from the Servant of Sin. She herself had, spiritually at least, returned to Vensor.

Flores shook his head and attempted to force matters back how they had been. Vensor shone. The moons sailed. The workers in the sky accepted the souls of the dead. What did he know of Heaven, of Vensor's divine plan, to accuse God's acolytes of fraud? Flores nodded. What indeed? He had seen enough! Amina had broken the law; Wijah erred. The human chords of jealousy and fear were apparent among the priestesses. How clear becomes the tarnish once idols become familiar, he thought. Plainly, he decided, the Fomenter of Strife sought His own in each heart that beat, even in God's own house. Gila-sa had usurped the most Sacred Spring of God.

With this thought, Flores curled upon the wide bed and slept.

A soft scratching sounded from the door. He turned and someone removed the bar. The door opened.

A lone priestess stood in the light of a glowing brand. The guards had vanished; black night absorbed Flores' sight through the window panes. The priestess entered the room and held the torch to a lamp, lit it, then moved back toward the door in silence. Flores followed her with his eyes, expressionless.

She stopped, pulled the door shut, and threw back her cowl.

"Nara," Flores said.

"I am pleased. The one from the city recalls my name."

"I hope I pronounced it correctly." Flores bowed his head. "I apologize for not knowing the proper form of address for a Sister."

She hesitated, then said, "That will do."

"You spoke to me."

Nara breathed deeply. "Nara will do her prayers later and ask for forgiveness."

Flores glanced at the door, which hung ajar.

"You need not think of escaping," she said. "The Temple is alert to your violence so long as you remain within its walls. The entire floor is sealed and guarded."

Flores nodded, noting the delicate line of her jaw, her lustrous skin, her bright, enveloping eyes. "Why must Sisters never speak to men, Nara?"

"Everyone knows that," she laughed.

"Not I."

"Because Sisters are holy. That is why we live behind walls. Men are by their nature strong and violent–they cannot live in harmony with Daughters of Vensa or even with themselves."

"Do you believe that?"

"I have seen the violence of the city from the wall. It reminds us always that we must never allow men the freedom of the Temple."

"Are you so peaceful then that you have no violence?"

"Of course. We are Sisters."

"And your holy laws are never broken?"

"Never!"

"Then you must not be a Sister, because you are speaking to me again."

She paused, then laughed. "No act of ours could change our nature. Though the day has shadows, no one would say it is night. Sisters are holy and pure by virtue of their sex and forever unspoiled by the greed and passions of men. Our Queen and what we see teaches us this truth."

Flores looked puzzled. "Your 'Queen'?"

She laughed again. "But you have not seen the Queen, so of course you would not know." She shook her head. "Men! How can you know anything? Vensa keeps you ignorant for your own good. For the good of all, but especially for Herself."

Flores dropped his legs over the side of the bed and straightened his back. "There is no use pretending to me, Nara. Neither men nor women can hide their true nature–not even through cassocks."

Nara looked at him strangely.

"You–as all of your Sisters–are a gila. Even Amina. In truth, you are all servants of the god of fire, Atasan."

Nara permitted half a smile to form.

"Servants of Atasan? Is that what you now believe?"

"Yes. I don't know how or when, but you gila-sa have seized the Temple for your own purposes and have corrupted God's laws, even in his most sacred function of the calling for sons. And you have murdered or otherwise disposed of Vensor's true priests. Now you deceive the men of the city to gain their food and treasure."

Nara laughed again, deeply amused. "So a defiled one has been in the Temple for a day and now knows all its secrets, even the inner thoughts of Vensa."

Flores hesitated, glancing toward the courtyard which lay empty and bathed in amber moonlight. "I know that there are no true heirs."

"Heirs?"

"Yes."

"And what is an 'heir'?" she asked indulgently.

Flores felt uneasy again. He suspected that he had revealed a weakness to a dangerous enemy and backtracked.

"An affair of the city. You wouldn't know of it."

"A direct descendent?" She guessed. "As with animals? How entertaining! You men think of the funniest notions. Not to know your own parentage, or the manner of your birth.... Ah, the Queen handles you so well. You follow her instructions perfectly and never guess that you live in Her city at Her allowance, but think it belongs to you and even invent a name for it–Ven. But it remains merely the outer slums of the Temple of the Goddess Vensa as it has for centuries past and shall for centuries more."

Flores listened quietly, trying to master a deep and growing disturbance.

"So gila-sa have 'invaded' the Temple?" She laughed softly again. "And how many of our errant Sisters from the outworld have you brought to the postern in a century? Ten? Fifty? Your violent masculine mind, which seeks to impose rigid forms on everything, surely can see that the numbers alone are lacking. But then a thousand gila-sa could not do what you suggest, for each that you return undergoes the Ritual of Penitence."

Flores frowned. "You could have exterminated Vensor's priests long ago and your numbers grown from a few to many–the city brings food for a multitude. You would never go hungry."

"And how could their numbers grow without men?" Now the tone was humorless and bitter. "Would their children drop from heaven like a hail of flesh?" Nara eyed Flores more closely. "No, our fallen Sisters of the outworld have always been slaves of men, despised even while desired. We Sisters, the priestesses of Vensa, who have been here since time began, rescue our errant Sisters from the men of Maalstrom when we can and bring them to justice. We are strong in justice. Here in Vensa's Temple we bring our sinning Sisters to salvation for eternity." She looked at him strangely again. "But, Flores, by the Will of Vensa, even a holy Sister of the Temple, slave to no man, needs a man at least once in her life."

She stepped forward and halted directly before him.

"Flores..." Nara lowered her eyes and seemed to grow small. Suddenly Flores felt that Nara was infinitely more vulnerable than he had realized, that she was but a small, unhappy child lost in a wide, threatening world and in urgent need of protection, a terrified waif whom only he could protect and reassure. Almost of its own accord, his arm lifted and reached out to embrace her, protect her. With an effort he brought it back to his side, but she noticed and stepped closer, smiling.

"If I speak for you before the Queen," she asked, "will you grant me my wish?"

"It seems that your Temple is self-contained and perfect. What could you possibly desire that is lacking in all your prayers and purity?"

Nara reached out. His hand again moved and she took it and raised it slowly to her mouth. She kissed it, then rubbed it on her flawless cheek, lashes flicking.

"Love, Flores. I need love–or I'll die." She looked up into his eyes and wrapped her arms about him.

Flores shook his head, then pushed her away.

"Don't you understand?" she hissed. "They'll be back soon. I have no time to explain!"

Flores backed away.

"Life, Flores. I need life. Give it to me!" She clung to him and whispered, "I can make your mind sing."

He pulled back evading her grasp.

"How can I make you understand? Don't you realize that you are the first male within these walls in decades? It is my chance for life! You must give me life!"

"Why don't you leave the Temple? The city is full of men, if that is what you want."

Her expression was incredulous. "Don't you understand? You think the Temple walls were built to keep men out? They were built to keep us *in*! If I were caught escaping, it would mean the Ritual of Penitence for me as well. And even if I did escape, how long would I survive beyond those walls in a world where women are only clever animals, birth a sign of bestiality, and love a capital crime? Most of the outworld remains ignorant of our very existence! And those men who do know us, and appreciate us, must guard us, imprison us in secret, or face the anger of all. Can't you understand? For me, the outworld holds only slavery or death. The walls in your mind are the truest bars of our prison. Escape has been tried many times–and has always failed, will always fail, unless...."

She moved close again, still hesitant, but driven.

"Unless I could find someone...one man...like you." She stopped, trembling with hope and fear.

Flores stepped back. "I don't know what you're talking about, but I don't let animals touch me in an intimate fashion–even pretty ones."

She halted, stunned. She tried to speak but only stuttered, her face contorted with rage, shame, and outrage. Finally she spat, "Vensa! That scheming gila! She thought it through so well! She keeps flowers out of the Temple on pain of death, and she keeps you men in such ignorance that when you see a woman you don't even know what to do!" She swirled, took a step toward the door, then turned again.

"And Amina!" A haughty imperious expression flashed across her face. "You think I don't know that you gave Amina life? Ha! The whole Temple knows! And we'll have her hide." She raged hoarsely, stamping her foot. "Somehow she persuaded you, she got around the law. How? Tell me!" She stepped forward again. Flores stepped back and she halted, panting with desire and anger. Then, with icy finality, regained control.

"Let me tell you what awaits your woman–as it awaits all Sisters caught outside the Temple. The Ritual of Penitence! The first day, your precious love will wait without food or water. The second day, she will kneel beneath the whip and pray for forgiveness. The third day, she will carry the young unaided to the highest floor of the tower where, if she does not step with care, she will die! Three days without food–three days without sleep–three days to remember her crime and regret what she did. I myself will make certain the Ritual is completed. When the tower peals three times, three days after its start, she will have performed her last service, for the Queen–or for anyone!"

Nara turned and hurried to the door.

"Your woman will die, Flores. By our sacred law I myself will push her into the high pit on the third day. Remember! Listen for three peals from the tower. Then remember another who was once willing to put on paint for you!"

With a last lingering glare of the purest hate Flores had ever felt, Nara exited and quietly shut the door. The bar was again lowered into place. Whispers indicated the return of the original guards.

Flores sat upon the bed, and thought.

The next morning a delegation of Sisters arrived armed with the usual pinwheels and Flores was escorted to the rotunda where the six halls intersected. Flores did not recognize his escorts, and they entered a previously unexplored corridor. Through the glittering windows the noble saw a dome expand as they approached. Where the hall met the dome the party entered an antechamber and a wave of moist heat flowed over him. Flores' gaze was riveted by a phalanx of scarlet and crimson eggs the size of large gourds laid carefully upon shredded cloth and tended by priestesses who hovered over them and rearranged the cloth, inspecting and shifting the gourds with care.

They bent low and entered a second chamber. Here were more orderly rows of lozenges, smaller and incomplete, and the priestesses hurried about with skins of liquid, pouring white streams upon them. The chamber echoed with a delicate mewling and Flores paused to look more closely at one–at first he could see nothing but a tangle of pale flesh. He leaned further. Something moved unexpectedly amidst the wet crimson flesh and took form, and Flores saw a tiny mouth open and cry for its accustomed nourishment. He stepped back. His escorts directed him forward again.

A third chamber followed. In this chamber the lozenges were complete, but here took an ovoid shape, each lozenge turgid white and small as a clenched fist. The rows expanded to fill the room. The nether side of the chamber was formed of huge blocks of poorly joined ashlar, and Flores halted before an assemblage of cowled priests with their ubiquitous ceremonial pinwheels. A metal curtain of imbricated leaves, emanating a steady breeze of warm moisture, blocked his further passage.

Here stood Wijah, her expression petulant and dour as ever. As they approached, the old woman slipped behind the curtain. Soon she reappeared to the sound of sloshing water. The old woman addressed something that moved heavily behind the pendant leaves.

"The offender from the city is here, Goddess." Flores looked at Wijah; she returned his gaze without interest. "And we are prepared for his violence," she added.

Water splashed behind the leaves. A guttural coughing or clearing of a large throat came to them, the rumbling filling the chamber. Then a deep voice spoke, uttered with difficulty, its pitch low and strained.

"Has my daughter...shown signs?"

"No, Goddess."

A full minute passed. Flores slowly became aware of slow labored breathing from behind the metallic curtain and wondered what his own verdict was to be. He decided that if necessary he could outrun the priestesses, but knew that his ignorance of the Temple's corridors must in time impale him upon their blades.

The voice strained again.

"Our daughter has greatly sinned.... Her crime opens the gate to eternal fire for her soul, and for all her Sisters. Evil has come to our Temple."

Flores looked down, his brow drawn.

"Prepare a stone for the tunnel–our purity will not be tainted again. For Our daughter, Amina–the Ritual of Penitence. For the child from the city, his presence is an eternal danger. Return him to where he was found, and seal the entrance."

There was a splash and the breathing stopped. The Goddess was gone. Flores was returned to his prisoner's chamber and, this time, both exits secured.

A week passed and they came for him. A dozen priestesses, Wijah and Nara among them, accompanied him to the hall through which he had originally been brought and directed him to enter the adjoining storage room. They proceeded to the second chamber and Flores found it had been cleared of the barrels and chests that had previously filled it. The room had been altered to accommodate a large ramp of timber arranged so as to guide a huge circular stone, a slab from a ruined column, to the mouth of the corridor exiting upon the cavern. A simple contrivance of ropes and pulleys held the drum in place – for the moment.

Amina was there. She was haggard; apparently she had labored much, for she leaned upon Aleka and her eyes were closed. Nara was near. She glanced alternately at Amina and the stone drum, a look of sly triumph in her eyes.

Wijah initiated the reaction that would, immunologically, expel the intruding organism from the Temple host.

"By decree of the Queen," she informed her attending Sisters, "this corridor and the impure realm beyond are to be sealed forever from our Temple. For the welfare of her eternal soul and in penitence for her sins our Sister Amina, daughter of Vensa, will herself release the stone over the entrance and loose the sand that will fill the tunnel. The corrupt one from the outer world is to be returned to the cavern from where he came. It is wrong to condemn him, my Sisters, for he only follows his nature and cannot hope for enlightenment. But as for Amina, it has been decided that she must undergo the Ritual of Penitence."

Her Sisters took her arms, but Amina was too exhausted to react and merely stared upon the ground. Flores, who also stood motionless, detected no sign of surprise in her expression.

Wijah stamped her crosier and made mystic signs with her hand.

Laughter ringing from Nara as from a bell-tower, the dark priestesses set up a din with shrill piping sounds and dragged Amina toward the taut cord and the stone obstruction.

Flores glanced at the tunnel. The crumbling door had vanished and the entrance gouged to fit the drum. The shaft of the tunnel was impenetrable to his gaze, but he could make out in the torchlight specks of sand already dropping from the roof to the floor. No priestesses stood between him and the entrance.

A ceremonial pinwheel of blades was pressed into Amina's hands. She shook and almost dropped it. Wijah waved her staff and pointed.

Flores was to leave.

Now.

Suddenly, he took several quick steps to the side of Amina. Snatching the pole from her hands, Flores cut the cord. As a menacing grinding filled the chamber, he took Amina's hands and dove into the tunnel, yanking her after. Recklessly they ran, through hissing streams of sand that poured from above and enveloped their ankles in a dying light suddenly extinguished to the impact of a quake. Amina fell. Flores pulled her through the pouring torrents without pause. He slipped in the shifting morass and scrambled forward another yard before falling and fighting for breath, the dark tide sucking at his limbs. With a final effort, he broke free and slid out of the tunnel on a wave of sand, Amina by his side. Behind them, the tide grew until the tunnel was entirely blocked.

CHAPTER 14

CATACOMBS

Slowly Flores regained his breath. Through the darkness he could hear Amina gasp.

"Are you familiar with these passages?" he asked. "Amina, if you refuse to speak to me now, we will both die."

"No," she managed. "I know only the main passage, from the Temple."

"Well it leads but one way. Come." He took her hand.

They climbed a flight of steps to another tunnel, followed it, and turned again. Soon they lost their direction. Their progress was slow, but, after what seemed a great length of time, a light began to shine ahead, and they hastened as they neared its source. With a cry of joy, Flores glimpsed a jagged slash of light. He scrambled over boulders and peered through an irregular crack in the rock to stare upon a terrazzo floor lit by an aperture in a high domed chamber. They were again inside the Temple.

In his mind's eye Flores saw the sweeping mosaic and gilded plate, the nude Goddess reclining in anticipation, her winged lover rushing to embrace, and the raw cleft tearing the work asunder. In silence, he waved Amina back and they began to retrace their route, then halted. Instructing her to wait, he returned and wormed through the cleft, disappearing in the labyrinth of the citadel. A few minutes passed and he reappeared with a torch. Amina had fallen asleep and for a moment Flores feared she was ill, but, upon shaking her, she opened her eyes and smiled.

Despite the light of the torch, more time was spent in cramped passages before the two descended a last flight of steps onto the cavern's uneven floor and again glimpsed the luminous deserted city, the rushing waters of the channel imparting an illusion of life and movement to the dead structures. Negotiating the narrow ledge, they halted before the same cave in which Amina had first found Flores. Amina was exhausted, and Flores lifted her and carried her within.

"No!" she cried. Pulling free, she ran into the city. Flores feared he would lose her, but she stumbled and fell. He ran to her.

"Return to the cave. I will nurse you as you did me," he said.

"No!" She shook her head. "Rest here...please." She looked into his eyes.

He nodded. "Here."

Flores cleared away the dust that overlay every surface within the cavern and lay her upon smoothed flooring between two intact walls. They were safe. There would be no pursuit from the Temple, he was certain of that, and the city itself was lifeless. He lay beside her, and they slept.

When Flores awoke he stood and breathed deeply. Amina continued to sleep. The brand had burned low, but still cast sufficient light to explore. He took the torch and returned to their little cave to see whether anything useful remained. But the cave was empty; the blanket and food and candle had been removed. Returning empty-handed, he sat and waited.

Finally, she woke up. Upon seeing him, she suddenly wrapped her cloth more tightly about her; but then relaxed and smiled and permitted the folds of the garment to loosen. Amina seemed no worse for her ordeal, and it seemed to Flores that she had recovered more quickly than had he. Already she stood and stretched as if nothing out of the ordinary had happened in the past few days.

"Will we remain here and live in these tunnels?" she asked with bright innocence.

Flores laughed. "Of course not. We shall leave these caverns at once. That much should be possible. But entering Ven and traveling Maalstrom—that is another matter." He gazed at her in the weak light for a minute, his eyes moving over her exposed face and neck.

"What is it you find interesting?" Amina lowered her gaze. Flores was struck by her shyness. She did not merely seem vulnerable, as did Nara. Amina *was* vulnerable. He felt a surge of protectiveness, more powerful than with Nara, as dark images formed of soldiers seizing her and handing her over to grim eunuchs in cassocks. Then she looked up and smiled, full of confidence again. He shook his head clear and looked away.

"Come with me," he said. "I know a way out."

Plunging into the crumbling city, they aimed for the far side of the cavern. For the first time, Flores was able to inspect the ruins closely and perceived that, far from being mindless or random as he had first believed, the architecture consisted of a single continuous hexagonal structure held together by mortar that had long since lost its strength. The lightest pressure, he discovered, was sufficient to tumble entire piles of masonry in clouds of white dust, leaving the many gaps or crenels that he observed. How long had the cells stood, he wondered? For what purpose had they been built? He shook his head at the strange ambition of the builders and returned to his task.

After some searching, they found the area where Flores had first fallen. In the glow of the cavern's luminous minerals, the roof seemed much lower and the mountain of debris considerably smaller than he recalled. The pinhole that he remembered was clearly visible in the live roof of the cavern as a darker aperture against the surrounding black rock, the gap still unrepaired, snapped timbers still suspended from the ceiling. It was evident that when the flooring had collapsed, he had fallen through this gap and landed upon a high rock-ledge adjoining an ancient flight of steps. Apparently at some time in the past the ledge had been used by the Serclaslers for dumping—trash was intermixed with a carpet of rock and dust loosened from the roof. He had fallen, he now realized, but a few feet to the ledge, and rolled with the hill of gravel and debris to the floor of the cavern.

With the extinguished torch, Flores could almost reach the aperture. Several wooden beams lay about, and he set about constructing a crude ladder. The work was difficult in the brittle light, but, tying two of the beams together with strips of cloth torn from his shirt and Amina's habit, he soon completed the task. Slowly Flores clambered up the beams, using the cloth as handholds. At times he halted to listen. He had no way of knowing whether his activities had attracted the attention of Serclaslers on the floor above—perhaps mute guardsmen waited even now with drawn swords.

Cautiously he raised his head. The chamber was dark and silent. With some difficulty he drew himself within, then glanced into the adjoining rooms and corridor. All were empty. Calling to Amina, he grasped her hand. With a loud report, the floor split. Amina screamed as another section of flooring collapsed, doubling the size of the gap and dislodging the ladder. Straining, Flores finally pulled Amina into the room. She scrambled forward and stood, but half the floor had gone and the side of the room with the privy, including the pipe that led to the Suma, had become permanently inaccessible.

Flores sighed. Once again they were trapped. Unable to return to the caverns or escape to the river, only the bleakest alternative remained: to disguise themselves, wait until dark, and attempt to slip past Numsenmur's sentinels into Ven. Even should they be successful their prospects for survival in the city were poor.

Cautioning Amina to silence, he inspected the corridor. It was apparently still empty, but the light thrown forth by the wall-lamps was too dim to be certain. They quietly entered and for a moment Flores peered at the spot where he knew a secret niche lay. He was tempted to throw their luck in the direction of the wayward youth Crestal, but felt unsure of his reception. At their last encounter Flores had been an important leader of the city. Now he was a condemned criminal.

Steps sounded. Flores yanked Amina into an open door and they found themselves on a landing in a torch-lit stairwell, the stairs wide and massive, curving up and to the left. He glanced back. The steps sounded louder and were joined by others. Taking Amina by the arm, he ascended the stairwell. They had gone no more than half a revolution when they almost collided with a figure coming the other way. Flores looked up with his heart in his throat, fully expecting to face the Lord of the Serclasers himself.

The newcomer jumped back. Before them stood a solid man of medium height, thickly muscled and unarmed. Poised to run back up or to fall upon them as needed, he was too bewildered to do either. The man stepped closer. His eyes grew large. He pointed at Flores and spread his hands.

"Tilsis!" Flores scrutinized the servant's face to ascertain his sympathies. "Tilsis, you helped me once. Help me again. You must get us out of the palace."

For several moments the slave stood motionless, as if imagining the consequences of his collaboration should they be discovered, or counting the possible rewards should he turn them in. Voices emanated from below. Tilsis motioned them to follow and re-ascended the stairs. Soon Flores stood before a massive door of iron-backed rorewood, an irsrem pane on one side revealing the stuccoed roof of Numsenmur's palace, a dazzling yellow in the light of the afternoon suns.

Opening the portal, Tilsis motioned that Flores and Amina should wait, and closed it behind him. Several moments passed, and he reappeared. He flashed a series of hand-signals, from which Flores gleaned that he and Amina were to descend the stairs again and seek refuge in another chamber. Flores nodded and indicated for Tilsis to lead the way. The tramp of boots again carried from below. By an unfortunate turn of luck, they had arrived at the very door which those whom they had almost encountered below were seeking. The servant stepped halfway within the chamber, and signaled again, more energetically. A moment passed, then Tilsis swung the portal wide. Flores entered and stared upon a broad bay window and an elaborately carved partition, behind which an obscure figure moved.

Tilsis pointed to another door, which opened on the apartments of Crestal's inner sanctum. Leading them within, he indicated a panel that stood open across the room from the outer door. Flores and Amina entered the narrow aperture. Tilsis shut it behind them. Instantly they were plunged into darkness, but Flores had already recognized the secret passageway that Tilsis had used months earlier to usher him into the presence of his master, Crestal.

A report of fists upon the door of the outer chamber and loud voices raised in anger carried to them through the thin wooden panel. A pencil of light penetrated a crack in the woodwork and Flores noted that their passageway circumscribed the room and adjoined the sill of the outer chamber door. Quietly he moved toward the door until the conversation became distinct.

"Where is your obedience, servant?" bellowed a voice. "Kneel before your chief." Boots shuffled on the landing and the voice sounded again. "You would profane the sanctity of your king's private chambers with your gaze? Avert your eyes! Yes, like so. It is for your king only to inspect these rooms."

Heavy boots sounded through the doorway as Numsenmur, King of the Vensors, entered the first compartment and opened the door to the second chamber.

The door closed and Crestal's voice drifted clearly to Flores. "My lord, you have chosen to honor me."

"Enough of that. What are you doing without your veil? I've told you that you're never to dispense with it." A hand descended upon flesh and Crestal cried out. Flores glanced at Amina. A pillar of light revealed puckered brows and a downcast eye.

The boots turned. The inner door opened, then shut, and the harsh voice rang again from the first compartment.

"You oaf! They are both present. Why do you waste my time?"

"No one was here, I tell you." Flores recognized the voice of Ust, emanating from knee level as if he addressed the floor. "My soldiers banged upon the door for half an hour and none came to answer. They do this often of late and defy my authority. But now I have caught them. Against your express orders, they left their chambers. The eunuch and his slave were both gone!"

"Do you mean to say you entered these chambers? I gave strict instructions."

"I did not, sire!" Ust answered hastily. "I sent for the keys and a bade a slave enter. The slave searched the entire apartment room by room and reported that they were empty."

"Yes?"

"Then I had the slave killed, as per your orders that any who enter beside your eunuch and his slave should die without delay."

Numsenmur rumbled approval. The boots turned and re-entered the second compartment. "Have you been out of these apartments?"

"No sire, I would never–" the thin voice squealed as if in response to a raised hand.

The chief of the Serclaslers grew calm and his voice assumed a gentler tone. Numsenmur breathed deeply. "I give you all that you need and more. The choicest foods, the rarest objects. If you desire more slaves, I will prepare another.... But from what I hear even silent mouths find ways to talk. Are you not happy, Crestal...?"

His only answer was the creaking of the wooden floor.

"What can I do? You cannot mix with the others–ever. You know that would be unwise. Always have I granted what you wish and what is in my power to deliver."

The sound of quiet tears drifted.

"Dear Crestal, you are my favorite, and have ever been. It is my wish that you come into my arms willingly and with pleasure. Won't you come into my arms? As you did once before?"

The lighter steps moved away and Numsenmur breathed more heavily. Flores felt his cheeks burn. He had no desire to hear such from his enemy.

"There! You are ever thus. Why do you hate me so? Each day, for your sake, I court death and dishonor. Since the first night that you came I have treated you well–but you are ever cold. Do you wish me to return you to your previous owner? Or turn you loose in the city? No. You know what that would mean. Here you live in safety and in comfort and are beyond all harm. So, bestow a kiss on your Benefactor."

A moment passed and Numsenmur quickly inhaled.

"You still refuse me. So be it. You will never win this struggle. Now that I have you I will not release you. Any man who touches you, any who speaks to you, I will kill with my own hands. Devil that you are, you have bewitched me since you first arrived. Is it not enough that you corrupt my flesh, you would corrupt my soul as well? But I am the master of this place. If I discover that you have left these rooms, I will crush the life from you myself, spell or no! For the remainder of your days, none shall visit you, but you will remain within these rooms till you rot. In the end, you will come to me willingly, or you will die in this tower–alone."

The boots turned, the inner door was swiftly jerked open and slammed shut. The boots approached the outer door.

"Tilsis!" Numsenmur said. "I must say something to you. Listen well. You continue to draw breath for one reason only–because I remain confident that you cannot betray my secrets to anyone. If I suspect that you have communicated with anyone but your master, you will be replaced immediately, to your infinite misfortune. Remember that." The boots turned.

"As for you, you bumbling idiot–"

"Sire!" Ust protested meekly.

A fist connected with an unprotected face, and Ust gasped and collapsed upon the landing.

"Perhaps this will teach you to listen to a slave!" Numsenmur growled. "Be thankful he no longer lives to contradict your story. If you continue to waste my time, you may join him. Now, post two guards at the tower entrance below. They are not to leave the landing, but are to halt all who approach these chambers." The outer door slammed and Tilsis replaced the bar. The boots descended the stairs, leaving the chambers in silence.

Some moments later, the panel opened and Tilsis motioned that it was safe for Flores to exit. He did so and entered the outer chamber.

Crestal-Nidrenmor of the Serclaslers turned to greet him. Silhouetted in the window, the merging suns flaming about his head like an aureole, the youth stood in a modest black cassock of the eunuch guild. His trimmed hair was of two colors: dark where cut, straw where uncut, the straw blending with the yellow of the rooftops. His amber pupils were obscured by curled lashes of so deep an indigo that they matched the blackness of the cloth. About his torso, limbs, and neck flowered modest folds of coarse material. Only his head and hands were visible, but they could not hide his moderate stature and slender, almost thin, frame.

Yes, a child, recalled Flores. He noted that the tears had vanished. Even as he watched, the hard, disciplined look that he had seen months before reasserted itself. The youth peered at him and seemed to forget his own troubles.

"Flores, where did you go? We looked for you throughout the–"

The Turlicum Lord silenced Crestal with a wave of the hand.

"Worry not, dear Crestal. I am well. For a time I lay ill in the caverns that underlie this place, tormented by thirst and fever, but cared for by the kindest soul to be blessed in the eye of God." Crestal smiled, the sun glinting in his eyes. "This person spared of himself nothing, and stinted so that I should eat and drink. When I burned, he comforted me–day upon day he thought only of my health."

Crestal lowered his glance, then looked up at Flores and breathed deeply.

"And this is he–Amina of the Temple of Vensor." Amina entered the room.

In mid-breath, Crestal halted stiff as ice.

Arranging pillows in a chair for Amina's comfort, Flores indicated that she should sit. "Have you any food, Crestal? Amina is famished, and tired. He has been through much."

The youth finally forced himself to speak, reddening. "For the love of Vensor. A priestess!" Amina risked a sideward glance at Crestal and a quiet look of serenity and smugness settled briefly on her lips. An indescribable expression transformed the youth's face, reflecting confusion, shock, disappointment, incredulity, and–other emotions?

The youth turned and Tilsis brought a bowl of dunmelons. "Where did she come from?" His voice rasped as if struggling to control extreme emotion.

"From the Temple, of course."

Amina sat and her gaze settled on the melons. Flores crossed to her and offered her the bowl. She selected one.

"I think some new attire would be in order for 'him.'" Flores still could not bring himself to use the forbidden vernacular, although he noticed Crestal had not hesitated. "Not to mention a bath for me. Then I can start thinking of how to depart Ven."

"You've been *inside* the Temple?"

Flores thought a moment, then answered.

"Yes."

"So that is why Numsenmur could not find you. He searched the entire palace and only last week the catacombs. But how did you return? How did you get in?"

"Those catacombs lead indirectly–or rather, led–to an old postern of the Temple." He looked at Crestal with nonchalance. "My visit to the holy Sisters was unexpected, but not terribly disagreeable." He broke into a broad smile. "I even managed to settle a score as I left. However, I don't recommend the Temple as a vacation spot. The hospitality of the priests leaves something to be desired."

While Flores spoke, Crestal stared at Amina, who said nothing but sat next to Flores, eyeing the floor. "With the exception of my guardian Amina, I should say," Flores added. "He has had some difficulties with his peers. You might say that he has suddenly developed an irresistible desire to see the world–the outworld to be exact." He looked out the window. "And how goes the war? Has Nesos arrived?"

The youth swallowed. "Nesos has been camped before the walls for over a month, Flores."

The Turlicum turned suddenly. "A month!" He paced the room, staring across the yellow rooftops to the city, then sank into a chair. "A month in the catacombs and Temple."

"Numsenmur announced your execution to the public the day before you vanished. The king searched everywhere. Everyone knew whom he sought."

"What 'king'?"

"Why, Numsenmur, of course. He turned the Assembly into his throne room. The city believes you dead, murdered in his dungeon. The civil war ended soon after it began. Some clans tried to hold the gate against him but were ejected. Then they tried to hold the outer city, but Nesos arrived with an army and Numsenmur closed the gate against them and shut them all out. They fled. Now Neset-sa ring Ven and have burned all the bridges. And they have stopped the river traffic to starve us–the malkops have been busy."

"But our garrisons? They are in the three valleys for two hundred miles! Where are they with our allies?" Flores demanded.

Crestal shrugged. "There was fighting in Lesel and Sish when the king's–Numsenmur's–men tried to take command. And our allies? The garrison in Toor was massacred after the Battle of the Plateau. But that was before. I have heard nothing new for days. Except that many of our vassals are there–" he pointed, "–with Nesos.

"And what of Nasvetin?"

"I have heard nothing."

"So we have lost the war!" Flores breathed deeply. "And Ven will be next." He stood and stared over the rooftops again. "And what of my son, Mesret?"

"No one has seen him. He was never executed, in public at least. Perhaps Numsenmur has him locked away somewhere, but not in the villa or we would have heard by this time. Numsenmur has not mentioned him to me."

Flores nodded. He felt tired and his eyes began to shut. Amina had already closed hers.

"We need sleep." He approached the consort of Numsenmur. "Speak the truth, Crestal. Can I trust you? One signal from you would mean my death, and Amina's also."

Crestal looked at Tilsis.

"Have no fear, Flores." Tilsis glanced at Amina. "Me, at least, you can trust." For some moments the Turlicum stood beside Crestal, contemplating the swiftly changing sky. The afternoon was already drawing to a close and shadows grew in the hollows and angles of the palace crenelations. The noble stared moodily beyond the city to where the Amanus-nama began. The terraced cliffs of the mountain range piled one atop another into the distance. Them, without another word, Flores turned, walked to the couch, and collapsed. Tilsis draped blankets over Flores and Amina and removed the fruit. Crestal turned. While his eyes took in the wide expanse now succumbing quickly to the onrushing night, he quietly tapped his foot.

When next Flores awoke, it was late evening and Tilsis and Crestal sat together across the room, the servant motioning silently and Crestal whispering. Amina still slept. Soon the others noticed that he was awake.

Crestal approached.

"Better?"

"I can survive another day or two," Flores replied.

Fresh clothes and water had been placed beside him. Tilsis left, then returned with more food. Crestal had Tilsis fill a ceramic tub with water and Flores bathed.

"We were lucky to get this," said Crestal, while Flores dressed. "The hens and lyarts are all rationed. Now only these dunmelons remain." Flores leaped upon the victuals as Crestal continued. "Food is getting low; everything is rationed–Numsenmur won't allow us our usual privileges." The youth seemed indifferent. "But the ducts from the

Temple run as full as ever. We won't die of thirst."

He grew quiet while Flores ate.

After finishing, the Turlicum stood. He walked to the windows where small flames could be seen flickering in the suburbs. "Crestal, you have helped me again. Why?"

The Consort of the King of Ven stared into the night. He looked disconsolate and glanced at Tilsis as if he wished the other could explain or that Flores had not asked.

"I...I am not of Ven."

"No," said Flores. "Otherwise you would not be so young."

"You speak of me as if I were a child–I am not...I–" The youth looked at Flores, then dropped his gaze again. "I am of a far city. I was captured as a child and sold into slavery." He compressed his lips and looked away.

Flores said, "Your city–of what name?"

"I cannot remember. I was a child. But I was trained by the Eunuch Lord of my captors."

Flores paused, regretting his comment. Flores felt again that he was intruding on something private, something about which he had no right to know and which could only complicate his affairs. But his curiosity refused to let the conversation die. "Eunuchs are in demand. They have their place."

Crestal focused on the flames in the distance. "I don't remember my clan. All I recall is riding a reven in the hills, then an ambush–many dead, some captured. I was sure I would be rescued. I wasn't. Instead I was carried by warriors to a strange city where their Eunuch Lord accused me of being a servant of Atasan. I was told I must repent, and cooperate. Then came the training. Finally I was sold to Soorkrul, then to Numsenmur."

He dropped his gaze and Flores, again embarrassed, looked out the window. "If we could bridge the floor below, we could crawl through the pipe as before and leave Ven."

"No longer."

Flores glanced at Crestal. "Why?"

"This end was mortared to keep rats out. Even if you covered the floor, you would need a team of slaves with picks to open the culvert."

Flores put his chin in his hand and thought. "We need a reven, but that would be difficult."

Crestal glanced at the priestess through narrowed eyes. He straightened his back. "Tilsis can get one."

"But then we must get past the Neset-sa. That may be the greatest difficulty."

Crestal stood while Tilsis carried the last of the water out the door. "Well, there are the gills."

"The what?" Flores asked.

"The gills–Numsenmur has devices that he took from the scribal school. He's worried and thinks he may have to sneak out of Ven, so he took them from the scribes. Tilsis saw him swim beneath the surface of the Suma like a fish."

Flores stared in surprise. "Tilsis, is this true?"

Yes, the servant motioned. He made gestures about his head as if outlining some object.

Now dressed, Amina joined them.

"I have even thought of using one myself," Crestal continued. "Tilsis saw Numsenmur and another leave the workroom. They went to the reservoir and sank into the water. Numsenmur swam below the surface for an hour–he could have swum to the sea if he had liked."

"Can you get them?" Flores asked.

"I don't know. They are always guarded by at least two warriors."

Flores said, "We'll need two...and one reven."

Crestal glanced at Tilsis, who nodded. As Crestal disappeared into the inner chamber, Flores noticed again the contradictions of the youth's appearance, the slim body wrapped in the bulky robes of the guild, the tender hands and clear face without trace of beard, the closely trimmed hair. He wondered about his isolation in the tower and Numsenmur's fear of visitors. If he was not to so certain of the Serclasler's piety, he might almost suspect Crestal of being other than what he seemed....

৯৹ ৪৩ ৎ৶

CHAPTER 15

ESCAPE

The following day they prepared Flores' escape. In order to lessen the chances of Flores or Amina being recognized and the alarm raised, they decided the attempt must be made at night. While the suns sank behind the western horizon they hurriedly prepared. A sword, a dagger, and two extra tunics were strapped and packed, but no food since it could not be expected to survive submersion in the water. The guards on the tower landing would be easy to evade–the fugitives would use the secret stairwell, as Tilsis often did.

The guards in the workroom where the gills were kept presented a more difficult problem. There was no way to circumvent their guard post and obtain the gills. Using Tilsis' knowledge of the guards' schedule, Crestal and Flores conceived a plan: If Tilsis could trick the guards into leaving their post, even temporarily, once they had escaped, it would be the guards' word against that of Crestal that Tilsis was involved. Who would Numsenmur believe? Two mercenaries who had abandoned their station, or his favorite consort who would swear that Tilsis had been with him and whose testimony would be confirmed by the guards stationed on the stairwell?

After Flores and Amina obtained the gills, Tilsis would guide them to the reven-na stalls, which had no sentinels at night, and then return to Crestal's quarters while the fugitives slipped quietly into the Suma. A dangerous game, should they be discovered–but what choice had they? If they remained in Crestal's apartments, they must eventually be found, and the aid that Crestal and Tilsis had already rendered become known. Their choice was simple: gamble or die.

Deciding where to go once they had made their escape presented new problems. Since the Neset-sa occupied the lands around Ven, Flores and Amina would have to travel by water, which the gills, Flores hoped, would enable them to do. This meant north, south, or east. Each direction had its dangers. North was not only upriver, but through the Falls of Sish, requiring a portage around perpendicular cliffs, the waters both above and below fraught with treacherous pools and back currents for miles. East was also against the current and led from open steppes, now combing with Neset-sa, to the ruins of Ror and the drylands. Flores had no supporters in the east and could only expect a summary fate.

South led to Asan and the southern sea, now watched by Neset-sa and more enemies of Ven. However, far to the north in the vassal city of Nasvetin, perhaps still under garrison, ruled a noble in Flores' employ. Before the war with Nesos, the town had been a Turlicum fief. It seemed their best hope. The only way to reach this distant outpost was circuitous–south, then west, then north, then east, hundreds of miles through forest and wilderness. A difficult journey, with all the dangers of the wilds, but more likely of success than a more direct route, and–perhaps more important–less likelihood of discovery for a gila.

There was no question of leaving Amina. As Flores pointed out, without his assistance she could not be expected to survive. No city on Maalstrom would allow her within its walls. To every Vensor but Flores she would be slave, victim, or threat. Flores himself would be in danger as long as she accompanied him. He mentally filed the problem away. Once in Nasvetin he would deal with Amina–or with his companions' objection to her. He would think about it.

At last all was ready. Evening had come, and, as Flores and Amina tightened the straps supporting their packs and stepped into the secret compartment, the Turlicum noted in surprise that Crestal followed. The youth wrapped his swathed garment about him more completely than usual so that only the eyes shone.

Tilsis was apprehensive, but Crestal peremptorily waved them on. "I often climb these stairs, but tonight I will walk the corridors of the palace as well, even if only for a few moments. I cannot live forever in this tower, Flores. I wish to accompany you and watch. If you refuse, I will scream–or order Tilsis back to my chambers."

With a glance at Tilsis and Amina, the noble shrugged and together they entered the stairwell. Minutes later, they emerged in the lowest level of the palace. The fugitives had taken the precaution of providing hooded cloaks for Flores and Amina. The palace seemed devoid of inhabitants. Most slept, but many, as Tilsis informed them by pantomime, had sneaked out to steal roots from the city's gardens.

Hurrying through halls and chambers, they descended a stairway, and Tilsis led them down a long, darkened passage that led to the solitary entrance to Numsenmur's secluded workrooms. They approached the entrance in silence. Within an empty side room they paused, waiting until the sentinels were changed. Then they allowed more minutes to pass in case the departing guards returning unexpectedly. Once they felt certain no one would interrupt them, Tilsis advanced to the door and peered through the small barred window. Flores followed.

The anteroom was little larger than a cubicle, and two armed men sat, surreptitiously taking swills from a skin sagging with watered-down wine. One muttered, glancing occasionally at a second inner door. He breathed through clenched teeth. "Smil, you're a fool. These eyes saw the bridges sink to the bottom of the Suma, and even if their mounts can swim the river, the men cannot. And what would they do once over? The banks are too steep. Our warriors would chop them up and the river would take them to the sea." He unstopped the skin for emphasis.

"As usual, Usud, you miss the essence of what I say," replied Smil. "Of course, a main attack will be from the northeast. It abuts out and can be assaulted from two sides. But how can you ignore half the city? We abandoned the southern slums to them and they could send cutthroats swimming over while Vensor rests."

Usud rubbed his neck and again glanced at the inner door. "What does the chief cares so much about in there that he thinks they may come here? What do you think?" He stared inquiringly at Smil. "Gold?"

"More likely a live lyart. And Serclasler puts us here to keep it safe from Vens, not Neset-sa."

"Humph. May Vensor gather his strength quickly and light the valley. I would rather the Neset-sa attack just to stop this endless waiting." His stomach rumbled. "If I saw one now I'd cook him before he was dead."

A knock sounded upon the door. The guards grabbed their swords and stood.

Tilsis stood so that his face was visible within the window. He waved.

"Ah, so it's you." They eased their stance.

"Well, what is it?" sneered Usud at the mute.

Tilsis motioned that they should open the door. Smil looked at Usud and the latter nodded. Smil unlocked the door and opened it.

Tilsis entered the room with Flores behind and presented a letter forged by Flores that instructed the guards of the workroom antechamber to report on an upper level to help in supervising the division of the confiscated wealth of a noble.

Smil watched them warily with his sword still half-drawn and passed the paper to Usud. Usud glanced at it, front and back, and handed the document back to Smil.

"Looks good."

"Yes, it does," answered Smil.

They stared at the intruders without moving. The servant gestured to the pair again with more force.

Smil glanced at the paper, turned it over, and again handed it to Usud. "So is it all right?" He rocked on his heels.

Usud peered at the calligraphy. "Yes, Smil. It is."

With a shock, Flores noticed that Usud held the paper upside-down. Neither could read.

"Sirs," said Flores from beneath the cowl, "may I compliment you on your remarkable learning. Thank the gods and Divine Vensor that good Tilsis and I have by sheer chance stumbled upon two scholars here in the workrooms of the king. For you see, as the two of us were given our assignments by the king himself–whom you know is a most learned man–we were instructed to read the scroll ourselves to learn the details of our instructions, but being lowly people, and I only newly employed, we were too afraid to reveal our ignorance."

Usud looked at Smil and the latter scratched his head.

"All we know, therefore, is that you are released to supervise the division of the property of the Lord of the Turlicum, a large part of which has been collected in the supply chamber upstairs. What a relief that you can inform us of what our assignment is in return!"

"Um..." Usud turned the paper over and glanced again at the squiggles. "Property?" he inquired. He unstopped his water skin and drank. Smil thought a moment then took the paper and held it sideways.

"You two men–uh, employees–are to go downstairs to the room before the forbidden room–" He peered askance at Usud and pushed out his chest. "–and remain there while Smil and Usud–if they are the ones on duty–supervise the division of the spoil in the supply room." He paused again. "And until Smil and Usud can go upstairs and verify their orders." He smiled broadly at his cleverness, rolled the document, and placed it in his belt.

"A new employee, eh? Well, look about you. But don't touch. And don't go into those other rooms. The chief'll have your skin if he catches you in there! And if you are to get along with the boys, we'll have to have a look at you." Before Flores could stop him, Smil grabbed Flores' hood and flung it back.

"So that is what you look like. I was beginning to wonder if you had a face."

Flores' heart leaped into his throat and Tilsis grasped the handle of his rapier but Usud walked to the door without a second glance. Flores let his breath go.

Smil took a step to follow, then turned. He looked closer.

"Just a moment. You know, you look like one who recently disappeared from within this villa..." His eyes widened. "Why, you're–"

Smil fell like a rotted trunk beneath Flores' fist. The impact of a sword haft ensured that he would not awaken soon. A single yelp escaped his companion before Tilsis' hands found his throat, and the pair rolled across the floor, the soldier thrashing wildly for his weapon. A blow of his skull upon the floor ended his efforts.

Wide-eyed and speechless, Crestal and Amina stood within the entrance. Flores and Tilsis tried the inner door–it was locked. Procuring one of the guards' irsrem swords, they forced the jamb free, then butted the door open. A short flight of clapboard stairs led from a landing to the floor of the workroom below, and together they dragged the unconscious guards swiftly down the steps.

The inner chamber was large and filled with rows of worktables and strange appurtenances suspended from the ceiling and walls. On its far side was a cabinet with a metal door chained shut. Tilsis led Flores to the cabinet where their eyes fell on the chain.

"Irsrem!" Flores said, crestfallen.

Tilsis inserted a rapier and pulled, and Flores joined him, together exerting their full strength, but without effect. Ten times their strength would not be enough to break the iridescent bonds.

A hiss from Crestal alerted them.

Tilsis indicated an open storeroom behind the entrance and the intruders dragged the guards within, leaving the door ajar.

Moments later a man entered, carrying a tied sack. He spoke to himself. "Now what has happened to those thieves?" The newcomer looked about him with disdain. "I've told them clearly: Someone must be guarding these apartments at all times. I step out for one moment, and what happens? They abscond." He sniffed. "Or perhaps Our

Grand Monarch needed them to arrest children in the Orphanage and neglected to replace them." His voice dripped with spite and sarcasm. "Oh, what a glorious reign our king has had. How the city has prospered. How fortunate we are to serve Your Enlightened Majesty." He bowed in exaggerated salute to no one.

A gleam of recognition shown in Flores' eyes as the man passed and lay his sack upon the table. The man was finely garbed, and sported a rapier. He muttered to himself as if in a quandary. Emptying the sack upon the table, he examined its content. An object lay before him made of rubber and a cup with a surface that looked very much like reven gills. The noble placed the cup over his mouth and strapped it behind his head. He breathed and air moved in through the cup and out through a nozzle underneath. Removing the contraption, he eyed it covetously.

The man took up the device and crossed to the cabinet. Flores moved to watch. The man drew a key from a chain around his neck and inserted it into the irsrem lock, then hesitated. Withdrawing the key, he walked back to the table.

"Why?" he hissed, the sound echoing in the workroom. "Why should I serve Numsenmur? For mir? Of what use is silver if the entire city dies? What use are slaves if there are no soldiers to enforce my will?" He struck the table with his fist. "No! Why should I run about risking my life for him while he prepares to desert his own people? So he promised not to leave me behind—I'd sooner trust an orphaned thief." He eyed the device again and spoke softly. "No, I will not leave this for him. I will tell Numsenmur that Yezd erred, that the next lung will be ready in two days. By that time, I will be gone."

With a look of nervous triumph he whirled and made for the antechamber.

"Good evening, Sir Ust." Flores blocked his path, his blade drawn and glinting. Ust's expression shriveled like paper before a torch. A faint rattling became audible from decorative chains round his wrist.

"It's not possible. You're dead!"

"Then why not join me?"

Flores took a step. Without warning Ust's blade leaped from its scabbard and plunged for the Turlicum's throat. Flores deflected the thrust and drove Ust back with repeated blows, hammering him as if he would crush his enemy by their impact alone. The Loyalist countered with unexpected strength and maneuvered himself between Flores and the steps. Upon sighting Flores' companions appearing near the exit with drawn blades, Ust paused.

"Flores! Why do we fight?" He lowered his rapier. "Don't you see we are on the same side? I have entered the ranks of Numsenmur's enemies! Permit me to demonstrate my sympathies and we can work together to overthrow the Tyrant."

Flores replied, "If you now are one of Numsenmur's enemies, then this war has three sides." He rushed Ust, and in a moment of desperate parrying, struck Ust's blade to the floor. With his elbow he slammed Ust against the wall and pinned his throat. Flores motioned and Tilsis tore the key from Ust's neck.

"Where is my son?"

"He's... safe...not here." Ust coughed and Flores loosened his hold. "Numsenmur never had him," Ust whined. "That is why he was so angry when you escaped–he had no one upon whom to wreak his vengeance. But," he nodded insistently, "I know where he is. Just permit me and I will take you there myself."

Flores reflected on this while Tilsis unlocked the cabinet and removed two of the underwater breathing devices. Warily Flores permitted Ust to stand.

Crestal drew closer. "He has seen us," he said to Flores.

Ust blanched. At that moment, a quiet sound emanated from behind Ust and the room's occupants saw upon the landing a small man, leaning heavily on a cane. Snivet.

Shoving Flores upon Crestal, Ust flew up the steps. With a high-pitched squeal, Snivet turned and limped to avoid Ust's oncoming form. Too late, their bodies collided and Snivet plummeted to the stony floor of the workroom where his cane snapped.

At the exit, Ust paused to catch his breath.

"Yes! I will take you, you Turlicum oaf. Follow me, if you dare, to the Abyss of Atasan!" He leaped out the doorway and shouted as he vanished in the corridors of the palace. "The Consort and his slave have stolen the king's property! Help!"

For one long moment Crestal and Tilsis stared, unable to move. There was no going back. Flores grabbed the sack that Ust had dropped. Tilsis plucked another gill from the cabinet, paused, then snatched what remained. The servant retrieved the blades from Smil and Usud. Moments later, all four threaded corridors at a dead run with four devices in hand, three more in the sack, and rapiers bared. They turned a corner and climbed a stairwell several steps at a bound aiming for a back exit that let onto the palace grounds. Near their goal they paused, lungs heaving, and Tilsis peered cautiously around a turn into another antechamber.

By the light of a torch, two men leaned tiredly, their backs turned toward Tilsis, the moonlit court spread brightly beyond. Flores had planned to pass this guard post later–now they would have to depend on their wits and their strength. Already Flores thought he heard signs of pursuit.

One of the guards turned and tapped his fellow. They grabbed their helves as they turned. The first sighed. "Ah, so it's our eunuch-mute, the pet of our lord's favorite. Well, what do you here?" They peered at him with contempt.

Tilsis made some incomprehensible gesture with his hands.

One of the guards nudged his companion. "You know they say he is not too bright. But the way he curries his master's favor I suspect he is cleverer than us–or perhaps has more stamina." They guffawed as Tilsis drew his sword and fingered the honed glass.

Suddenly they paled and yanked their weapons. The servant's blade severed the jugular of the speaker, who collapsed in a bloody ruin. Crashing backward, his companion made a desperate parry with his sword. Tilsis slapped it aside and pierced him through, leaving the blade jammed in the wall. The fugitives left him pinned and screaming as they secured his sword and dashed into the yard.

To their right, beyond a moat, was a labyrinth of shallow canals and railed walkways with storage and feeding bins of fish, grain and tubers. These were the stables of the reven-na, roofed with a broad, flat pergola of wood and glass, held aloft by numerous pillars. Built to catch the rain and add it to the flow of the canal, due to ingenious planning, it was constantly cleansed with fresh water through four-hundred-foot channels from the Suma.

Picking three trained and dependable reven-na, Tilsis lured them from their stalls to the walkway where the animals clawed impatiently while the three adjusted saddles. One sank back into its stall and had to be coaxed out again with barbed prods. Crestal mounted one, Tilsis and Flores the other two. The Turlicum pulled Anima onto his reven before him. This took no more than a few moments, yet it seemed to them like an hour–they could still hear grisly sounds from the guardroom. Flores wondered why the general alarm had not been set.

The four donned breathing apparatuses and carefully adjusted them, thankful for the simplicity of their design. No sooner had they strapped them on than a dozen soldiers streamed into the courtyard from the palace. Despite their urgency, they made no noise, but clustered together whispering excitedly and peering about. They looked up and Flores realized why no alarm had gone off–the upper story of the huge left wing of the palace was lit. Numsenmur was home and the guards were panicking, fearful of reporting the escape of his favorite consort, opting instead to search in silence. They fanned across the yard, probing every shrub and shadow with their rapiers.

The escapees attempted to move away from the men, but the gloom under the pergola was not complete, and as they lashed their beasts through the maze of walkways, they were limned against the night. Their pursuers cheered in triumph–their prey was sighted. From the villa a loud metallic clanging began, as the alarm was finally turned.

Desperately the reven-na scrambled, slipping on the clapboards, breaking railings and startling the animals still penned. They reached the gate beside a deep basin. Flores slashed the rope that tied it. Tilsis kicked it open.

As a clump of shouting warriors pounded the walkway behind, the reven-na took several mincing steps and soared. For one breathtaking moment the riders clung, eyes tight, as the reven-na hovered, violet tongues tasting the air, tails snaking in anticipation. They slapped the water and sank. Within a few brief seconds, the beasts had shot far away.

CHAPTER 16

WILDERNESS

Sedrech-Nurlemnev of the Turlicum raised a cupped palm to shield his gaze. The rising heat distorted his view of the plain. He squinched and rubbed his eyes. Far across the browned and yellowed surface appeared a shade of deeper brown like a pencil mark. The mark slowly broadened to a smear, then vanished in another trick of the rolling hills.

Sedrech glanced about him. In either direction stretched a line of men eyeing his movements, each squatting alongside a prostrate reven spaced one every twenty feet. The heat wrung sweat from his face, and a dark cloth wound about his brow managed to take some of the sting from the suns' glare. At his feet the grass was hot to the touch, the natural green long since withered to brownish yellow. Nothing escaped the drumming rays. His reven breathed in shallow puffs, its gills flexing, and curled its snake-like neck to gaze at him without comprehension. He spat on its gills and stroked it.

Out here, Sedreck reflected, things are always the same, but worse. In the spring the land is flush and fertile, and the crops mature quickly after the winter's frequent rains. The hills and meadows bloom with flowers and verdure enough for endless grazing. Then it fades. Nvediteg holds back his rain and the breath of Vensor wilts the land in a few short weeks. The lush plains wither and the crops begin to falter. In haste the people bleed the Suma, the Hedronmas, and the Tlaam, irrigating their fields so the grain can complete its cycle and seed before harvest.

Then come the rum-na. Out of the late autumn drylands the herds swarm, aiming instinctively for the three valleys and the rich, wet grain, and the annual campaign to divert them, conducted by the outlying Vensor cities, is renewed.

The smear reappeared. It was twice as wide and continued to broaden. Gradually the dark brown obscured the lighter hills. A vague rustling drifted through the shimmering heat and the men looked to each other for reassurance. The advancing mass gained another ridge and sank into a shallow depression at the edge of the plain where the men crouched. Beyond, atop a far ridge, Sedrech glimpsed a brief, bright fluttering.

Suddenly, a belt of shaggy beasts rose up, swaying like a roving forest in a gale. Sedrech smiled faintly. Such absurd creatures, he thought. Harmless as individuals, the menace lay in their numbers and their scurrying about at breakneck speed. Without natural predators, and possessing limitless reproduction, they multiplied each spring at fantastic rates–until their food was gone.

The leading rum-na had two pumping, bird-like legs, a mass of bushy feathers, tiny arms with grasping paws, a short, craning neck, an erratic revolving head with a large, flat beak, and a stiff shock of feathers springing from each temple like whiskers, shaking with each step. The ones before him were as large as Vensor-sa, though they could grow taller. On some, the whiskers were puffing out and bills yawning cavernously in reaction to imagined threats. Their teeth and bills were harmless, but their numbers could bear one down even as the beasts tried to hop away.

Without warning, the animals in the vanguard switched direction and skittered to the right; swishing and scraping swept over the men like rocky surf. As in a school of fish, the lead animals became the flank as the vanguard paralleled the waiting pickets.

Quickly Sedrech motioned. The men to his right leaped to their feet and flapped poles with bright streamers attached. They jumped and shouted as their mounts struggled erect. The herd angled slightly, away from the men.

Sedrech groaned. The direction was wrong. If the animals passed on the right, they might dash away and wander about for days before he could intercept them. He signaled again. On his right the men mounted. He impatiently motioned them, signaling a difficult maneuver: a dog leash sweep designed to redirect the flow. The vanguard turned again and set to collide with the main body, then the horde ebbed and recombined. Sedrech eased; they would have a second chance to intercept the herd.

"Commander!" The man on his left pointed.

Startled, Sedrech observed a dark mass emerge from the left, previously obscured by a subtle rise, He gripped his reins. His eyes lit.

The onrushing rum-na had halted. He signaled again and the dog leash again began to swing. The animals angled left, as desired. Sedrech shouted and the men about the center leaped to their feet. Again the rum-na compensated to the left and Sedrech smiled. Then, as they secured their mounts, Sedrech saw a small stream of rum-na that extended beyond his right wing. He realized that his men had failed to connect with those far bits of color. A knot of animals reversed, then a larger group. As Sedrech groaned, the main body of the herd followed. Hastily he galloped to intervene, but knew he could not catch even the slowest of the beasts. The stream of tawny animals grew to a flood and Sedrech's tired troops separated in the confusion.

The horde dispersed into a hundred motley groups of hopping, bounding animals, stampeding erratically in all directions. Several reven-na panicked and collided, pitching their riders beneath taloned paws as twisting clumps of rum-na drove them down. The men still flapped their streamers through a spreading cloud of gritty dust, but the campaign seemed foiled. The commander swore as several weeks' effort fell to waste.

At that moment, the wild and fickle rum-na restored Sedrech's fortunes. A mass anchored itself and began to retract the scattered herd. The men to Sedrech's left had risen to their feet in dejection, but now the sight of their billowing flags triggered a sudden flight. The rum-na rushed to the left, puffing yawning, tearing tufts of withered grass, more groups tamping after. The vanguard did not pause when, short moments later, the brown plain dropped beneath their feet; bills flapping voicelessly, splay feet kicking, they tumbled off a precipice to crash on the rocky slopes below. The rasping torrent did not slow or turn but continued to plummet until all but a few remained. A large number of the horde continued to rove aimlessly, but an equal number lay on the unyielding rocks below the cliff face.

Slowly, Sedrech's stunned troops picked across the lacerated plain. Small groups of rum-na cantered about. Here and there, young ones had been trampled; they stumbled in a daze or crawled, dragging broken limbs. Yellow dust hovered eerily over the field like mist silhouetting the bobbing figures. Converging in a wide arc, the men guided their reven-na toward the ravine. The dust was settling fast. A tired party of riders appeared from where the rum-na had first entered the field, as was frequent in such expeditions, much too late to matter.

Sedrech pulled loose his headcloth and wiped the grit from his brow.

"In twelve years, Revtal, I still cannot outwit or even predict these mindless beasts."

"At least we've earned our worship and preserved our friends in Nasvetin from starvation," Revtal pointed out.

"Not that they will appreciate our efforts." Sedrech stroked the neck of his reven to calm it. "And I cannot say I blame them. Were I in their place and it was my city occupied by foreign soldiers, I would be no more hospitable. After all, we do cart most of their food to Ven."

Sedrech mounted as a warrior appeared on the horizon from the direction of Nesvetin, his reven moving at top speed. It was apparent that the rider was a courier from base. He directed his mount toward the commander and dismounted.

"Word, Sedrech, from Ven," the warrior said. "Nesos of Neset has laid siege to the city. That is why they have been silent. Toor and Sish are in revolt and Nasvetin is plotting against us."

Sedrech nodded and spurred his reven. The courier opened his mouth again and the commander halted.

"And there was other news," said the courier.

"Yes?"

"Our Lord Flores is missing."

ᦇ ᘒ ᘓ ᦈ

Flores opened his eyes on a flickering world of rushing shadows. A swift blast of deliciously cool water wrenched his head back when he raised it, and he weathered the pull just long enough to see where he was. He was enveloped by darkness, and he thought of the pit and chilled. The darkness passed to reveal rough walls of the moat on either side, marching forward to converge at some hidden point beneath the water's shimmering, star-laced surface. Between his arms, Amina clung to the outstretched neck of the reven, with her eyes shut. His own arms passed around her, pinning her body beneath him. Before and behind he could see Tilsis and Crestal, eyes closed to the current, heads pressed against their breasts. Flores' reven swam joyously, moving in easy, sinuous lateral twists despite its barreled body, head swinging from side to side, snaking between the water rather than through it. Its muscled tail twitched in captivating repetition, each stroke sending it forward effortlessly like a fish, its gills working lustily, its tongue darting out to taste the water.

The walls vanished and the swimmers arched far above the bottom of the river, which was lost in quiet darkness. Flores could see further than he would have supposed, but his companions remained no more than vague shadows, and Flores strove to overtake them. A purple cloud of fish engulfed him and passed. A wall of wriggling dots drew aside just as he pulled at his reins. Having been raised solely for land and permitted only the freedom of their stall reservoirs, the reven-na had never before swum in the river. They showed a certain nervousness, but exuded a boundless pleasure at propelling hundreds of feet without encountering a grating. Crestal's mount whipped after one of the fish that swam by in hundreds, and for a moment they feared they might lose control of the animals. However, the beasts responded at once to the familiar tugs and kicks.

They surfaced and hovered; Tilsis signaled to orient them. He was difficult to make out in the darkness, but soon they understood, and within a short time the animals broke into an easy stroke southward toward the sea. They came up cautiously, unsure where they might be. However, the city was far behind. It looked peaceful–the city of the suns, scuts and spires shining in the starry waste. No mark of war or hatred could be seen, but they knew that a host of foes watched, honing weapons, eager to drown those shining spires in blood.

Flores readjusted Amina's mouthpiece as Tilsis alerted them to several small boats–smugglers slipping food past the blockade. Amina was again able to breath. They submerged and resumed their journey south.

Morning arrived in a welter of soft rays. Before them, an array of fish, weeds, and crawling life of the riverbed shone in the rising light. Tilsis swam close and touched Flores' arm. A fourth reven swam beside them. Small and slim, apparently adolescent, it followed for a time, then, when the others slowed, snapped away. Flores surfaced, hoping to see some sign of it again, for neither he nor the others had ever seen one undomesticated. With a start, he caught his breath. The others came up in time to see a herd of wild reven-na slither onto the river bank, and turn to gaze, their grey hides glistening with rivulets.

By late afternoon they were exhausted. They had been in the water more than half a day and, surfacing together, decided to leave the river for the far bank. Previously, they had been unable to do this, for the west bank of the Hedronmas was an unscalable cliff for many miles to the south of Ven. Their journey south was calculated to take them beyond the sheered rock, where they could gain the forest to shelter their journey north to Nasvetin. However, they had not surfaced in an uninhabited area. A small island split the river, its steep shores lifting to a rock-strewn escarpment. Flores had known of several islands in the middle Hedronmas, all belonging to nobles of Ven. This, he soon realized, was the largest, the famous villa of Senkin of Tooselwat, grandfather of Sruk. It was built of limestone and marble stripped from monuments in the subject cities of Lesel and Asan. Sruk had no son to occupy the villa, but the island might now provide a sanctuary for warriors of his clan who failed to gain the protection of the city. Reining their mounts toward the arc of vegetation paralleling the west, the travelers clawed out of the water onto the muddy ground. The bank sloped into a line of trees. There, in a spot hidden from passing eyes, they let exhaustion take them.

When Flores awoke, Tilsis was sprawled beside a twisted bush tied with three reins. The reven-na lay with legs folded and necks huddled, their snouts flat on the soft loam of the forest floor. Amina was gone, though a patch of crushed grass lay near. Crestal lay near Flores, sleeping soundly. Flores' stomach rumbled. Having brought no food, they would have to forage. A breeze threw his hair and chilled him. Winter had set in and they would need fuller clothes. But their bellies came first. The thought of crustaceans sizzling over a campfire came to mind. Flores belted his sword and started down the path toward the water.

Footsteps sounded on the path ahead and Flores paused, then stepped behind a tree. Amina came into view.

She jumped. "Oh, you frightened me!"

He laughed uneasily. "I did not mean to."

Amina had torn what remained of her cumbersome robes and now walked with ease, exposing the full expanse of her neck and upper breasts, together with much of her legs. What remained of her robe was still damp with river water and clung heavily to her limbs, leaving little of her body unaccented. The rest of her legs glowed yellow with the dust of flowers. She shivered and rubbed several spots as if they ached and slapped an insect away.

"The days grow colder," Flores said. "We should find better clothing. Thick tunics would do nicely."

Amina nodded. "I...was hungry," she said.

Flores nodded and together they descended the path to the riverbank. Just within the covering of the bank's vegetation, Flores halted and pointed. There, in the mud of the bank were the tracks of a sike, apparently left when the ungulate had come to drink. The Turlicum peered about for further signs. His stomach rumbled in anticipation of the good eating it would make if they could bring it down. Shielding his eyes to gaze across the water, he froze. A thin column of smoke curled upwards from the island of the Lurenmurgs. He stared. "We should leave the river. I don't know whose smoke that is, whether Sruk's clan or Neset-sa. Either way, we're in danger. So long as they remain on their side of the Hedronmas, we should be safe, but we should not remain here for long."

"There are some rafts upriver," ventured Amina.

It was Flores' turn to be startled. "Rafts? Are you certain? Were they boats, or timbers roped together?"

"I think timbers, I'm not sure. Is it important?"

"Timbers are for reven-na. Come." Flores started up the path.

Tilsis and Crestal were awake. The noble informed them of events, and they re-saddled the beasts. The youth, with Tilsis, disappeared behind a thicket. When they returned, Crestal had torn his cassock and re-sewed it in the manner of trousers so that he could ride in modesty. Securing the surcingle, he stirruped a foot and swung his leg over the round torso of his beast, the smallest of the three. Flores watched, amazed. The youth's talent, or knowledge, was entirely unexpected and unprecedented for the eunuch.

Crestal looked up and shrugged. "It feels natural somehow, as if I were raised this way."

Flores arched his eyes. He turned to Amina.

The priestess gazed in the direction of the river. She looked at them with a blank, helpless expression.

"Have you never been out of the Temple?" Flores asked.

She shook her head and looked about her in confusion. Her tunic was thin and she began to shiver. The cough of an animal carried from the distance.

"Can you ride a reven?"

The priestess looked at the animal and stepped back. She shook her head.

Flores laughed. "So until today you have lived your life in hibernation, flattering the gods, and have never lifted one finger to do anything practical. I'll bet you never swam before, either. I'm afraid that means that if we leave you here, you won't last long. You'll die of exposure—or worse."

Flores looked inquiringly at Crestal. The youth had turned away.

"Tilsis," Flores called. "Can you take her behind you?"

In response, the servant lifted her and plopped her unresisting on his reven. He mounted in front of her and linked her arms about his waist.

Flores reflected on his employment of the forbidden vernacular. He had not wished to acknowledge the fact that Amina was a gila, not before the others at any rate, but found it now came easily. He filed it for later reflection and adjusted the reven-hide saddle. He mounted, and within minutes they were threading dank avenues of forest.

The grade was steep. Away from the river the ground sloped rapidly toward the plateau, rising to moderate elevation above the valley. Near Ven the land was lush only along the rivers. The rain fell in late autumn and early spring, there would be no snow as was known in the far north. Here in the lowlands, water fell intermittently year-round. Verdure thrived on the slopes and ridges, waving fronds of greenery, and arced shoots latticed the sky so that soon the path grew narrow and thick copses forced them to retrace their steps. To make better progress, they dismounted and led the reven-na by hand. As they climbed, the woods began to clear due to lack of soil. Broad outcroppings of rock and broken stone spread beneath their gaze so that the reven-na frequently stumbled or slid and picked circuitously around cragged bolts or thorns.

They were famished, but at least not chilled. While Amina walked casually about, Tilsis and Flores set to work. The servant set about making bows. This took some time, for the first shoots sampled proved too brittle. Only on the third try did he find the proper density. The arrows proved more difficult, and after several attempts at flying wobbling shafts into unconcerned birds, they decided to find more suitable wood.

They followed the path up. The Hedronmas, civilization, war—all had fallen far behind. Ahead was only the plateau, sloping gently skyward, again thickening with mottled plant life. It was peaceful, no sound of beast or bird, only the faint cricking of insects and wind through leaves.

Finally, Tilsis found the right foliage—a patch of siriolus, stems straight as ramrods. Tilsis hacked them free, noting the lengthening shadows, and stripped bark off nearby tubers. He folded it twice for feathers. Emptying his pack, he produced unused spurs and broke them upon a rock. Soon he brandished a clutch of arrows. Just as the suns sank in the west, the servant brought down a sike. They dragged the body to a lee of boulders and Flores sparked a fire while Tilsis flayed the pelage.

The skin was staked to dry and the quiet night underlay with crackling wood, its fluxing tongue softening the chill air, while the four lay to sleep or contemplate. Amina, still wrapped in priestly clothing, seemed immune to the temperature. Crestal slumbered, dreaming fitfully of a mysterious future and forgotten past, his youthful body already taking to the wild. Tilsis, the muscled servant, his hair growing out, slept curled, his shoulders hunched; he lay where he could see his master, Crestal, when he opened his eyes.

Flores gazed into the fire, trying not to listen to an exchange of small, still voices. Far away, amid a silent crush of people, the youth on his knees by a bier of wooden scaffolding had his prayer answered as two malkops, pale with unearthly beauty, lazily flapped. Their burden, a noble with a jewel studded reven helm, slowly receded to a dot on the far horizon. The camp's fire popped and the scene changed. Beneath glittering stars a brace of knotted arms dragged away a paunchy, mumbling noble, bleeding from his thigh, and a thin white-haired man, fearful, but resigned to his end and to the rules of the deadly game that had made it necessary. His end was dignified; he would not spoil his name by resisting. But Flores could see only the jeweled reven helm vanishing in the sun. He stared through drifting curtains, keeping vigil, then slept.

When the spreading light of day drew the land to life with flitting wings and cycling hums, Tilsis crushed roots in the basin of a concave stone. He coated the inner hide of the sike-pelt with the acidic foam and worked it in by makeshift pestle, then set it to dry while he dressed the flesh. Crestal was intrigued, and would have liked to help if he had known what to do.

Flores did not wait, but was soon stopped by the servant, and coached on how to hold his blade and where to cut. Amina stood and stretched. After a time the noble glanced up, and rolled a dismembered head in Crestal's direction. Crestal shuddered and tried to look away, but with a resigned shrug pulled the head to a convenient seat to worry it with a knife.

Tilsis looked up and motioned. Flores laughed. "No, Crestal!" He came over.

"Leave that alone. Tilsis wants to bury that part; it's too much trouble."

The youth sighed, his hands smeared. With a grimace, he turned the beast's hackneyed countenance to a boulder.

"If you want to help, come watch Tilsis. He knows." The two joined the servant as he dissected the last large cuts of meat and wrapped them in fronds. His bloodied knife was soon cleaned, and before long the choicest cuts were packed in bags, and the rest nicely pinned beneath stones and rubble.

The party mounted and took up the trail.

The day continued warming and none felt the chill of the previous night. Flores wondered if their new coat was finished and how it might fit, till he was elected to carry the drying pelt. He then wondered why they bothered at all and tried to stay upwind as much as possible.

For the next few days the four refugees ambled west, following the shelving slope upwards unhurriedly, each gaining rest or conserving energy, thinking of the long trip ahead. The weather grew colder and for a space of several days they sheltered in a gorge, fanning flames until Tilsis landed more game and tanned the skins. Then, with food, clothing, and tools, they felt prepared to resume their journey, and threaded paths up and west again.

The land was rich and ribbed with life. Chilly gusts threw whorls of leaves, smothering limbs and faces with clouds of loose splendor. Under a warm azure sky, the travelers verged the summit of a final ridge and looked upon a sea of mottled green and bronze. Woody tops listed in the capricious wind like whitecaps, while golden clouds fell in woody avenues and sunlit fields. They descended and penetrated the cavernous arcade.

Crestal sang quietly to himself. The youth still wore his eunuch dress, clinging to the voluminous folds with strange persistence. Flores wondered at this. He would have thought that the youth would have taken the first opportunity to rid himself of the symbols of his humiliation, but the youth clung more tightly, never removing the tattered clothing within sight of either Flores or Amina. Cold stream baths were supervised by Tilsis alone. Amina, on the other hand seemed deliberately to display her limbs, and displayed an almost supernatural disregard for the cold. Finally, however, she discarded her robes for a collection of animal skins, and could hardly be persuaded to do so in private.

Riding, Crestal peered at Amina for a time through the corner of his eye. Finally, he turned suddenly to her and spoke in his thin childlike voice. "Amina, why would a priestess wish to leave the Temple?"

Amina reflected, smiling shyly but saying nothing.

The youth came nearer. "Didn't you like it inside the Temple?"

"I don't know what to tell you. It's so different from everything out there," she said.

"How did you spend your time?"

"I cared for the Queen with my Sisters, and fed Her." Amina shrugged as if all was now explained.

"The Queen?" Crestal pursued.

"Yes, the Queen."

"I'm not understanding."

"The Queen–Vensa."

Crestal still did not comprehend, and Amina smiled submissively. Flores watched her. At times he wondered whether her smile was a facade. It seemed as sincere as any. "I've always been happy," she continued. "I don't know. Wijah was kind–before. But then the sacred chambers changed. Wijah became mean and abused me. Now–"

"And who is Wijah?"

"The High Priestess since Kura died. She relays the Queen's instructions to all the holy Sisters." Amina pouted. "But for a time I have been unhappy. Wijah makes us spend all our extra time praying or doing extra duties for the Queen."

"Do you like working for this Queen?"

"Oh yes! She is kind. She gave us life; we are her tribe. We owe her worship."

"Even though she makes you work?"

"We all love her. We pray for her happiness always." She smiled brightly.

"Then why did you leave?"

"Once Kura praised me in front of Nara, when Nara had done the work. I said nothing–I was too shy to speak." Helplessness transformed her expression. "Nara became angry and accused me of stealing her praise. Ever since, she has hated me. Now, with Wijah, Nara prays hard and gets much recognition–and I don't. They both hate me."

"Even though it wasn't your fault," Crestal exclaimed.

She shrugged.

"How did you meet Flores?"

"I used to look for places where I could be alone away from Wijah and Nara. I was in the cellars."

Crestal passed a subtle glance over to Flores. "So you found the caverns through an opening in the Temple...and there found Flores."

"I found him." Amina shrugged again and smiled. With that, she ceased talking.

Flores looked at Amina. She glanced at him, then lay her head upon Tilsis' back and smiled. The suns grew suddenly dark. Flores shook his head to clear it, but a frown had settled upon him. He turned to Crestal.

"Where did Tilsis learn his craft?" he asked the youth.

"Woodcraft?" The youth glanced at the servant, his form bobbing rhythmically. "I don't know. You can ask him."

"How would he answer?"

"The way he always does."

"Is he of your house?"

Crestal looked at Flores. "Of Numsenmur's?"

"Yes," replied Flores. He had not wished to speak the name of his nemesis.

"He spent time outside the city as a youth. Why the sudden interest?"

"It's not sudden."

The youth turned, locks lifting in the breeze.

"The rest didn't happen till later." Flores gazed still wondering.

Crestal continued, "He showed promise with a sword. Then one day, his tongue was cut out. That meant he had been chosen for Numsenmur's personal guard. He served thus for some time, trained by Numsenmur himself until he incurred the master's anger. It was my hand that stayed the lash. Now he'll do anything I ask." For a moment his lips pursed and the haughty cast Flores had seen before returned. The look brightened. "It's like I'm his heir. Me a servant of At–" He bit his lip. "Me, a eunuch and a slave."

That night they lay around a crackling fire in silence. Flores drew his shaggy pelt close and traced constellations in the sky. A small clump, Teknos, lay at right angles from the mass of myriad lights which followed a wide smear that spanned the horizons. The ecliptic of the suns and moons and the several planets angled widely from the bright smear, called the Abode of Heaven.

How strange that he should be here, he thought. I sleep under the sky in the western wilds in the company of a mute slave, the consort of his enemy, and an enigma from the Temple of Vensor who had called him the founder of her tribe. I could abandon her, he thought, but to her the wilderness was a new world, strange and menacing. Where would she go? Gila or not, she was helpless and could not return to the Temple.

Flores shut his eyes and tried to recall the moment of their first encounter. He could not. When he awoke, she was already there, singing and rocking. Even now he felt her eyes upon him, like a spirit of another world, one new, unsullied, untouched by war or death. Shifting in the brisk night, his gaze met her saucered pupils, gazing across the fire. For a long moment they stared. Then Amina's eyes shut, and Flores slept.

With the suns to guide them, the four turned north. The first step of their journey was complete. The trees hugged, still thick, and parted occasionally for meadows and brush. Flores contemplated the training of Tilsis. The noble found this interesting–and frustrating. Here was one who knew all the secrets of the security of Ven's ruling despot: how he fought–which way he leaned, what weapons he preferred and which he avoided–every idiosyncrasy a rival or assassin might desire. And whom could he tell? Flores shivered. Who else would go so far to attain his ends? Sruk had more honor, Sendas less nerve. He had indeed miscalculated, and to his sorrow. He rubbed his right hand. It was ever Numsenmur. The Serclasler was more than one third of the Triumvirate and had been all along. Sruk had the tongue, Sendas the money, but Numsenmur alone possessed the blade and was not afraid to wield it. However, Flores thought, one does not need a tongue to fight, or gold. All one needs is a weapon and an opponent. Tilsis could reveal his knowledge in other ways. One day Flores proposed to spar and soon probed the servant's abilities unceasingly, with an eye to what might one day be useful against Numsenmur.

On the third day Flores' eyes were opened that Tilsis was probing as well, and like a shorn mask, the noble perceived the training's full extend–the deft handling of the reven, the tilt of his rapier, the unconscious pride that shone only when desired, an inner awareness that he was the equal of a tempered Simet knight, but an awareness subtly mixed with bitterness from the knowledge that his low status would always outweigh his abilities in the eyes of others. Each day they paused to practice. Flores, the knight trained from childhood in the skillful use of violence, with Tilsis the slave, driven by Numsenmur to excel or die.

It was during this time that Flores lay one evening and watched Amina, as he often would after the others had drifted off to sleep. For days now he had felt an indefinable something, a soft prickling, a drift of wing on cerebral landscape. An unseen presence followed him around the clock, nudging, obtruding, distracting and filling his mind at each restful interlude, pushing him to do something, daring him against all sense or purpose to do...what? What does one do with this unprecedented mystery, this Sister of Vensa, this gila of Maalstrom? The legendary powers of gila-sa over Vensor-sa seemed so much exaggerated nonsense. She was friendly, she listened, she smiled often and spoke little, and, worst of all, she did just as he had commanded when he first had met her in the cave beside the catacombs–she kept her distance.

Flores gazed at her as she slumbered across the clearing, his eyes drifting as if an undiscovered world underlay her robes. She lay so gently, dovetailed so perfectly with a man. What was it about her that turned a stone of memory, which his mind glimpsed open but each time hastily barred shut? The images before his eyes swooped upon him and took their place beside rock and tree and flesh and bone and sky and child. He shook his head–it was too confusing. Amina moved fitfully by the campfire flames, raising and dropping a bare, dusky elbow. Her crow-black hair draped the edge of a saddle with furrowed tresses curling like a dust-laden twister, the glossy strands suffered little from the elements. Her limbs seemed to him to be an unusual color, dark, not like that of night, as he had previously thought, but rather that of twilight, or of a winter afternoon heavy with billowing nimbus and sagging rain, a color with a touch of open ocean, as reflecting the azure sky, but so engrossed with earthly qualities that it reflected more lead than blue. With expanding pupils, the noble watched her fur part and open to his gaze. She lay bare, her rounded chest rising in restful slumber, soft swollen hummocks dual like the Deity, slick swarthy skin glabrous from lashes to midriff.

Her eyes slowly opened. For a moment she stared. Then she raised upon her hands and, without looking away, crawled close to nestle alongside her lord. Her eyes, big and deep as a ewe-vok's, enveloped Flores. Parting distended lips that tensed faintly in a transient suggestion of fear, her mysterious olive-shaded mouth then relaxed as she felt his arms encircle her. A sultry half-smile, curved like a new and timid moon, wrinkled one cheek only, and a liquid end of tongue emerged to moisten lips, like the cap of a tropical iceberg waiting for a careless ship, or a fleshy fulcrum capable of tumbling mortal empires. That night, in a nameless cove with the mad moons rushing above, Flores possessed Amina. Across the clearing, a youth lay awake with half-closed eyes and heard.

೪ ಐ ೮ ೩

CHAPTER 17

THE REVEN CLAN

The men escorted their unprotesting prisoner through the sunlit court-yard. Walking proudly, the captive did not bend or bow his head and his captors had not added to his indignity by fettering him. He was lit-tle threat. Unarmed and unarmored, the best he could hope for was a quick escape on strong legs. His guards each wielded blade or dagger beside military irsrem plates, and running seemed little good, for the walls of the courtyard rose on every side, low but sturdy and alive with warriors. The captive had no such thought, however. He could achieve his purposes more effectively by cooperation. His gaze skipped over the courtyard. All the accoutrements of war milled within his vision: tendered mounts by the hundred, soaking in a king's ran-som of scarce water; mud-brick hutments laid methodically, detach-ments trotting from walls to buildings and back; parties of dusty outriders trotting in an opened gate. The prisoner's escort impatiently hurried him up several steps onto an informal veranda cool with shade. A stolid, weather-roughened man of calm demeanor leaned back in a skeletal wooden chair and motioned the newcomer to sit alongside several packing crates that lay before him for use as a table. A scroll curled and a metal signet ring rocked where his fingers had touched them.

The captive sat with straightened back and gazed at his host. He chuckled in a hollow tone. "I thank the Urlis that they let me see the day the Pearl of the Twin Valleys is crushed. It will only happen once, and the tide of history will cleanse the land as if your tribe had never been."

His host looked upon the writing fixtures with an indifferent eye. He smiled, sheepishly it seemed, and glanced up as a second prisoner, also unbound, was led in, and as a third was brought. At a gesture from the host the guards ringing the captives straightened.

A pair of riders dismounted foaming reven-na, entered swiftly, and kneeled.

"Our emissaries were refused, governor. They answered the summons with arrows and are massing men across the square. Another party made it past but now they've closed the streets. I've given the order to saddle mounts."

The governor nodded, turning his attention back to the three prisoners as the messenger left. He smiled again, as with suppressed smugness or a peculiar enjoyment of his predicament. This was embarrassing. Sedrech had been taken with this unexplainable undertow of humor since dawn and the unprovoked attack upon his garrison in the plaza. Who knew why? Perhaps because finally this was something different. Anyhow, he could not help but feel different since his promotion to governor and the doubling of his garrison. Those had wrought a change in his regard for this frontier post.

The second captive was an elderly man, a noble with greyed hair and eyes that glowed as though after a long sleep. He began to speak. "Sir captain, governor Sedrech, it is my fate that I always am in the power of the arms of Ven, whether pleading for leisure or reminding myself of unrewarded services." Sedrech leaned back again and listened attentively. "But the blue seas of fortune have finally changed, as one season must follow another, and now the perseverance of years have outworn fate itself, for the gods have seen fit to reward me with a different kind of interchange with the representatives of your resplendent city. I rejoice to inform you that I neither beg, nor cajole, but warn of the dire and manifold vengeance which my people of Nasvetin are now preparing to exact."

The other captives nodded their heads in agreement and looked solemn, ignoring the agitation of the guards.

"The Son of the middle Hedronmas, gleaming metal on his brow and glass upon his chest, lies now in the dust, prostrate, tremulous, see how he squirms with the horny foot of Neset on his neck; his clan is scattered, whelmed, warred upon through weald and wood, struck fiercely in steppe, and riverbank, and hammered down in forts in formerly servile towns. The Empire falls, Sedrech. It goes the way of Sish, Ror, and Sipan. It has outlived its vigor, and stumbles red-faced before younger and poorer men. The Vok-tail King beats upon the gate even now and the valleys reel in turmoil. The town of Nasvetin may soon know new masters, or perhaps at last live for itself alone, but we will chase your foreign clans from our sacred spring and they will flee in panic to their burning homes. This I have lived to see, even if I am now struck dead. For it will surely happen. My clans encircle you as you here encircle me. Your hostages will do you no good; my people have already performed the heavenly rites. We stand one foot in the nether world as of yesterday. I thank Vensor for the privilege of having the advantage of life, yet the immunity of death at once–my body to speak and watch, my soul to rest in the Eye of Vensor in quiet peace forever."

The elderly man paused, the glow turned to gloating in the light of his presage.

Sedrech leaned forward and pursed his lips, the tapered ends pulled slightly in another suppressed grin. The company did not notice and might have regarded the quiver as a grimace. The commander's attention joined that of the others as a fourth prisoner was escorted within and sat, a young man this time, attired in a rare and delicate tunic as were the other captives. Sedrech pinched a feather quill and rolled it absent-mindedly.

"Gentlemen," he said at last, "please accept my regret at having had to enlarge the number of hostages. I had wished to keep only a few heirs to important houses, and I've done my best to entertain and make you all comfortable, while bringing as little inconvenience as possible to your town. But the recent events have presented me with some difficult choices, dilemmas really, from which I must choose the one solution that will satisfy all. I'm sorry–I have not found that right solution. Now I can only satisfy myself. I welcome you, Matan of the Malamut." The elderly man bowed with respect. "You see that I have been moderate in my requisitions," Sedrech went on. "Your son, Amat, remains at large, and it does not look like he will join us, at least not as a hostage. And I welcome you Tanik of the Lemtelat," he addressed the young man who had first entered, "your father also remains free.

"Sirs, my policy appears to have failed for the moment. Your presence here as hostages has had no effect upon this morning's insurrection. Instead of halting, the revolt has spread and now includes the whole town as far as I can tell, and mounted Nasvetinians evidently have now blocked the streets so that we cannot communicate with other towns. But I see no advantage in freeing you, because your people would then have no restraint and would surely fight us, as your own words indicate, Matan. So I'm afraid I must make my policy harsher: Let none attempt to communicate with their kin outside these court-walls, or attempt to escape, on pain of death. For the next few days you will have to be in irons, though you may remain in the customary guest quarters and will have the usual servants and amenities. This will remain in effect until the present difficult situation is resolved. If I can be a better host in any way, in the meantime, please let me know."

"In Nasvetin," interjected Tanik, "the personal word of a noble binds better than the strongest shackles."

Sedrech's demeanor took an a serious bent. "But today, you are still part of the Republic of Ven, and you will be bound." He added, "It's unfortunate that this would happen just as your stay was ending, Sir Tanik, you also having spent much time with my predecessor. If we are victorious, I will see that you are excused your next duty. You may leave."

The hostages rose and filed out under close supervision of the guards, and Sedrech rose as several subordinate officers took their place, crests of reven-na claws upon the head of each.

The captain spoke quickly and choppily. "Teb, stay in camp, keep the gate open with the abatis covering, and watch our prisoners and our other property. You will maintain a mounted reserve day and night. Revtal, you will accompany Kus and myself in the decoy maneuver, then, after the battle, you will join Sterl in his return to the city of Nene. Kus, you will seize the granary by the plaza and thus initiate the engagement. If that doesn't draw the Nasvetinians out, then move house to house until you draw them out in some other way. Make it good; they must defeat us and chase us all the way to Sterl before he can spring the trap. No questions? Good, we begin in one half hour." The men left, then Sedrech called again. "Kus, let us go over some other minor matters." The officer returned and the two strode slowly around the scattered barrels, across the room and into a more comfortable chamber.

"News?" Sedrech asked.

"He took the emblem, but I think he only appeases us," Kus replied. "His sympathies are not with the Turlicum; he said openly that our predicament could be wrapped and labeled and placed on the doorstep of Flores Sumvensor, and that this one was too big to pass."

"Well, he is not a Serclasler."

"No, Tumlefler."

"Ah, of Laruca Venedol. I heard Laruca lies in the southern weald with a Neset pike in his gut," Sedrech noted. "But kin is kin, leader or no; what would we do without it? If Revtal can't be trusted, we will soon find it out, so I instructed him to ride with us. But you will be relieving Tes, not he. Until we've proof that Turlicum is dead, we will have no such disrespectful slander. Now be off and take care, my friend. I will join you soon." Kus nodded and left.

Sedrech continued toward the interior of the building, passing through several long-used chambers, each more decorous and more recently occupied than the one previous.

When the dust finally settles and we can again see clearly, he thought, and it happens that our Lord Flores lives, I think that may be the most unkind fate of all. He would have much to explain concerning his dealings with Neset. It is apparent that he is either a traitor or a coward–and swords are little inclined to listen to either.

֍ ೞ ೞ ֍

In the following days, with Amina on Flores' reven behind him, the travelers pushed deeper into the forest. The complexion of the country began to change. The fields and meadows which before had broken up the wood gave way to isolated lees and scattered glades. As the days passed, these pockets occurred less often and the band, still trailing north, watched the suns shift and hide behind waving verdure. The trees rose like cliffs and marched their green and brown mottled trunks interminably, soaring higher than any they had seen. Their boles and branches swelled and stretched as if they would usurp the domains of clouds, their strange ambition fed with no sane limit. The wanderers followed their twisted path unbelieving. Even the pale, light-starved growth of the forest floor inflated before them monstrously. Fronds and grey-hued flowers and other less unidentifiable growths engrossed amid piled beds of rotting humus.

For a week the refugees threaded through deepening darkness, their meager supplies dwindling as the game disappeared. They fell to rooting tubers and watched for tussocks of vokwort and spicerood, which would always be stunted and tough from lack of light. Redentine grass was eaten raw by them and their mounts–if the brittle stems enclosed any nourishment. Stunted sercotrope and cane yielded fruit, which provided their sustenance for a time. The sikes had long gone. However, other forest denizens showed themselves; they were delayed when an isia crossed their path, multitudinous legs rippling as it crept among the branches. And they gave wide berth to a forest ros, the predator's cough reverberating intermittently in the distance.

Despite fruit and roots, the four were again on the verge of starvation. The redentine gave way to toxic rosbane or lameweed, then the brush wilted and died leaving nothing for forage, and the trees lifted higher still, incomparably, their hypostyles spreading whorls across the suns and smothering their light so that the surface lived in perpetual twilight. Even mist was absent, the suns' rays unable to warm the dank ground.

The forest gave way to jungle and the jungle rose in competition with itself to the warmth of the terraced sky. It seemed as if the wood had pulled itself up and now stood on roots where before it had stood on trunks, and the ground was clotted with pale, diseased vestiges, debris melting down from the invisible boughs above. This had its advantage, however. With the density lessened, the three were no longer delayed by brush or thickets; they made better time, so they thought, till one morning they rose to resume their journey and realized they were lost.

There seemed no solution. Before the hollow eyes of Flores and his companions, the ligneous galleries duplicated at every point, repeating themselves without end like mirrors faced together. They decided it would be useless to climb–their bearings would again be lost long before they could regain the ground.

They could only proceed. More days passed, and with a slow relaxation, the trio perceived that the worst of the forest was behind them. The gloom slowly lessened in accumulating warmth. Fruit trees again were found and redentine for the reven-na.

Then one afternoon, as the band began to think they must look as pale and withered as the fungus weeds at their feet, they broke through crossed shoots and beheld the suns, gleaming on the calm floor of a forest glade. Their joy knew no bounds and Crestal threw his arms about Tilsis and kissed him with a laugh. Tilsis loosed his reven and the animal bore him into the streaming rays, cavorting.

They made camp in the spot, without counting the days, rejoicing and relishing their jungle fare as if it were a banquet. Flores and Tilsis sparred again and Flores, beginning to anticipate the servant's tactics, scored his first clear victory. Only when they had regained vigor and the weather had turned colder did they finally with regret abandon their garden paradise and resume their sojourn toward the north–now that they knew in which direction north lay.

So it was that they came to greener places where Vensor watched his own and pleasant paths beckoned. They trod on, comfortable and laughing, speaking of far valleys and villas in the summer, and love of life. Suddenly, Tilsis gasped. They had left the forest and the gusts of a winter gale whipped about them. The land was again broken, with outcroppings of rock and cleft ridges, and the travelers, after rounding a promontory, halted in surprise. Nested between dark ridges, and previously obscured by a jagged rise, loomed a stronghold of bulwarks and towers. The fields in its vicinity, those which at some time had been cleared of stone, were thickly overgrown with weeds and worts, and showed little evidence of ever having been actively worked. The valley wended naturally through these fields to the stronghold, and they soon saw that they would have to pass directly before the heavy twin portals to continue on their path. No hut or hamlet appeared to enliven their approach, no face or voice or plume of smoke rose within the high wall to relieve the quiet pressure of the rising bluffs. A fine mist fell as the gale gathered strength.

CHAPTER 18

MACIUS

Set within the portals of the stronghold was a smaller door, both of elaborately carved rorewood. As Flores and his companions neared the castle, this smaller door swung inwards and the aperture expelled a figure that bore upon them like a shot. Thinking they were about to be attacked by some new manner of foe, Tilsis turned his reven to withdraw and Flores drew his rapier. However, the man, who was un-armed, seemed not to notice, and delivered all his attention to his speed. As they watched, the door produced three more figures, each of whom followed closely upon the first. The latter appeared to suffer from some deformity or from the effects of a vile custom, for where the first figure ran upon his legs in the manner of a man, his pursuers, though obviously sons of Vensor and brandishing clubs and daggers, leapt forward as if they were animals.

Despite their strange progression, the gap between them steadily nar-rowed, due to the pursuers possessing a kind of primal strength. At a short distance from Flores and his companions, the fleeing man lost his footing. He rolled. In an instant his pursuers were upon him. One swung a club at his head. His intended victim caught the attacker's wrist and twisted the club free and used it to block a descending knife. His elbow took the knife-wielder's wind, and the club connected with the first ruffian, but the third assailant struck him in the side. He fell.

From their vantage point, Flores and his companions saw clearly as the third assailant, responding to a mysterious inner call, let fall the bludgeon and snarling leaped upon his victim. Pinning the man's shoulders to the damp ground, the creature spread his jaws as would a ros and snapped with hideous conviction. Flores and Tilsis had seen enough. As the ros-man's companions answered his cough and closed for the kill, Flores dropped Amina to the ground, and he and Tilsis spurred the reven-na forward.

Neither the animal-men nor their intended prey had yet seen the travelers, and, as two skin-clad mounted warriors barreled upon them with five-foot glass rapiers cutting the air, they halted. Growling, they backed away.

Suddenly one of the beast-men sprang into the air and landed upon the reven behind Tilsis. But his grip was weak and the servant managed to dislodge him, and the reven, disconcerted by the shrieking form at its neck, reacted as it would to any predator and sank its fangs into the attacker's shoulder. With a snort the reven shook the annoyance as it would a rodent and dropped it to the sward. A second beast-man leaped at their original prey. Flores engaged him. Roaring and screaming, the beast-man ignored the dagger and club that lay within easy reach upon the ground, and the Ven ran him through as if piking a cornered animal. The remaining one turned. He fled toward the hills that ringed the castle, every few feet turning his head to cough and bark. Flores made no effort to follow.

The former prey of the beast-men watched his saviors with nimble eyes and a blank expression. He felt his side where the club had landed. The man seemed near middle age but was, Flores noted, still vigorous. His skin was dark, and though his straight black hair was unkempt and had been rudely hacked with a bare blade, his face was entirely hairless, and Flores decided from his unkempt appearance that his chin had not been shaved but was always smooth. His lips were thin and compressed, his chin and neck more stocky than that of Flores, and his build strong from habitual labor, unlike the rational muscular development of the noble, or the massive natural endowment of Tilsis. His sturdy limbs had no trace of excess flesh, and, if not for his obvious health and vigor, Flores would have thought him in need of a meal.

Flores dismounted and cleaned his blade in the grass, then replaced it in the scabbard.

"What are you doing on my property?" the dark man demanded.

Flores looked up, startled. "We did not realize we were trespassing, sir. We meant no harm. Since you are obviously no longer in danger we will be on our way." He turned to remount his reven.

The dark man waved Flores away from his mount. "If that is true, then you are most welcome."

Flores hesitated.

"I am Macius," the dark man continued. His demeanor changed subtly. His face proved inflexible and responded but little. His body, however, was transformed as emotion flowed through it like electricity. His shoulders drew back, his spine straightened, and he repositioned his feet in the earth.

"Flores-Sumvensor of the Turlicum of the Republic of Ven."

"I should have guessed–a Simet noble. A rare event in these parts." Macius passed his gaze unobtrusively over Flores' companions.

"And Crestal and his servant, Tilsis," Flores nodded in their direction, "and last, my traveling companion–Amina."

Macius bowed deeply. "I am honored."

Flores pointed to the hills. "Might I ask, Macius–"

"*Sir* Macius. Of the city of Vedeg."

"My pardon, Sir Macius. Might I ask what manner of men those were, and why they wished to harm you?"

Macius thought a moment, then said, "Ruffians. Bandits. Until Recently, not a problem."

"They seemed insane," interjected Crestal. "Why did they act thus?"

Macius glanced at the castle.

"A cunning deception, really. They feign madness and pretend to be animals in order to frighten their victims. They were the last of a band that has kept me penned in this castle for months, watching day and night for an opportunity to kill and rob me. I dispatched several, but at last they found their way inside and came upon me by surprise. If you hadn't arrived when you did–" He drew his finger across his neck. "It seems, Sir Flores, that I owe you thanks for saving my life."

As he spoke, his body took on such an exaggerated pose of formality that for an instant Flores was not certain whether Macius was earnest or mocked him.

"I would be honored, gentlemen, if you would allow me the privilege of entertaining you as my guests." Macius pointed to the castle with its open gate, then to the hills. "We won't be bothered by the remaining one–he'll look for easier prey elsewhere."

The temperature was dropping and the rising wind threw cold sprays upon them. Flores nodded. "Your offer is welcome, Sir Macius."

Macius spoke as they hurried toward the gate. "I usually have no trouble from anyone in this area. I am a scribe, you see." He posed self-consciously, as if grasping a quill. "The locals have a superstitious awe of scribes. They won't come near. Even though I live alone after retiring to my clan estate, I have had nothing to fear–until recently."

They entered the stronghold and Macius shouted through the wind while closing the massive twin portals. "But I suppose that now has changed."

The mist became a downpour, and amid the cracking of thunder they hurried across a broad courtyard, and entered the chateau.

After leaving the reven-na in an adjoining chamber, Macius showed them to a large poorly furnished room and they sat about a low wooden table. The room was littered with strange objects such as a scribe of a high order might have, including lattices filled with scrolls, sacks of minerals and mysterious substances, tools of all sorts and sizes, and containers that gave off peculiar smells. Flores saw no sign of other inhabitants–shoots and grass covered the yard between the flagstones, and the roof above them leaked in several places.

"If you can spare me, I have some food remaining from my captivity–I shall prepare it for the occasion."

"But Macius," said Flores, "we have no desire to burden you. We have food–let us share it."

Macius paused, his body twitching with enthusiasm. "Let us throw it in together!"

He disappeared into another room. Some minutes passed and, while Flores was occupied with examining the scattered scrolls, Macius reappeared with several full pots and placed them before his guests.

"I fear," he explained, "that we have all had better meals than this."

They sampled the lukewarm broth and undercooked beans and found themselves in agreement.

Flores stood. "We have strips of sike-flesh remaining from our last kill."

He and Tilsis exited and in a moment both returned with arms laden. Together they and Macius fell upon the fruits and meat with relish, and rainwater washed it down.

After he had finished, Macius began to speak with new verve and animation, and responded to their questions about his home. "Vedeg is large and prosperous. I had only recently departed my city to return to my clan's estate here in the wilds. You can see that it has long been unoccupied."

"You must possess great wealth to contemplate restoring such a large edifice."

"I am a wealthy man, Sir Flores," he said, holding up a clasped fist. "But not in mir. Rather in the joy that comes from inner knowledge. In mir I am poor–the entire clan of retainers that my father once employed I had to let go, and the land around here is worthless. But I am content, for I have always been a favorite of Gethos, and even though I have no need for land and only a small need for mir, I know that one day I shall obtain what I need to restore my home and continue my scribal studies."

"What is the object of your inquiry, Sir Macius?" asked Flores.

The man reflected a moment, then reached for their shared goblet of rainwater. "The world." He drank and stood the goblet on the table, glanced once at Amina, then Crestal.

"In my younger days I traveled much, Sir Flores, and saw many things that I did not understand. I mean this in all sincerity, dear guests. My life has been a strange one from its inception. And I don't believe that the god of fortune has tired of me yet." He drained the goblet and replaced it on the table before them. "Not so long as I remember the burning spark that Divine Vensor has planted within me, as he has in all of us, to remind us that we are not alone on Maalstrom. It is strange, is it not Flores, that we are all subject to the eternal caprice of heaven?"

"Except for that which men take upon themselves, and bear responsibility for."

"I must confess that I don't believe that ever to be the case." Macius shifted and leaned against the wall. "I believe that we are all part of the sublime order, the plan of heavenly events, and that it is part of the divine plan to hide from men their ultimate purposes. We are all intimately connected, Flores, in ways we could never untangle, with each other and with the grandest events of the cosmos."

"An inspiring notion, Sir Macius!" Flores finished his meal and gave his whole attention to his host. Amina ate little and Crestal soon finished, but Tilsis slowly worked on the food placed before them by Macius, evidently possessing a stomach as well-forged as the pots.

"Do you in fact mean to say," asked Flores, "that one can understand little concerning mortals unless one knows something of the gods and their plans?"

Macius reflected a moment. "Yes. That is exactly so."

Flores looked at Amina and Crestal. "But what do we really know?" he asked. "We know the human order of things on Maalstrom—we are born, grow old and die. The Divine Plan, at least in Ven, is known only to eunuchs and sacerdotes."

"And to scribes," added Macius.

"Are you not a scribe?" asked Crestal.

"Yes, I did say that," replied Macius.

"Then tell us," said Crestal.

Macius shook his head.

"Yes," Flores smiled. "Tell us the Plan of the Cosmos! We have much time."

Their host glanced at the pouring rain through the window, then held up a finger and stepped to the lattice. Bearing a sheaf of papers, he returned and sat. He cleared his throat, and began to speak, referring occasionally to the paper before him.

"My friends, we live in the age of iron. I do not mean that we use iron, for though we do use it at times, civilized people now use irsrem for most of their works. I mean that the spirit of man is of iron–cold and hard and brittle. Forged in cauldrons with pain and effort, and corroding to dross in a few short years. Good only for war and death and the endeavors of the god of fire, it is now little used for building. So our age was born in pain and clashing, and all will falter and die when their brief lives end. Life was better in the Age of Silver; and better still in the Age of Gold. The Age of Gold was the first age, the age of glory and wealth and joy and life, when Man's ancestors, the immortal Zeyd, strode across the firmament breaking the giants with muscle and sword. Thus it was before the first revolt.

"Like the dawn of day, Vensor had opened his eyes in the midst of blackness and found pale stars. The stars were giants who loved fire and stone and hated all good-natured things. This was when he made his divine plan to fill the world with good and to do away with evil. So he searched and found the Zeyd upon a single star out of all that shine and ordained that they should serve his purpose. He gave them weapons and clever minds that they could do his bidding and make a place for themselves throughout the universe. 'Cleanse the sky of evil,' he said. And they did.

"But our ancestors were not of the flesh of Vensor nor of his blood; indeed, our ancestors were animals. They were mortal and weak and lustful and ruled by their animal passions before Vensor breathed his spark into them and civilized them. In their hearts they too loved fire and stone and they rose in treacherous rebellion against Vensor, who had done so much for them. At this Vensor became angry and swept the Zeyd from the universe. Thus ended the Age of Gold.

"Only a few Zeyd had remained loyal, and these Vensor loved, permitting them to live on only a few stars in the sky. Vensor repented of his anger and decided to help the remaining Zeyd. The Zeyd had killed all the giants but five; these were the strongest and they called themselves the Urlis. These Vensor placed in their service.

"Vensor spoke to them, saying to the first, 'I call you Talen. You will rule the beasts and bring forth hunger and the hunt to all things, and will appear in brown to all.'

"He spoke to the second, saying, 'I call you Gethos, for you are swift and blue. You are the restless sea which brings luck to men.'

"He said to the third, 'I call you Nvediteg, for though you are huge, you are also fast, and cannot be controlled. You are the black storm cloud that brings floods.'

"And to the fourth, he said, 'You are Tumsenet, for you are large, and slow, and green. I give you plants to rule, and will be worshiped under trees. You bring healing to all.'

"To the fifth and last, he said, 'I call you Nantifus, for you are small and scarred and very slow. You are the white mountains, and bring disease to the weak.'

"Thus He put all in balance, and the Zeyd prospered and lived long and happy lives. But Vensor grew sad, for though he had a clan and had brought light and good into the Universe, still he had no son. God wanted an heir, as do all living things, and now all things desire this, because it was God who first desired it.

"So Vensor begat his perfect and divine child, who was all powerful and all-knowing and perfect in every way. But he had a fatal flaw— envy. He wished to be the Creator himself and turned to Evil, saying, 'I am Atasan the Equal.' Then Atasan sought to bring forth, as did the Creator, and put his knowledge and power and will to the task. But what he made was not what he had desired, for he created the only thing missing from the universe: Chaos. And so was born Maalstrom, the natural world, in which all creatures save the descendants of the Zeyd consort with gila-sa, the world which forever tempts Vensor-sa with its corporeal snares, the world of feminine reproduction.

"Maalstrom is strong, ageless, and persistent. Not even the Creator Himself can vanquish Her, not even He can forever resist the tempta- tions of Her feminine nature, but, each night when darkness prevails, permits Maalstrom to mingle with His soul. Thus although Maalstrom was dumb and blind and mindless, it was beyond the power of any to control Her, and at the end of the Age of Silver, Her drive to reproduce overthrew the divine balance, plunging the Universe into the endless cycle of birth, sex, and death. As for Atasan, his act proved his undoing because at the center of Chaos was the Abyss of space and time, and Atasan fell into it where he remains today. And in imitation of Vensor, and to honor Him, and to protect themselves from Atasan's abomination, Vensor-sa now imprison gila-sa in His Temples."

Flores glanced at Macius, who was staring alternately at Amina and Crestal. During the narrative the priestess had made no sound but rested folded hands upon legs clothed in skins, skins that were now torn in places. Her eyes, formerly downcast in exaggerated modesty, slowly rose to receive directly the stare of their host. Flores frowned. He could not explain his uneasiness, and this made him frown even more deeply.

"One moment, Sir Flores." Macius stood and left the room. Soon he returned with several old but intact articles of coarse-woven vok-wool. "It occurred to me that you might be warmer with new clothing, and I happened to have these in my possessions. So, if you please...."

Crestal leaped up and immediately seized upon a dark enveloping cassock much like the threadbare one he wore. With Tilsis to assist he retired to a side room, changed, and returned in high spirits, once more modest from chin to ankles. Flores exchanged his furs for a new beige tunic. Tilsis did the same. Amina, who had taken somewhat longer examining the articles of clothing finally selected a chestnut gown that opened in the front, its cloth somewhat softer than the others. When the priestess returned from the side room, the others, who had not looked closely at the garment, saw that a crimson sun lay across its midriff with yellow rays spread outward to cover breasts and hips. The right hem of the garment was dyed ocher and crimson so that it blended with the sun-design. However, the selvage of the left hem had been sewn in jagged orange hue, so that when Amina sat and a dark knee extruded between the hems, although she had crossed right hem over left, as was customary, the orange selvage appeared, racing into view so that it seemed to split the sun on her abdomen like leaping flames.

Flores alone seemed to take notice of the peculiarity. Once the others had settled, the noble shook his head to clear it of the strange effect.

"But why didn't Vensor simply do away with Atasan?" Crestal asked. "Why permit him to create evil and death and still live?"

In answer, Macius looked to the scroll and resumed reading. "Thus, by the divine will of God, it is neither indifference nor necessity that enables Evil to exist, but Love: the love of parent for wayward child, of Father for disobedient Son, of God for his only Offspring–Atasan, Creator of Chaos. The True Creator, since he loved Atasan, permitted him to dwell in the Abyss hoping he would one day repent, though he had looked into the future and knew he would not. This was the end of Order and the long Age of Silver.

"And now is the Age of Iron, with space and time and death. Atasan, from his Abyss, eternally tests our will with material allurements and seeks to extinguish the divine spark within us with thoughts of war, hatred, and lust. Vensor, since he would not destroy his one true Heir, split and produced Vensed, who is not the true Son, but the sign of Vensor's love for all his children, the giving of Himself. Though his children remain subject to the death that time brings to all, we are exempt from the corrupt coupling of the rest of Maalstrom. Thus he gives us mortal sons to renew ourselves lest we succumb to temptations and all good be gone from the universe."

"And," added Crestal, "he gives his angels to take our souls to heaven."

Macius looked at Crestal in surprise. "Angels, you say?" For an instant his eyes widened in the flame of the lamp. Then he looked away. "So I have now made good my point. My fortunate life...its connection? This ancestral estate that has preserved me from the worst effects of poverty." He laughed. "I have even extended my own fortune to others, such as Yezd–" Macius hesitated, then explained, "–a retainer I once employed."

"We knew of a Yezd," said Crestal, reaching for an extra fruit.

Macius returned his gaze to Crestal.

"You were speaking, Sir Macius?" said Flores.

"My apologies," Macius said. "Sir Crestal, what did you say?"

Flores nodded. "We heard of a Yezd in Ven. Could he be the one you knew?"

"Did he mention me?" Macius asked Flores.

"I'm afraid that I have never met him." He looked to Crestal.

Crestal shook his head. "But he did have some strange devices."

Macius peered askance at Crestal.

"Sorry to disappoint you, gentlemen," interrupted Flores, "but I don't believe that I can manage further tonight. Tomorrow, with good weather, we shall ready our mounts and depart." Flores stood.

"Oh, but Sir Flores, the day has barely gone." Macius rose and gestured for the Turlicum to sit. "Sleep when you are old. I must pursue my point with you."

With a shrug, the noble sat. The others pushed away the remains of their dinner and settled into a relaxed sprawl.

Macius seemed suddenly reinvigorated. "You mentioned before

something about angels, Crestal. Well, some time ago I would have agreed with your comment and said nothing. However, I recently had an encounter that you may find interesting. Sometime last year I still had a few retainers here, including the Yezd whom I mentioned. This man was a vagabond who showed unexpectedly at my door, wanting work and a roof over his head. Having traveled much myself, I permitted him to enter and fed him. For some months he worked for me, then departed, but before he left he told me a very strange tale. This man had been for some time a sailor and adventurer, a rogue really, known among his seafaring friends as a daring fellow who never shrank from a difficult or dangerous task if there was a share of glory or loot to be had. He was also very audacious and strong.

"He related to me that once he was sitting in a tavern in the port of Vaw together with his friends devising plans for the attainment of sudden wealth. He began to mock his friends for their timidity and cowardice. He declared that only the boldest are favored by the gods, those who disregard all but their single purpose, and he loudly declared that he would shrink from no deed provided there was gold to be won or fame to be earned. If Vensor had a safe he would rob it, and pull Vensor's beard in the bargain.

"His friends were ashamed at their companion's boasting, and feeling the sting of his words, decided to put his boasting to the test. They challenged him before the tavern mob to do what no man had done and lived to tell of—to set his foot on the Isle of the Dead, and return with proof that he had done so. At first, my guest was dismayed because as the sailors knew the Isle is well guarded by the selks, which you call malkops. Any who venture beyond the island of clashing rocks, whether by accident or design, are immediately attacked by the flying creatures.

"But our friend took up the challenge, and the next day he set sail in a ship whose course would skirt the empty sea where rumor said the island lay. Weeks passed and finally the adventurer was put ashore in the furthest port the sailors knew—a string of huts, where the fishermen are all old and surly and care nothing for their mother city. He bought from them a lateen skiff and caught the wind. For weeks he plowed straight into the rolling waste as he had been told to do, putting all his trust in Gethos and the divine spark of God. Finally he spied the clashing rocks, a small speck of land with trees, a strip of sand, and a hollow cliff that sends brine into the sky with each heave of the sea. The precise location, since I have done some sailing, he related to me.

"Our adventurer, being a navigator of some skill, evaded the rocks and landed his boat on the narrow beach. He climbed to the top of the cliff and between the sprays of spume saw his goal: a white smudge of mist on the horizon–the Isle of the Dead. There on the cliff he waited, conserving his provisions. For he had devised a plan." Macius paused. "By the way, what manner of devices were they?"

"Devices?" Flores asked.

"Of your acquaintance, Yezd."

"Oh," said Flores and looked at Crestal.

"The strangest ever," said the youth. "One could swim beneath the water like reven-na!"

"His plan?" prompted Flores.

Macius cleared his throat and resumed his tale. "This sailor knew that he could never cross the intervening water by day, and, being a clever rogue, he suspected that he had as little chance to cross it by night, else someone would surely have done so before then, and re-turned to tell of it. The selks of heaven, which scan the skies above us even now, have powers and inscrutable purposes Vensor-sa have never guessed. So he waited. Many times he glimpsed them far above, soar-ing toward the Isle or away to scour the world in performance of their grisly task, sometimes several flying low with a heavy burden, other times darting from the upper reaches of the sky to swiftly skim the surface of the ocean. But never did they bother our adventurer, or even take notice of him. My guest eventually concluded that what he had been told was correct in that they do not concern themselves with what occurs on the clashing rocks and tolerate men there from time to time. But if men set their boats on the far side as if to approach their Isle–their anger then is sudden and terrible.

"Eventually the event our friend waited for occurred. The wind rose, and the skies darkened, and the clouds broke, spilling their burden over the vast sea and the tiny acre resisting its watery onslaught. Then our friend cut the lines that moored his skiff and set himself adrift. In the face of the storm, when nothing with wings could remain aloft and live, he raised his sail and skidded into the gulf. His little boat swirled and dipped, the waters tumbled and shook, but his nerves and his skill prevailed–he never knew how much time had passed, though later it seemed he had set out in the morning for that smudge of mist which on a day of fair weather would have required no more than an hour or two to reach, yet when his prow came ashore and drove into the sand with a final crashing of the waves the suns had long set.

"Oh, Flores." said Macius. "Those 'underwater devices,'" Macius chuckled. Does Yezd still have them?"

"No." Flores leaned back. "I do."

Macius swallowed.

"Or rather, I did. We–" He turned to Crestal. "What did we do with them?"

"Put them under a bush and covered them with leaves and brush, I believe. Why?"

Macius took a single, rapid breath.

"Simple curiosity. And where were they thus covered?"

Flores peered at Macius, then again to Crestal.

"On the Hedronmas, across from the island of–"

"Lurenmurg." Flores finished, looking at Macius with intensity. "The largest island on the Hedronmas with the largest villa. The western side of the bend."

Macius smiled.

"And what was on the Isle of the Dead?" asked Crestal. "What did Yezd find?"

Macius paused. "That he never told. But he landed upon the island and returned and lived to tell of his deed–not only to me but to others, most particularly to the sailors of Vaw, who welcomed him as a hero upon his return. And even today among the people of Vaw–and especially among the rulers of the city who had borne the brunt of his earlier exploits–he is the most famous and esteemed of thieves, and that in a city of pirates and thieves."

"But," asked Crestal, "how did they know he was speaking the truth when he returned? He could have gone anywhere and come back and just said that he visited the Island. How did they know?"

Their host nodded.

"Crestal," he spoke slowly, "how many funerals have you attended?"

He looked surprised. "Why, many."

"And you, Flores, and you Tilsis–many. Right?"

They nodded.

"And what happened to the deceased at those funerals?"

"They were taken by the malkops to Heaven, a place in the sky where the suns merge." Now Crestal seemed surprised.

"No!" Macius slowly shook his head. "Not to where the suns merge, but to a *real* place–here, *on Maalstrom*." He leaned forward, his visage expanding before them. "They were taken to a sunlit isle in the emptiest quarter of the southern sea where no man who breathes may go, but where all dead must. To the home of the selks, the malkops–the Sun God's Island of the Dead. When our hero returned to Vaw, he clutched in his hand the proof–the royal medallion of King Mulk of Vaw, which had accompanied the king on his death flight before the assembled multitude of the city."

Macius leaned back. "Final proof–if further was needed–was that the ruler, the old king's heir, Price Kot, seized the medallion and attempted to murder the rogue for his sacrilege. But, after many close encounters with the king's agents, he escaped, to arrive eventually at my door."

"Oh, then he never showed you the proof," Crestal said.

"True," Macius conceded.

Flores rose. "An entertaining story, Macius. How unfortunate that such tales occur only in the minds of men, and not in their deeds. But sleep calls."

The others stood and stretched.

"Macius." Flores looked at the Vedeg noble with interest. "Since you have been shut in here for so long and have no retainers to assist you in securing food, will you not accompany us to Nasvetin? I would return your hospitality in whatever way I can. You could ride with Tilsis."

Macius turned his unchanging gaze upon the Turlicum. His face revealed nothing of his feeling in response to this invitation, but something in the way his elbows moved apart and forward seemed to suggest surprise and gratitude. "Your kind offer is most appreciated. For the first time in months I am a free man. But I do not know if my destiny lies in Nasvetin. I will sleep on it."

"Please consider it. You are most welcome," said Flores.

"Yes," Crestal smiled. "Come with us. We will have fun together."

The dark man's gaze passed from Flores to Crestal to Tilsis, then paused on Amina. The priestess had stood with the others and was occupied with smoothing one edge of her new gown. The gap in her clothing that had revealed one thigh for the duration of the evening did not close when she stood, but expanded to reveal the full expanse of her smooth, lustrous limbs. Slowly she raised her eyes to those of Macius and blinked, her wide round orbs serious and innocent.

"I shall sleep on it," Macius said.

Macius led the way to his guest quarters. Once the door to the quarters had shut, and his guests had disappeared from view, the dark man turned, walked to the gate of the castle and quietly opened the portal.

Nervously, he stepped into the deeper darkness. His eyes took in the heavens and his lungs sucked the cool clean wind and for a considerable time he stood, watching and waiting and listening, while in the meadow night-spiders rasped the corpses of the beast-men before malkops arrived with the dawn. Finally a swift light appeared on the horizon and climbed high overhead and Macius smiled. He murmured thanks to the blue god Gethos, re-entered the stronghold—and halted in surprise.

CHAPTER 19

BONES AND IRON

Although it was a day of worship, Numsenmur wore plates of glass armor upon his body. He shifted his weight from one foot to the other with impatience. The numbers of Vensor-sa attending the calling for sons was less than usual but he did nothing to shorten the time involved; for the city's sake, if not for piety, the forms of the ritual had to be observed.

About him stood a half dozen bodyguards, slaves with their tongues excised. Numsenmur felt secure in their presence. He knew that whatever he said would not be repeated. He felt less secure in the company of his two other immediates–Ust-Terenol-Calomar and Dos-Senelwat-Hutsutsem, but they were the architects of the measure which, jointly, they now proposed to submit to the oracle. The King of Neset had proposed it; the noble Dos had negotiated the measure, and it had received Ust's endorsement. The King of Ven abhorred the proposition; they could chatter about truces and final settlements, but he was not deceived. He knew the capital of the Hedronmas and Suma was in trouble.

The siege of Nesos had begun one month before and continued to tighten daily. Wood for fuel was short, arrows were running low, and most important, the city was rationing its food. Each night fewer skiffs evaded the Neset blockade on the rivers. Everything except the water, which still flowed from the Temple, was rationed, with the severest penalty for violators. A cloud of winged malkops spiraled overhead to collect the corpses of the executed.

The voice of the magistrate rang announcing the arrival of another aristocratic house. No one moved. We're wasting time, thought the chief of the Serclaslers. Some of the nobles were dead, but most were either on the ramparts, or at home concocting escape plans, if not already beyond the battlements scattered throughout the valleys. He could not bring himself to believe that any Vens could have sided with Nesos. Other cities had joined the Vok-tail King–Numsenmur's men had identified warriors of Asan, Lunsen, and Toor–but none but the lowest and meanest coward or treacherous weakling would raise his hand against his own city, the guardian of his own Temple. He wished the magistrate would make haste. His skin crawled standing in the open plaza. Two attempts had already been made on his life. One week before, someone had shot an arrow at him, and the assailant was never caught. And only two days ago one of his own clansmen had tried to slip a stiletto through his ribs. His mutes cut him to ribbons, but why he had turned traitor Numsenmur could only guess.

Numsenmur flung his hand, cutting off the magistrate's speech. "Place the remainder in the orphanage!"

He signaled his attendants to carry the offerings into the Temple cellar. The city may be rationed, but the Temple must be fed; he had cut back on the offerings only a little. He wondered who had shot the arrow, or who had arranged for it to be shot? His allies, among the first to be suspected by any sensible Ven politician, were dead, incompetent, or missing–Soorkrul the Eunuch Lord, for instance, had not been heard from since the beginning of the war. What had happened to him was anyone's guess. Then he thought of Flores, but shook his head. Impossible! The Turlicum must be dead; he had vanished from his dungeon weeks earlier. Still, the man had an eerie ability to survive, seemingly for the very purpose of frustrating the Serclasler's plans. And the mysterious escape of Crestal and his servant would not rest in his mind. The guards in his workroom had sworn that Flores had accompanied them, though how he could reappear after a month's absence he could not imagine.

How the years have flown since they first met, Numsenmur thought. Flores' father had conquered the valley of the Suma after wars against Sish, Nasvetin and Tes. His triumphal entry into Ven had culminated in a speech and the adoration of the Assembly. "Turlicum is fame!" the Assembly had yelled, except Nidrenmor of the Serclaslers, Numsenmur's father.

Later, Numsenmur and the younger Flores, each hardly beyond puberty, had explored Ven's Nether Fields together, treading paths among meadows of yellow flowers interspersed with altars and monuments while their elders discussed ways to settle the differences between their houses. There had been an iron fence encircling a mausoleum with a statue mounted on the top, in memory of some ancient but now forgotten personage, and Flores had sat with his back to the railing to rest. Numsenmur blanched, and in response Flores had turned. He only had time to back his torso out of reach before talons sank into his arm. A predatory ros, shut in when the gate had inadvertently closed, had gripped him, seeking to drag the Turlicum Heir within reach of its naked, bone-white skull. Numsenmur could still hear its sharp cough and see its tusk snap. Numsenmur had stood. With pike in hand he had waited, ignoring Flores' cries, hoping the beast would do what he knew must be done one way or another. Finally, the claws released, and Numsenmur followed Flores back, returning later to assist in destroying the beast.

That had been the beginning. Flores not only survived, but within a few years, after the assassination of the elder Turlicum, had emerged in the Assembly as a rival of Sruk and Numsenmur. The war of the Turlicum against the Triumvirate had begun. For the many years since, Flores had thwarted the Serclaslers and the several houses which together had ended the older Turlicum's life. And Flores had always known, and Numsenmur knew that he had known, that the youth with the pike, the Heir to the Serclaslers, had chosen not to use it to aid Flores on that day in the Fields.

But the score now is even, thought Numsenmur. More than even. In fact, he was beginning to feel there was nothing he could do that would not finally be thwarted by Flores, that he would never be free of his vengeance. His plan for Nesos had miscarried, due to Flores; his principal ally was dead, due to Flores; even his son, for whom he reserved all the pride he possessed, lay somewhere in the wilds of the south, due to Flores. Then, the ultimate humiliation: the Turlicum had instigated Nesos' ejection from the Assembly. That was most unforgivable. He had returned to the Assembly by force of arms, but unbelievably, had been frustrated yet again by the man's disappearance out of his very palace immediately after he, Numsenmur, anticipating the coming execution, had announced Flores' death to the city–that from a man whose life he had saved! The ingrate! If he had not given warning on that day so long ago, Flores would not have turned, and Flores would not have been warned.

The pious requests and prayerful gratitude terminated and the Serclasler Lord, joined by Dos and Ust and the magistrate, climbed the steps to the golden idol of Vensor in the light of the flaming brands. The congregation below took up a slow chant of praise to the god. The magistrate stroked the gong. As the ritual encomium rolled from the magistrate's tongue, Numsenmur folded his hands and uttered a prayer. "Our Lord Vensor, Father of the Universe, Just and Merciful Giver of Life, Protector of the Sacred Spring, we beseech thee today to give your attention to your unworthy children in the following." Numsenmur unrolled the parchment and addressed the god himself. "Ven is under siege from the Neset-sa, and we suffer greatly. Their king has promised that if we open the gate he will spare the lives of all and will not violate the Temple. Should we do this?"

He stopped and gazed expectantly into the great round eyes spewing smoke that mingled with the steam of the chamber. After some minutes, a harsh voice rang out. "Silence, blasphemer! You violate the earth with your presence! You contemplate treason while my most loyal defender languishes in prison. We have heard of one noble in particular whom you have wronged–he is most worthy in our eyes. You must release–"

The voice of the god ceased as quickly as it had begun.

Numsenmur turned a sickly grey face upon Ust, who took a casual step back from the Serclasler Lord. Dos' eyebrows crawled across his scalp. A shadow dimmed the idol's smoky eyes, then a higher, shriller voice emanated.

"Pay no attention to what I just said. I spoke hastily. Repeat your request."

Numsenmur did so.

"I will answer your request in a moment."

Soon the voice resumed.

"My beloved children, I grow hungry. Go and bring food. You must not open the gate to the Neset-sa. Nesta is never to be trusted."

The Lord Serclasler heaved a sigh of relief and descended. It was truly uncanny how he kept imagining his archenemy, Flores, everywhere he went.

Several weeks passed. Then one afternoon, in the second month of the siege, Numsenmur clambered up the stairway to the parapets and gazed upon the wet, brown, undulating plain before Ven. A cold breeze whipped and flapped his cloak. His attention, together with that of his companions, focused on the activity below. Two weeks earlier, for the first time in the memory of the city, the Temple had opened its gates on an empty courtyard. The magistrates had entered, Numsenmur included, to inquire as to the cause of Vensor's anger and were addressed by the deity. Deliver food–more food–and soon. In desperation the plans were laid, then postponed by a series of assaults from the Neset-sa. For days they thought the city would fall, but the enemy's attacks slackened and then ceased. Finally Numsenmur sprang his plan: he opened the gate to release mounted men with orders to raid the Nesets' camp and seize all the food they could find. The surprise was complete, but the success only partial; for every barrel of ses they carried back, a Ven warrior fell to arrows or capture. The Neset-sa quickly recovered and pressed more allies into service. Their camps now blotted the rocky plain in all directions.

Now a new phase of the contest was opening, a phase which had summoned the Serclasler to the city's wall on the bright autumn morning. The torching of the slums had not moved the Vens, nor had the desecration of the Nether Fields. Now the captives which the Neset-sa had obtained from the failed foray provided the instrument for yet another stratagem of the Emperor of the Vensors. One by one, in succeeding rows, stakes were cut and, upon a rise near the city raised against the sky, a shrieking burden was impaled on each and left to flail just beyond the range of the arrows. Thus, Ven felt the fist of the Vok-tail King squeeze more tightly. Numsenmur seemed oblivious to the event, but as each stake was lifted, other Vens recognized the victim and hysteria spread. Several had to be subdued to keep from throwing themselves off the walls or rushing recklessly out the gate in futile efforts to free them.

Though personally repelled, Numsenmur, for the moment, felt a twinge of relief. The reason was perhaps not obvious, but it addressed Numsenmur's fear of treachery. A single hand could lower a rope to the enemy or several turn the wheel to open the gate. Cities had fallen before to the deceit of one individual. Numsenmur had increased the guards all round, and the execution of suspects accelerated. But after today he no longer need worry. After seeing the consequences of falling into the hands of the Neset-sa, no Ven warrior would dare let them in. The siege would continue.

A voice at his side directed his attention to a clump of mounted men which left the besieger's encampment by a far ridge, and approached the gate of Ven trailing yellow dust and winding between mounds of ash and charred beams–the remains of the city's suburbs. Beside Numsenmur the populace of the city were gathered thickly upon the walls.

The Neset-sa halted before the gate. One produced a hollow cone. He lifted the cone to his mouth and his bellow rang off the ramparts, momentarily drowning the tortured lungs behind him.

"King Nesos of Neset, Emperor of the Vensors, Brother of the Moons, has decided to make a magnanimous offer befitting his munificence and philanthropic nature. He has generously offered the post of viceroy of Ven to any individual who will open the gates of the city to its rightful and divinely guided ruler, the King of Neset. The new viceroy shall rule Ven in the name of the Emperor and no Neset shall touch him in any way. So pledges the Emperor, Nesos of Neset, who is known rather to die by his own hand than to break his vow."

Another captive, his arms bound, was thrust upon a spike by the executioners; then his ropes were cut and he was raised aloft. The cacophony was joined by another throat with its red stake. The emissary looked about him then called again.

"What do you say, Vens? Who will kill your chief, the Serclasler, and bring peace and prosperity back to your city? Who will be the first to open the gate and become Regent of Ven?"

Numsenmur inhaled, his eyes wide. Involuntarily he turned and surreptitiously watched his guards and captains. He inspected his armor and quickly tightened one plate. The lord motioned to a companion and arrows arched toward the emissary. Most struck the ground but one glanced off his armor and another found a chink and stuck fast. The announcer hopped swiftly away, clutching his arm where the shaft bobbed stiffly. Laughs and jeers followed, but quickly died before the steady jangling screams from the hill.

The king was now genuinely frightened. The thread of assassination from his archenemy and supporters had made him nervous. The defection of his consort, who had apparently sheltered the Turlicum for some days and was responsible for his disappearance, had pierced his heart and brought him to a pitch of anger he had never known, but the fear that now gripped his body and squeezed sweat from every pore was a new experience altogether. Terror settled over him like a tremendous weight. He turned to his captains and spoke a few low words, then descended to the street. His royal litter bore him to his palace.

For the remainder of the evening and far into the night, the King of Ven busied himself with an endless queue of curfew offenders, petitioners, and chiefs of allied clans in the course of forming or amending a series of schemes for preventing the fall of Ven. The only result was the stricter enforcement of existing rules or the more frequent patrolling of the city and its defenses.

Without premeditation or even awareness on his part, Numsenmur would end his conferences at almost the same time each night, and terminate his work. Over the weeks this habit had become almost invariable; he would summon his bodyguard of savage mutes and descend stairwells and ramps into the bowels of his ancestral edifice until arriving, on his lowest level, at the only entrance to a secluded series of workrooms. Here, in Numsenmurian fashion, he would confront the talented new scribe Yezd, who had been escorted six weeks earlier without notice from the municipal scribal school to these rooms, with all the apparatus that the scribal school possessed.

This visit was no different. Four sentinels stood within the anteroom and two more at the base of the steps in the workroom. Numsenmur ignored them and stalked past. Three men whose red scribal caftans swept the floor appeared in the doorway of the only entrance to a further series of workrooms to the accompaniment of acrid smoke. They bowed as Numsenmur approached and the despot's bodyguards laid clumsy hands upon their garments to check for weapons. Two of the scribes were middle-aged and carried stacks of bound scrolls and glistening yellow sheaths. Numsenmur's gaze focused on one scribe in particular, a slim man whose face was creased and wrinkled like an eroded hill.

The king paid no attention to the other two scribes, who were mere assistants of Yezd. The older scribe, who had already risen to fame within the scribal school in his brief stay in Ven, drew Numsenmur's full attention.

"Well?" The king was even less patient than usual.

"There is nothing new. The work continues." The ancient voice croaked.

"Four weeks, Yezd. I have given you all that you requested. The entire scribal guild now serves your commands."

Yezd eyed the sullen bodyguards surrounding him. His hands clasped and unclasped.

"I have begun another gill, but there are difficulties. We work with inferior materials. We lack–"

"Corta?" Numsenmur squinted. "Yes, so you say, but there is corta in every irsrem weapon and plate in the city." The Serclasler pointed. "I've given you the best rations, I've paid you enormously for the other gills, I've given you all the slaves and scribes you requested."

"It is difficult. We need new ore. It cannot be denatured from existing irsrem."

The other scribes nodded agreement.

Numsenmur breathed deeply and dropped his fists to his sides. "Then find a substitute."

The old man opened his palms helplessly.

Sweat beaded on Numsenmur's face. "Can you not deliver just one more gill?"

"The stocks were used. However, if you could send a crew up the Falls to obtain more corta–"

The king gasped in exasperation. He turned and made to leave, then pointed again.

"One more, Yezd! And you will be rich. But if you fail...." One hand curled into a fist as if crushing some fragile object. For one moment Numsenmur lingered, then he strode from the workroom, exuding fear-tinged sweat, a half-dozen heavily armed and silent guards in tow.

For a long moment, Yezd made no move, but stared upon the floor with his one blue and one yellow eye while his colleagues conferred in whispers. He blinked and peered about, taking in the ceramic and iron appurtenances strewn on all sides of the ill-lit smoky chamber. Then he too turned and was swallowed by the sulfurous darkness of the workrooms' interior.

৽ ৪৹ ୪৪ ৵

Dos-Hutsutsem-Senelwat rocked slowly forward on his heels and looked cautiously to the left, then cautiously to the right. Like a pendulum he swung back and eyed his two companions, then rocked forward again to inspect the hallway. He turned and motioned to his two companions to follow.

Sendas wore leather pants and jerkin covering a common tunic. His feet were covered by the boots of a low-born attendant, which had been requisitioned for the evening by his master. Covering his head was a cap with projecting flaps which he held close.

The second man, though burdened with hidden accoutrements, was apparently slim, with clipped beard, uncertain glance, hand perpetually contacting the dagger at his side. One hirsute cheek often wrinkled with the distaste one might feel if forced to endure the perpetual company of boors.

Sendas and Ust stepped softly and sought to appear inconspicuous. Halting before a simple wooden door, Dos signaled them to enter and quietly shut the door behind them. The ex-ambassador completed an affectedly casual inspection of the empty room and returned his attention to his comrades as they removed their caps.

"Last chance, sirs." Dos searched the faces of both of them with his owl-like eyes. "Beyond here there is no going back."

"Back to what?" replied Ust. "The city falls, or starves. Either way, we go with it. We've sworn for ourselves, our clans, and our city. Even now the tyrant prepares his own escape, awaiting only our deaths to signal his departure."

"Without doubt," Sendas nodded. "I have lived to regret most years of my life, the years I carried our cause in the Assembly, frequently alone. Now, to think how I furthered this absurd man's career, put him upon his throne, as it were, as if I, or anyone, wished him to lord over our fair city in such an impertinent manner. You're correct, Sir Ust. We've sworn to undo the monarchy, to be disloyal to the Loyalists, to reduce the Triumvirate to atoms–its remaining atom, that is."

Dos arched an eyebrow and calmly queried them.

"Do you have your weapons?"

"Right here, Sir Dos." Sendas placed a hand within his shirt and came up empty. "A moment." He dug deeper. Ust produced two more daggers beside the one at his belt, one deep blue and a vicious eighteen inches of honed iron, the other razor-edged irsrem.

"He will enter first," continued Dos, "and leave all but two of his slave soldiers behind. We will have one opportunity as he walks in the door–just one. When we finish him, there will remain several more slaves in the hallway against the five of us. They won't matter. Since Numsenmur took me into his confidence, I've learned that no one in the palace would much regret his, shall we say, timely demise." Dos leaned toward them. "You would be surprised how communicative a man without a tongue can be."

Ust glanced at Sendas and blinked.

The Molersal searched more pockets. "Sir Ust, since terminating your employment in the palace–"

"And canceling the tax base of my house," interrupted Ust.

"–Numsenmur has varied his schedule," continued Dos. "He fears assassination everywhere. But near midnight, he always visits the workrooms to check on his scribe's progress, in fact almost precisely at midnight just before he retires. The king has placed extra guards in the anteroom and two in the workroom itself to keep his scribe from absconding."

Sendas removed his jerkin and placed it on a bench at his side, revealing a second leather jacket beneath the first. "Getting cold nights, you know," he explained. He removed a baldric and began to unroll a wide cummerbund.

Dos intoned, "The extra guards within the anteroom left in late evening, since these hours are the least busy on the estate. They will return in the early morning. Of those on duty now, the two in the anteroom will be relieved by you. The two in the workroom are already with us. They permitted the Turlicum to steal the king's property and were punished for their role. Without Numsenmur's knowledge, I transferred them back for tonight and have persuaded them to join us."

"I have it!" Sendas unwrapped the last of the cummerbund and shook loose a dainty instrument, presumably intended for paring nails, and far too small to harm anything unwilling to cooperate. "In the clan for generations," he explained. "Notice the gilt and silver work. Ordinarily, of course, I would never consider removing it from my estate, but for this occasion, being of such import to the city, a civic duty so to speak, I felt that here was the perfect occasion. 'Sendas,' I said to myself, 'here is an opportunity to do something for Holy Ven, a deed to live in song and epic for a century, and what better opportunity to use–' "

"Sendas!" Dos and Ust shook him by the arms.

"Here, take one from Ust," Dos said.

"One of mine?" said Ust, as Dos seized his longest blade and handed it to Sendas. "I really think it would be better if I am equipped as planned. I'm funny like that, the slightest difference in plan and–"

"If you insist," interrupted Sendas, accepting the blade. "Many thanks, Sir Ust."

Ust glared at Dos. "Most welcome, I'm sure."

While placing the dagger in his belt–which had underlain the cummerbund–Sendas seemed puzzled.

"Should we not have swords like the other guardsmen?"

Dos walked behind the bench and pulled two swords with scabbards from a roll of cloth. "These are for appearance. The room is too small for several to wield swords."

The ambassador peered deeply into their eyes, searching for traces of fear. "Gentlemen, there must be no mistakes. We will have but one chance. When he enters–we strike. All together."

"That is our motto," said Sendas. "All together."

"No turning back," whispered Ust.

"For Ven and Temple," intoned Dos. "And the end of tyranny."

"The monster's death and the people's rights!" added Sendas.

"For freedom and the liberties of Vensor-sa everywhere," hissed Ust.

"And," rejoined Dos in a hollow voice, "no matter how fiendishly he tortures us, or how long...no betrayal!"

"No betrayal!" echoed Sendas.

"Through blood and flames," Dos said, clasping their hands in his. "Through torture and the rack! Unity–till the deed is done."

"Till the deed is done!" repeated Sendas.

Ust eyed the door and swallowed.

Dos reconnoitered the hall again and Sendas and Ust donned their caps and buckled the swords to their belts. Dos returned and signaled.

The bright exterior of the palace of Numsenmur concealed a murky heart within, and no corridors or chambers were murkier than the pits through which the threesome now passed. Air weighed heavily and stagnant and was damp and smoky from flames and alcoved lamps permitted to burn too long and gutter. The Serclasler, as did his ancestors, had relegated the less pleasant tasks of his household to these regions, or those tasks which, for whatever reason, he wished to remain beyond the prying eyes of the uninitiated. Few people descended to these crooked halls at any time, and none without good reason. Dos hoped none had reason this night.

The ambassador carried a small lamp suspended on a chain to light the gloomier passageways and swung it from side to side as he walked, leading the others. He raised an arm and listened, then waved them forward again.

"I would prefer that you not be seen, despite your disguises," Dos said. "That is why I let you in by the side door. No one has seen you except from afar." He paused and turned his large bird eyes upon them. "It could be unpleasant if you were recognized."

Dos resumed his walk. "I was there when Numsenmur interrogated his jailers, the ones who lost Flores. At the time, Numsenmur believed they had been bought by his enemy. It was dreadful." Dos looked at his companions again. "They were Numsenmur's experts and knew the hideous possibilities and mortal consequences of their deed." Dos swung the lamp toward them so they felt the heat. "Bones and iron, gentlemen. Bones and iron."

Ust glanced behind and loosened his weapons one by one to ensure their quick availability.

They rounded several corners and passed into a particularly dark area.

"Halt!" hissed Dos.

Ust stumbled and dropped a dagger, and Sendas, thinking they were about to be attacked, snapped his rapier free and clattered the blade against the wall.

Dos calmed them. "I thought I had heard someone. It is nothing."

They breathed deeply and resumed walking.

Finally Ust and Dos indicated the door of the scribal workrooms to Sendas, and, as Ust and Sendas watched from the safety of an obscure corner, Dos approached to peer through the bars of the small window. The door suddenly opened and the Hutsutsem struggled to retain his composure as two men appeared with drawn blades. The ex-ambassador spoke rapidly.

"Good. Such vigilance! You have passed my test. The king shall learn what a fine job you are doing here in his pits. He shall learn from my own tongue that you deserve a promotion. And higher pay!"

The guardsmen stood straighter upon hearing this.

In the darkness Ust whispered, "I've been thinking, Sendas, perhaps this is not the best time to execute our plan."

As the guards re-entered the chamber, Dos summoned his companions from the shadows with a rapid covert motion.

"In fact," continued Ust, "while we stood here, another plan has come to mind. In this plan, you see, we–" Sendas adjusted his scabbard, drew his sword, and with raised chin, marched to do his duty. Ust caught his breath, swore and hurried after. Sendas had just returned his blade to its sheath when Dos and the guards emerged and stopped in front of the door. As the nobles approached, the sentinels peered, their gaze passing from head to foot.

"Your replacements," informed Dos. "Newly hired and enjoying the king's full confidence."

"If you ask me," grumbled one of the guards, "his full table too." He glared at the newcomers.

Dos turned his owl-eyes full upon the two guards. "Would you care to repeat yourselves, sirs," he asked, "in a voice loud enough that the king may hear?"

Their faces lost some color.

"Meant nothin' by it."

"Good. Depart."

The speaker tapped his friend's shoulder and they walked away. One glanced back. "Too well fed–if you ask me."

After Sendas and Ust entered the anteroom, Dos closed the door behind them and crossed to the far side. He tapped twice on a second door. Two common soldiers stepped from the dimly lit interior of the scribes' workrooms, a sharp smell of sulfur accompanying them. Both were garbed in attire similar to that of Sendas and Ust.

"You said you would be here an hour ago." The man spoke with ill-concealed suspicion, his hand resting on sword helve. "It's almost midnight." The two regarded Dos with an habitual wariness of those of superior rank. "Who are they?"

"The less you know, Usud, the better. Close the inner door."

The two hesitated, then obeyed.

"Now lock it. Good. We want no interruptions."

The other guard spoke. "Where is it?" His eyes searched the newcomers for evidence of something unseen. "Sire," he added respectfully.

Dos looked briefly at Ust without expression, then withdrew a small package from under his robe and unwrapped it.

"Fresh lyart!" The two famished men fell upon the meat and speedily devoured it, only hesitating to unsling a skin of wine that Usud had cleverly positioned behind him while speaking with Dos.

"Drink, Smil?" he offered to his comrade, somehow smiling with a mouth gorged with flesh.

"Love to." Smil directed the stream in happy disregard of the disapproving glare of Dos. Usud snapped a finger and held out a palm. Dos produced a sack of coins and deposited them. He glanced at the other nobles and explained, "Sometimes love of country coincides with love of money."

While they ate Dos organized the plotters. "We haven't much time. Finish and go to the table." Smil and Usud moved without pausing in their feast and sat upon the small table used for receiving minor functionaries.

"Now, Ust," Dos said, "the right side. Sendas, the left. Good! Perhaps we should douse a lamp to increase the gloom?"

"Yes, good idea," said Ust. "Then I can get him from the dark. By surprise." Ust grinned his dagger disemboweling an imaginary enemy.

Usud shook his head. "Will arouse his suspicion," he mumbled.

Dos nodded. "Of course. Keep both lit. The flames are low enough for our purpose and the corners are dark." Ust swallowed. He stood by the door, hugging the wall, and involuntarily began to slide deeper into the gloom.

The conspirators waited. Sendas drew his sword again and cut the air. He removed his cap, and with nothing better to do, draped it over his sword's tip and raised it aloft where it became tangled in sooty cobwebs.

"Where is the scribe Yezd?" Dos asked Smil and Usud.

"In the farthest chamber, working alone as he has for days." Smil finished and wiped his mouth on a sleeve.

"He's a weird one for you," volunteered Usud. "Always burning and mixing, reading scrolls and breaking canes over the backs of other scribes." He looked to Smil for affirmation. "We stay as far away from him as we can."

"Oh, yes," he nodded. "As far as we can without deserting our posts and being whipped." He stopped talking and absently ran his hand up one side as if to massage recently acquired scars. Both guards grew quiet and the room darkened before the weakly flickering lamps.

Dos hissed. "Listen!"

The others looked at each other, then sprang to alertness. All watched the narrow barred window for a silhouette or approaching shadow and Dos moved away from the window's line of sight into the room. He slunk to the aperture and cautiously peered out to survey the long, poorly lit corridor.

He shook his head. "Nothing." He turned and crossed the room and began to unlock the inner door.

"By the way, Sir Dos," said Sendas. "Where is your dagger?"

The noble turned his round eyes on him in surprise. "My dagger?"

"Yes. You said yourself that a dagger is better than a sword. Where is yours?"

"Dear Sendas, I thought it was understood. I will be the reserve. Should one of you fall into trouble, I will be there to back you up. I'll be recognized–I'm not in the guise of common ruffians like you and these guards. Better if I wait in the workroom." He turned again.

"Not for one moment," called Ust, drawing his sword half out of its scabbard.

"Indeed, Sir Dos." Sendas let his cap fall. "To think such a thing."

"Look now, sir," said Usud, feeling every inch the ruffian, but resentful of Dos' comment just the same, "Smil and I don't like people who leave their dying to others." Smil nodded and carefully laid a poniard on the table for emphasis.

"However, on further reflection, a reserve is most useful just behind the front line."

"*In* the front line," corrected Ust.

"*In* the front line," echoed Dos, re-locking the workroom door.

Usud opened a tall cabinet and handed a long wooden pike with a artistically fused irsrem blade to Dos, who accepted it with reluctance, and took up a position behind Sendas, where the butt of his spear knocked against the far wall. The menacing complex of spurs and blade aimed directly at the midriff of Ust, who did not fail to apprehend its potential. Dos' face had resumed its usual imperturbability. He whistled softly as he inspected the ceiling.

"Here," hissed Smil. "Something is happening in the hallway." He stepped to the window and peered.

"It's past midnight," said Ust. "He's late."

Smil watched and listened while the others braced for an attack from unseen hordes. "There, that is what I saw. A lamp went out."

The others relaxed.

"A lamp?" Sendas scratched his neck. "Does that happen often?"

Usud sat heavily in the chair behind the table and swigged wine. Smil shrugged his shoulders. The others breathed more easily.

Dos said, "Wait...that's what I heard before. Someone dropping a lamp."

The others looked at each other.

"There," said Smil, still gazing through the window. "Another lamp went out."

Usud ran to the door and peered, and rubbed his chin.

Ust bared a dagger. "He's late, I tell you! Why?" He sheathed it again, and drew his sword.

"And another," Smil hissed. He turned and began searching for an escape route.

"He's overdue," said Usud. "He's never been this late."

"But why?" Ust flattened himself against the wall, then slowly peeked through the window on the gradually darkening corridor. He pulled away while Sendas and Dos looked through.

"Soon," observed Sendas, "we will not be able to see the corridor at all."

"But someone in the corridor could still see us," said Dos.

Ust clapped a hand to his mouth.

Usud collapsed into the seat and stared at the floor. "It's *him*." He shook his head. "He plays with us. We're found out!"

Smil buried his face in his arms. He burst into sobs.

The pike in Dos' hands wobbled and Sendas and Ust each watched the morale collapse in the face of the other.

"Tonight, of all nights of my life." Usud pulled the stopper of the wine skin entirely off and proceeded to drain it.

"Listen!" hissed Sendas.

All remained still and heard quite clearly two sounds alternating in the corridor some distance beyond the door: a muffled thump as from a giant war club beating rhythmically upon an unprotected skull, each thump followed by a clashing and scraping of metal on metal as might the iron sword of assassins when approaching their prey through darkness, sometimes followed by a long metallic scrape. The scrape would be followed by a moment's pause before the club beat again.

The sound grew louder, then stopped. For a moment silence reigned, then the scraping rang with twice its previous volume in a veritable din of noise.

Smil leaped and stared out the window, his face filling the opening and tears running down his neck. "The last lamp is out!" He backed away from the door and tore his hair.

Ust hopped from one leg to the other, taking deep breaths, spreading his arms wide with each inhalation. He halted, puffed, then began hopping again.

The hollow thump resumed and grew louder.

"It's the rack for us!"

Usud beat his fists upon the table.

Sendas tried to groan, but choked; he prayed and drew his dagger.

Dos spread his arms heavenward and began a complex series of manual religious affirmations.

Smil rose to his feet. Possessed of a fresh reserve of courage he calmly pointed an accusing finger at Usud. "Traitor!" he shouted. "This was your idea!" He called toward the door, "Hurry, before he escapes! A traitor to the king! His name is Usud!" He cupped his hands to bellow louder while Usud, pale as death, unbuckled his scabbard and sword and slid them across the floor toward Smil.

Sendas fell back against the wall and slowly turned the dagger toward his own chest, sweat flowing down his prayer-muttering cheeks; Ust howled and flew higher with each bound.

"It's Numsenmur's slave-soldiers come for blood," boomed Dos, "their mute war-cry more terrible than any voice!"

"Divine Vensor, just this once!" screamed Ust.

"I'm coming, Father!" yelled Sendas.

"It wasn't my idea!" shrieked Dos. He pointed to Sendas and Ust. "They forced me! Blackmail!" Dos picked up the spear. "I'll help you, my king. Leave them to me!"

Sendas collapsed as Dos rushed past, pole in hand. The epicurean spoiled the ambassador's aim by inadvertently falling across the handle and forcing the blade down, where it lodged in the far wall.

"He made a pact with Nesos," shouted Sendas, transferring his grip to Dos' legs. "He went to Neset and joined with Flores!" Dos pitched heavily to the floor and Ust began jumping upon both him and Sendas.

"Traitors! Thieves!" yelled Ust. "They've stolen the king's property! Help!"

Smil and Usud tumbled about, pummeling each other.

The door to the corridor opened.

Snivet stood framed beneath the lintel, his beady eyes wide with shock. A worn crutch propped his right shoulder and both hands clutched a wide copper cauldron filled with still hot lamps from the corridor's alcoves. He thumped his crutch, took one step and shook the metallic lamps, then clumsily spun the cauldron producing a raucous scraping sound.

"Someone give me a light," he whimpered. "I can't find the stairway."

At that moment, the door to the workroom exploded in a sheet of flame and smoke. The crumpled door fell flat and Sendas, Ust, Dos and the others beheld a towering figure in red cassock. His face was a mass of bags, tubes, and cups as he emerged from the sulfurous interior of the magician's lair. Each hand glowed with flame as the figure advanced.

Dos and Sendas regained their feet with the agility of athletes and began a competitive scramble for the outer door. With surprising strength Ust lifted Dos entirely off his feet and swung him round to face the onrushing demon. Sendas caught Ust by one arm, and when Smil and Usud attempted to pass, all three thrust them down. Snivet managed a single step before the onrushing mob fell upon him like an avalanche, flinging copper lamps about and breaking his crutch.

Behind them, the crimson nemesis strode confidently forward, pausing every few steps to toss its flame upon the floor with vigor. Each bomb produced a bright flash and a gush of white smoke. Usud and Smil, enveloped by the fumes, faltered and clutched their throats. They fell and lay still. As the Simet-sa of Ven vanished in the direction of the distant postern leading off of Numsenmur's estate, Yezd took his own course and vanished up a winding staircase.

⤳ ೞ ೪ ⤶

CHAPTER 20

TUMSET

The storm passed. Flores and his companions awoke and re-entered the room where they had dined the previous evening. Their host did not reappear, nor was he in any of the adjoining rooms. They waited. After a time they began to call, then searched the many chambers and corridors of the ancient chateau. Evening returned, and the travelers ate and slept and once more awoke and still Macius had not returned. Concluding that he had departed the estate, which was unsurprising knowing as they did of his long confinement, but with deep regret that their affable host had decided not to accompany them on the remainder of their journey, the four travelers re-strung the saddles on their revenna, packed the remaining foodstuffs, and resumed their journey to Nasvetin.

Flores still wanted to make for that city, not because he knew that succor awaited him there–no more than a chance remained that his retinue had survived–but because until such time as Ven might again be free and independent, the Turlicum had no place else to go. Having once been famous, he reflected, he could expect to be no less notorious. Upon exiting the castle, the travelers turned north, circumventing the ramparts of the keep, and soon exited the bluff-enclosed valley. Around them the quiet hills expanded, the sky shone clear and warm, and the meadows kept the forest at bay so that for several days their progress was quick and effortless.

Amina seemed to blossom as the spring progressed. Ensconced behind Flores on his reven, the growing warmth soon induced her to open her robe more than before so that the others at times glimpsed bared limbs or curving breasts. She often smiled or laughed in fresh innocence at everyday events like the passing of a butterfly or the arrival of a cloud. Though they conversed but little, Flores was never to be found far from Amina during this time, and, when not mounted on his reven before her, the Simet noble hovered constantly in her presence like a moon about its planet. And when dismounted, he would perform the most menial of tasks for her comfort with apparent spontaneity, surprising himself by his behavior as much as Tilsis and Crestal.

He could offer no explanation. At times, especially when the thought uneasily surfaced that Amina was after all a gila and that he, Flores, was committing the crime of feminality with each night that passed, he would shudder and direct his thoughts to take refuge in the memory of the debt that he owed her and would tell himself that she was not just a gila, but a special one, a gila of warmth and beauty, motivated by wellsprings of altruism, a gila who had once saved his life, and that Amina, *his* Amina, could not be what the nimble-tongued sages and unctuous eunuchs had slanderously proclaimed.

She, and perhaps other gila-sa as well, were not the enemy of Mankind, Flores thought. No, his lips would say, his eyes gazing upon her yellow-sun abdomen as she knelt or walked or smiled. This dark-haired, dusky-limbed mirage that inflamed his days and nights could not serve the interests of Atasan, the Fomenter of Evil, the eternally ungrateful child of Vensor. Then Amina would rise and wander, and the Lord of the Turlicum, watching her every move askance, would quickly, nervously follow.

On occasion, while Flores' attention was elsewhere, Amina would wander beyond his view, and the Turlicum, heir to generations of haughty pride and leadership, would suddenly frown and his eyes flash. Hurrying from trunk to trunk, from clearing to clearing, he would search and peer until he had once again found her. But their rendezvouses would entail no deep sighs of relief or passionate embraces–only a resumption of Flores' perpetual nervous hovering. But Amina would always turn and laugh and sometimes throw her arms about his neck and invite him to kiss her. Amina smiled constantly upon him during these days, beckoning, laughing, and when the darksome velvet night arrived and the fire burned low, the priestess from the dark Temple of Vensa, the gila-woman of Atasan, did nothing to deter his ever more passionate, ever more insistent advances.

The others showed little interest in their affair. Used to ignoring the affairs of nobles, Tilsis remained devoted to his master Crestal, in a platonic relationship long established. The youth at times would laugh with the others, but it gradually became apparent that a subtle tension had grown between Crestal and the others since their first days in the forest. Crestal did not blossom as did Amina, and would at times withdraw wholly within himself for long periods, saying nothing to the others nor responding even to the accustomed signals from Tilsis. Neither did he gain weight as did the men, seeming as arrested in his physical development as in his affections. Remaining closely attached to his bulky eunuch's clothing, the youth continued to disrobe and bathe far from the gazes of Flores and Amina and under the protective guard of his devoted and vigilant servant, a procedure which all came to accept without comment.

In their trek to Nasvetin the band had gone too far north and decided that they must head southeast in order to circumvent the mountains that grew and took on detail with each day of travel. The countryside again became thick and forested and began to grow less rocky. Pools and streams appeared, then a wide river. For a time they followed its bank, skirting a dense jungle of verdant growth that paralleled its northern shore, before the riders were forced back into the deeper forest by the intercession of a lofty ridge, the last southern spur of the ranges to the north.

Arriving at a gradual embankment that seemed to lead to a crevice that could serve as a pass over the summit, the riders directed their mounts up the slope and found themselves on the cusp of the ridge. One side of the cliff continued to rise in the direction of the river, high and impassable, while the further side lay outspread, nothing impeding their view of the wooded country beyond but a few bushes and trees that sprang improbably from the barren clefts about them.

Each saw the clearing at the same time.

A steep slope dotted with bosky outgrowths ran down to join a level stretch of ground relatively free of the interminable forest that had obscured so much of their journey. To their right the wide, sluggish river flowed around the cliff's base in an easterly direction, thick copses standing on its bank. These copses for the most part had been felled to form a large artificial clearing in the forest. On their left a path exited the forest-wall and entered this clearing, now overgrown with brush and undergrowth, to arrive at the face of the cliff, where visible below their right, a half-moon portal of opaque irsrem glinted darkly in the cliff shade. The gate was of such proportion, and the surrounding cliff-face so naked of any habitation or civilized dwelling, that the surprised travelers instinctively recoiled and returned to stare from behind the ridge-trees. Immediately to their left, amid a clatter of vitreous armature and irsrem pikes, the forest emitted a clutch of reven-na mounted by a score of well-armed warriors.

Flores recognized the upward curving shoulder armor of the city of Tumset, one of the more distant Vensor cities and fiercely independent, having defeated a Ven army in the distant past, and having resisted all efforts of Ven to establish peaceful relations since, preferring to foment rebellion in Ven's northern provinces. The Turlicum had only a moment to inspect the passing soldiery as his attention was immediately drawn to the main body of the expedition, which followed close upon the soldiers and the reven-na.

First came a litter of wooden panels, sealed shut with strips of thin copper nailed about the edges of the box and carried on the shoulders of eight muscular slaves. Two men whose chests were bare except for crossed leather belts walked alongside the litter, trailing whips tiredly in the dust. Next came several wains hauled by small lyarts and piled high with cloth and barrels. Following these, a lengthy procession of prisoners trudged into view, exiting the forest in a single file and moving slowly across the clearing. These apparently had marched a considerable distance, as attested by their haggard and listless condition, and obvious need for food, drink, and rest. Their condition did not surprise the observers ensconced on the ridge. Slavery, after all, was part of the natural order of things, having been long decreed by Vensor for the less able in life. But even slaves were children of Vensor and could not be punished with complete impunity. So, in reaction to the scene that unfolded below, Flores felt outrage rise within, now, upon his return to civilization, even as he had felt outrage upon his departure from Ven the many weeks before.

The lead prisoners of the queue, the members of which were linked neck to neck by a continuous chain of irsrem, stumbled and fell, causing the prisoners behind to lurch and stumble as well. The procession came suddenly to a halt. The leader of the expedition, his armor bright with gold and silver filigree, turned his reven at the onset of the disturbance and spurred his mount past the train of wagons and the litter to where the slaves had fallen in the scurf. His features were clearly visible to the spies on the ridge. They seemed the features of a Simet noble of quality and training, the nose prominent and aquiline. The lips were thin and pursed, but responded easily to his mood, as if governed not by the head but by the heart. His head was bare, his hair pale and light as if bleached by the suns. His cheeks and chin were shaven, but his locks long uncut, the strands having been braided and permitted to dangle across his broad back.

By the leader's side rode another brightly clad officer of similar appearance, so similar in fact that he could have been a twin of the first. His reven loped in time with the other beast, braid dangling, the same metalwork shining in the suns.

A bellowing sounded from amidst the disordered queue. Turning his eye to the center of the procession, Flores' gaze lit upon a bright sparkle that seemed to rise and fall with the howling, visiting each slave in turn and leaving flicks of red where it touched. An upraised hand swung the cruel whip with its metal tip once more and the prisoners, clad only in grimy skirts, moaned and began to rise to their feet with a great shuffling.

At first Flores could not see the agent of the commotion. Slave drivers with whips flanked the queue, but their whips hung by their sides unused, themselves drawn by the tumult to stare. Then the crush cleared and among the prostrate slaves appeared a figure whose knotted forearm rose to unleash the punishment again. Flores noted the studded leather bandoleers of a professional slave-driver, observed the casual indifference of a man long inured to the sufferings of his profession. The driver was abnormally short, which explained why Flores had not seen him before. He was not so short that Flores would have thought him a dwarf, but the slave-driver's frame bore just hint enough of dwarfism as to bring his lesser height to the notice of observers, but perhaps without gaining the human understanding or pity that a more extreme deficiency might have evoked. His curtailed height seemed to have detracted nothing from his sinews, however, which should have clothed a frame of much larger proportions. The legs were knotted to match the arms, and the man's back was of such width that he seemed at times to be more mineral than flesh, as if a stalagmite had developed some means of shambling about the countryside.

Unlike the Tumset officer who now rapidly approached, the features of the slave-driver in no way matched his torso and limbs. Whereas the other slavers wore their hair long, often accompanied by thick moustaches, the slave master's hair was short in the style of Ven, and his ears much larger than usual, which lent a diabolic aspect to his appearance, joined as they were to the cramped body and clean-shaven face.

The peculiarly sinister appearance of the man was not relieved by the indifference of his expression, and his actions soon confirmed Flores' initial impression. Floggings were common enough among Vensor-sa, and excess in their implementation frequent. But the sight of the fist gripping the handle of the whip, rising to apply the metal-tipped lash once more, and needlessly since the sight of the raised whip alone was sufficient to impel the slaves to stand and begin to shuffle forward, caused a purple hue to flush across Flores' neck and face.

"Malag!" The two officers reined in their reven-na beside the slaver. "There is no need of that," said the first officer. "They now move. We have arrived at the river. A few more steps and we may all rest."

The grimy forearm slowly lowered as the slave-driver turned his leaf-flanked head to stare upward at the gold-encrusted soldiers.

"Your concern is strange, Sir Tem," said the slaver. "Are these slaves or honored guests?"

"I remind you again, Malag, that these men are not merely slaves, but former soldiers of Tumset. They may be accused of slackness and hence sold into servitude, but so long as they remain in my care and on the territory of Tumset–"

"Only the forest belongs to your king now, Sir Tem," interrupted Malag. "By order of your king this clearing belongs now to my master."

"That is so. But while they remain in my care, which they shall until the payment that your master has promised my king is in my possession," Tem's voice rose, "you will treat them with more respect than is usual for those in your trade."

Mild surprise settled on the slave-driver's features as he glanced over the ragged procession and its connecting irsrem chain. He permitted himself a grin and with his whip touched the chain that joined the slaves.

"Respect?" he repeated to himself mockingly. The slaver dropped the whip to his side and smiled, revealing a row of healthy teeth. Flores wondered whether the driver's repulsive exterior might hide other overlooked qualities, then shook his head. What did it matter? He had learned enough to realize what the travelers had stumbled upon–a secret, illegal slave trade by citizens of Ven with Ven's enemy to the north, Tumset. Probably for the mines of Maanus to dig corta, he supposed. But why pursue a slave trade in this lonely, distant outpost, when slaves were plentiful throughout the empire and more easily secured from other sources?

On the path below, Malag lowered his head as if furling a flag and motioned the other slavers to commence walking toward the cliff, where the green and red-flecked gate had begun to sink into the face of the barren cliff. The driver glanced at the captives. Their eyes remained fixed resignedly upon the ground. His whip snapped in the air and the caravan lurched forward and spilled into the clearing.

During this exchange, the second officer had sat atop his reven at the side of the expedition's leader. His gaze rested mostly upon Tem, and seemed to express a tangle of emotion centered on some obscure but intense dissatisfaction. At the crack of Malag's whip, he turned his gaze suddenly upon the slave-driver and shouted venomously. "Loose your whip once more, slaver, and I shall personally cut the hand that holds it from your arm! It is a scandal that scum like you should be permitted to accompany Tumset soldiers, and a greater scandal that your master should be allowed to possess Tumset land, much less to trade in Tumset slaves." The captain's hand clasped his sword's helve as Malag took in his breath and glanced surreptitiously at the other slavers. Several stepped forward, expressions of confusion and outrage upon their faces, but Malag said nothing.

Instead he forced a smile and dropped his gaze. "As you wish. You know that you have only to state your desire, and I shall fulfill it as best I can."

Pan jerked the reins of his reven and spun about. With a leap he came even with his superior, Tem. Emotion caused Pan's voice to carry further than he had intended, and again Flores and his companions heard the exchange.

"This slaver has disgraced us throughout the journey, Tem. Why do you allow it?"

Subtle movements among the warriors drew Flores' gaze momentarily. The warriors glanced at each other as if each shared the same concern.

"It was not my decision, as you are well aware. Our instructions were to sell the captives to Malag, not to inquire as to Malag's further purposes."

Pan swore. "A scandal. We should have whipped this insolent fellow when first we met and sent him and his men on their way. To think that we allow such to occupy Tumset land. If I were in your place I would put more value on loyalty to kin–"

Tem jerked his reven to a halt. "But you are not in my place! And until you are, I thank you not to speculate–or give advice where it is not requested. We act under the direct orders of the king of his guild master. And while I am in command there will be no dissension in my ranks, or words from my second officer." Tem paused to see that his words had had their intended effect. Then he spurred his mount forward. A few moments later he halted his reven and turned. "Come to my tent this evening, Pan. I shall have instructions for you. We can discuss them together." Tem slapped the side of the reven and rode across the clearing, dismounting by a large flat wain, where soldiers had begun to unload canvas and stakes in preparation of erecting several tents. At a distance of five hundred feet, the dark gate continued to open, silently and with monotonous slowness. The slaves staggered to the riverbank where they collapsed into the water and quenched their thirst alongside the reven-na, the animals hissing and rolling in the muddied water as their tenders sought to restrain them with hooks. Ignoring their charges, the slavers, excepting only Malag and a few personal attendants, passed through the gate into the cliff and vanished into darkness. Several minutes passed and the heavy portals slowly shut behind them.

Soon a dozen tents, dyed grey and brown, were pitched beneath the suns. Flores and the other travelers turned to leave. Crestal had already retreated some distance down the slope, having departed at the first sign of the warriors and their cargo. Then Flores signaled the others to wait a moment longer. In the clearing below his vantage point, the sealed litter was again lifted and carried by its bearers to the entrance of the largest tent, which had been pitched in the center of the clearing. A score of brawny arms bore the mysterious ark within. Malag and his attendants followed. Flores furrowed his brows and turned to view the sky. Approaching the western horizon, the twin orbs of Vensor threw a dense pall over the cliff-shrouded grove, still alive with movement as soldiers piled brush and thorn bushes about the clearing to form a makeshift stockade. Others took up positions at the entrance to the central tent. Like bloodstones, their starry helmets glinted feebly in the dying rays of the suns as Atasan prepared to claim his due, and the habitants of Maalstrom again awaited the untender mercies of the eternal Adversary of Men.

With care to prevent a spare noise alerting the soldiers to their presence, the wanderers withdrew behind the shelter of the ridge, descended the slope, and re-entered the forest at its foot. Penetrating some distance to ensure that the light from their fire would not announce their presence to those in the compound, they halted their mounts in a small clearing masked by a canopy of trees and prepared to bed for the night.

Flores let Amina slide to the ground, then himself dismounted. Tilsis soon lit a fire, feeding the flames with dry sticks while Crestal gathered grasses for a bed. The youth seemed even more morose than usual and once buried his face in Tilsis' chest. The pair soon drifted off to sleep, lying together on the side of the fire opposite Flores and Amina. Despite the exertions of the day and Flores' continuing obsession with the course of events in Ven, he again possessed what he had begun to regard as his privilege and right, lying with Amina and tasting those wan and contented lips of lustrous ebony. Afterward, he collapsed into a sleep at once moribund and restless, images of Ven inextricably entangled with the Temple and the enigma that had come into his life.

The night wore on and the fire burned low and the wood grew still as a pool in a mountain glen. Overhead a small patch of sky, outlined by drifting leaves, revealed a sprinkle of stars composed as if in some occult design, symmetrical but meaningless except to those with the key to knowledge. Had there been eyes to see, they would have glimpsed a red-rimmed moon emerge slowly from the forest and from its pitted and fiery surface primeval rays cross the intervening waste to arrive finally at the clearing, as if drawn to their imprisoned kin now reduced to barren ashes among cold stones. A chest began to heave more deeply, a pair of eyes opened to glimpse the last sliver of sinopia as the satellite vanished in the foliage. The figure rose, gazed briefly at the sleeping forms, then stepped silently into the forest.

Minutes passed. Walking with exaggerated caution, now halting to listen, now hurrying to overtake a swiftly moving object, the figure moved with definite if unobvious intent. The trees streamed past and suddenly the ground rose in a gradient, sloping rapidly upward to a barren ridge sheltered by stunted trees and flanked by a towering cliff. Gaining the summit of the ridge, the figure surveyed the Tumset soldiers' compound. Torches marked a path through the thorn-bushes and tents; more flames flickered by the larger tent in the center. Soldiers nodded sleepily at their posts. Shadows suggested other sentinels among the reven-na and the slaves.

Crestal blinked away tears, and fingered the blade of a dagger. He glanced backwards, stepped onto the far slope, then slid to the grove at the foot of the far side. Once in the grove, the youth pulled his ever-present robe above his knees, and crouched behind a shrub. Drawing his dagger, he peered into the darker patches around the outskirts of the compound.

A short distance away, a shadow emerged. Crestal caught his breath.

Striding without pause into the light of the torches as the sentinels shouted in sudden alarm and drew their weapons, was the priestess Amina of the Temple of Ven, a calm smile exuding confidence and serenity.

Warriors rushed to the camp's entrance. The soldiers' rapiers and pikes soon surrounded the priestess and she halted, arms forward with palms up, still smiling, but now with quiet patience, her yellow-sun abdomen rent fully in two to expose her nude body in its entirety. The warriors' expressions changed from alarm to curiosity. A moment later the weapons were lowered and the youth's jaw opened in surprise as several warriors closed about their charge and escorted Amina into the compound. The flaps of the large tent parted and she disappeared within.

The camp quieted and the soldiers returned to their stations. Patiently Crestal waited. Finally, with tears now firmly suppressed, he crept forward, circumventing the torches and the guards, until he penetrated the encampment and found himself between a shrub and a grey wain. His eyes remained fixed on the large tent at the center of the camp and the soldiers by its entrance. What had induced Amina to come? What plan was being laid by the priestess and her new friends, who were known enemies of Ven? If he could approach that tent, hear what was said, he might learn, might save his friends from a similar plot that had crossed his path once before. Behind the tent, Crestal detected a patch of darkness. Crestal stepped to the edge of the clearing.

Someone moaned–the youth paused to stare across the clearing. There, alive with torchlight, stood a strongly muscled man with smooth pate and bulging bicep. Slowly the bicep slackened, allowing the victim in his grasp to moan, then the arm re-closed about the man's windpipe and something cracked. Tilsis let the corpse drop. Crestal raised a hand and their eyes met.

"Intruder!" A Tumset warrior materialized directly in front of the youth. Still rubbing the sleep from his eyes, the warrior pointed to Tilsis and the body at his feet. "Invader! He has killed a guard!" The soldier suddenly grew silent, puzzled by the liquid running down his arm. The dagger struck again and his jugular exploded gore. The warrior collapsed. With knees shaking, Crestal gazed upon the wet dagger in his fist as if upon a disembodied ghost. The weeks in the wild had had their effect after all.

Tilsis gestured to the youth. Back! While there is still time! About him the enemy spilled from every tent, and, as Crestal made no move, the servant stepped into full view of the sprouting torches, and drew to him the eyes of every soldier.

CHAPTER 21

THE ENIGMA

"One thousand golden mir! A wondrous payment that even your wealthy masters should welcome."

Malag allowed his lips to settle in what he believed to be a smile, but their unfamiliarity with that expression permitted only a smirk to form.

"Such was the agreed upon price." Tem gestured to one corner of the tent.

Malag nodded, and his slavers crossed the interior of the canvas chamber to stack bags of gold upon the carpeted ground.

Tem sniffed. "There is no call to be appreciative. A contract is a contract. And your masters are no less wealthy than mine."

Malag ceased his vain attempts to lighten the mood. He turned and snapped his fingers to hurry his men.

"There is still your part...." The leaf-adorned head bent to eye the Tumset chief more keenly as if alert to the possibility that a contract was not a contract until completed.

The chief rose from his stool and pulled aside a tent flap to reveal an adjoining cloister. Within the other chamber stood the gilt palanquin, flanked by eight Tumset slaves. Lifting the palanquin by parallel bars, the slaves bore it within the first chamber, still sealed, still silent. They placed their burden at the feet of Malag. Lowering it slowly and with care, they withdrew.

Malag approached the litter. He ran his fingers around the hammered copper edges, his practiced eye inspecting every nail. For several moments one enormous ear was pressed to the upper surface of the box. Malag frowned. Finally he straightened and again traced the outlines of the litter with his fingers. He seemed satisfied.

"It has not been opened. That is good. As you know, my masters insist that their cargo not be exposed or molested in any way." The slavers surrounded the litter, took hold of the bars, and hoisted it upon their shoulders. Malag turned and bowed his head. The smirk returned, his manner betrayed by ill-felt intent.

"One moment, slaver."

Malag paused as his slavers exited with the palanquin. A look of confusion and apprehension stole over the slave-driver's visage.

"Yes, sire?"

Pan spoke. "For weeks we have carried that palanquin across the barren wilds at great effort and cost to please you and your masters, and still we do not know what it contains. I wish to know. It seems a very plain box, and since it has been opened only briefly and always in your presence, it seems that you alone know its contents. It cannot contain a living creature, as no animal would suffer such treatment in silence. Yet it bears openings for air to enter. What did we escort, slaver? What do your masters value so highly that they should pay our king such sums for its safe passage?"

Malag gave a genuine, mirthful smile, but said nothing.

Pan continued. "All my kin, the prisoners whom we shall so disgracefully turn over to you in the morning, are not worth but a fraction of the sum that you have paid tonight. What interests your masters so that they are willing to part with such a fortune? And I have learned that this is not the first such litter my king has delivered to this fortress."

Malag's eyes sparkled. "True, good sir," he hissed in his most sarcastic tone, "no animal would suffer such treatment—at least any animal you would be familiar with. But then animals have not the power of reason, nor the capacity to suspend their natural desires for the sake of further gain. The well-trained and the well-motivated are worth their weight in gold, as any employer dependent on talent and discretion well knows."

"Enough, Pan," interrupted Tem. "Off with you, Malag, and your box. I have seen all I wish of it. I do not wish to lay eyes on it again. It has been a heavy charge and an annoyance and what it may contain interests me not at all."

The slaver opened his mouth as if to speak, but he decided to remain quiet. He swung his foliage-like appendages and took a step toward the entrance. He halted as the flaps drew aside. Two Tumset warriors entered on either side of an enigma that wore the yellow sign of Vensor splashed across an ocher robe.

Malag retreated and stared, eyes narrowing to a slit. The warriors directed the newcomer to stand in the center of the tent. It silently obeyed, gaze averted, delicate hands modestly clasped.

The Tumset chief sat up, his brows rising in curiosity. "What is this?" he asked.

One of the guards approached. "He entered the camp, sire. Lost apparently. Saw the fires. Says he needs food and water. We searched him. Um...he is–" The guard glanced at his charge, "–unarmed."

Tem fell silent. Pan too stared, deep in thought.

"What an odd looking creature..." Tem pointed for the benefit of Pan. "Have him turn for me."

The guard looked at the newcomer and drew his forearm in a circle. "Turn for the captain."

The figure turned, sedately, eyes on the carpet beneath its feet.

"What do you make of him, Pan?"

Tem's second glanced at his superior, surprised out of his reverie. "Humph. He is no warrior."

"No, but pleasing. And I'll wager he knows his business–and that a priest taught him."

Pan sneered and returned his careful gaze to their guest.

"Now without the robe," said Tem.

The guard approached his charge and carefully but firmly removed the cloth and let it fall to the carpet.

At sight of their guest freed of the cumbersome garment, Pan frowned in deeper contemplation. Tem's brows climbed higher on his forehead. Someone noisily inhaled.

"Again," said Tem. "Turn, I say." The captain rested his jaw upon one palm as if contemplating a mathematical theorem while his guest joined its hands together again in a feeble attempt to preserve some semblance of modesty. It slowly turned, eyes still averted.

"No, no," added Pan. "Lift your hands, like so. I wish to see."

Upon viewing the anatomy of their guest without obstruction, Pan turned his gaze upon his commander, who returned his stare with equal incomprehension.

Tem shrugged. "Poor child is deformed. Feed and clothe him, and let him rest. Then I shall interrogate him and learn where he hails from."

Again someone inhaled sharply and a voice hissed. "What do you mean by this, Tumset?" Malag stepped forward. He halted beside the newcomer. "What is the meaning of this outrage?"

Tem and Pan stared at Malag, puzzled in turn by the slaver's behavior. Malag laid one vise-like hand upon the creature's arm and yanked so that the newcomer fell to its knees. The slaver glanced around the tent as if searching for something.

"How do you happen to be here?" he shouted. "Did you take it upon yourself to do this, or were you tricked by these Tumset thieves into thus exposing yourself? Either way, you will return with me and you will pay for this indiscretion with much pain!"

A sign from the Tumset chief and the two guards who had brought the newcomer grasped Malag's arms and forced the slaver to the ground, pinning him beneath their knees.

Tem cleared his throat. "I don't know what has angered you so, Malag, but it does not please me to see my guest treated in such a way. Tem stood. "Pan, take our guest into the other tent."

Pan escorted the newcomer into an adjoining chamber, then returned.

"Guest?" spat Malag. He struggled and the two guards dug their knees deeper into his back, making no effort to restrain their pleasure at doing so. "My masters...have paid...you promised me...the palanquin!"

"The palanquin? Whatever has that to do with this poor deformed creature stumbling about in the night?"

Malag sputtered and Tem signaled for his men to release him. The slaver stood and brushed himself, his face a bright crimson. "You promised to deliver the palanquin to my masters!"

"What do you mean, Malag? We delivered it but moments ago. You yourself inspected it and your men carried it away. The palanquin must be within your master's palace at this moment."

"I saw only a sealed box. I heard nothing as I should have–no sound of any kind."

Tem's brows rose again. "So a living creature it was. Well," He shrugged, glancing at Pan, "that is no longer my concern."

"We had a sacred contract!"

"You are becoming tiresome, Malag! I have said the contract is fulfilled. We owe you nothing more. Tomorrow we shall depart and I warn you, do not try to detain us. My soldiers itch to test their blades on your skin and I doubt that I can restrain them much longer–nor do I wish to."

Malag gasped. He glanced from side to side, making guttural noises. The dam burst. "You owe me nothing, you say? Nothing?" He shouted. "I'll tell you what you owe me–one gila! That gila! Whom you have released from the palanquin and now seek to force to your own pleasure! When my masters open the palanquin this evening, I have no doubt what they will find there: rocks and stones. Which you substituted for this gila while I slept!" He stamped his foot and one hand grasped the dagger obtruding from his belt. "I claim this woman for my masters as their rightful due!"

Tem stood. His lips pursed.

"I will tell you but once more, Malag. I was ordered to deliver one palanquin and not to inquire as to its contents. That is what I have done. I owe nothing more to you or to your masters. Tomorrow I shall leave the slaves, as I promised. For them you have paid and I shall abide by my word. But this creature does not belong to your employers, or to you. If it is indeed a gila–and this fact has not been established–then it is my duty to return the creature to the Temple in Tumset and not to permit the likes of you to endanger your souls by consorting with the creature."

"Only priests may escort gila-sa! When my masters, the holy priests of Ven, learn that you violate the law of Vensor–"

"Enough!" Tem held up his palm. "Leave my camp at this moment! If I see you again, Malag, you will join the other slaves, and you may be sure that your welcoming will be none to pleasant, although I myself will take the greatest pleasure in it. I care not one whit for you or your masters, who should look to their own necks lest someone take the trouble to inform the authorities in Ven of your masters' disgusting and illegal traffic! I wonder how your city would receive that knowledge? That is my final word." Tem breathed heavily, his cheeks glistening.

For a long moment Malag stood before them, holding his breath, his glance stabbing from Tem to the guards then back to Tem, searching for the words that would release the prize and restore his reputation with his masters, whose rage at losing their cargo only he could know. Beyond them a breeze lifted the flap to the other chamber and revealed a pair of smooth tanned legs where the newcomer stood in shadow, listening silently, one brown toe tracing an obscure pattern upon the embroidered carpet. With a vigorous motion Malag summoned spittle, cast it noisily at the feet of Tem, and ran from the tent.

Tem exhaled. With a sweeping movement, he scooped up the discarded gown and strode into the adjoining cloister, Pan close behind. As in the first chamber thick carpets were strewn about, but here were accompanied by a small table, two fold-up chairs and a tangle of soft furs. A single torch flickered in a socket set in the tent's central pole, and thick smoke hung in the air circling lazily until passing through a vent in the uppermost stretch of canvas.

Gently the chieftain offered the robe to the newcomer. His guest accepted the garment without comment and put it on, then Tem sat and studied his new guest in the soft light of the torch.

"Approach me."

The woman came, dwarfed by the visage of Tumsenet, the totem god of Tumset, which was sewn into the carpet. A few steps from the Tumset officer, she paused. A clatter of armor carried dully from the direction of the tent's entrance where guards walked their duty. No guards stood in the chieftain's chamber. Whatever transpired within, none would disturb the Tumset chief's private quarters.

"Can you speak the language of Vensor?"

A moment passed and his guest nodded, gaze still upon the carpet.

"Good. Then what is your name?"

"Amina." She raised her eyes and for a moment her lips seemed to tremble, although it might have been a trick of the light.

Tem turned to Pan again. "It is a pretty creature." The chieftain returned his chin to his palm. "Despite its...differences. And somehow, in a strange way, attractive, I think."

"Of course," replied Pan. "It is a gila."

"Is it?"

"Are you blind?" said the second chieftain. "You heard Malag. Look! It is not like us!"

"You are ever hasty, Pan. We should question this creature to discover its nature."

They both resumed their observation of the newcomer.

"Amina," said Tem, "will you turn for us again?"

She turned. The robe escaped her grasp and fell softly to the carpet.

"What should we do with it?" inquired Tem.

Pan glanced at Tem and sneered. "You ever ask the advice of those you scorn. Is it not clear? The gila cannot remain here."

"And why not?"

"Can you not see what it is? Does not your very soul coil in horror in recognition of its nemesis?" Pan stared, still absorbed by the play of shadow and light upon Amina's bare torso. "You are not deaf. Listen to Pan, your advisor. You know the penalty for harboring a gila as well as I. The camp knows of its presence. Word will spread. And Malag makes no empty threat. By now his eunuch masters know as well, and if they inform our own eunuchs in Tumset, and should they inform their master.... I fear Malag is right. If this creature remains in the camp, we shall be in violation of the Law of Vensor, and the penalty will be severe. It cannot remain. It must depart, or," Pan swallowed, "someone must take it away."

Amina stooped and retrieved the robe. She draped it over her shoulders but at a gesture from Tem did not place her arms within the sleeves. Her exposed breasts seemed to swell in the half-light and her nipples grew and hardened beneath the stare of her interrogators. Her face reddening, she averted her gaze.

The Tumset chief rubbed his chin and glanced at Pan. The second officer seemed in a trance, unmoving except for strong, steady breaths.

"I do not fear Malag. And you may be right concerning the men, not to mention the king and the Guild. But our duty is clear. It would be best if this creature–this Amina–remains here in my tent, under our personal guard, while the expedition returns to Tumset. Assuming, of course, that this is indeed a gila." He leaned back in his wooden fold-up chair.

"I wonder.... Amina is such a pretty name."

Pan looked askance at his chieftain, a look of disgust and horror twisting his features. "I do not like your language. You know that it is a witch, a sorcerer."

"We do not know that," said Tem.

"You know what your eyes see! It is an emissary of Atasan, a priest of the Adversary of Men, the enemy of Vensor and all His children. You know as well as I that it cannot be allowed the run of the camp, which is why Malag had it sealed in the litter. The creature is a master of trickery, a menace to us all. It must have used sorcery to escape. I repeat–let me take it into the forest...." He swallowed again. "I could take it myself to Tumset and deliver it to the Temple. Or I could leave it...in a shallow grave."

"I do not approve of your taking the gila into the forest alone. If the creature is as dangerous as you say, then you yourself shall be in peril, or others you may come across."

"I can handle this creature, this witch, of Atasan."

"You judge too harshly, Pan. That is another of your faults."

"And you judge not enough, but hear and obey all."

"Silence! I have heard all I wish from you as well as Malag! Hold your tongue in this tent until I ask for your opinion!"

"I shall hold my tongue when the safety of the men is assured!"

Tem stood in exasperation. "Pan, not one more word! Since we left Tumset you have done nought but disobey and carp on my leadership. Now in my very presence you would defy my will? I shall have you in chains upon our return to Tumset!"

Pan looked away. He snorted. "You will do nothing. And you know why you will do nothing."

Tem, whose words had seemed stronger than his emotion, calmed. He lowered his eyes and sat heavily in the chair. His gaze wandered about the interior of the tent for several moments, then lit upon Amina.

Amina stared at Tem in wide-eyed perplexity.

He leaned forward as if nothing out of the ordinary had occurred. "Tell me, my dear Amina. How came you to be wandering in the forest? Were you encased within Malag's palanquin?"

Amina closed the robe about her torso and stared at her feet.

Tem frowned. "Your harsh words, Pan, have upset the creature." He spoke gently. "Listen, child. Do not be alarmed. No harm shall come to you." He glanced at his second. "You shan't harm the creature, shall you, Pan?" Pan shook his head. "Indeed," continued Tem, "you shall have the best that I have to offer. My tent is yours."

She looked up and smiled.

"Now tell me. How came a fragile creature like yourself to be wandering in the forest by night?"

Amina shrugged her shoulders and stared upon the rug again. "I was traveling with friends when we separated. I don't know how...." She raised her eyes and pulled a lock of black silken hair to one side. "It was dark...I became lost." She shrugged again. "I searched but could not find them. I saw your fires..." She smiled. "Here I am."

A low sound emanated from somewhere beyond the tent, carrying low and distant like the call of a distant predator. The eyes of both men remained fixed upon Amina. One delicate, well-formed finger adjusted the hem of her garment and for a brief moment a red dagger seemed to flash up one thigh towards her abdomen, though whether it was a trick of the firebrand or some design on the garment previously obscured was not apparent in the trembling light.

"Please, Tem," said Pan, "let me take it alone to Tumset–before it is too late. Being Simet-sa, we are not as vulnerable to its wiles as the soldiers. In the forest there shall be no danger...to the men...in the forest...."

"I think not," interrupted Tem. "True, being Simet-sa, and therefore closer to Vensor, we are not as vulnerable. However, it is not only dangerous, but valuable as well. To escort a gila alone in the wild would invite attack and brigandage. Look, it is tanned and well fed. I am certain that it did not escape from the palanquin. She speaks the truth, and may have an escort searching for her even now. Our duty is clear. We shall guard it well and return it to the Temple in Tumset. And then we shall split the reward. Thus, we may benefit while we protect the expedition and any others we may encounter from the power of its sorcery. And in the meantime," Tem looked at Pan, "it shall not leave my tent."

Pan returned his glance with a glower. The darkness in the tent's interior seemed to have deepened and the second officer felt an unfamiliar and obscure, but no less strong, emotion stir deep within. Oblivious to Pan's deepening gloom, Tem smiled upon his guest.

All three started–a shriek pierced the air. From outside the tent swords clashed, then the camp as grew suddenly silent again. Tem and Pan entered the reception chamber as six Tumset guards threw aside the flap and entered, dragging the body of a man. They let it fall heavily to the floor where it lay prostrate and silent. Several of the guards bore the wounds of a rapier.

"Am I to be allowed no privacy?" shouted Tem. "What do you bring me now?" His eyes fell upon the body. "Who is this?"

An elbow jerked and the body, strongly muscled and with closely cropped hair, opened its eyes. A large knot had risen upon its head and purple bruises rapidly spread about its torso. The Tumset guard by his side let loose another kick and the man jerked.

"Infiltrated the camp, my chieftain. The devil strangled a sentry not far from your tent and killed two men before we felled him with a lucky blow." He glanced down. The intruder stirred again, and the guard delivered another kick.

Tem passed a quick glance over the intruder. "Look." He pointed. "The skirt of a Ven. I sense Malag's hand in this. Hold him up."

The guards glanced at each other, then cautiously lifted the man from the floor and stood him on his feet, his weight requiring the strength of four. He opened his eyes and stood on his own, though weaving.

Tem stepped forward. "Who are you, I say?"

Their prisoner made no answer.

"There is no use pretending, we know you are a Ven. Simply tell us who sent you and what your orders were and it will be easier for you."

The man said nothing, but shook his head to clear the throbbing. He turned his swollen gaze about the chamber, noting each occupant in turn.

"Tell me, now. Was it Malag? Or was it his eunuch-masters?"

Tem signaled to Hut. The crew chief swung a fist, but before It could connect, his victim ducked. With a leap, the prisoner drove into the clot of Tumset guards like a wrecking ball, felling the lot instantly. His massive hands closed about the neck of one and snapped his vertebrae like a twig. The hands reached for a second neck when a Tumset knobkerry rebounded off his skull and he again collapsed.

"Must I do everything around here?" Tem dropped the knobkerry. "Take him out. He is obviously one of Malag's men, sent to assassinate me or to spy upon us. Put him with the slaves.... They will know how to deal with one of Malag's slave drivers." He winked knowingly at Hut, whose neck had narrowly escaped the fate of his companion and was now massaged by its nervous owner.

When the rambunctious–and dangerous–intruder had been removed, Tem turned and re-entered the further cloister, where a different sort of danger, one of infinite more attraction, craved his attention. Amina had made no move since Tem left, but continued to stand quietly before the officer's chair with her head bowed. The robe had been drawn across her breasts and her arms were folded. Upon the return of Tem and Pan, she looked up and smiled brightly.

Tem's mouth twitched. Turning, he closed the flaps to his private quarter and tied the strings. Pan watched Tem as he did this and his previous look of deep gloom returned.

"You may leave, Pan."

The second officer said nothing, but stood.

Tem turned to stare at him. "I said, you may leave." Pan lowered his gaze. Without a word he turned and vanished.

The chieftain walked to his chair and sat. For some minutes he rested, his chin resting on one palm while he regarded the gila before him, Amina, who waited patiently, calmly, deep drafts swelling her rounded chest in steady alternation. Finally, he stood. Amina stepped closer. One delicate finger touched his arm and a serene smile formed gradually upon her lips as she raised her face and gazed into his eyes. Sweat beaded upon the chieftain's cheeks. Two small hands clasped his and the woman took a step back, drawing the chieftain after her. A moment later they halted. Still smiling and without shifting her gaze from his, the woman sank slowly to her knees. No sound disturbed the silence of the chamber except the gentle guttering of the torch, no movement drew their eyes from their mutual embrace. Tem sought to raise one hand but it would not obey. Frozen, he stared as the delicate hands began to work, calmly but swiftly removing his clothing. When he stood before his guest entirely disrobed, the enigma parted her mouth and reclined upon the furs strewn upon the carpet, her hands sliding slowly along her inner thighs, a moan of pleasure escaping her lips.

Tem gasped. He fell to his knees, his face suspended inches from hers. As he stared, her eyes seemed to expand and suddenly he felt he was plummeting, drowning in those dark liquid pools. Moments later he shuddered, reddening, conscious of the stare of Pan upon his back.

He wheeled and confronted his second officer.

"Did I not order you from this tent?"

Pan stood before him, disrobed as well, breathing hard with passion.

"Do you think there are no limits to what I shall tolerate?" Tem screamed. "Do you think I will overlook this as well?" Tem noticed the shining blade in his second's hand.

"Wha...what do you plan to do?"

Pan's visage froze as if in calculation of a hard deed. "You have guessed."

Tem caught his breath. "You're insane. You don't know what you're doing—"

"I'm afraid it's you who does not know what he is doing. But I can save you from this act."

"What do you mean?"

"You have violated the law of Vensor and tarnished your soul. But don't worry—your body shall not be buried, but shall be tossed in the meadow to rot and be torn by animals and thus your soul shall find its way to heaven."

Tem glanced away from Pan to Amina. The woman had covered herself with a brindled fur and gazed upon the nude pair over one edge with furrowed brows. Pan followed his gaze.

The chieftain saw his opportunity and lunged. The pair closed. Tem succeeded in loosening his assistant's grip on the weapon. The blade flew across the chamber and came to rest by the tent flaps. Tem swung a fist but missed. Pan returned the blow and partly connected, sending his chief sprawling onto the floor. Before he could recover the knife, Tem grasped one of Pan's legs, and together they rolled. Hands found their mark around a neck. Moments passed. With a last convulsion, the victim heaved and a dull rattling sound followed and Pan rose and stared upon the floor where Tem lay.

Pan turned. Amina had not moved but gazed at him from the tangle of furs. He approached, hands bared and outspread, his face, formerly taut and worried, now transformed by a broad smile. The woman relaxed and let the covers drop again to expose her bare torso. Her arms rose to embrace him and her knees parted to receive him and Pan strode confidently forward, needing no guidance or assistance. Panting with desire, he wrapped one muscled first in Amina's raven hair and pulled her to him. For a stretch of time they remained thus, the flames and shadows alternating in a chiaroscuro play.

Again and again Pan gorged his appetite, but remained unsated. Over and over he thrust, drawn by the enigmatic smile resting gently on the devilish lips before his gaze, ever moist, ever hot, but unmoved, as if taunting him to satisfy her, her breath purling sweetly in his nostrils, her fingers tracing outlines on her dark swollen breasts, her nails nicking, drawing blood on his skin. He drove on. The sweat stood out like beads and began to pool and roll, glistening on her dark nipples, which rose like nuggets. He grew thirsty from excess and began to gasp. He shuddered and wished to stop, but another glance at the mysterious landscape in her eyes spurred him on again.

He could no longer breathe and again he shuddered, and then opened his eyes in surprise. Seeking to inhale, he found the pools of night no longer focused upon him but on something that rose behind him. Amina recoiled in fright. He struggled to his feet and turned, but a sudden obstruction about his throat tightened, and the steel-like hands suddenly removed and he inhaled a deep draft of air, then screamed. Twice–thrice–and again the blade struck home, sinking deep into his lungs.

Pan fell forward upon the floor, bruising his face, and found himself staring into the eyes of Tem, who also lay prostrate, a blade protruding from his back, and blood flowing from his mouth. "What shall we do, Tem?" He asked himself. "I don't know, Pan," he answered. "What do you suggest?"

Amina clutched the furs tightly about her, staring at a squat dwarfish creature that leaned over the body of the Tumset chieftain, the only corpse in the room.

"So die, Tumset scum," he snorted. "Let's hear you babble to yourself now. For once you will have no surprises. For me, or for anyone!"

Shouts and the din of arms and armor carried from beyond the tent. Yellow lights flew past, visible through the canvas, torches in the hands of running warriors. Behind Malag the flaps to the reception chamber flew open and a crew of slavers entered, brandishing clubs and swords. A Tumset guard lay sprawled behind them.

Malag turned to Amina, a smirk rippling his lips. He leaned, grasped the brindled fur that covered her in one hand, and yanked it aside. The smirk deepened. One paw closed about her dark arm and the woman was lifted to her feet effortlessly. He grasped her and shook her so that her head almost snapped upon her neck.

"So you left the palanquin after I cautioned you to remain hidden." He shook her again and her black hair flew. "And you removed your veil, revealed yourself to these scum of Tumset, and allowed them to view what not even I, trustee and confidante of the Eunuch Lord of Ven, was permitted to see–although I often risked my life for your welfare. But now, by Vensor and Atasan, I shall see what others have seen! And I will have my pleasure as well." For a long moment the slave master held Amina at arm's length, his gaze enveloping her face and torso, now flickering, now lingering, thick slaver accumulating about his mouth. His lips terse and motionless, he reached out a broad palm and slowly brought it to one ample breast. He cupped it and gently squeezed. Amina stifled a cry of fear, then slowly exhaled. The slave-driver's eyes rose to meet hers and found that a smile had transformed her visage. He blinked. Snatching the fur, he wrapped her quickly within it. Then flung her over one muscled shoulder and hurried from the tent, moving almost at a run despite his burden, his lungs sucking small, passionate breaths.

Emerging into a night alive with flame and shadow, Malag paused. Before him, a wounded Tumset warrior attempted to crawl to safety away from the tent's entrance where the slavers had cut him down. Malag barked a command and his minions fell upon the injured man with axes, quartering him with savage glee. The slave-driver turned his glance toward the west where the dark cliff-face of his master's fortress loomed, all but invisible in the darkness. He knew the opaque portal stood ajar, having released the slavers in their sudden assault on the unsuspecting Tumset-sa. With a last stealthy glance, Malag lurched toward the cliff, his underlings in tow and Amina over his shoulder. Passing another tent, a shadow loomed before him and swung at his head. He dodged, and an unlucky companion took the rapier thrust in the neck. The Tumset warrior swung again and cut down another slaver, then the remainder closed about him and he fell before an avalanche of swords and axes. Malag waited until the weapons had done their work, then resumed his stealthy march. As they approached the portal, the cliff-side plunged their path in blackness and they paused, their way obscured by the sable shadows, their minds confused by the tumult in the camp. Behind, the shouts and flames grew as fresh bands of slavers, arriving from some unknown quarter, joined the struggle against the Tumset-sa.

"The torch," barked Malag. "Where is the torch that we left by the entrance? Where are the guards?"

"A torch, comrades!" his men echoed to their unseen friends. "Light a torch in the entrance so we may find our way."

A torch sputtered and was placed in its socket at the entrance to the tunnel where the portal had withdrawn into the cliff-face. The ember cast its feeble light across glittering walls and stamped earth. Reflected in its pale glow stood one man, down-turned sword grasped firmly before him, bodies strewn awkwardly about his feet, their eyes still, their limbs unmoving. His unsmiling face shone red; his stance blocked the slavers' path into the fortress.

The slavers halted in surprise. Malag released his burden, and, still gripping one delicate wrist, the slave-driver thrust Amina into leafy undergrowth where she remained in shadow, her gaze averted, her free hand drawing the fur more tightly about her shoulders. Still uncertain as to whether the figure before them was friend or enemy, Malag peered more closely. His brows furrowed as he noted the unwashed clothing, the lack of noble headgear, the common sandals, the dagger belted in the style of a poor man, and the unkempt beard of one of the pedestrian class. The intruder wore neither the skirt nor the leatherwork of a slaver. Malag felt anger rise within–the slaughtered bore the bandoleers and baldrics of his comrades. The slave-driver spoke, making no effort to disguise his contempt, but apprehensive lest more intruders lie hidden in the darkness.

"Aside!" Malag said. "You have no business here."

As if chiseled in stone, the intruder made no move.

Malag grimaced. "Speak, man. What do you here? You are not of Tumset, and you do not work for me. By what right do you interfere in my affairs?"

The man said nothing, but fingered the butt of his sword.

"I warn you. Only once more shall I ask. Who are you, and from where do you hail?"

A moment passed.

"A stranger."

The slaver's lips twisted with sarcasm. "Nothing more? You have no name?"

The intruder lowered his eyes until they rested on a ring upon one finger. The ring bore the sign of the Turlicum. He glanced up again.

"You need not know it."

Malag's eyes narrowed. Again he took in the common raiment and style of the intruder. Stepping back, he turned to his men. "Cut this dog to pieces. Then scatter them throughout the valley."

Without hesitation, the two axe-wielders leapt forward. They separated and closed upon their intended victim from two sides to catch him between them. Flores remained still till they came close. Then, even as they swung, he leaped and pinned the nearest rogue against the wall of the tunnel. A clattering sounded as the axe lodged in the wrist-guard of the rapier. The dagger found its mark and the axe-wielder screamed. Flores ducked–the axe of the other slaver clove into the skull of the first, cutting short his shriek. Flores twirled. The movement carried the sword in his left hand across the neck of the second axe-wielder in a single smooth movement. Body and head, almost severed, fell to earth with a dull report.

The others stepped back. Malag glanced behind him as if unsure of the outcome of the battle in the camp, and wondering whether he might have need of a quick escape into the fortress. He returned his glance to the mysterious figure that blocked his path, in the process letting his eye pause over the figure of Amina who still crouched in shadow by his side. He peered into the darkness that surrounded them. Suddenly he realized–the intruder was alone.

"What is the matter with you? He is but one. Get him!"

With a cry the entire band, excepting only Malag and his charge, pushed forward brandishing their weapons. A swordsman closed with Flores, thrusting and shouting, sparks flying where the iron contacted irsrem. Flores parried and backed into the shadowed tunnel until his attackers were crowded together. A club swung, interfering with the thrusts of the swordsman. Flores nicked the arm holding the club and its owner jerked it back and struck the swordsman. Immediately Flores' rapier sank into the swordsman's chest. His dagger locked with another dagger, then he pulled the sword free, and with the same motion lopped off the hand that held the club. Still grasping the club, the hand turned several flips before landing in the midst of the remaining thugs, who stopped their advance to stare in horror upon the severed organ. Meanwhile, Flores lifted his sword and faced the man whose irsrem dagger remained locked in the tang of his own. The slaver sensed what was to transpire and paled; Flores' visage darkened. His victim sought to disengage, but Flores passed the edge of his rapier under his opponent's armpit and then withdrew, with terrific force. The arm flung as had the hand of the other unfortunate. Again Flores twirled and a second poetic motion drew the rapier from groin to stern, opening up his victim so that his organs exploded.

Another step and the slavers had had enough. Routed, they fled back to Malag, where they stood, the remaining nine clutched together, their silence interrupted only by the whimpering of the one who had lost his hand. A companion tried to staunch the blood gushing from the stump.

Malag stared at the nemesis before them, who calmly awaited the next assault, sword down-turned, blade and tunic red with gore. The slaver again glanced behind him. The flames and shouting in the Tumset camp continued unabated.

"What is wrong with you cowards?" he shouted. "Have you become old men to let this fellow defeat you?"

"He is well-armed," they wheezed, "and clever–"

"He is alone...even if he does fight like a Simet warrior." His gaze again wandered to Amina. The underbrush blocked Amina's view of the tunnel and, still fearful of exposing his treasure, Malag pushed her deeper into the shadows so that she remained invisible from the tunnel's entrance as well. He looked again to the figure looming before them.

"By what right do you interfere in the affairs of the Eunuch Lord?" Malag said, his tone almost pleading.

Flores made no reply.

"You should know my master is powerful. He is Soorkrul, the Eunuch Lord of Ven. This is his fortress. This is his land. And he brooks no meddling in his affairs. In his name, I grant you one last chance to avoid his rage, but only if you depart this moment and never return. If I inform him of your interference, I warn you his anger will be great. He does not bear the death of his clansmen well. And once he learns of your deeds he will not rest until your head stands upon a pole. I grant you this one last chance to live, but only if you depart now."

At the mention of the Eunuch Lord, Flores' eyes glinted. When he awoke to find the camp empty, he never thought that his old nemesis might lay behind it. So Soorkrul was the power behind this illicit trade beyond the ken of Ven's Assembly. But why? He nodded. Doubtless to provide a place of refuge from the uncertainties of Ven's politics.

And, he reflected, Soorkrul's presence here would explain his long absence from Ven. The Eunuch Lord himself may have ordered the attack on the Tumset camp. Then, realizing his thoughts were distracting him from the task at hand, he shut them out. Learning calmly on his rapier, his eyes re-focused on Malag. Suddenly the slave-driver grew quiet and stared as if through Flores, or behind him. A sly smile crept over Malag's face and he returned his attention to Flores with renewed confidence.

"Then you," he hissed, "shall pay the consequences. What did you think, coming here and interfering in our affairs, in the affairs of my master? Did you think you could murder his underlings with impunity? How long do you believe you can hold out against my soldiers?"

Flores' eyes glimmered with contempt at the thought of the slavers as soldiers.

"An hour?" continued Malag. "A day? Surely you realize that we will overcome you finally and cut you to pieces–if you are lucky. Perhaps you will only be injured. Then we will take you alive and we will string you up and slice you slowly, or perhaps nail you to a pillar. Think of that–of being dismembered at the leisure of your tormentors, your skin stretched and nailed to our fortress gate while you yet live –"

During this recitation, Flores kept his attention on Malag and his men. Suddenly the sound of creaking leather rose close by. Flores froze–he had forgotten the tunnel at his back. Swiftly he dove and rolled out of the tunnel's entrance across the beaten earth. Swords and clubs struck the earth in pursuit as the tunnel disgorged a fresh gang of slavers who had approached from behind in silence. He alighted on his feet, only to face Malag's men as they fell upon him from the other direction. Never, he thought, desperation rising within, had he found himself in such a hopeless contest. Never had he had such need of all his talent for self-preservation and mayhem.

The slavers closed about him, raucous shouts ringing out triumphantly in expectation of a swift end to the one-sided duel. He cut one down immediately. Another he caught in the thigh. A third lost a hand. But the rest continued to press and a club struck his forearm, the force of the blow almost breaking it, leaving him numb with pain. A chill seized him, as he recalled memories of his youth when he had first engaged a real opponent and swordplay had become more than play. He permitted the chill, which froze the untrained into immobility, to transmute into thrill as he savored the rush of adrenaline. Then, with an act of will he reasserted control and achieved inner calm. As the smell of ozone permeated the air, his sword wove an impregnable wall between him and the motley band, who were, as he reminded himself, mere thugs–no match for a Simet warrior.

But even thugs might overwhelm a warrior should their number be sufficient. Again they pressed him and another blow glanced off one shoulder. Flores staggered and almost fell. With a supreme effort he forced a stabbing rapier back with a spray of sparks and gutted its owner with the dagger in his right hand. As the man collapsed, he lunged again, seeking to maneuver himself to the cliff wall in order to protect his back. But they threw him back, encircled him, and moved in for the kill.

"Wait!" Malag approached, dragging his captive roughly behind him. His squinty eyes took in Flores' features; his leaf-like ears listened to the sounds he made as he panted from exertion. By his side Amina slowly straightened again, but staggered, fatigue now swiftly overtaking her.

"I wish to see my men cut you down," Malag hissed joyfully. "I wish to look upon your face wet with blood. I promise that you shall not die until you see your organs torn from your body and arranged before your gaze."

Flores slowly caught his breath and focused on the creature that had appeared at Malag's side, whom the slave-driver had heretofore hidden in the shadow of the undergrowth. For one instant his eyes drank in the exquisite features of the most beautiful priestess on Maalstrom. His gaze locked on the vise-like fist that held her within its grip, a fist that belonged to the power behind his enemies, to him whose life was dedicated to the elimination of gila-sa from Maalstrom–to Soorkrul, the Eunuch Lord.

"Amina?"

In surprise he watched her eyes rise and meet his own. A tired smile crept over her face. Her feeble hands lost their hold on the fur draped upon her shoulders and it slipped below her breasts. Upon Flores' utterance, the dwarfish slaver ceased his gloating over Flores' impeding death. With a guttural cry of rage, Malag struck Amina upon the side of her face with his hand.

Amina moaned, then cried out. "Flores!"

Like a phoenix, Atasan sprang to life in the hot sparkling night and breathed His fiery breath across the sullen landscape. The smoky pupils in Flores' face glowed like gems in anticipation of a revenge that would gladden the malkops for months to come. As if in response, silver wings flashed above. Attracted by the fires, malkops had already gathered, like flies eager for the feast.

Malag dragged the priestess to her feet. A finger pointed at Flores. "You know this man?"

She nodded, almost imperceptibly.

Malag's face turned crimson, then purple. He stopped breathing. With one arm he held up the priestess, with the other he pulled back and unleashed a fresh series of blows. She collapsed.

"How, slave? How, you gila-whore of Atasan? Is there anyone you do not know? Have you surrendered your pleasures to all on Maalstrom but me, your chief benefactor?"

Even as Malag shouted, Flores began a complicated spinning upon one leg, his sword and dagger twirling. The slavers stared in confusion, uncertain where to intervene. Suddenly he rolled and engaged the nearest with his legs, tumbling him to the ground. His dagger found its mark, then he was on his feet in the midst of them, slashing and piercing. One he opened like a fish. Another he thrust through the neck. A third sprang back, clutching his intestines, while a fourth grabbed at his eye and shrieked, colliding with the others.

"Come, gila-bitch," Malag bellowed amid the screams of the injured. "You will pay dearly for your disobedience!" Amina's voice pealed higher as the slaver dragged her into the tunnel mouth. Flores breathed hard, then set his jaw. Dodging another thrust, he straightened, grasped his dagger by the blade and hurled it. By an unlucky turn of fortune another slaver stepped into its path and took the blade meant for Malag.

With one last cry from Amina, Malag disappeared into the ill-lit tunnel. A creak sounded—the portal was closing. Emerging from one side of the tunnel, the massive irsrem door began to slide shut, glinting green and ox-blood in the flickering light, the dark crescent steadily narrowing. Desperately Flores strove to scatter the slavers and follow, but was thrown back. Once the gate had shut he could never enter, never see her smile again. Again Flores rushed to the attack, and again was foiled. The slavers were learning to anticipate his moves, their rapiers now hovered before him like the glass bars of a shrinking cage. Tiring rapidly, Flores engaged another pair in swordplay, sparks spitting, the irsrem flashing with starlight where gore had not yet coated the glass. The slavers closed, revenge in their eyes for the carnage that

Flores had inflicted on their comrades. No thought remained of re-treating or of sparing him. This time they would kill him, or die.

Suddenly one of the slavers stumbled. A second gasped as an arrow appeared in his chest. With a shout, a band of Tumset warriors burst into the clearing from the direction of the camp, pikes and swords in hand, releasing arrows as they came. The slavers turned and Flores sprang between the last two remaining between him and the tunnel and propelled himself toward the mouth. With one last heave, he flung himself between the portal and its meet. Another instant and the pow-erful gears would crush him. He sought to enter–something held him back. What mysterious force had intervened to thwart him yet again, now, at his hour of greatest need? He glanced down and discovered his sword was caught in the jamb. Twisting, he entered the tunnel, but, forced to choose between his sword and his hand, at the last moment released the weapon.

The gate slammed shut.

With a chill Flores realized what he had done. As the hollow report reverberated the length of the empty tunnel, he realized that he had entered the abode of the Eunuch Lord, populated by his armed min-ions, in secret, and without weapons and without any manner of es-cape. The blackness of the tunnel mirrored the blackness that descended on his soul.

CHAPTER 22

ILLUSIONS

The king of Neset was less certain of his victory than the famished defenders of the city. The half-clad youth at his side hardly drew his gaze. The cooperation of the Heir to the House of Turlicum, the newest addition to the king's harem after Mesret's escape from the city, inspired little confidence within him. Nesos knew the fickleness of newly won allies. Word had come that morning of the progress of a relieving army. Vens from the Suma were reducing the vassals' cities one by one and would eventually force the Nesets away from the capital, or besiege them in turn. The contingent from Toor had fled the previous night, and, should the deserters return, it would not be as allies of Neset.

Ven must fall. Nesos awaited his traitor.

The king snapped his finger and, with his guardsmen, exited his blue and white tent into the darkness. He crossed the main part of his army's encampment, picking a path among fires and tents and refuse and tethered reven-na. Occasional knots of men reveled drunkenly within tents; other tents stood disturbingly empty. A few of the men grumbled, but most were silent, especially when Nesos walked by. After a time he found what he sought: an unassuming bell tent of soiled linen in the midst of the encampment. None stood watch at the entrance; the flaps drifted in the errant breeze. Peremptorily, Nesos posted new guards. The king passed through the flaps alone.

A man of moderate height stood before a table that bore several lamps, peering into a small mirror that he held in one hand. His back was toward the king. Nesos entered and the man lowered the mirror and turned. Hesitating, the king glanced at the entrance, then smiled, his mouth opening in surprise. A mass of subtle wrinkles folded upon the face of the tent's occupant as the man by the table bowed.

"Homd!" blurted Nesos. "How fortunate that you have arrived. I have much need of your counsel. But first I wish you to help me find my illusionist–"

Nesos blinked. Before him stood not his high advisor, but his knight at court, Sterleric. The knight lifted a cup of mead that had materialized from nowhere.

"To your health, O King!"

Nesos could detect no alien inflection in the voice. Sterleric himself might have delivered the toast. "What is this?" he growled, his pitch rising in outrage. "You dare to imitate a traitor whom I have executed? And one of my nobles as well? Take care, illusionist. Ply your art at dinner parties only–meddle with affairs of state and you will find little entertaining thenceforth."

"As you wish."

"As I command!"

"Indeed."

Nesos frowned. Something in his illusionist's tone disturbed him, or perhaps the momentary, almost undetectable delay that had intervened between utterances. As they spoke, the man was in constant motion. No longer did Sterleric stand before the king, but his image was replaced by that of an aristocrat with silver hair and rich adornment. Nesos did not recognize him, nor the portly noble who succeeded the aristocrat. A series of unknown visages passed swiftly before the worried gaze of the First Born of the Vensors. Then the blur coalesced into the complete head of Towt, another knight of Neset, sapid and weak. But his body was that of an acrobat, an absurd combination that brought a chortle from Nesos. The king's mood lifted.

"You are still learning your art, I see." Nesos nodded with pleasure. "Practice well, for I have need of your services."

The illusionist assumed the guise of one of Nesos' guardsmen who stood by the entrance to the tent. Nesos smiled again and continued.

"Three weeks ago I announced that any Ven who should open the gates to me would rule the city in my name. But I have yet to obtain results. No traitor has appeared to end this bloody affair and permit us to return to our homes in Neset. So I need a...specialist. Someone who could enter the city and do the job himself."

"Of course," the guard responded. The warrior blurred and melted, assuming the image of Nesos' entertainer-contortionist.

"For this 'performance' I will reward you well–riches beyond count. And, of course, you will be free of your chain. But if you wish your reward, you must return to me and continue to serve me."

"Chain?" the contortionist inquired, his brows shifting in puzzlement. Both men glanced at the contortionist's feet. No restraining device of any sort could be seen. He moved one leg and the invisible links clanked.

Nesos smiled. "How much time do you need to prepare?"

"I need...no time." The contortionist vanished, to be replaced once more by the dead vizier. Homd breathed deeply. "I have been waiting. Only your pride has kept you here so long."

The king's jaw again dropped. He closed his mouth and frowned. The elusive figure again launched into a complex evolution of strange and alien faces and Nesos shifted his feet uneasily.

"Soon then? In the hours before dawn?"

A stranger appeared before the table and nodded gravely. Nesos turned and strode toward the exit. From behind his back came a familiar voice.

"Soon. In the hours before dawn."

Nesos felt his skin crawl–the voice had been his own. Swiftly he turned, rage twisting his bearded face into something unrecognizable. But he beheld only a crippled old man leaning hard upon a wooden table, an iron chain wrapped about one leg. The King of the Vensors regained control. This was too much, he thought. After Ven falls–no more. As he passed beneath the awning, Nesos touched the seal of his finger to reassure himself of his own identity. His royal signet ring must never be removed.

In the hour before dawn, when the last number of sentries walked the parapets of Ven and those who did were tired and sluggish, a lone man emerged from the shadows of Ven's streets and approached a dozen soldiers who sat about the wheel which held the bar across the giant irsrem portals of the city. At the sight of him, two sentries stood and drew their blades. The figure hurried upon them.

"Wait where you are, sir," called one of the guards. "State your business." The others looked but did not rise.

The intruder kept walking, a look of severe disapproval on his insolent face. He stopped and flexed a massive fist.

"A strange man walks upon you in the night and you lie about in comfort? You dogs! You'll have Neset knives at our throats."

The sentries stood and shook themselves alert; the two guardsmen recoiled. The block-like fist connected with a jaw.

"Release the bar!" In confusion the sentries exchanged glances. Had they heard right?

"Now, idiot!" His fist ascended to strike again and the guard forgot his jaw and grasped the iron wheel.

"But, Lord! The Neset-sa!"

"Do I have to cut out your hearts and open the gate myself? Don't you recognize your king?" The newly adopted emblem of office, a jeweled scepter, was flashed briefly before them. "There is a party of Vens beyond wishing to join us. By Divine Vensor, open the gate now before the Neset-sa discover them."

A score of hands cranked the wheel pulling the bar from the gate. Once the bar was clear, Numsenmur-Nidrenmor-Serclasler gripped the handle and slowly swung one heavy portal wide. He gripped the other portal and swung it also. Then he waved two of the men to his side.

"Throw a torch into the darkness. When our men have entered, shut the gate quickly. If the Neset-sa get in, it will be upon your heads."

Numsenmur turned and walked toward a side street. He disappeared into the gloom. For a moment the sentries stood dumbfounded. One picked up a torch and sent it soaring into the night. He poised to hurl a second when his companion restrained his arm.

"Wait."

A wave of soft drumming came to them, like a low pitched rumble of thunder far on the horizon. Several men looked up and scanned the heavens for dark patches of thundercloud, but the stars and gibbous moons shone clearly.

The Vens appeared. A knot of reven-na with carapaced riders hurtled past and rushed in the direction of the plaza. The sentries watched them vanish. Another group materialized and raced through, then a third. The guard, still holding the wheel, stared in surprise at an arrow lodged in his chest. A second shaft joined it. Screams and shouts drifted from the interior of the city and a flame sprouted; bands of men crossed the intersection and clashed.

Vens poured from the gate's barracks and rained arrows from the walls, while the invading Neset-sa dismounted and ringed the area around the gate. Other Vens swarmed from side streets, seeking to swamp the intruders, but without success. With the first light of dawn breaking in the east, the main body of the army of Nesos rolled over the desperate defenders and irrupted into the city.

Morning passed. As the sounds of fighting dwindled, two grey lyarts with upthrust tusks thumped beneath the lintel, towing a golden-gilt chariot on spoked wheels. From each hub gleamed hammered silver— on one side scowled Nantifus, the god of disease; on the other Nvediteg hurled lightning. A pilot of wooden rails was suspended from the animal's yoke, displaying Ven captives spread-eagled. In the car upon a dais stood the Emperor of the Vensors, King Nesos, jeweled staff in hand. A driver stood lower with the reins.

While further cohorts followed, brandishing a forest of hirsute vok-tails, the king directed his chariot along the Way of Nevsonhet, past the rambling cloister of the Guild and entered the main plaza of Ven. The city had been wholly surprised and the corpses were few.

The chariot came to rest before the grounds-gate of the Assembly Hall. Nesos entered. A conspicuous throne had recently been installed at one end of the hall among the tiers of benches. How thoughtful, he mused. He sat upon the throne and spoke to his warrior chiefs, and leaned back to wait.

For the duration of the morning Nesos sat as his soldiery fulfilled his orders. In singles and pairs, the Simet-sa of Ven were brought, some struggling, some willing, some dead, the last being dumped in-formally in the arena. Among the living were Dos and Temes, Scroy and Renel, Hama and Abb, and sixty others—a half dozen had been killed in the night. Still Nesos remained silent, perched upon the throne, finger flanking face.

He waited.

The suns reached zenith. The fighting had long ceased and the Em-peror's patrols penetrated every cranny, every cubicle of the city. Fi-nally, in mid-afternoon, the doors to the plaza opened, and a warrior walked onto the floor of the Assembly Hall. The man wore an archaic iron helmet with slumping falcon's wings, vitreous armor, and bore a jeweled scepter. A Neset soldier behind him carried a broad iron sword. The man with the scepter strode casually to the center of the chamber, stepping over the corpses of Ven Simet-sa, and stared at the King of Neset, who watched complacently from the throne.

Nesos moved his finger and the man approached. When the benches blocked his progress, he mounted them and strode upward until he stood directly before the throne of the conqueror. Handing the scepter to Nesos, he knelt. Rising to his feet, Nesos took the iron sword from the Neset soldier, and offered it to the kneeling warrior. The warrior took the sword, stood, turned, and removed his falcon-winged helmet.

"Let it be known," announced the King of Neset, "that the Emperor of the Vensors keeps his word. Men of Ven, look upon your new viceroy, who shall rule the city in the name of the King of Neset: Num-senmur-Nidrenmor-Serclasler!"

Numsenmur smiled for the first time in months–a wide, grand smile.

The king of Neset clutched the arm of a chieftain and whispered. The chieftain produced a parchment and read something to Nesos. The king cleared his throat. "One man in particular has not been found." Nesos rubbed the royal seal upon his finger as if unfamiliar with its fit. "I offer a standing reward of ten thousand mir to anyone who can bring me one Flores-Sumvensor of the Turlicum."

Even as he spoke, beneath the hall of Vim, a crew of soldiers strong-armed a struggling figure down a dark, mortared corridor. The man's hands were tied, his head covered by a sack of black cloth, and a gag muffled his cries of rage. Behind them iron bars clanged shut and a lock turned.

CHAPTER 23

HALL OF MIRRORS

The rough-hewn tunnel receded darkly before Flores until vanishing in the depths of the mountain. He began to walk. From beyond a turn in the passage, a ghostly light glimmered, but the passage remained plunged in darkness so that Flores could barely make out the floor beneath his feet and the sharp stone angling obliquely from the walls on either side. He moved slowly, suspicious that some mechanism might be present to foil enemies who have forced the entrance. Ahead loomed a patch of deeper sable. Although the tunnel floor seemed solid, Flores moved leftwards to the tunnel wall. Inching forward he felt the path with a sandaled foot. His left hand found what seemed to be a depression or handle carved in the rock. Leaning further, he discovered a series of depressions. He paused–his foot found a small protuberance set within the floor, near the wall. He felt further. The nubs were also in a series, extending laterally across the passage. Gripping the handles, he lowered his foot and pressed the nearest nub. The ground fell away with a roar, leaving him clinging to the handles, his feet dangling.

Pulling himself up, he found that a narrow ledge had survived the collapse. A common device, he thought. The darker patch ahead would be a second pit, with a narrow bridge spanning it, intended not only to lull gullible intruders into mounting the bridge, which would be designed to collapse the moment they reached the central span, but also to distract intruders from the ground beneath their feet as they approached the pit and bridge. The moment they first encountered the row of projections, they would die, impaled on stakes set in the bottom of the pit. Flores traversed the ledge using the hand-grips until he once again felt the solid floor of the tunnel beneath his feet. Then, stepping more lightly, he advanced to the edge of the darker patch. Again he moved to the left and found a second ledge with grips set in the rock. Swiftly he crossed, bypassing the bridge and its pit. He began to run. There would be no more pits. Eunuchs would not inconvenience themselves more than what he had already encountered.

The tunnel jogged left. The light flickered more brightly, emanating from an open door on the right. Without peering within, he halted to listen. Hearing nothing, he risked a quick glance. The chamber was empty of life, but apparently served as a barracks, with a row of mattresses lying upon a series of low daises. A single torch, now almost extinguished, smoked in one corner beside a wide mirror. The smoldering ember had drawn his eye from as far back as the gate. Flores lifted the torch from its socket and swung it. It burst into flame and he halted in shock. A stranger stared at him from the mirror–wild-eyed, unkempt beard thick and tangled and framed by broad shoulders with a lean body clothed in a torn tunic, soiled with patches of gore. He caught his breath–then laughed. That was what several months in the wild had done! He looked younger. And stronger. New muscles had appeared on his neck and his face had darkened. But he felt no joy for his new toughness. His thoughts remained centered on the city of glass. Health and skill meant nothing unless they led to victory over the Triumvirate and Soorkrul. No happiness could enter his soul while his enemies lived.

His eye focused on a flash. Across the room, the accoutrements of soldiers lay strewn where the slavers had left them. The scabbards were empty, except for one. Flores drew out a two-piece irsrem wrist dagger with a flexible, attached arm-guard that extended to the elbow. A rare and expensive weapon, such as only noblemen might possess, intended mostly for ceremony, and abandoned by its owner. What prompted the slavers to leave it? Flores wondered. Any weapon would do for them. He admired its fit, and understood. Of course–it was made for a left-hander. For most that made it a mere curiosity. Now, if only he had not lost his rapier.

At least he was again armed. His confidence renewed, he turned to leave, then paused. Feeling eyes upon him, he spun, his new dagger at the ready. The room stood as empty as when he had entered. Nothing was visible in the chamber but furs and mattresses and the single plain mirror that spanned from wall to wall. Well, thought Flores, even slavers may be vain at times, especially should their employer be the eunuch Soorkrul. Reproaching himself for his unreasoning suspicions, he left.

Penetrating more deeply into the fortress, and jogging swiftly but silently, Flores passed more chambers, some with signs of recent habitation and some filled with barrels or other domestic items. Each chamber was as empty and silent as the first. A quick search of the following two rooms produced neither Malag nor Amina. And to his annoyance, he found nothing to replace the clumsy wrist-dagger that he wore. Each chamber did, however, display a feature similar to the barracks-room he had first encountered. Each had been constructed with a broad mirror on its far side so that the first image he viewed upon entering each room was himself. He shook his head. He could not understand the eunuchs' obsession with their appearance, but the illusion of greater space offered by the mirrors was welcome.

In the corridor he again halted to listen. He could hear no sound such as Amina might make if she was near and Malag forcing her to his will. And he decided that he should not call to her lest he reveal his presence to Malag and be overwhelmed by his minions. He felt certain that the slaver had not seen him enter the fortress.

A series of larger rooms now opened before him, apparently interconnected communal chambers arranged around a dining area. Again all were empty. Could the eunuchs have dispatched their entire garrison to attack the Tumset-sa? Why? Flores wondered. What could have aroused Soorkrul's eunuchs to such an extent? Nevertheless, the fortress was large, and other complexes far from him might still be occupied, perhaps even housing the Eunuch Lord himself. At the thought of Amina lost within these dark chambers, strong-armed by Soorkrul or the evil dwarf Malag, Flores felt strange emotions stir. Why should he care what happened to a gila of Atasan? What if she had once saved his life? He had saved her from the punishment of the Temple, escorted her through the wilds, fed and clothed her. What more might he owe a servant of Atasan?

His brows furrowed as he jogged from corridor to corridor, glancing into every room. The strange emotions settled upon his face and he felt something wet upon his cheek. Then, with an effort of will, he pushed the tears aside and told himself that Amina was not the reason he had entered the fortress–the reason was Soorkrul. The chance to harm an enemy had been too much to pass up. The discovery of Soorkrul's hideout, whose existence the Eunuch Lord had kept secret from the Assembly, had made him curious. If Flores could save Amina at the same time that he explored, so much the better. Honor required no less. But if he could not save her–his life was worth whatever injury he might inflict upon his enemy.

He halted. Upon the stone floor lay a jumbled gown, with a small bit of yellow extruding from beneath one fold. He picked up the garment–a rising sun threw rays across its midriff. It was Amina's. He caught his breath and from somewhere a silent voice swore that if she did not live, if she was harmed in any way, the dwarf and a host of slavers would soon reside on the Isle of the Dead. The anger passed, leaving him confused and hesitant. Again he reminded himself that his purpose was not to rescue the priestess but to injure Soorkrul. He moved to toss the robe aside, but at the last instant placed it within his belt.

He glanced down the gloomy corridor. The tunnel was lit by more of the smoky torches and lamps that had illuminated the previous chambers. The hall sloped down, although whether the ramp led deeper into the ridge or back toward the entrance, or in some other direction, he could not tell. Strange smells wafted from ahead; one hinted of fodder and dung, another was less mordant but bore a trace of sickly sweetness. He could not recall where he had experienced the odor in the past, but he knew he had and that the scent meant death. He paused to re-examine the spot where he had found the gown. There was no mistake. It lay squarely within the tunnel.

Flores set off at a run.

The passage flickered with torchlight. The floor was smooth, though grew rougher as he progressed. The strange smells grew stronger, as did his sense of danger. He stopped. A vague sound drifted as from a great distance, rumbling and rustling, though whether it emanated from a living throat or from the eternal stresses of the subterranean abode of Atasan, Flores could not discern. It ceased, and he resumed his advance. Vertical panes of glass, mirrored like all he had seen thus far, were embedded in the walls, providing an illusion of a phalanx of unkempt warriors stealing along a host of darkened corridors. Again the sickly sweet smell impinged upon his nostrils. He glanced down and saw his arm shake. He gripped his thigh to steady it.

Abruptly the tunnel terminated and opened into a vast cavern lit by a hundred flames. The flames were cast in perfect order, their red tongues licking in such flawless unison that he wondered what devilish art the Eunuch Lord had employed to bend the very forces of nature to his will. Then he realized that the chamber was simply a larger version of the tunnel, and that he had entered a single room, larger than most, but made to appear larger still by the burnished mirrors that covered every surface, including floor and ceiling. The entire panorama was lit by a single torch set above the threshold overhead, which was reflected a hundred times, leaving him giddy as he contemplated the multiplicity of images. As if suspended in air, he stood while the vagaries of the cosmos whirled about his head, nought existing but he and the unsteady sensation that seized him when he peered into the maze beneath his feet. The thought obtruded, making Flores at once fearful and exuberant, that Soorkrul might be more than Flores had realized, not merely a son of Vensor, but Atasan himself, having enslaved Chaos and brought it to his abode to assist in slaying his enemies.

Then a light appeared and shined upon a familiar upturned face, drawn tight in horror and fear. The perfect features of Amina were not obscured by her emotion, nor by the flickering light behind her. Flores' heart rose. The nude torso of the priestess was suspended by her wrists from some higher chamber toward which her expression of fear was directed. Venting a cry of rage, he rushed into the chamber of chaos.

A multitude of warriors approached the cavity where Amina silently screamed, her face upturned in horror. The light flicked off and the Turlicum slid into a wall of polished glass. Before Flores could regain his balance, a metallic clanging rang out and he knew that a new sheet of glass had descended to cut off his escape. With difficulty, he rose and stood. The floor beneath his feet was polished so smooth that each step threatened to tumble him upon his face. He glanced about. Where had he seen Amina? Where was the tunnel that led to this diabolical chamber? He struck the glass with his dagger–the weapon slipped across the surface as easily as had his sandaled feet, offering the irsrem blade no hold. He paused and ran one hand across his eyes. When he reopened them, the cavity had reappeared across the chamber. Within it was Amina, again suspended by her wrists, now staring in horror below her. Again Flores scrambled to his feet, gripping the dagger and propelled himself forward, anticipating the slide across the slick glass so as not to tumble. But he could gain no momentum and before he had crossed the chamber, falling several times in the process, the image had vanished. Where Amina had been, he reached out his hand and felt cold glass. He saw only himself staring back in anger.

Flores cursed his own stupidity and bumbling confidence for having rushed headlong into the fiendish trap. Shouting, he swore revenge come what may upon his and Amina's tormentor, and smote the floor and walls, half invisible in the flickering torchlight. Finally, after what seemed an eternity of headlong rushes and humiliating pratfalls, he halted. Standing in the center of the room, he thought. Several facts had become clear. First, although he could not see his tormentor, his tormentor could see him. Otherwise, he could not extinguish the light each time but an instant before he reached Amina. Second, even should his tormentor not extinguish the light, he could not hope to reach the priestess, since a panel of glass stood between them at all times. Third, since his tormentor, meaning Malag and perhaps others as well, could not be moving Amina from one location to another with such rapidity as he had observed, they must be shifting insubstantial images of her. Finally, in each image, Amina had not actually been harmed, but only threatened, and Flores began to suspect that she would not be harmed. After all, she and others like her were the objects not only of this game, but of Soorkrul's entire expensive scheme, with its fortress far removed from civilization in these western wilds.

Slyly, Flores nodded to himself. Yes, it was not she who was en-trapped and tortured, but he. Rather than driving blindly toward the illusion, as he now termed it, why not search for a way out of the trap, which might hold further terrors for one who had expended all his energies in fruitless pursuits? Quietly he resolved not to approach the next manifestation, but to search carefully for the source of the light or some trick of the mirrors, that might lead to a hidden exit.

The image returned to life across the room and Flores observed that although Amina appeared frightened, she was not harmed. He made no effort to approach her, but instead glanced about for the light's source. Nothing was visible save the host of silent warriors. Then both the image of Amina and the single torch that lit the room were snuffed out and Flores found himself plunged in blackness. What new trick were his observers readying to unleash, he wondered?

He had not long to wait. With a rasp of glass on metal a sudden smell filled the room, assaulting him not only by its strength, but by the pain that it evoked from the depths of his mind. The sickly sweet aroma curled within his nostrils and, despite the darkness, or perhaps because of it, his eyes saw a wide field of brightly lit altars and a fence of steel bars round a mausoleum, and a predatory beast startled from its angry meditation. Crazed with rage and hunger, the beast roared and flung itself, the bars bending from its hideous strength. Pain shot through the length of Flores' body, and his eyes turned down and glimpsed the claws of one prehensile paw embedded in his right forearm and wrist, the shredded flesh already mangled beyond repair.

The picture flicked off and Flores sensed something moving in the shadows about him. A slithering sounded, then a low angry rumble as the beast searched for its prey. Flores knew what he had next to defeat. The slithering paused and a moment later the lungs of a jungle ros loosed a roar of deafening volume, as if offended that a mere human would dare to breathe in its presence rather than die from fright.

Flores crouched, dagger lifted to protect him from a sudden rush. How could he defend himself, armed as he was with a clumsy wrist-dagger, barely able to stand where his sandals contacted the polished floor? He felt the blade shake. Then he breathed and steeled himself, and reflected that, unlike the last occasion when he had faced such an animal, he was now armed. This ros would not escape unharmed. The torch reappeared and the beast, larger than Flores had expected, saw him and leaped.

Flores sought to jump back and to one side, but slipped and fell. Stunned, the Turlicum muttered a quick prayer to Vensor that his corpse be exposed to Heaven's angels, and prepared himself for the end. A moment passed and nothing happened. He sat up. The ros scrambled for footing as he himself had scrambled, the bowed claws unable to grip the glass. Angry roars filled the chamber as the limbs of the beast flailed in vain.

Its efforts calmed. The bony, fleshless skull of the animal, with its single down-curved tusk and two up-curved eye-teeth, ceased its maddened coughing and focused its two beady eyes upon Flores. The creature began to advance with less difficulty and soon built up momentum. Too slow to escape, Flores fell beneath the impact of one savage paw upon his arm guard. He collapsed and rolled out of reach, but the creature fell upon him and seized his forearm in its prehensile talons. Desperately Flores sought to disengage, but failed. Amid ferocious roars, the animal proceeded to drag him toward its jaws. Flores flailed. Moments later, the tusks snapped upon his arm with enough strength to split iron. Yet the irsrem held, and Flores thanked Gethos for leading him to this weapon rather than to a more flexible and vulnerable one, which he had first desired.

Sliding his feet beneath him, Flores managed to stand. The beast slipped. It released him. When it returned to the attack he used the arm-guard as a shield, maneuvering it between the ros and himself. His lack of footing again undid him, however. He slipped, and talons raked one shank, scattering blood. He rolled out of reach, stood, and caught one extended paw upon the blade of his dagger. The injured ros unleashed a shattering series of roars. Flores backed off. The ros followed. Again its claws raked, leaving streaks of red across his side and chest. He rolled. The animal sought to pounce, failed, and again abandoned itself to a paroxysm of scrambling.

Regaining his breath, Flores calmed. About him a hundred bloodied warriors faced a hundred ros-na amid a forest of smoking torches. How sad, Flores thought, that his tormentors could not see by the full light of day. How typical of eunuchs that they would deny even this to an enemy. A warrior should die beneath the open Eye of Vensor.

Flores exhaled. He did not know how much time had passed since he had awakened alone by the fire in the forest. He was tiring quickly, soon he would no longer be able to defend himself. As the ros again gathered momentum, Flores lifted his weapon in salute to Vensor. It was fitting that his life should end as it had begun–facing the symbol of all his enemies, a ros. Stepping back, he braced for the last rush.

Perplexed, he glanced down. His foot no longer slipped. The last swipe of the ros had ripped off one sandal and, to his amazement, his bare foot now gripped the glassy floor with perfect traction. He stepped again to test it–his footing was sure, solid. Quickly he kicked free the other sandal and crouched, prepared to challenge his enemy with new confidence. As the animal neared, the jaws split and roared and the beast of Talon rose on its crooked doglegs to gather him in its bloody embrace.

Flores spun free and when again he turned to face the ros, a red gash had opened along its flank. Its roars thundered, shaking the chamber like the voice of Nvediteg, as its inflamed brain sensed the mutilation. Again it rose to seize the puny human and rend its weak flesh. Flores spun to the opposite side, opening another gash. But the Turlicum tarried too long and was repaid with a rake across his own chest. He poised to contemplate his injures. His blood, and that of the ros, now coated parts of the floor. If the contest did not end soon, his new advantage would vanish as the floor grew slick with his own gore. He thought, then stepped forward.

Advancing to the center of the chamber, he shouted, taunting the animal. Snarling, it again launched itself in his direction. Judging its speed carefully, Flores turned and ran toward the wall. With the beast behind him, he climbed and flipped. Alighting behind the onrushing ros, he found what he sought and plunged his blade deep into the lower spine of the beast. A savage twist and he spun away as the animal exploded in rage and anguish. It recovered and again attacked. Flores backed away. Detecting a slowing of the back limbs, he compensated with a slower climb and flip. Again the blade sank home, embedding itself in the same wound. Another twist, and Flores leaped clear. A second paroxysm of anger showed no movement from the ros' paralyzed rear limbs.

Still seeking to bury its fangs in its accustomed prey, the ros dragged itself after Flores. The warrior now approached with calm and stared with pity upon the dying creature. The black eyes, shot with green, glared hatred. Flores realized that he, in the mind of the beast, was merely another one of its tormentors. Methodically, he delivered further thrusts to the spine until no sign of life remained except a low rumbling in time with the creature's breathing.

Flores stared soberly upon the carnage. Could he expect such merciful treatment from his own enemies? From somewhere a gasp of anger and disappointment emanated, echoed through the chamber. Flores glanced up. His observer must be closer than he had suspected, probably in an adjacent room. Recalling what had first drawn him into the chamber, Flores expected to glimpse Amina again in torment, but once more the torches vanished and the chamber plunged into darkness. He chilled. A second time he heard the rasp of glass on metal as the sickly sweet odor of a ros filled the chamber.

Flores sprang toward the sound. The gasp had come from somewhere above. Since someone must be manipulating the trapdoor, and that person must be apprised of events in the chamber, the passage that released the animals into the chamber of glass must therefore lead directly to that of his hidden observer. That passage was now opening, and Flores realized he would not have a second opportunity to traverse it. Without the torchlight to confuse him, he found the panel easy to locate and waited in silence as it widened. A slithering followed as the next ros sprang into the chamber, eager to quench its hunger with human flesh. As the light flicked on again, Flores dove into the passage.

The panel slammed shut. Flores found himself in a narrow culvert. Moving quickly, his dagger out-thrust before him, he emerged in a wide chamber, his view of its dark interior blocked by vertical bands. His fingers closed upon the bars of an iron cage. He peered across the murky room and detected the outlines of a series of cages leading to the far side of the chamber, each cage separated from the next by an opaque panel. The first two were empty, their panels already raised. These were, as he realized, probably the very cages that had released

the two ros-na he had encountered. A low rumbling sounded from beyond the panels indicating the presence of other beasts should their
master have need of them. Flores shuddered. What would have transpired had he remained in the chamber of glass? One ros, even two,
he might kill. But a dozen? His tormentor had laid his plans well.

From somewhere a human voice rose, agitated. Flores glanced up
and saw the rim of a balcony or split-level some eight feet or so above
the chamber in which the cages stood. The shifting torchlight bathed
the rim in a ghostly corona; as Flores watched, a hand appeared over
the coping and took hold of a thick rope that led to the panel separating
him from the next cage. The hand pulled, enabling another ros to traverse the culvert leading to the glass room. Further along the balcony,
past a spiraling stairwell, the hand appeared again to release a second
panel. Then a third. Its owner was taking no more chances. A series
of low rumbles grew as Flores fumbled for a device that might open
his cage before the animals detected him. Just as his fingers located
the latch, talons sprang from the darkness and sent Flores sprawling.
He stabbed on reflex. A shrill scream indicated he had found his mark,
but the talons struck again, this time seeking to grip his forearm and
drag him toward the powerful jaws that snapped in the shadows.

A head appeared over the balcony, the face obscured by the corona
of torchlight behind it. Attempting to discern the cause of the commotion in the cages on the lower level, it oscillated. The head bent, broad,
fan-like ears waving, then withdrew. A moment later it returned and
the lash of a whip struck the cage.

"Scum of Talon!" the head hissed. "Obey me, I say! Enter the chamber and slay this intruder. I cannot be certain of his death till he lies
torn beneath fang and claw. Now enter the chamber, the lot of you."
The lash returned, striking the bars of the cage before the head again
vanished behind the wall.

The whip distracted the ros from its duel with Flores, and the
Turlicum wrenched his arm free, and slashed, tearing bone and skin.
Again he fumbled for the lock. The latch sprang and he clambered
from the opening. Wasting no time, he immediately released the dagger, seized the nearest rope with both hands and climbed. The shriek
of a woman spurred him to greater effort. A moment later he emerged
at the top of the balcony and pulled himself over.

On the upper level amid smoking torches a dwarfish creature with
wide shoulders and narrow waist stood with his back to Flores, facing
Amina. The priestess of Vensa was suspended from a metal frame gib-

bet that had been swung over a rack of glowing coals. Above her an assemblage of blades and pins circled, edging ever closer. To one side, a contrivance of tubes and panels shined upon her torso, the image transmitted along further tubes to various locations on the walls of the chamber of glass, the interior of which lay fully revealed to Flores as he stood upon the balcony, as if nothing intervened but air. Inside the glass chamber, he glimpsed a famished ros gorging upon the body of its dead companion. Amina's eyes were closed. Her chin nodded upon her chest and her unclothed body glistened with sweat. Crouching, the creature turned a knob and the rack burst into flame. Amina awoke and shrieked.

"Do you feel it, daughter of Atasan?" croaked Malag. "Do you feel the kiss of your master? Pain has Atasan visited upon this world, and pain is what Vensor repays Him with. It is the currency of flesh, the language all understand. There can be no truce between your master and mine. As a soldier in God's holy war, I accept no less than total victory! What's that–you would renounce your evil ways? Ha-ha, you cannot! It is your nature to seduce, as it is mine to surrender. We cannot change our natures–neither you nor I. This much the guild has taught me. But before our holy union, you shall suffer for the crime that you force me to commit. You will pay dearly for my lust!"

A guttural cry tore itself from Flores' guts. His hand re-closed upon his gory dagger which locked back into place with the arm guard. Blinking from the sooty atmosphere, he stepped forward as Malag turned, his impish face frozen in shock and surprise. The Turlicum took several small steps, then sprang full upon Malag as might a ros from its den, his warrior soul reduced to its most elemental instinct.

In mid-leap, he froze, then rebounded.

His grumble of outrage ceased. In shock and incomprehension he dropped to his feet, staggering to remain erect. Dazed, with bruises swelling about his face and head, he reached out one hand and felt– cold glass. On the other side of the invisible partition, Amina had again lapsed into unconsciousness, and Malag, slave and slave-driver to the Eunuch Lord of Ven, opened his mouth and exploded in laughter as he gazed upon Flores. The dwarf flicked a switch and the glass wall shuddered soundlessly into the floor. One hand raised a thick wooden club. Flores attempted to ward off the blow, stumbled. The club sent him plunging into the stairwell.

Cautiously Malag approached. He leaned over the stairs to eye Flores' crumpled form at the bottom of the landing. The slave driver breathed deeply, a brightness about his eyes. Turning suddenly, he swung the gibbet away from the rack, and released the chain that suspended Amina. His muscular arms lifted her easily before him. Trembling with excitement, one gnarled hand slid briefly, sensually, over her slick ebony skin, now pausing to massage, now tracing the curves of her slick torso.

Throwing her limp form over one shoulder, he opened a wooden door. He passed through, locked it from the far side. Halting to listen, he cocked his head as if to detect some subtle but familiar sound. Corridors sped beneath his feet, his stealthy advance silent but for the panting of his labor.

At an intersection, Malag paused before a series of mirrors sunk into the walls. He fell to his knees, and crawled beneath their lower extremity, dragging the limp Amina behind. Similarly avoiding other mirrors in his path, he arrived before a small chamber cluttered with barrels and bales, the dreariness of one corner barely relieved by a soiled muslin rug and tattered furniture. Here he halted and carefully placed the object of his passion upon several stuffed dirty grey pillows. Again his hands wandered across the fleshy landscape that opened before him, sweat from the abducted corpus mingling with the slaver spilling from his open, impassioned mouth. Once again he paused to listen, ears waving like antennae for the slightest deviation from the normal band of noise. Malag tore loose his skirt. Leaning low over his captive, he raised her arms above her head to render resistance useless. Amina's eyes remained shut, her teary face smooth and calm. With exquisite care his tongue tasted the sweat on one side of her neck. He moaned. He settled full upon her.

"Slave Malag," interrupted a voice. "We commanded you to take possession of our lawful property which the Tumset soldiers stole, and to deliver it to us. We did not command you to take possession of the gila yourself."

The slave-driver jerked upright, hastily covering himself with the muslin rug. His face was white and his body shaking. His eyes shifted from Amina, whose outspread form left no doubt as to his intentions, to the several black-clothed eunuchs who stood about the threshold of the door. Their expressions were unruffled, unconcerned; their words soothing, confident.

"Worry not, Malag. We know the failings of the flesh best of all."

"I...I sought only to prevent the creature from escaping," he blurted.

The eunuchs smiled–tolerant, indulgent smiles. Two more entered the storage room, lifted the inert body of the priestess, and carried it out.

"You shall not be punished–too severely, that is."

Malag paled.

"Anyhow, we have erred," one said. "When we learned from you that the Tumset-sa were entertaining a gila in their camp, we assumed they had stolen our cargo and substituted rocks in its place. So we dispatched you to retrieve our stolen property, using whatever force was necessary. However, we neglected to inspect the palanquin ourselves. It seems that the gila our holy brother in Tumset sent us never left the palanquin. When we opened it, we found the body wracked by poison. The pouch was still in its hand. The gila that you...rescued...was not taken from the palanquin, but has appeared from elsewhere. We have no explanation, but we are fortunate that by this stroke of luck we have another to send in the place of the dead one when we ourselves return to Ven. And Maalstrom is fortunate that we detected this creature before it consumed the children of Vensor with its evil energies. And you, Malag, are especially fortunate, else we must had sent your head in place of the dead gila."

Malag swallowed, and began to recover some of his color.

The eunuch sighed and smiled. "It will be good to see the father of cities again and hear the voice of our beloved teacher, Soorkrul. Our absence has been long, and we have heard no news from our master, or Ven, for many months." He sighed. "Such is the price we of the order pay for our devotion to reason and light."

"Master, I..." Malag's chest swelled. "I foiled an intruder who desired this woman. He lies by the Guest Chamber even now, unconscious. He deserves death for his sin and his violence–"

"We will decide who deserves death," interrupted the eunuch. He paused to ensure that Malag apprehended his full meaning. "We have found the captive. He is strong and will be useful pulling an oar on our sacred galley."

The eunuchs turned to leave, then paused. "It is not for you to kill him, or anyone, without our word."

In the hall beyond the eunuchs, a large body of slavers and mercenaries armed with clubs and pikes began to tramp past, heading for the eastern gate.

"The soldiers of Tumset have killed many of our servants," the eunuch continued. "But we have many more. Accompany them, Malag. All who resist are to be killed. Those who renounce their clan, and demonstrate this by executing one of their comrades, may live–so long as they serve our holy order. The rest you will kill. Scour the surrounding country well, and fear not the wrath of the king of Tumset. Our trade is worth more to him than the lives of a few of his soldiers. This trade must remain secret–it is our desire that none who may have learned of the contents of the palanquin should escape. If the outside world learns of this incident, Malag, it will go poorly with you. Now go. The degree of punishment for your transgression will depend upon your success in accomplishing your mission."

Malag again swallowed. Averting his gaze, he clothed himself and vanished in the mass of dour slavers traversing the corridor.

CHAPTER 24

"THE TURLICUM IS DEAD!"

Flores awoke to a drumming in his head. It was long before he could move. The ground swayed, aggravating the throbbing, but the movement accelerated his return to consciousness. Slowly his eyes opened despite a swollen brow that interfered with his vision. He struggled and sat upright. He was within a cavernous grotto, the roof of which was lost among a profusion of stalactites. Gradually his eyes focused on the source of the drumming–from the far side of the cavern a waterfall spilled into a broad dark lake. The impression was beauteous, he thought, and he would have enjoyed the spectacle but for his more immediate surroundings. The ground swayed again and he discerned the outlines of a large slave galley of the holy priests of Vensor with oar-seats and gangplank. In the center stood a long, low cabin for passengers, its outer panels carved with representations of all the gods save Atasan, the signs of exaggerated masculinity obtruding obscenely as was the wont of eunuchs.

An elbow struck him. He attempted to shift out of the elbow's range, but was prevented by a clattering of irsrem. A length of irsrem chain joined his ankles; another chain intersected it, running beyond his vision in either direction. Before him a wooden oar was suspended. Along the galley sat a crowd of dirty men with other oars, cursing and jostling from lack of room as the boat prepared to push off.

A familiar form appeared on the gangway. Malag directed two slaves to lower a plank and assisted several black-clothed eunuchs in boarding from an adjacent pier. They took no notice of Flores, nor of the other oarsmen. Flores marveled that Malag had allowed him to live after their encounter in the fortress. What purpose could the eunuchs' slave master have other than to subject him to more exquisite tortures? What might his fate be should the slave-driver or his masters discover his true identity? Flores did not wonder at their lack of recognition. Indeed, he had hardly recognized himself in the mirrors, given his bedraggled and dirty appearance. His injuries, which were fortunately superficial, made him even less familiar, not to mention disagreeable to the eye. He hoped that his anonymity would continue and turned his signet ring in to face the palm of his hand.

After the eunuchs had entered the cabin, a dozen slavers with pikes came on board, followed by the crew, who took up posts beneath golden globes mounted fore and aft in imitation both of genitals and the suns. The ropes were then released, and the galley floated free of the dock. Flores took up his oar and upon the crack of a whip began to pull.

A stony aperture appeared before them. With a few more strokes, they glided into the glare of the noontime suns. Flores glimpsed tufts of smoke, remnants he assumed of the Tumset camp. Neither mortal nor reven was visible in the clearing. Then the river turned and the galley, golden globes and phalluses glinting in the suns, entered a wilderness of forest.

Flores sat near the stern of the vessel on the port side, not far from the steersman. Eyes shadowed from sleeplessness, the steersman watched the muddy riverbanks drift by while other crew, two forward and one aft, tested the water with poles or diverted driftwood from the hull. Someone groaned. Flores looked at the oarsmen. None seemed grossly mistreated or near death, but it was plain no effort had been made for their comfort. From the bench beside him, one breathed upon his neck.

"You're a son of Gethos, Ven. A blue orphan of the seas."

The man's appearance repelled the noble, although he realized that his own appearance must be little different. His companion's beard was dirty and uncombed, his face soiled, his hair equally neglected.

"We're both orphans," the man continued.

Flores attempted to ignore him, but as the prisoner showed no inclination to cease speaking, the Turlicum finally replied. "Good sir, we are slaves destined to be sold to a foreign city or to live out our lives behind an oar on this galley. Here we sit, Divine Vensor knows where, unable even to fly to Heaven should the ship sink beneath the waves. How, good man," Flores eyed him carefully, "have you determined that we are lucky?"

His companion leaned forward and grinned. "Because we're not going to the mines of Maanus!" He indicated several oarsmen in the forward half of the galley. "That is their destination," he nodded know-ingly. He cautioned Flores to silence. "Heard it from a guard. If they knew, they would drown themselves, and us with them, at their first chance."

Flores glanced at the unfortunates and thought he saw worried looks. Perhaps they knew. The Mines of Maanus.... Yes, he thought, he was lucky if that was not his destination. But what was in store for the rest of the crew?

"That's the best part," his companion replied. "Not for me, because I'm from Tumset. You, on the other hand, are from Ven–I know be-cause you talked in your sleep. You, my friend, are going home." He gave a vigorous pull on the oar and hummed cheerily.

Flores ceased rowing. His friend took one arm. "Oh, I know. You're happy now, but before you get your hopes up–you won't be allowed to stay. After Vensor's holy servants debark in Ven, their ship will re-turn to the fortress. I don't wish to live in Ven. When I was a youth, I was apprenticed to a merchant. We visited the city of Ror. I saw the famous Lord Turlicum himself when his army took the city. Many were killed, the city's Temple profaned. You Vens have no mercy, no respect for tradition. So I don't wish to live in Ven. But you will get to see your city once more. Yes, we are lucky. I may never see my own city of Tumset again, but at least it's not the mines for me. And when we return, we will serve the eunuchs with swords instead of oars."

Flores was puzzled. "You would serve the eunuchs though they have enslaved you and killed your clansmen?"

Telmoc, as his companion was called, peered at him. "And why not? My clansmen sold me into slavery." He attempted to spit over the side and instead hit Flores' arm. "All I did was criticize our king. He is op-pressive and violates our laws and does nothing while the eunuchs build an army and take our land. Now I wish nothing more than to turn my weapons against him. The others, you ask? Yes, most are of Tumset also. All sold to the eunuchs of Ven as our king has done for some time now, giving little thought to his own city. Except those." He indicated the half-dozen at the far end of the vessel, those destined for the mines.

"They are from Vedeg. We took them captive when we took their city. Our soldiers took it, destroyed the entire city, burned its Temple." His chest swelled with pride.

"How can that be?" interjected Flores, recalling the words of Macius.

"I heard that Vedeg was prosperous and at peace."

"The peace of death," laughed Telmoc. "I myself helped throw down its gate a year ago. We still have not disposed of all the captives. We sold many to the mines of Maanus. They have no city or Temple now. No one cares what happens to them. They are as good as dead."

Flores smirked as he resumed pulling the oar. "Has *your* city no mercy then, no respect for tradition?"

Telmoc glared at Flores. "That was different. The men of Vedeg were scoundrels, planted grain in our fields, competed with us in trade."

Flores nodded. The end of Vedeg was a familiar one. And should Nesos win his war with Ven, Ven would share its fate, its citizens scorned and sold to the mines. A chill shook Flores as he thought of his former companions in cramped hot tunnels, extracting corta from its bowels, never to see the light of day. He shook his head. What had happened to Crestal and Tilsis, he wondered? What paths did they tread? When he awoke in the camp they had already departed, as had Amina, though their mounts remained.

Flores sighed. Try as he might to forget her, the image of the priestess remained within him. Her powers were strange, unearthly. During their journey through the forest he had tried to accept her as a rational being like himself, but he knew that she remained altogether different. She was a gila. He had known that from the first moment he saw her in the glow of the candle, but had not wished to admit so. He could not flee her beauty. How sensible that the priestesses of the Temple, the gila-sa of Atasan, should veil their enchantments from the rough gaze of men, how wise since others of their kind possessed similar charms. He himself had fallen to those charms and become a criminal, guilty of feminality. But, far from destroying him, Amina had saved his life. So, although perplexed, for his involvement with Amina he would always be grateful. However, he reminded himself, that must be the limit of his feelings. He was bound to provide for her as payment for her assistance. But the debt mattered no more; the priestess remained in Soorkrul's fortress, at the mercy of the eunuchs.

Flores clenched his fists about the oar. Why could he not forget her? The more he strove to free himself from the tangle of his emotions, the deeper they drew him in.

The snap of a whip drew him out of his reverie. He glanced up to see Malag standing over him, a cold smile settling upon his face. No, reflected Flores, he has not forgotten. The smile transmuted into concentrated hatred and the dwarf's hand wandered to a second whip tipped with metal such as Flores had seen employed on the Tumset slaves. Flores cringed, then a noise from the front of the boat distracted the slaver. A eunuch had exited the cabin to take in fresh air. Moving swiftly away, Malag cracked his whip over the head of other slaves, leaving Flores to his oar.

Towards the end of the second day, the galley came to a sleepy river port with a quay of neglected clapboards. The ship pulled alongside and a motley band of soldiers with ill-fitting armor boarded the vessel and removed the slavers whom Telmoc had previously indicated. The Vedeg slaves were few and in poor health and, far from decreasing the strength of the crew, their absence freed the remaining oarsmen to row with greater vigor. A faint sorrowful rattling of chains drifted on the wind as they trudged toward the distant mountains. Flores felt pity; he knew from Assembly reports how the corta pits swallowed lives.

"The mines of Maanus," said Telmoc, pointing to a far white patch. "We're lucky. Downstream all the way to Ven."

For another day they rowed. The right bank took on new character. A ridge emerged and the forest on its summit grew wild and thick, its base offering little opportunity to beach for the night. On the left, however, the country still lay flat but for the range that grew steadily in the distance. The bank stretched green and rolling before their gaze. Finally, the slavers dropped anchor. The prisoners were permitted to step off the ship to attend to their bodily needs, but the long irsrem chain remained in place to prevent any break for freedom. After the slaves had stood about and stretched their legs for a time, they were allowed to lie on the bank for the night, and Flores watched the moons weave their mysterious pattern until the lapping wavelets on the side of the boat finally lulled him to sleep.

At dawn they resumed their journey. The right bank grew wilder and the ridge more precipitous until it became a cliff. The left, on the other hand, grew hilly and shorn of vegetation. Then the far range loomed suddenly before them and Flores recognized the tall peaks of the Amanus-nama, the Amanus mountains, white with snow.

Then, as the galley rounded a bend in the river, the lookout shouted and pointed. Slaves and crew gazed upon a pair of ruined smoldering huts. Soon more smoking ruins appeared on the bluffs. The slaves grew restive and wondered what they might encounter when they arrived at the city of Sish, next on their itinerary. A range of hills drifted by, and the drivers remarked on the absence of river traffic.

Finally the wide plain before the city hove into sight and they stared in silence. The field before the city was covered by a vast camp of warriors, tents and totems outspread before its walls, reven-na trampling its crops. Near the gate a skirmish was in progress. The besiegers loosed arrows while the defenders replied in kind. Even the eunuchs, hitherto reluctant to leave the cabin, came on deck to watch.

The galley came even with the harbor, its stone breakers and wharves jutting into the river. Suddenly the steersman leaned hard upon the rudder and sent the galley careening away from the city as a flotilla of canoes emerged from the wharves. Malag and several assistants, formerly distracted by the scene before the city, lashed the slaves into full exertion to put as much distance as possible between the galley and the approaching flotilla, while the eunuchs' soldiers readied their pikes to resist boarding. From the bank near the encampment, more craft appeared. The canoes of the besiegers raced across the water, the men paddling madly in a race to intercept the skiffs from the city. The two fleets converged. A furious battle ensued with arrows flying at narrow range and men leaping into the skiffs of their opponents.

As the fleets engaged, Flores opened his mouth in surprise. The men from the bank flew totems of Ven. He stood and shouted, waving his hands. In unison, Malag and several slave drivers exploded and fell upon him with a withering series of blows and lashes. He crumpled back onto his bench, but continued to eye the skiffs. If he could only free himself of his chains long enough to attract the attention of those warriors...but it was hopeless. As the city vanished from sight, the two fleets remained locked in combat, neither willing to admit defeat, the Vens more concerned with preventing their enemies from seizing the priests' galley than in taking it for themselves.

By nightfall of the following day they reached the portage. A series of shallow rapids fell away as a spur of the Amanus Mountains, the northern flank of the Falls of Sish, intersected the Suma. Malag, backed by a dozen armed slavers announced that the captives were to carry the galley down a series of rocky gorges until they had passed the rapids, where, having refloated the galley in the river and the prisoners again chained in their places, they would resume their journey to Ven. In the meantime the anchor was dropped and the men rested in preparation for the morrow.

When morning came, the drivers pulled the boat to the bank and, for the first occasion on their journey, the chains that had burdened the slavers for the duration of the trip were removed. While this operation was executed, the galley was turned over to dry in the sun and the captives allowed to stand and limber their legs under the close supervision of the slaves. Finally the order was shouted to lift and the prisoners raised the boat and staggered away from the river toward a jagged formation of rock. Aware that should a prisoner wish to escape this would be his best opportunity, Malag and his assistants ringed the boat with drawn swords.

Rounding the crag, they descended a steep gorge and Flores' spirits sank. The drivers observed them so closely that he could see no opportunity to evade them.

A shout rang out. The galley was slipping. The slaves strove to halt the slide, but slowly, inexorably, the massive vessel picked up speed. The slavers beneath the front staggered–those beneath the stern lost their grip, and with a shudder the galley sank, sliding in mud and gravel. One of the prisoners screamed, then gurgled as the ship slammed against a rocky wall with a sickening crunch of bones.

"Lift!" shouted the slavers, their whips snapping across the bare backs of the slaves.

Ignoring the crushed corpse, the slaves hoisted the boat aloft. They resumed their march. Presently another high tor blocked their progress and the slavers directed the captives along a path that circumvented it. Emerging upon a broad plateau stretching away toward broken country beyond, the slaves halted–a short distance away a body of cavalry padded across the meadow. Flores stared. Their leader wore flayed rum-na claws.

"Vens!" Flores shouted.

The slaves lowered the boat.

Shouts of outrage rose from the eunuchs and their slavers.

"Pick up that galley!" snarled Malag. When no one moved, he unfurled his whip with the metal tip and laid it upon several backs, beginning with Flores. With a low cry of rage, the Turlicum crouched and flung himself upon the slaver. They went down. Immediately the other slaves broke away from the galley and began a wild dash for the mounted men. Flores wrestled free and joined them.

The leader of the cavalry drew his blade and sprang forward to meet the slaves and their guards. His men whipped out rapiers and followed. With joy upon his face Flores ran to meet them. One word and he and the other slaves would be freed, the eunuchs whipped and sent on their way, and the Turlicum would resume his rightful place as head of the most powerful clan in Ven, once again prepared to vanquish his enemies. Once more Maalstrom would know justice, once more Atasan would see that evil cannot triumph over good.

"Halt!"

The Ven chief pointed a rapier at his chest. Flores stopped short. Behind him the other slaves halted in their tracks.

"I know you," said Flores, his voice breaking despite his effort to summon a semblance of dignity and control himself. "You work for me."

The haughty captain cast a supernal glance upon Flores' chains and the dirty moccasins that the slavers had exchanged for his riding boots. "Oh?" replied the officer, smiling. "Doing what, my good man–shining your boots?" He winked at his men.

"No. You are one of my officers, a Turlicum. And well paid for your services."

"Well, then, how fortunate that we should meet. Maybe we should introduce ourselves so we can pay each other social calls." The soldiers guffawed.

"I'm afraid I don't remember your name. If only–"

The officer tired of the joke. "Too bad. I'm afraid I don't recall yours either." He urged his mount past Flores and addressed the eunuchs. "Holy brothers, are you in need of assistance in controlling these rabble?"

The chief eunuch arrived, limping and holding his cassock aloft to avoid the dirt. "Indeed, sir," he wheezed, "but only to replace their chains. They are an unruly lot and they shall be disciplined for this breach of trust. But, kind sir, I am certain that we can handle them without assistance once they are again restrained."

Flores stepped forward, outrage upon his face. "What is this?" he shouted. "You dare address eunuchs when your lord stands before you on foot and in need?" The eyes of all turned upon him, amazed.

"'Lord'?" the officer repeated, unsmiling.

Flores inhaled and his eyes narrowed. "Indeed. Look close, captain. For I am Flores-Sumvensor of the Turlicum."

Surprise settled on the officer's face. Carefully he peered at Flores. For a long moment he eyed his uncut hair, battered sun-burnt face, the tattered rags hanging on his limbs, his full dirty beard. He threw back his head and howled with laughter.

"Fool! Flores of the Turlicum died in the pits of Numsenmur months ago! Now get back and pick up that boat. We'll have no rabble breaking laws in Ven territory."

His booted foot planted itself upon Flores' chest and the officer thrust him to the ground. Then he turned and his reven hopped away.

Flores struggled up, held aloft the signet ring of Turlicum, a reven paw inscribed upon it. "This ring," he called, "proves what I say–"

He was gone.

Flores cringed as Malag laid another weal across his back. Turning, he beheld the dwarf flailing madly with his metal-tipped whip. Sputtering with fury and possessed by an evil joy at having found a pretext to avenge himself on Flores, Malag sent his victim staggering backwards with the force of his blows, bleeding in several places, until the hand of the chief eunuch fell upon Malag's arm.

"Enough. I understand your frustration with this slave, but we need all our hands to haul the boat. We have lost several. Do not deprive us of another."

Slowly the paroxysm subsided and Malag calmed. At his command, the slaves again raised the galley aloft and resumed their journey, made more miserable by the lashes of Malag and his slavers, even less restrained than before by the eunuchs.

The remainder of the journey passed without event. Malag watched Flores with renewed hatred, and occasionally the Turlicum noticed Malag eyeing him with curiosity as if contemplating some obscure possibility. And once, when Malag stood next to him on the gangplank, he noticed him staring at the ring on his finger, although, since he kept it turned toward his palm, nothing of its inscription was visible. Had the dwarf believed his claim at the portage, or had he finally recalled Flores from public events in Ven? Moreover, since their abortive escape, the attitude of his fellow slaves toward him had changed. Several eyed him with resentment and made him the butt of jokes, as if he were the author of their troubles, while Telmoc, who occasionally received a blow meant for Flores, no longer spoke but ignored his every attempt to kindle conversation.

Flores soon began to wonder whether he would be killed by his enemies in Ven or murdered on the journey by his colleagues seeking petty revenge. Stinging from the impact of Malag's lash, which the dwarf laid upon him with increasing frequency when the eunuchs were not on deck, and, lacking even the solace of casual interchange with the other galley slaves, Flores gradually sank into a sullen, dark indifference.

After the last portage the Suma narrowed, the striped cliff-side gaping like a wound before the steady onslaught of the river on the tableland. Flores wondered at the fate that had thrown him inexorably upon his enemy. He blinked and saw the wounds on his hands, running red on the corpse of his father, then grey in the pits of Numsenmur's palace, and dirty green between the jutting quays of Ven. Though the sky was calm and bright, clouds roiled interminably, clouding his vision. Rage, despair, hope, resolve, hatred, regret welled up in wrenching unstable succession.

The galley neared its goal. Around him, chains shook with each pull of the oars as the spires and domes of the city of glass drew closer. Flores felt no joy; the moment of his execution neared. The galley touched an empty dock and grew still. The slaves dragged themselves to their feet, and Flores found he could move only with the greatest effort. He glanced up. The harbor was devoid of people. Unusual, he thought, but then the city had been at war when he departed, and for all he knew was still at war, though why no one had attempted to intercept the boat he could not imagine. Directing a dozen soldiers to clamber ashore, Malag entered the galley's cabin while other soldiers threw ropes and drew the galley to the dock, tying it firmly. The eunuchs emerged in a body then climbed ashore and peered about them in confusion.

Life had not returned to Ven. Flores wondered whether the eunuchs knew of the war with Nesos, coming as it had so swiftly and cutting off communication with the valleys. He sat on the jetty, burying his face in his arms. His depression was so overwhelming that he remained unmoved even as Neset-sa sprang from the surrounding sheds to attack the eunuchs' soldiers amid sudden screams and shouts. Rude Neset warriors tore amulets from the necks of the eunuchs–the priests protested and Neset pikes were thrust into them, their bodies collapsing on the quay. Flores made no move until a sword prodded him to his feet. Neset slave drivers quickly chained the oarsmen of the galley together to form a caravan. Even the presence of Malag, now chained with the other prisoners, his mouth open with shock and chagrin, drew no interest.

"Move!" a Neset ordered.

Their first stop was the public baths. A haze dropped upon him as the water cleansed his body, stinging the many small cuts inflicted by Malag's whip. But Flores' soul was elsewhere–treading forest paths with a gift from a different world, a mystery he could not understand, but craved, a sweet ideal. How he had enjoyed those green paths and yellow meadows in the company of Amina! How clearly he could see her even now beside him, their path winding in the suns. Then a hulking brute blocked it, a brute with tawny beard and a cough like a ros. The dagger-like claws reached. With a cry, Flores leaped to subdue the beast. He struck it.

Yells erupted and the lash of the ever present whip brought Flores back as the slave in front of him regained his feet and resumed walking, casting apprehensive glances over his shoulder at the madman chained behind.

In surprise Flores found himself pausing in front of the Temple gate. Staring upon the pavement, he raised his head only when he heard the chains unlock toward the rear of the caravan. With the aid of several soldiers, the Neset slavers removed a thin slave wrapped in a cloak, whom they had removed from the cabin of the eunuchs' galley. The Neset-sa approached the gate of the Temple where a small postern reserved for accepting gifts without ceremony opened to receive them. The cloak was removed. Flores froze. His eyes drank in the black hair, the curving body, the sad eyes, the perfect lips. The Neset-sa chained her to iron rings in the open door. The door began to close.

"Amina!"

The flawless eyes turned and found Flores. Two perfect arms lifted toward him.

The postern shut.

Crying in rage, Flores lurched forward, dragging the caravan after him until a Neset slaver lashed his back, raining blows amid a spattering of blood. Even then Flores would have continued to press forward, determined to reach the Temple, but Neset pikes thrust against his skin. While a crowd of Vens and Neset-sa gathered to mock them, the caravan jerked to its feet and resumed its weary march.

The band followed the Way of Murfenmas to the central market of the city and spilled into the plaza. Neset guardsmen shouted to the populace to yield, and Flores was struck by the din of the ritual that apparently had been underway for some days. In the center of the plaza a vast concourse of Vens, free and slave, young and old, escorted by rough Neset-sa herdsmen, shuffled past a figure perched atop a high mound. The crowd rendered some sort of homage or obeisance, and, having completed their task, were permitted to disperse. Skirted Neset-sa herded the newcomers into the dense queue and pushed them forward, disregarding their cries of distress. Other conscripts were chosen by some obscure criterion, some being suddenly and rudely thrust into the vast river of people, while others were permitted to pass the queue unmolested. Flores could see no obvious criterion for the distinction.

As the slavers neared the mound, the crush became greater and a net of whips flicking overhead forced them to accelerate. A slave near Flores slipped and brought down several companions, including Flores, evoking a caning from Neset-sa pikes. Regaining their feet, the slaves rushed forward. Finally Flores saw their destination. Atop a pyramid the size of a building, rivaling the Assembly Hall in size, sat the princeling Sedsednon, swinging his arms in vigorous enjoyment of his burgeoning glory and squealing in anticipation of more. The pyramid consisted of shoes of all types: sandals, boots, laced, tanned, all piled indiscriminately together in unending terraces that towered above the multitude. Those that rolled down the slope were intercepted by slaves and cast back to others on the side of the hill, who struggled to maintain the colossal monument to the imagination of the heir to all the lands of the Vensors. A tiny shriek carried to Flores from the minuscule figure enthroned on the pinnacle as Flores' turn came to remove his worn moccasins. He threw them; another slave tossed them higher. A few moments later, the caravan having performed its duty, the Neset drivers resumed command of their charges and directed the caravan toward the auction block in the merchants' district of the central plaza.

The crowd at the block was small, consisting of foreigners come to profit from the misery of Ven. They were for the most part disappointed, since few had died in the conquest and the city itself had not been sacked. Furthermore, the commotion in the square distracted many traders and the ritual itself drove off most of the citizenry. For this last fact, Flores was glad. He knew that the moment of his discovery would be his last. In line before the block, Flores shuffled, resigned to a life of servitude.

As he moved slowly forward and his ears absorbed the cries of the slave sellers, he realized that he listened for a different sound, the ring of three peals from a tower, and though he told himself that it was too late or that it did not matter, that a few happy moments on a forest trail meant nothing, still he listened.

"This is he."

Telmoc pointed. No chains encumbered his wrists and he stood free and separate from the caravan. A Neset guard planted the blade of a pike against Flores' chest and the oarsman took hold of his hand, pulled loose the ring, and handed it to the soldier. One warrior released his bonds; another pulled Flores from the column of slaves and motioned that he walk. More soldiers gathered and Flores had difficulty getting his breath. He had always thought that the moment of death would be painless, that he would be numb or dazed or unconcerned. He wasn't.

Accompanied by Telmoc, the soldiers escorted Flores across the square towards the Assembly Hall, the newly freed slave walking beside the foreign soldiers brightly, his head held high. They crossed the Assembly gardens then entered an annex of the hall of Vim, the hall that stood above the state prison cells. As his cell door slammed, enclosing him in the most complete blackness he had ever known, he thought he could hear the jingle of a bag of money changing hands.

CHAPTER 25

THE HALL OF VIM

Flores sat. The pain grew and became unbearable, clasping him in its snake-like tentacles. Amina, here, in the Temple! The seconds passed and soon would end in the ring of a gong, rolling from the acropolis across the city, and she would die. Flores shook his head. He forced her from his mind. She was, after all, a gila. Why should he care? He had his own troubles. He could never escape from his cell beneath the hall of Vim. Even if he could, his own people no longer knew him. His own captain had said as much–he was already dead.

The time passed without food or drink. He saw nothing; not the least ray of light entered his cell. The only means he had to measure time was his breathing. He counted his inhalations, and, at fifteen per minute, tried to estimate the time that had passed since his arrival, to know when the suns were down so that he could sleep.

A prickling reminded him of an old disturbance, an ancient guilt. He knew why this had happened: The gods first make mad whom they would slay. The cell precedes the tomb, the judge the headsman, however similar they be. He had been impious and scornful of the heavens. Why not? His father was allowed to die while his enemies had prospered. But he had transgressed further–he had been openly callous, leaving piety to his rivals Numsenmur and Sruk. And in surprising ways he had been vindicated. As he had learned, no god spoke in the Temple. But he had gone too far. His indifference had become scorn. Worse, he had consorted with a servant of Atasan and committed femininity. That was the crime of Flores–he had loved a woman.

He caught his breath. With an almost palpable chill he felt the darkness of the cell penetrate his soul. He was sinking. He closed his eyes. The snakes began to writhe. Suddenly a dark-haired angel with blue-painted face wrapped him in a cloak and offered water and bread to his lips. He ate. He sighed, then rose and chased her through golden woods and spun with her in open glades.

He exhaled and resumed counting. Then slept.

The darkness split, and a lamp shot its light about the room. Flores cried out and rolled to hide his stunned eyes. Slowly the pain eased and he tilted his head to look. A large man with a bushy black beard and crafty expression stood in the glare of a flickering lamp held aloft in his right hand. Two men in glass armor with pikes filled the entrance behind him. The large man motioned them beyond earshot.

"Did I not tell you, Flores Assemblyman, that your city is corrupt and worships Atasan? As fire cannot match the suns, the god of evil cannot thwart the will of his own father, Our Lord Vensor. Your people involved me in their plots with no thought for the consequences, either for myself or for Ven, and they have brought ruin to their city. And did I not say, Flores, that I would keep my word? The Serclasler of Ven is now my viceroy and obeys me, though he was my enemy before. I have fulfilled my oath by appointing him. But Sedsednon must rule; to him I have also sworn. Vensor would blind me if I violated my oath to the Serclasler and he is killed at the hand of a Neset, so I will permit you one final chance for life, a last act of revenge, a final chance to settle the quarrel that for so long has split your city.

"Soon my men will return. They will unlock your door. They will escort you to the hall of Vim. There you will find my viceroy. My men will give you a sword. Only one of you may exit alive. The winner goes into exile, the loser to Atasan. The choice is yours. None but I know that you breathe within these walls. Those who brought you to me I have ordered killed."

Without waiting for an answer, Nesos backed out of the cell and servants brought trays of food and drink. The door was shut and the night returned.

Flores ate and slept. Time was gone. He ceased counting. His life had begun again, a rebirth measured in hours. Exile or rule or death mattered not. Beyond the mausoleum was, and perhaps always had been, oblivion. Life post-Numsenmur was inconceivable. And the woman, who even now underwent torment at the hands of Nara and old Wijah? He could do nothing. It was again an affair of the Temple.

He thought of the task ahead.

A hunger grew, bubbling like spume, a thirst for a time and place that he finally knew, climaxing in one instant a lifetime of havoc. The desire swelled and filled him so that he panted, his mind racing through memories of exercise yards and endless drills. A lifetime of practice and test with sword and pike was for this instant and this instant alone; from private yard to forest glade with a servant, his life coursed like an arrow to its goal. His one remaining purpose, the only purpose he had always held or meant to hold, he could now see clearly, far more clearly than the phantom world through which his body had recently moved. He saw an irsrem blade of world dimensions with razored tip tearing redly through a statue, the dying howls of a ros soothing the chaos inside.

Flores stood and began to follow the ancient patterns as he was taught and the newer movements derived from the habits of reven-na; pivot, volt, cabré, strike. The hot wind of the ritual of Atasan once again stirred. His skin grew slick, his muscles tightened, his balance improved in the dark.

And his hearing. Gradually he became aware of an occasional sliding sound emanating from somewhere outside his cell. First would be silence, then a short gasp as if someone sought to catch his breath, followed by a scuffle and a rough sliding. It would start, then stop, then begin again. Finally it ceased.

Much time had passed and Flores sat quietly in the blackness of his cell when the jingle of keys announced the return of his keepers. He did not turn his head from the light but closed his eyes. He stood, then very slowly opened them. The same two men who had accompanied Nesos stood in armor outside the cell, their swords sheathed, bearing torches. They waited patiently, unconcerned.

Flores walked out.

They rounded a turn and a guard indicated an open iron gate with keys still in the lock and a stairwell. Flores lifted one foot to climb when the sliding noise came again, louder than before, apparently from an open pit a few steps away. With a glance at his escort, Flores reversed himself.

"No need for that," said one. "None may look except the king."

But Flores kept walking and the other guard put a restraining hand on the one who spoke. Carefully the noble peered over the side of the pit. For a moment he saw nothing in the shifting light. Then his vision focused on a man standing calmly in the center of a square well, just deep enough to prevent the most agile from escaping. The man looked up. For the briefest instant, Flores thought he looked upon a stranger, someone he could not recognize, but the light changed and with a shock he stared full upon the face of Mesret.

"Father, please let me out."

The guard rejoined him and casually pointed toward the stairwell. They did not know.

Flores' elbow hit one in the face. He turned and sent the other tumbling into the pit. A swift movement sent the first crashing to the door. Flores stepped on his chest and withdrew the man's rapier. Deftly he pulled it across the guard's neck and the man's head rested lamely on the reddening stone. Quickly stripping the man of his skirt, Flores lowered it over the side, and Mesret, having retrieved the sword of the other guard, clambered with little difficulty up the cloth and out of the pit.

"Nesos took me and put me here. He did not harm me, though. I'm all right."

Flores sensed none of the old antipathy that his son had previously held for him. "You must leave," said Flores. "King Nesos has let me out for but one reason–to kill Numsenmur. It is a wish I will fulfill. He is pushing Numsenmur aside for Sedsednon. If I survive, I will be pushed aside also."

"Sedsednon? He will destroy the city..."

"Why should Nesos care? Ven is his enemy."

"But I have other purposes," Mesret said.

"What?"

"Nothing, Father."

Flores nodded. "You must leave. Try to disguise yourself, but get out of the city. A Ven army with Turlicum is at Sish. Go there."

Mesret smiled. "Yes, Father."

Flores had been buckling on sword and scabbard as he spoke. When he was done, he and Mesret climbed the stairwell to the upper floor. It joined a corridor that led to an antechamber of the hall of Vim, and Mesret, with a last tender glance, disappeared in the opposite direction.

Once out of Flores' sight, Mesret walked boldly with his sword sheathed. He entered a room where several Ven workmen were occupied repairing furniture. He crossed the room without pause.

"Lord Serclasler!" one cried. The workmen stood respectfully and bowed their heads until the viceroy passed. Numsenmur strode through a second room and down a short hall. Vens with daggers maintained their customary vigilance by the door and stood in surprise.

"Sir Sruk!" They looked at each other in surprise. "We thought you had died."

"Do I look dead to you?" Sruk chuckled as he exited the building.

A band of well-armed Neset-sa loitered by the complex. They straightened and shuffled to release their tension.

"As you commanded, O Brother of the Moons, none have exited the building."

"Good. You're doing well." King Nesos walked into the garden and was lost to sight among the trees.

৯ ৪০ ৫৪ ৶

Numsenmur-Nidrenmor of the Serclaslers passed through a corridor and entered the banquet chamber of the hall of Vim. Twenty Neset-sa soldiers accompanied him and silently dispersed to the several exits. Numsenmur watched hesitantly. He had brought his glass rapier, as habit dictated, but not his armor plates. Since his act of treachery he had felt secure; he trusted the word of Nesos. But as a former head of state, he craved insurance. Recent events had left him wondering if he would soon regret his deed–his authority was plainly slipping. His own people, the Serclasler clan, still obeyed him, but the other clans more often than not found ways to frustrate his orders. And King Nesos was openly contemptuous and used him like an errand boy. With Nesos' recent indulgence of Sedsednon, Numsenmur felt a nervous apprehension. Clearly, he was no longer treated as a viceroy. Could Nesos' plans have changed?

He watched the Neset soldiers cover the exits. Why had he been summoned here? Nesos was nowhere to be seen. Disgust twisted his mouth. These Neset-sa with their shaggy beards were unwashed and boorish. It was unfortunate that the cultured capital of Ven had been subjected to their foul habits. The whole city would have to be cleansed when they left. But, he noted, he had at least saved the Temple. No vulgar herdsman would desecrate the heart of Ven. Nesos had promised.

Numsenmur wandered to the center of the chamber and examined the two sunken trenches and walkway that ran the length of the hall where he had celebrated many a festival. Light poured through the roof and threw jagged trapezoids upon the floor. Dust filled its rays. From the corner of his eye he saw the Neset-sa, framed at the far end of the room between pilasters, part and admit someone who strode casually into the room. Not Nesos, he thought. Must be waiting, like me.

He turned.

Flores walked slowly, unwilling to hurry the moment. He wanted to savor each second, etch it within his memory, so that in future ages, whether in Heaven, Maalstrom, or the Abyss, he could recall it complete, a balm to match the emptiness within. His hands tingled from contact with the charged, naked blade held close to his side; if Numsenmur did not look closely he might think it sheathed. Flores neared the lone figure standing silently in the hall, the light of one trapezoid cutting a swath across the figure's face. Only the left side shone. Flores remained in shadow until quite near. Pressing the hilt of his sword to his right breast, he stepped into the light.

The other turned.

The Turlicum Lord impressed the scene upon his mind, missing nothing, his unblinking eyes recording all with mechanical efficiency. He saw Numsenmur's cheeks grow pale; the tawny beard jerk once, twice, the block-like hand palsy and begin to tremble.

Numsenmur opened his mouth. For a brief moment he tried to call, to summon his mutes and slaves to cut the vile organism, like a cancer, from the world, to squash and obliterate it, to stamp it as he would treacherous subversion. But before the sounds came, a new light gleamed; around his eyes the folds of skin sagged and set, not to be moved by human agency.

He brandished his rapier. "My gills...my consort," he croaked. "Where are they?"

The Turlicum stepped forward, his whole being focused in perfect concentration. In answer, he extended his sword.

"Then we have no choice–" Numsenmur lunged in mid-sentence, aiming at Flores' sword arm, but the Turlicum parried and Numsenmur's blade scraped half its length, producing a chain of sparks, before he leapt back in reflex. Flores feinted twice to edge his enemy toward the open trench beside him. Numsenmur saw the tactic and backed further, away from the sunken ship. The Turlicum lunged and the air exploded with furious clashing, leaving a sharp odor of ozone in their nostrils. Numsenmur gave ground and allowed some seconds to pass as he gathered his faculties. Finding his voice, he yelled.

"Soldiers! Are you blind? This is an enemy of the king!" Numsenmur halted to shout louder. "Take him! There is a reward!" His voice reverberated through the chamber, then died. Several Neset-sa pulled their swords free of sheathes and huddled more closely by the exits.

So that was it, Numsenmur realized. He was viceroy so long as he breathed. Therefore, he must stop breathing. And not by the hand of a Neset. Numsenmur clenched his teeth and glanced behind him.

"So it's an alliance of traitors and devils." Numsenmur pointed his blade. "First I'll finish you, enemy of Ven, then will be the turn of Nesos, the enemy of Vensor himself." He looked about him again. "I see they have left it to us." He smiled stiffly, his skin still white. "I will perform this execution myself."

The Serclasler fell upon his enemy with vigor and sought to use his greater muscle to full advantage by hammering him into submission. However, the blade of the Serclasler was not iron, but irsrem, and bore little weight. With some effort Flores resisted the onslaught. Their blades contacted, the flash illuminating the length of the hall, and Numsenmur threw his weight upon him.

Flores fell.

The Serclasler's blade whistled. Flores tumbled into the trench. With a beast-like growl, Numsenmur rushed to pursue and thrust repeatedly at the twisting, dodging target. The Turlicum tightened his grip on his sword and connected with Numsenmur's boot. No flesh was touched, but Numsenmur stepped back. Flores rolled across the walkway and into the other oar-trench.

Numsenmur leapt to the walkway, but his bulk slowed him. Flores clambered out. He regained the floor.

The currents of dust spun again in an angry clacking of swords which lit the chamber's environs like distant lightning. The figures twirled, Numsenmur seeking to close and crush Flores with his weight, Flores searching to feint the Serclasler into slipping or tripping and to pin him with a thrust. The bared feet of the Turlicum lent an unexpected agility to his struggle.

Numsenmur unleashed all in another attempt to overwhelm his nemesis. Flores bent and twisted, too slow–the honed edge opened a red streak down his chest. Desperately he lunged at an angle only attainable with the left hand, a parry which frequently had disconcerted Tilsis. Numsenmur yelled and broke off, clutching a bleeding thigh. The Serclasler turned and without warning leaped and fell full upon him, pinning Flores to the floor. Flores struggled but could not move.

"A last word, traitor?" hissed the ros, its voice echoing from the fields of the nether world.

Flores' pupils closed to a point. "Silence, blasphemer. You violate the earth with your presence."

Numsenmur went limp; his jaw slackened. Spider-like he crawled off Flores, the sweat rolling off his contorted face.

The Turlicum rose. He rushed upon Numsenmur.

The Serclasler took one step and slipped upon his back. With horror, Numsenmur watched his rapier fall and Flores' foot fling it away. He was helpless.

Flores dropped a foot upon Numsenmur's chest with such force that the Serclasler gasped. The tip of Flores' blade halted at Numsenmur's neck.

For a moment, Flores stood in perfect silence. His foe swallowed from exertion. Gradually Numsenmur caught his breath and calmed. Finally the beaten man whispered: "For your hand?"

Flores shook his head. "For Turlicum. And for Ven."

He raised his arm to strike the final blow, the maw of the netherworld opening to receive his enemy, conscious of the soldiers who had come close to escort the victor to Nesos,...

A gong rang.

The arm paused.

From somewhere far away an ancient memory returned, a memory of joyful days under the open sky and the wondrous creature who risked all for him, for love alone, and now would die, at this moment, in the innermost reaches of the Temple, after torture and abuse from the jealous priestesses of Vensa.

A second gong echoed.

Flores trembled.

He awaited the third and final ring that would announce the end of the Ritual of Penitence, and cut short the life of the only person to bring happiness to him, the hum whose pitch would freeze the heart within him and break it in pieces.

Like a thunderclap it came. It washed through the hall from end to end and returned to crush an empty shell.

His gaze returned to the defeated foe beneath him. Hatred welled up like poison and spread to encompass his limbs, his head, his soul. He would not live in vain. The arm lifted.

The hall reverberated with another ring.

Flores looked up. *Four* rings?

A moment passed.

The metallic hum passed over again, and yet again.

Numsenmur gasped. "The Temple! The Neset-sa are in!"

In an instant, Maalstrom returned with all its boiling passions. It was not the Ritual of Penitence–the Temple was invaded. For the first time in a millennium, the gates were open.

She lived!

Flores looked upon his stricken enemy prostrate before him. Numsenmur's jaw was open, sweat and dust lined his face, blood seeped from his thigh. The beaten man wheezed, his eyes glazing. Instinctively Flores' sword arm lifted to strike, the hunger of his vengeance, the impetus of his life, still demanding satiety in a flow of blood.

Again the hall reverberated.

In Flores' mind he could see Amina, tormented, carrying her heavy burden up a winding staircase, and Nara pushing her into a great dark pit and laughing her tinkling happy laugh; then the Temple, consumed in an orgy of flame and blood as Nesos roared with laughter.

The Neset-sa stood near. Nesos awaited the completion of his orders by his slave.

Amina called.

With a cry of triumph and joy, Flores flung himself upon the Neset-sa and scattered them like straw, leaving corpses in his wake. He made for an unguarded door. Behind him he heard Numsenmur gasp and blades clash anew.

CHAPTER 26

VENSA

Nesos waited calmly for news of his assault. The Assembly Hall shined bright in the rays of the suns and his newly confiscated jewels were resplendent on his fingers. He stretched his legs and settled more comfortably on his throne, noting the rough edges of the workmanship. He had not bothered to polish it; the hall would be next. He would burn the entire city, in fact, after looting the Temple. But the Temple came first. The citadel would doubtless consume days of his time. First they had to kill all within, then there would be gold and silver to cart off, and much else. It was common knowledge that a city's Temple contained the best that a city possessed. After the Temple... who cared? The rest to the flames. The bodies could fall where they may. Then he would deal with the one who had dared to impersonate him on that previous night.

Returning from a brief absence, Mesret, the Heir of Turlicum, sat beside Nesos, relishing his status as the newest consort of the Emperor. Neset soldiers flanked him, gathered about the throne. More rows stood on the floor of the chamber. The Simet-sa of Ven had been again summoned and gazed helplessly as the cries and sounds of violence carried from the city. Several of their number lay prostrate at the spot of their resistance.

A bearded Neset warrior in glass armor entered the hall and approached his king. He whispered in Nesos' ear. The Emperor nodded.

With a wave of his hand, Nesos summoned his captains, then announced, "I have just been informed that my viceroy of Ven, the Lord Serclasler, has been assassinated. The criminal who committed the foul deed, Flores-Sumvensor of the Turlicum, is at this moment undergoing state execution for his abominable act and has confessed that he had assistance from citizens of Ven." Mesret said nothing but nudged closer, one hand stroking the Emperor's bare arm. "In retaliation I have ordered that the Temple of Ven be burned and that every third noble be slain."

The Assembly erupted with shouts, pleas, and screams. The Neset guards blocked the exits and herded the Assemblymen back onto the benches where they cowered.

Another runner entered and approached the Emperor. Climbing the tiers, he bowed at his feet. "Vens are attacking, my king. Spies opened the gate and the city is in revolt."

Nesos nodded, then spoke quietly to his guards. "Stop them. They cannot force us from the city. And if the people aid the invaders, kill them all. Now bring me my son." He smiled. "It is noon. Let the people of Ven look upon their new king." He began to laugh, softly at first, then the low rumble echoing through the hall.

His commanders had left and Nesos sat calmly, awaiting news of the glorious victory, when a commotion at the entrance drew the gaze of the Assembly. Several Neset-sa backed into the hall, their swords flashing. One Neset fell, followed by two more. Before Nesos could intervene, Numsenmur-Nidrenmor of the Serclaslers burst into the chamber, alive as ever. He turned to face the Emperor.

"Traitor!" The Serclasler breathed hard and pointed his sword. "You ordered me killed! You," he panted, "are the enemy of all Vensor-sa!"

Nesos stood with eyes wide. Several men rushed to engage the intruder, but Nesos threw up his hands and called them back. "No! You must not kill him! I have sworn before Vensor!"

Numsenmur gripped his irsrem rapier more tightly, and dove into the ranks of Neset soldiery in an effort to gain the throne. In moments several more Neset-sa had fallen beneath his blade and the soldiers began to return his blows parry for parry. The assembled nobles shouted, the swords clacked, Numsenmur roared, and the excited warnings of Nesos were lost in the noise and confusion. Suddenly the Serclasler paused. A Neset pike had found its mark. He lifted his rapier to strike and another ripped home. As the chamber quieted, a half-dozen weapons penetrated the body of Numsenmur, each wielded by a Neset warrior. The Serclasler stumbled. For an instant he gazed upon his enemy. One hand reached outward. He fell upon the benches, twitched once and lay still.

Nesos held his breath, his eyes round with fear.

"I swore..." his voice trailed off.

The chamber had fallen silent. Neset soldiers stood about the massive corpse sprawled upon the tiers, its eyes still focused on the massive hewn throne. Nobles and soldiers stared, all awaiting the next move of Nesos. The Emperor glanced about him, his gaze flitting from man to man, as if death lurked in every heart and hand.

His voice trembled. "I must never look upon this city again! Or lay eyes on anyone of this land!"

Nesos took one step, then stiffened. Like a contortionist, he attempted to reach his back with both hands to relieve the searing pain. He swiveled and locked eyes with his assassin.

The youth Mesret stamped his foot and screamed. "No! I won't let you! You can't leave me behind! I must be your consort!" Mesret snatched another knife from the belt of Nesos and plunged it into the Emperor's chest. "Your consort! Your consort! I must be your consort!"

The king's eyes, still wide with superstitious fear, grew vacant. He collapsed backward and rolled down the tiers of benches to stop at their base in a bloody ruin.

The hall exploded. Mesret vanished beneath an avalanche of Neset warriors. Soldiers and Assemblymen alike crowded through the exits to make good their escape.

♔ ❦ ❧ ♔

Flores raced through the gardens of the Assembly Hall, his bared feet uprooting tufts of grass.

The Assembly gates were open. Several Neset warriors stood within and gazed at a disturbance in the plaza. Flores shot through them. Surprised shouts rang out, but Flores was already far within the square.

People scurried in all directions. Angry Vens wandered with naked swords looking for Neset-sa, many flinging stones. Bands of Neset-sa were killing any who crossed their path.

Sedsednon was still perched upon his mound of shoes, now swelled to gargantuan proportions. His small outline could be seen swaying and gesticulating at its peak and he shrieked in a tiny voice. At the base of the mound surged a crowd of Vens with torches. Flores saw the flames leap and grow. The arrival of a party of Neset cavalry and the massacre of the Vens did not retard the flames.

Flores made for the Temple at a dead run.

Minutes later, he entered the square before the citadel. The portcullis was up and hundreds of Neset-sa were flooding into the courtyard.

Frantically the noble ran to make the entrance, ignoring the desperate and outraged Vens that collected around him, armed with anything that might end the life of a Neset. The Neset-sa turned and formed ranks to oppose the mob; Flores heard the squalling of infants in the courtyard behind them. From the direction of the city gate, a body of cavalry arrived and the Nesets retreated into the courtyard of the calling for sons. The portcullis staked shut while arrows drove back the Vens.

Flores' gaze was attracted by a party of familiar figures among the cavalry. "Revd! Isav! Mosum!"

The three reined in their mounts and stared, stunned. Each bore an expression of helplessness, wrung with the weight of the impending catastrophe in the Temple.

"Flores!" Isav and Revd flung themselves off their reven-na almost on top of their lord and embraced him so that they spun. Then Mosum grasped his hands and shook them until his teeth rattled. The Turlicum paused. He looked questioningly up at a fourth rider who did not dismount. Isav and Revd dropped their gaze and let their hands fall to their sides.

"Sir Sedrech,"Flores called. "Don't you recognize your lord? Surely the elements and obstacles that the gods have placed in my path have not altered me so much. The bones of my face at least remain the same." It was then that Flores noticed the strange clan insignia that Sedrech and the others wore.

Sedrech directed several warriors to dismount and encircle Flores.

"My lord…I mean to say, my former lord, it is my unfortunate duty to place you under arrest in the name of the people of Ven and the Assembly in exile." The warriors disarmed Flores, and Revd and Isav and Mosum allowed themselves to be pushed away without protest.

"Why?" Flores' voice was little more than a whisper.

"The world has believed you dead, Flores, and your clan has been disbanded for some months. Little thought was given to this possibility arisin. But, since you plainly are not dead, I am compelled to execute the last ruling of the Council regarding you, and hold you until trial for collaboration with the Vensor Emperor, King Nesos of Neset."

The Turlicum glanced at his old friend from the Assembly. Mosum looked to the ground. "I am sorry, Flores. It seems I can never defend your interests in your absence. I tried."

Flores seemed to shrink at his words. He placed a reassuring hand on Mosum's shoulder, then gazed at the Temple where the gate had completely shut, barring the city from interfering while the Neset sol-diery proceeded with their grisly task.

"It matters not to me, Sedrech, how you or the Council judge me when the war is won and the Neset-sa driven from our country, but first listen to me and obey one last order from these lips, for the sake of Ven and the Temple of Vensor. If you don't...all within the Temple will die."

Those who heard him speak looked from Flores to Sedrech with a blend of mistrust and hope.

"I know of a secret passageway into the Temple," Flores continued. "It leads from the palace of Numsenmur through an underground cav-ern along a path accessible to men on foot. I am certain that it is open and unsuspected even as we stand here."

Several warriors prodded their reven-na close to Sedrech. Among them was a youth who wore no clan insignia but whom Flores imme-diately recognized as the Heir of the Serclasler tribe.

Lirsus pushed his reven forward. "I will vouch for the actions of Turlicum, Sedrech," Lirsus said. "I was present at his meeting with the enemy and I saw him in the battle." His voice rose as he spoke. "Our expedition was defeated by the desertions of the Simet-sa, Ust and Simlet, who fled in the midst of the fighting and sought to pin the blame on others. Turlicum was in no way responsible, but gave his best against Nesos in the battle that followed."

For one moment Flores and Lirsus locked eyes, then a scream carried to them from the Temple. They looked up and saw a black-swathed figure on a balcony above the gate fall beneath a Neset sword.

"Lead me to the passageway," Sedrech pleaded.

Flores swung upon a reven and hopped toward the palace of Num-senmur while the news spread.

Soon Flores led a column of men through the labyrinth of tunnels beneath the Temple, Sedrech at his side. With torches to light the way, Flores moved unerringly to his goal. The crevice yawned before him just as it had months before. Scrambling over the boulder, the noble dropped to the gritty floor of the Temple. The Vens swarmed after. The split belly of the reclining woman disgorged warriors by the hun-dred as her divine and flawless lover smiled above.

Flores found the stairway of polished granite and followed it through darkness. He burst open a door and stepped into the sunlit corridor. Boots stamping behind him, he swept into the rotunda. Five priestesses lay sprawled in dark pools. With a mysterious sense of urgency that approached panic, the Vens raced along a hall littered with black corpses and occasional bodies of Neset-sa, swords and ceremonial pinwheels dropped randomly about. Through the clerestory, Flores watched the dome of the Queen's chamber grow.

They entered the first chamber and humid heat hit them. Row upon row of magenta gourds lay neatly, but some near the aisle were smashed and showed a sickening movement within. A clot of robed guardians lay piled at the entrance in a welter of crimson and dark cloth. Several priestesses knelt and chanted rhythmic prayers. Others moved in a daze among the eggs, still tending, paying no heed to the latest wave of invaders.

In frantic haste, Flores seized the nearest priestess and shook her. "Where is the high pit?"

The woman covered her mouth, made a superstitious sign, and resumed chanting.

In disgust he flung her aside.

The Vens entered the second chamber with its smaller, paler pupae. More carnage greeted them. Harsh rings and shouts from the next room drew them on.

Flores tore aside the veil opening on the third chamber. Neset-sa were vanishing behind the imbricated curtain which led to the very center of the Citadel. Other Neset-sa were crushing as many white, fist-sized eggs as they could while repelling the sharp thrusts of outraged priestesses armed with pinwheels. Pausing in their gory task, the warriors easily cut down the interfering women.

An incomprehensible sound exploded from Flores' mouth and the Neset-sa turned. With a cry, the Lord of the Turlicum leaped upon them. The clacking of glass swords rang, mingling with the cries of the dying. Flores finished one with a thrust to the armpit and dashed for the last chamber, the sacred heart of Ven. With a sudden swipe he lopped off a carelessly extended arm, then paused to listen. A deep guttural roar filled the room, seeming to shake the walls, a tortured and labored sound like the dying exhalation of some great beast. The skin on Flores' arms and back prickled. He crashed heedlessly through the metal leaves, the curtain clattering into a jumbled ruin.

Flores froze.

Dozens of Neset-sa warriors strove with an equal number of shrieking priestesses, flailing and slashing with abandon. The bodies piled high with each passing second and lay in two dense paths upon a narrow concentric stonework that encircled a deep vat of water. Within the Sacred Spring of Ven, the first among Vensor-sa and the most inviolate, floated a vast, swollen thing, grey and drifting like a capsized ship. Bright streams of crimson flowed from a score of pikes and spears embedded in its flesh, rigid as quills. Flores blinked and saw a dark hill crowned with stripped trees. When he found the head and its absurdly small eyes looked into his own, he grew ill.

A Neset warrior with flushed skin and distorted grimace flung his hand and those who had cast the lethal weapons unleashed more. The head split and roared, sputtering in the froth. The tiny limbs kicked. Red streams stained the pool in a deep brown cloud while bodies of priestesses and Neset-sa slowly sank and vanished in the depths.

Flores engaged the Neset-sa near him and forced one into the water. The pressure of the Vens pouring into the chamber from behind rapidly overwhelmed the remainder, excepting the commander and a few others who fled to the far side and escaped through another exit. The door slammed shut and bolted.

The groans and shrieks of bedlam smote Flores as he viewed the scene, but his mind was elsewhere. Where was the high pit? Who could tell him? Everywhere he looked, the black acolytes of the Goddess Vensa prayed or chanted or dragged shattered bodies, their hysterical shrieks reverberating through the chamber. Two opened a barrel of ses and attempted to feed the drooling mouth of Vensa. The island of flesh drifted out of reach.

The noble grabbed one of the vacant women and forced the food from her hand. Sedrech and Isav joined him.

"Where is the high pit?" Flores shook her hard.

The woman looked at him in a daze, then dropped to her knees and wailed a prayer.

Flores became aware of labored breathing from the thing in the pool. A choking seized it and Vensa coughed horribly. The room was filling with Vens, awestruck by the spectacle. No living memory prepared them for the scene.

The head inhaled. Vensa forced the air out painfully through obstructions in her throat.

"My daughter Nesta has won...you're too late, my children...now her city will grow..."

The great body heaved and rolled. A tiny hand clasped the rim of the stone walkway and stabilized the floating mass.

It breathed again. "I know her, my children...she will seek to kill you all, because you came from me. But she too is of my loins. When I found the sacred spring and dug my pool with these hands, the world was empty, and she not even conceived..." She breathed hoarsely. "My daughters are wayward and must be watched...they become corrupt and abandon me." Tears flowed down her cheeks. "How ungrateful they are to fight me for my birthright..."

The hill coughed convulsively.

"Now my city will die and fall to dust...for you, my children...."

The hill listed and the hand lost its hold upon the walkway. With a low hiss the head slipped beneath the surface and spouted froth. The mountain shuddered and rolled. The murky water grew still but for the slow bubbling of the spring.

The cacophony of the Queen's chamber quieted. The Vens continued to crowd the room and organized spontaneously into a procession so all could satisfy their morbid curiosity. The priestesses began to tend their maimed comrades, ignoring the dead thing that floated in the pool. They understood better than the men the momentousness of the tragedy. Far better that the city or its priestesses had died.

Flores watched. His body no longer fought, but his mind still raced. One phrase cycled endlessly in his ear: the high pit...the high pit. He turned to leave but something caught his eye.

The walls of the Queen's chamber arched skywards on all sides of the room and would have met high above the center of the pool to form a perfect dome except for a round gap, an orifice through which open sky was visible. This gap now admitted a figure the size of a man. Slowly it circled, gliding lazily upon wide wings, spiraling downward in practiced, easy swathes. While Flores watched, it momentarily paused, and interrupted its spin to flap higher. Then it sank. Like a stone it plummeted for the pool snapping amid gasps of the watching Vens into an agitated hovering directly above the corpse of Vensa.

A mournful wailing rose from the Sisters. "Atasan! Atasan!"

The thing lit on the bloody corpse. Flores could see it clearly; man-like arms, human-like legs, its limbs thin but knotted with dark muscle, stiff green plates about shoulders and chest, evidently integral to its flesh. Flores could not turn away. Mandibles working and compound eyes glinting, the creature sniffed and crawled jerkily over the corpse of its lover.

An angry buzzing hummed through the chamber and the creature jumped and soared. Once it circled, passing its inscrutable glare over the occupants. Then it flipped and sped from the chamber. The priestesses knelt and sobbed.

Flores retraced his route though the rooms of eggs and pupae and returned to the rotunda. Perhaps he was too late after all. How could he know? Vensa was dead, and her priestesses silent, or insane. The three days were almost up, if not already. He must find Nara. How long would it take to search the Temple? His mind searched back to that distant day when as a prisoner he was confronted by the desperate and angry Nara. "I myself will push her into the high pit," she had said. The first day she fasts, the second she prays, the third she carries eggs to the highest level of the tower. And, "If she doesn't step with care, she will die." What could Nara have meant?

An idea dawned.

Flores gripped his sword and ran. He flung open the door of the tower and began to climb. Spiraling without pause, he took the stairs by threes, following them up, level upon level, each succeeding window revealing a smaller, more distant city, immersing in a flood of shadow.

After a time, he slowed. He marveled at the great height of the spire and its stolidity. Every step of stone demanded the stamp of a foot, evoked the protest of a resisting calf. Despite his caution, his sheathed sword tapped each step; he slapped it back in irritation.

At the last and highest level a trapdoor halted his ascent. Through a final aperture at his side, Flores saw the suns touch the horizon, almost fully merged.

A frenetic voice wheezed beyond the hatch, its high pitch clearly audible over the low moaning of the wind.

"Here! They come. We must push them to the ledge."

"No. You must work without me."

"What? What is this?"

A tinkling laugh answered. "You foolish old woman. Did you really think I would concern myself with Her one moment longer than I must?" She laughed loudly in the blowing breeze. "For the first time in centuries, men are in the Temple! Not one, but hundreds. I'm ready for the sting. Do you imagine that I would not choose the freedom of centuries over the slavery of a short, barren life serving Vensa?"

"Wretch! How can you think of such? How dare you forget your duties to Vensa!"

Flores heard thick cloth tear.

"Aiyee! One comes forth! We must place it on the ledge!"

"No, old woman! If you wish to obey the Queen then you must work alone–"

The cloth ripped louder.

"It is out! It lives! The others–quickly!"

"I came here for one purpose only–" A high-pitched whistling penetrated the trapdoor and window. "And when Amina falls down the shaft to the realms of Atasan, my task here will be done."

"You ungrateful woman! How can you forsake your Goddess? You, a mortal, would rival Her in all Her divine glory? How dare you desecrate the Temple by drawing breath!"

Flores heard bodies tumble and someone shriek. The trap slammed as he emerged onto the cold windswept floor of the open platform. The circular stone floor was littered with dark-red lozenges, each perhaps a yard in length. Thick posts supported a massive iron framework from which a wide brass gong suspended, and below the gong plummeted the tower shaft waiting in the growing darkness for an unlucky stumble In deference to the malkops, neither the shaft nor the platform's edge bore handrails.

Wijah kneeled over the supine forms of Nara and Amina, the thick handle of a whip brandished in her hand. The old woman stared at the blunt handle as the cold wind fluttered strands of her hair. Hatred, outrage, anger flashed across her face. Slowly she rose to her feet and, ignoring Flores, carefully towed and rolled the red cocoons to the tower's edge. Malkops glided and flapped in the declining light, hovering nearer to retrieve them. One cocoon had ripped, and its pale malkop staggered and whistled and flapped its new wings uncertainly.

Flores rushed to Amina's side and cradled her in his arms.

"Amina, I have come!"

Her tired eyes opened. For a brief moment, they stared into his own and a smile lit her face. Then they shut. Flores worked his arms under her to take her to the stairs when suddenly a screaming reven landed on his back. He rose to dislodge the clinging and biting form of Wijah while avoiding her nails which sought his eyes.

With an effort he pulled her off. Holding her two wrists in one hand he carried her to the stairwell and placed her within. She screamed and struggled with furious energy.

"Begone, priestess!" he yelled.

Flores closed the trap and turned, but Wijah popped it open and clambered out, screaming and mad as ever. Flores swore. Picking her up bodily, ignoring her kicking feet and fists, he walked down the stairs to a landing. There he placed her on the stone and tore strips of cloth from her cassock. In several minutes he had tied her neatly and placed a thick gag upon her mouth, and, satisfied that she would cause him no more trouble, he remounted the stairs to the upper platform.

"Anima! Vensa is dead! We can remain together–"

He stopped.

The platform was empty but for the howling of the wind. Cocoons, Amina, Nara–all had vanished. And the malkops no longer circled.

Maalstrom
Vedeg
Tumsenet
Klopus
Nene
Nasvetin
Tes
Lunsen
Sish
Toor
Ror
VEN
Tlat
Lesel
Asan
Sipan
Neset
Ud
Lim
Vaw

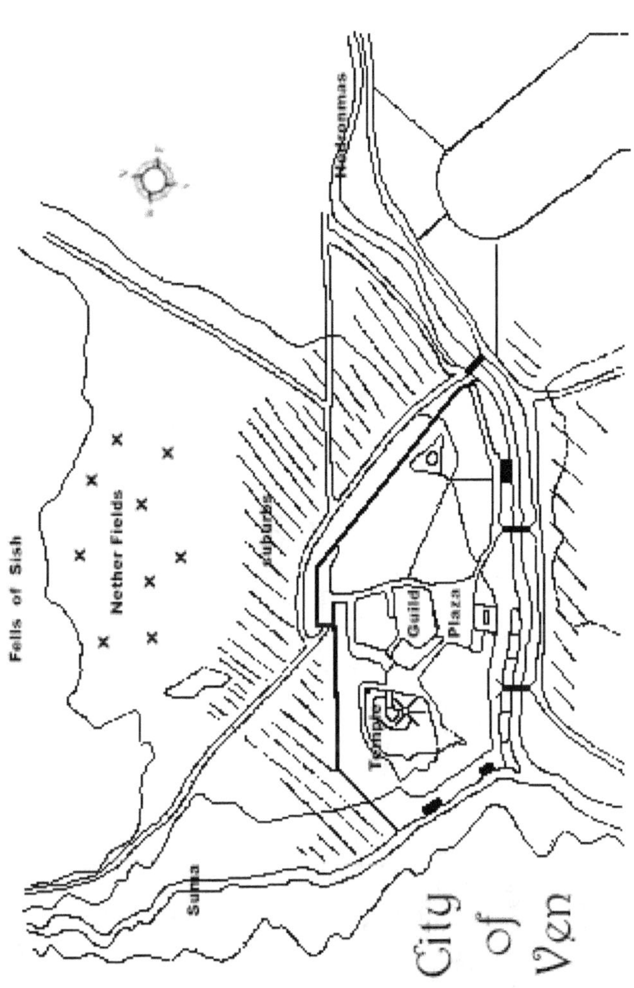

Hadsammas
Fells of Sish
Nether Fields
Suburbs
Guild Plaza
Temple
Suma
City of Ven

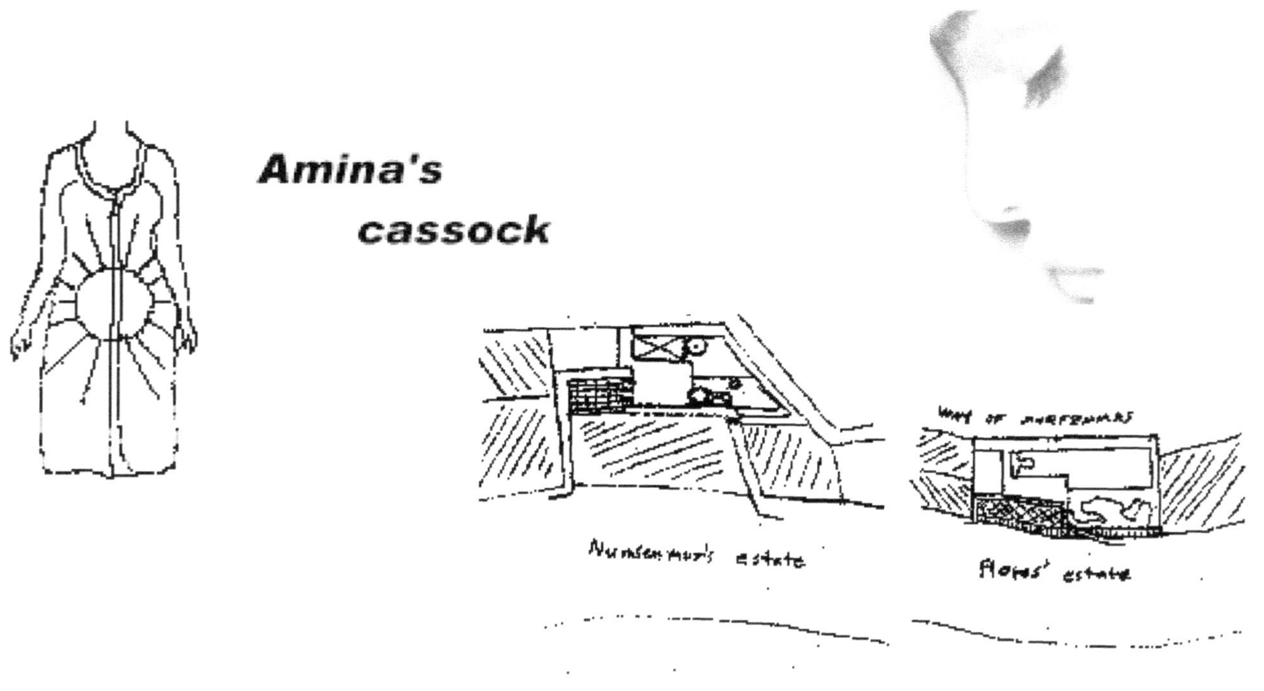

Amina's cassock
Nurnsenmun's estate
way of maelstroms
Flores' estate

MAALSTROM
by Glenn L. Roberts

Flores of the Turlicum

NOTE FROM THE AUTHOR

Maalstrom was begun in the autumn of 1975 on a manual type-writer "in a smoke-filled haze" as a twenty-year old sophomore in college. Most was completed in two months.

The story: long ago, colonists from Earth landed on Maal-strom, a newly discovered planet circling a double-sun. Some women colonists became infected by a predatory species of na-tive wasp which caused the women's DNA to merge with the wasp DNA. Abandoning the other colonists, the 'infected' women secluded themselves singly in brick shelters which they built around water springs and began giving birth insect-fashion, their male offspring living outside the birth-shelters and their female offspring confined inside.

These 'wasp-queens' found their lifespans greatly extended. Vensa was one of these original colonists, already thousands of years old when she gave birth to Flores and Amina, her original brick shelter, which Flores stumbled across in the cavern, crumbling, and long since surmounted by an imposing cloistered Temple.

In the way of all mortals, Flores will die, but Amina will live for millennia and, if adequately protected by the unruly men exiled to the 'outer slums' of Her City, give birth to many genera-tions. Her manipulative and selfish behavior is essential to the survival of her quasi-insect species, to which Flores belongs.

The changes in DNA were not confined to the colonist-queens, however, but also created the malkops—or 'selks,' resulting in a complex biological interdependence between the various queens in their temples, the men in their cities, the malkops flying above, and Atasan.

That is the background—a swashbuckling Conan-style tale of bloody encounters that can be read merely for fun.

The symbolism goes further.

Maalstrom is the product of an education in anthropology, ar-chaeology, and the psychology and sociology of religion. Reli-gious myth—or, since that is a redundant phrase, just Myth—organizes all human societies. It is social glue, the com-mon values and thought patterns that hold a people together and enable them to communicate and cooperate. Myth is not only for 'those primitive people over there'–it is everything that *you* know, and what you *think* you know. A human without Myth is the ultimate contradiction; there never has been, and never can be, humans without Myth.

Every person with unique values and insights knows well the consequences of straying outside the boundaries of a society's Myths. They become heretics.

Flores is such a heretic. Or rather becomes one through the process of discovering the biological realities of his insect species, and the supra-factual nature of its Myths. These myths are enforced by an interplay of custom, religion, economics, ideology, and ultimately raw force. No society for long allows heretics to publicly undermine the social glue that allows its society to function. Thus the City of Ven rejects Flores.

But Flores, by his Will to Power, will not be stopped by convention and searches for a way to transcend his society's Myths and acquire Ultimate Knowledge. The crystal bracelets are the mystical insight that grant this Knowledge. Yezd is the shaman who transmits the technique. The selks are the semi-divine Messengers who guard access to Heaven, and, if properly ritually addressed, will transmit the Hero's questions to the Divine.

Atasan is an anagram for Satan, the Ruler of the physical world. In Maalstrom, I provide an insight into the role of this Ruler and, I like to think, a unique and provocative explanation of the existence of evil (see Macius' rendition to Flores of Maalstrom's dominant Creation Myth while in Yezd's castle).

Maalstrom and *The Selk King* are a single story separated by a cliff-hanger ending. In *The Selk King*, in the Chapter titled 'Revelations,' the reader will find the solutions to the many puzzles underlying Maalstrom's plot–just before Flores, having acquired mystical insight using his new-found shaman's technique, storms the ramparts of Heaven.

But don't expect me to be *your* Shaman. Whatever you know, or think you know, Myth lies heavy not only on Flores' perception, but on the reader's as well. Behind the Veil, Secrets lurk. Such is the nature of Reality, on alien planets like Maalstrom as much as Earth.

Maalstrom and *The Selk King* I hope remain as relevant to the Seeker-of-Knowledge's efforts to break free of Society's conventions and penetrate the Veil as when written. Dark, insightful and Just Plain Weird.

—Glenn Lazar Roberts
June 15, 2016

Dreams of the Dark Lotus

If you enjoyed this
Dark Lotus Book
please post a

REVIEW

on the
following websites:

www.amazon.com
www.goodreads.com
www.siriusreviews.com

Thank You!
—Glenn Lazar Roberts